VOX MACHINA

STORIES UNTOLD

AUTHORS

JESS BARBER

MARTIN CAHILL

REBECCA COFFINDAFFER

AABRIA IYENGAR

SAM MAGGS

SARAH GLENN MARSH

RORY POWER

NIBEDITA SEN

IZZY WASSERSTEIN

KENDRA WELLS

CRITICAL ROLE

VOX MACHINA

STORIES UNTOLD

RANDOM HOUSE WORLDS
NEW YORK

Random House Worlds
An imprint of Random House
A division of Penguin Random House LLC
1745 Broadway, New York, NY 10019
randomhousebooks.com
penguinrandomhouse.com

2025 Random House Worlds Trade Paperback Edition

Originally published in hardcover in the United States by Random House Worlds, an imprint of Random House, a division of Penguin Random House LLC, in 2025.

Illustrations on the following pages by Adrián Ibarra Lugo.

ISBN 978-0-593-87425-7
Ebook ISBN 978-0-593-87424-0

Printed in the United States of America on acid-free paper

1st Printing

BOOK TEAM: Production editor: Jocelyn Kiker • Managing editor: Susan Seeman • Production manager: Erin Korenko • Copy editor: Laura Dragonette • Proofreaders: Alissa Fitzgerald, Julia Henderson, Jacob Reynold Jones

Book design by Alexis Flynn

The authorized representative in the EU for product safety and compliance is Penguin Random House Ireland, Morrison Chambers, 32 Nassau Street, Dublin D02 YH68, Ireland, https://eu-contact.penguin.ie.

FOREWORD

Liam O'Brien

Storytelling has been at the center of my life from the start.

My childhood was littered with things to read. On any given day in grade school, I'd have a book or two to chip away at during recess or on the drive home. My summers were full of road trips in upstate New York, the windows down, a novel transporting me to one far-off place or another.

Our family home was perched on the bluffs facing the New York City skyline, which means my folks were able to get me to the theater early and often. *Magic.* Here was a place where words could leap off the page and I could see character and story come to life in front of me. When I reached high school, I found my way into the drama club and got my first taste of performing. I fell in love with Shakespeare's plays, among others, and explored them in class and onstage. I joined our school's forensics club, passing over debate for the far more enticing prose and poetry.

It was also at this time that I really delved into tabletop role-playing games. Like the theater, they offered me and my friends the ability to write our *own* stories and bring them to life for one another. And those different games we played led me to even more books. Longer-form fantasy series. Science fiction. Whole new worlds to explore, with characters and tales that I still love and remember to this day. I would read novels about *anything*, from Dickens to Dostoyevsky, but if I'm being honest, it was always fantasy and adventure that hooked me the most.

Eventually it was time to head off to college, and for whatever reason, I spent less and less time escaping into fantasy and tabletop games and leaned more heavily into my studies as a young actor at NYU. It might be that I was just more drawn to the theater at that time. Or perhaps some part of me believed I needed to put away childhood things in order to be an "adult" and a "very serious actor."

I spent years plunking about the boards, both in New York and around the country. Eventually I tripped into voice-over work, which led to many years of happily bringing all sorts of stories to life in animation and video games. And it's at this point that I think many of you reading these words will know what comes next.

Be it chance or be it fate, a circle of like-minded, uniquely creative actor nerds in Los Angeles decided to break out some dice and graph paper and tell a little story together around a card table. A birthday gift from one friend to another, although I know now that very first game we played was a gift to all eight of us. One that delights and thrills these many years later.

I still shake my head in wonder at it all. How we spun a simple little adventure in an apartment one night that led to my friends and me becoming a family. Here were seven other people just as enraptured with story and character as I was, and for several years we would come together over Brie cheese and dice to return to the world we had created together, beat by beat and chapter by chapter. We couldn't get enough of it and counted down the weeks that stretched between our games.

Eventually (and implausibly), we were offered the chance to bring our game into the public eye and share our tale with an audience. We were giddy at the prospect of it but also unsure if there would be much, if any, interest. We were in love with the adventure we'd been spinning, but it seemed unlikely to me that people outside our magic table would share our passion for any considerable amount of time.

I have never been so happy to be wrong.

The eight of us at the heart of Critical Role have now spent more than ten amazing years exploring the world of Exandria and beyond. What began in the little swamp town of Stilben has expanded out across multiple continents and planes of existence, through the chapters of three sprawling sagas. There is no longer a week that goes by that we aren't digging our hands into some aspect of storytelling, and the last decade has been the most creatively rewarding period of my life. Every moment has been magic.

But I think what is most incredible for me has been watching our world and its characters take on a life of their own, leaping out of *our* imaginations into the minds of so many others. To know that what we've created means so much to so many people, in the same way the books I grew up on mattered to me, is incredibly humbling. Our story and world have spread so far and wide that the eight of us can no longer populate their expanses on our own.

Luckily, we don't have to. Our storytelling has been collaborative from the start, and we now get to build our world with a whole host of amazing people—actors, artists, writers, you name it. I spent a good many years as a young artist in dogged pursuit of creative work. So getting to invite others to join us and *share* in that storytelling? It is the best.

Which brings us to this book.

This is an incredible collection of stories told by a delightfully talented circle of writers. I'm happy to note that some of these authors are friends, while for others, this was my first chance getting to enjoy their talents. Every single one of them has made Exandria richer with their tales.

Vox Machina is our family of heroes that first captured people's hearts. But they didn't do so alone. At every turn of the story, we met other incredible characters. Some of them helped our heroes; others hindered them. Some were famous, while a few favorites were deeply infamous. We fell in love with them all. And many of them had us wondering about *their* stories. Their struggles and origins. Their innermost thoughts. Their personal tales have been obscured in the mists on the periphery of our imagination, yet to be explored.

Until now. The scribes of this collection have pulled these tales out of the ether and expertly set them down for posterity in the pages of this book. My deepest thanks to all of them for giving us such an intimate look at some of our most beloved characters. I am grateful for their storytelling.

Anyway, I think that's probably enough out of me. Go ahead and turn to the next few pages. That's where the adventure begins. I trust you will enjoy it.

CONTENTS

VOX MACHINA

STORIES UNTOLD

UNDER GOLDEN BOUGHS

Martin Cahill

By the time I was born, there was no more Calamity. There was only the silence of a world brought low by war. Just the held breath of survivors, waiting to see if destruction would return. The absence of gods, who, in compromise, left to save what they could.

The earth reeked of death, the sky scorched with fire. Even the very ley lines of Exandria shook and quivered, as fragile as glass, terrified in their own way.

Exandria was a smoking ruin. Though it yet lived, it would be ages before it thrived once more.

Before he left beyond the gates his siblings made for themselves, my creator came to the world he loved so much one last time.

And there, he planted me.

I can tell you only what I recall, and what I recall is very little. But there will always be something about the thought of my progenitor that sends me back to the moment of my own creation: Why did he make me? And what did he wish for me?

In the deep roots of myself, where all my feelings and thoughts live, if I try very hard, I can conjure the image of him at my planting. You, whose mortal eyes are not made for it, cannot stare directly into the sun. But I, whose body was made for my creator's light, can vaguely recall the details of him.

There was weariness in him, though you'd not know it by looking. There was a meagerness to his core, which pulsed with frenzied brightness, but to me, it was clear he ached. And though no mortal could discern them, there were wounds within his molten visage that would not heal for generations, patches of darkness swallowed and held away from the world he loved.

My creator. My parent. The Dawnfather. Oh, my father, shattered from a long, heartbreaking war.

Within his corona, a crown that is the sun itself, there is light. Fire. Destruction. Creation. Judgment. Severity. But gentleness, too. And yes, kindness.

As I was lowered into the scorched, blackened earth, high in the mountains, that was what I remembered most: even the supreme sun may handle the smallest thing with tender care. Hands, each a burning bonfire, buried me deep into the soil. His divine warmth wrapped around me like a swaddling blanket.

How long he stood there after, I could not say. Not that I could even think yet, let alone speak. That would come later. But I can imagine it, his loneliness. His unfiltered rage. A shadow to my father's sun.

My father stood there for a long time and, in doing so, showed me what my tasks were to be: To watch. To witness. To stand for as long as I could. To shine, regardless of the dark. And, in shining, to see and know all around me.

Of course, he left at some point. I couldn't tell you when or why. I imagine he heard, from somewhere beyond the stars, the words of his siblings, calling him home before the closing of the divine gates, wrought of pure will. Or perhaps it was the plea of a faithful, beseeching his light and aid. I know it was most likely some other horror that needed his might, but I'll always hope for him to find joy when he expects conflict.

Either way, he left. And before he did, he laid a massive, hot palm across my planting site. I can hear his sigh even now, as though sound were steel, carved into my very heart.

To hear a god exhausted.

Someday, my limbs would be large enough to hold him. For even the sun needs comfort and rest. But then I was still but a seed and could do nothing.

I can see him standing now, lighting every angle of the Alabaster Sierras, like the dawn.

And like every dawn, he leaves.

The light fades, and in my seed, I slumber, dreaming of sweet, sweet sun.

LIKE THOSE WHO RAISE THEIR voices in worship, scattered throughout the city around me, I have never known exactly what purpose my father had for me, but, like them, I hoped. Hoped to one day know. Hoped to one day fulfill it, to make him happy and proud.

But I believe I can say with assurance that what began to happen to me in my slumber was something he had not and could not have anticipated.

Yes, I began to grow, unfurling from my seed in fits and starts, nourished by rain and light, the nutrients of the dark earth. Yet, there too was something else in the soil. Something different. Something divine.

For didn't the blood of the Knowing Mistress water this earth, coagulated and still beneath the surface? Didn't some small part of the oblivion that was defeated linger here, flaring in long stretches of starless shadow? And even my father—hadn't his divine gold lit the valley and mountains like a pyre with his wrath?

All this divinity, blood and shadow and light, it had changed the very earth I had been planted in.

And so, as I grew from the sustenance all growing things need, there was another nourishment that I drank in. The taste of myth itself became a part of my core. When those legends found root within me, I began to change in ways beautiful and unexpected.

With the blood of the Knowing Mistress, my mind began to form. Thought and cognition. Reason and emotion. Idea and memory. All churning and braiding together, carving pathways through me, as though consciousness were a carpenter's knife that, year by year, defined me with care. Each sunrise, I awoke with new understandings of my existence and Exandria at large. Leaves fell, and I knew it as gravity, autumn, color, and weight. Flowers budded and bloomed across me, and I knew metabolism, sunlight, stars, summer, heat, and beauty. Snow accumulated on my bare crown, and I knew cold, slumber, hunger, winter, and want. I began to know this world in its complexity and reveled in the education.

At times, memories of the Calamity would burn in me, that horror and heartbreak of the ages, when cities fell from the sky and the air itself was aflame. From them, like the Knowing Mistress, I knew sorrow.

From the deep shadow of an oblivion I had never met but feared nonetheless, I came to know dread. Though I knew it was chained once more, in a space beyond reach of mortal and god alike, I could still taste it in my roots. Its unending fury, its terrible hate, its mindless hunger . . . whatever it was, it left a stain on Exandria, a world it could not help but yearn for, for no reason other than it was made to devour. Months would pass before a vision from its smoking shadow would rear inside of my mind, fuliginous flashes of deepest umbra, a chaos so vehement and unsatisfied it could drink the sky dry of stars and still wish for more. And yet, this fear, it was an education. Especially coming from an alien being I could think of only as my parent's very antithesis. As I was born in sun, so, too, I came to understand the shadow.

And as the years went by, as I grew from thin stalk to stolid sapling, from the smallest of timber to a budding tree, my very soul was brought to life by my father. The Dawnfather's touch left divine magic in me—just the smallest spark, and yet . . . it was enough to feel through my roots the deep and loving song of the stone far beneath me, trading gossip in tectonic shifts. It was enough to taste life on the wind that flowed over my branches and around my growing trunk; in my slight golden leaves, I caught the flavors of birdsong and beetle buzz, learned the differences between rain cloud and snowstorm. And his spark within me, yes, gave me just enough reach to know and feel the ley lines of Exandria. Roads of pure magic, forged even before my father's time, before even the elemental spirits began their joyful dance. If I really focused, I might be able to know their aurora, converging above me just as night arrived. And on those days of solstice, I did not even need to concentrate; the ley lines danced for me, an audience of one.

Ah, life. Beautiful, complicated, bittersweet life.

As I grew, I felt it, the terrible conundrum.

Life ended. Death came for all. Even with that spark of sunlight in me, I knew it the way the sea knows water, and the way fire knows heat: even I, someday, might die.

I had already shut myself off from all the little deaths I felt in and around me. The spider ensnared by the jay's quick beak. The flowers that suffocated beneath the first snow. One evening I even saw the smallest pinprick of a star simply vanish, gone wherever stars go when they cease their blaze.

It changed me, that shadow of oblivion I had supped on. And yet I was not ungrateful for it—to know the void, to have some sliver of it within me, as I had a mind of knowledge and a soul of sunlight. For in holding it close, that darkness, I understood the promise of life: to rise with the light, to experience and know all there is, and to one day slumber in shadow.

I cannot imagine the conflict that took place on the soil where I am planted now. That restless, many-limbed oblivion; the bleeding breast of the Knowing Mistress, leaking wisdom; the Dawnfather's blade like the core of the sun.

I am a marker of that conflict. As I grow, I know more than I ever dreamed I might.

I know history can change in the blink of a mortal eye.

And so it did.

I had a working knowledge of mortals, those myriad peoples of the world whom my father and his siblings loved and protected, watching over them as I watched over this valley, these mountains.

But I hadn't met any until a bright and blustery summer's day when I sensed a line of beings, marching through a mountain pass like ants. I could taste salt in the air when I sensed in that direction and could only imagine the hulking wooden ships they had made to come to a land as new to them as they were to me.

As they approached, I felt their language in the vibration of stone and wind. A new emotion welled up within me, I who had been content for decades to stand and grow and feel no hand of time on my trunk.

Giddiness. I felt giddiness! A pure joy, like a child made excitable by the discovery of the new. I recognized words. Words! Language had been but a concept, but here it came, in shapes strange and soft and spiky, shushing and hissing and rounded. Oh! Language was a lovely and delightful thing. I tasted new metals, steel and brass and gold in the form of rounded coins. I tasted worked leathers and heavy boots, felt their tread upon my grasses. The tang of sweat, the pump of blood, the soil of another landmass under their nails!

I could also taste exhaustion and fear, a weariness to each step that fell to the earth with little rhythm. Something had happened to these mortals, and I suddenly wondered at the state of those ships, and how exactly they had arrived.

It was an exhilarating moment, and, like the sun above, I watched them all come down through the mountain pass, beaten and delirious themselves. Who knew how long it took to travel across the world? I knew from memory that powerful wielders of magic could open the air like a door and go where they wished, but not these people. Wherever they came from, whatever they sought, they had done so on their own power, by their own will.

Is it odd that for a moment I felt a sense of pride? Kinship with this group who had made it to the land I called home? I wished for them to see it as beautiful, and as they wept to see the green of my valley, and the gold of my boughs, I knew they did.

It was some time before they turned their attention to me. First, they gathered water from the nearby streams, shouting with delight at its coldness and fresh flavor. Next, they set up a series of tents, driving stakes into the dirt, securing them with rope. It wasn't until the sun was just about to set that finally two individuals came toward me, stopping just under the spot where my branches reached farthest.

One of them spoke, their voice deep and robust, strong and soft at the same time. "And what do we make of this, Sunfather? One look and it may actually be big enough to patch the damage to our vessels and perhaps even build another at their side!"

The other mortal was older, parched in the way that no water could quench. And yet I could sense jollity in it, curiosity. "Ah, my lord, I've no idea. I'm no shipmaker, just a holy man trying to help steer a flock more lost than most. 'Tis beautiful, though, that's for sure. There does seem to be something to it, something I . . . recognize." Then, "Would you pardon an old man's intrigue?"

Before I could process their words, a hand was suddenly on my trunk.

I had . . . never been touched by mortal hands. My branches swayed, and I know the light of the sunset caught them in dazzling bursts of rose and amber.

I heard the voice let loose a deep breath, as though he were as moved as I. And then the warmth on my trunk changed, growing into a feeling I was familiar with, faintly: a warmth that went from a candle to a campfire, a greater fire than I had believed mortals could make on their own.

When I finally recognized it, I could have wept myself free of leaves.

Whoever this old man was, he touched me with the same warmth as my father.

As I came to the realization, the old man gasped as well, and I could taste the tears that suddenly appeared in his eyes, full of divine awe. I could only imagine that, as I had recognized his connection to my father, he, too, felt the light reflected inside of me.

He turned to his companion, laughing with joy. "Ha! Oh, Lord de Rolo! I—I don't know how and . . . I don't know why, but within this tree is—is the divine light of the Dawnfather, the Dawnfather himself!" He laughed again and put both arms around my trunk as far as they would go, embracing me. "I'd sooner chop myself in half to be used as stern and hull than harm a leaf on this divine tree. Maybe he has guided us here, my lord. He looked through time and saw our trials at sea. He gave us this tree, this beautiful golden gift as bright as the sun itself, to stand for us. For any who would come here! We were being watched all along, my lord. And this? This is a sign, exactly as we prayed for. A place of rest. Of safety. We may not know our next move, Lord de Rolo, but while we figure it out, we have found heavenly succor."

The old man wept into my bark, and could I weep, I would have done so with him, for as much as he thought I was the gift, he was wrong.

The touch of my father, the first since my birth, was truly the dearer boon.

As the sun sank below the horizon, I heard the first voice, Lord de Rolo, mutter under his breath, as though through a smile, "Well, then. Very good, I suppose. Would hate to be the man who comes between a priest and his tree. Until you can tell us your name, bright one, we'll just have to call you the Sun Tree. Fits until we come up with something better, yes?"

Had I the chance to have spoken with him, I'd have said not to worry himself.

It was perfect.

THE CITY WOULD NOT COME to life for many, many years, but the spark that would see it built was born that day.

Not that that was what these wayward mortals were determined to do. Beneath my shadow, these shipwrecked pilgrims milled about and explored my valley, more having come through the mountain pass toward proclaimed safety.

Safe enough, anyway. Those first weeks included the hunting of dire wolves and cougars, the setting of magic traps and small abjurations, maintaining some sort of guard at all times. As this Lord de Rolo and his crew, including his wife and several small children, began to set up life, those in his employ, or possibly command, began to secure the valley. Game was hunted, berries were foraged, water was gathered, and it brought me joy to see the resources of my valley, the timber of the nearby wood used for housing and structures. I did not envy my brethren; I was grateful not to have been felled myself.

I knew this dance, life and death, and so was more concerned with the mortals who made it their job to survive. Even if many talked of leaving come spring—of rebuilding boats and ships, mending sails, consulting maps—a part of me knew they would last beyond the winter. My valley was beautiful, its resources plentiful, its scars of war long healed and ready for renewal. I would not be surprised if some left, but I knew what everyone else did not: many more would wish to stay.

I don't believe they knew they were making a city. As I remembered the lessons found in the blood of the Knowing Mistress, cities were far too large a concept to pursue, too massive in scope to be held in the mind's eye. Infrastructure and maintenance, politics and government, these things were snakes consuming their own tails, endless and twisty, ever-changing yet always the same. No sane person pursued such dangerous and exhausting serpents.

But I also knew that cities came to life of their own volition. People with common goals and mutual respect lending aid and resources, their calloused hands reaching toward one another, each lifting the others in synchronized care. It is in these acts, these moments of charity and community and justice, hunger sated, shelter given, thirst quenched, that the soul of a city is forged. Once the soul of a city is made, those who gave their heart and breath and blood to it can withstand any devastation or horror.

History is cemented on such foundations. And on such foundations, monuments of society can be built.

Lord de Rolo, his wife, and other members of their crew often met under my branches to discuss how they might come together and survive the coming cold. Some weeks had passed, and many wondered how best to bring order. Already, there were a fair number of people arriving from the wreckage, ship lumber and supplies in hand, each with base needs to be addressed.

When Lord de Rolo began to speak, I sensed a natural leadership within him; I'd have to keep my eye on him and that name he carried like a saber.

"First things first, everyone. Winter is coming on, and we've no idea its harshness compared to our old home back east, so we must move forward with caution. Supplies are limited, yes? And our scouting parties are only willing to range so far in unfamiliar land. So," he said, using a branch of mine that had fallen, "here's what I propose."

Through the vibrations in the soil, I traced the shape of the future along with Lord de Rolo. His vision was humble, but I knew in that first sweep of circles—a large outer one and a smaller one within—much could be built. He spoke of walls as much as he spoke of gates; ways to protect from within and means to bring others inside. "I'd see to our own protection first, of course, but we also need an ability to range, hunt, and gather only what we need. We're to be back at sea come spring, and I'd rather the local flora and fauna not curse my family name for picking the valley clean, if we can help it."

The group chuckled as he continued, painting a vision of just enough shelter, food, and resources to see the snow through until thaw. "By which point," he said, marking off a little circle in the middle, "we can gather here at our lovely, bright friend, pay our respects to the Dawnfather, and cast off. While we're here, it will be the heart of our new life. The Sun Tree. We *are* calling it that, yes, Sunfather? One of my little girls has suggested Goldyleaf and Mister Bright Trunk, so if I could assure her we've already got it covered, maybe she'll settle for naming a local hill or something?"

The older man from before laughed and nodded. "Oh yes, Lord de Rolo. I have felt it every day, stronger and stronger. The Dawnfather planted this tree some time ago, maybe even pre-Calamity. It's not just his light that resides within; it seems the tree is a convergence point of other magical tides. Maybe your wife, the good doctor, could study it some more with me," he said, pointing to the woman at Lord de Rolo's side; I could taste her magic, which waited on vellum pages at her side, patient.

She adjusted the small spectacles on her nose and inclined her head to the Sunfather, pushing a lock of dark hair behind her ear. "I'd be happy to, Father. I've been somewhat distracted by proper transmutation of the materials we're scavenging, but in the evenings, there are certainly faint flows of light visible, at least to one of my persuasions. Merits more study, absolutely."

Lord de Rolo chuckled and put a hand at the small of her back in comfort. "Well, if you can make any of those lights visible to all, my darling, the Dawnfather knows our crew of survivors could do with a little delight. In the meantime . . ."

Many days went by with this small council meeting under my canopy, and I sheltered them from the coming cold and gave what light I could as night came on, earlier and earlier each evening.

In the mornings, the Sunfather would sit with me and sip a cup of tea. He would tell me of his life before arriving on these shores, in a land called Wildemount. A small town called Deastok. Friends and loved ones left behind. "My heart aches, but I know someday I'll see them again, yes? And we are all still under the light of the same sun. There's comfort in that."

When she was not busy leading engineers and mages, Lord de Rolo's wife, Frida, took lunch with me, bringing her children, Greta, Dane, and

Isabella, along. When the children played in the burgeoning town square, she would murmur to me of her fears and her dreams, research book open on her lap. "Winter comes, and I feel like my children. Like we're all playing pretend when we should be terrified. And yet, aren't we doing the best we can? I know we are. And when we try our best, it is a comfort to know it couldn't have been any better, that we gave all we could. It is a tenet of science and the arcane as much as it is one of religion and the divine: at a certain point, one knows all one can truly know, and everything after is just . . . faith."

When the children tired, she'd swap books and read them stories of fantasy and myth, flights of fancy that took them from the decks of pirate ships to the clouds of Zephrah, from the back of a battlefield horse to a city called Emon, the jewel of Tal'Dorei.

In the evenings, Lord de Rolo himself visited with me, leaning his back to my trunk, sipping something hot and spiced from a small silver tankard. He didn't speak much but stood with me as though we were two surveyors, coming to see the future being built around us. It was one of the few chances he had to be alone—though not really.

Throughout the winter, houses sprang up every few days, their roofs sloped like the hull of a ship turned upside down, a small nod to what brought these people here, a reminder that even the past can shelter you, regardless of its form and weight. Snows came and went, freezing muddy ground and bringing joy to the young and consternation to the old.

As the flower unfurls in sun, as the caterpillar reaches for its wings, so too did these survivors grow toward something they couldn't even imagine.

All the while, I relished in my name. The Sun Tree. Like any good name, it was true. As the winter entered its fullness, more and more people came to me, leaving small candles or beads, tiny metal trinkets or preserved flower petals. It seemed they believed me to be a conduit of my father, and, like a struck tuning fork, maybe their offerings could reach him through me.

I didn't know for sure if that was true, but I sincerely hoped it was: I had begun to care for each of these people who called me and my valley home.

But unlike myself, the little camp had not yet stumbled upon a name. Many were tried, and yet, they all slid away—not true enough, not fitting. And why name a thing that would be going away?

Until the day Frida de Rolo approached her husband at the crest of winter's ending. In her hands was a piece of mountain rock, jagged and pale. "Husband! My love, look what we've stumbled upon."

With a flick of her fingers, the rock began to glow, beautiful as a luminous green moth. "On the eastern slope, I'd asked a few of my engineers to test for samples and learn what they could of the region's minerals when we found this. I have never seen anything like this, my love."

An eyebrow arched over a small pair of gold-rimmed glasses. "Darling wife, you have my permission to blather."

She smiled, redness spreading across her pale cheeks. "Don't flirt with me right now, Darius de Rolo, or I'll not tell you of our discovery. Now then, I've only been analyzing for a little while, but already there is something strange about this hunk of rock. Something about the convergence of ley lines, maybe? A mixture of the Sun Tree's divinity and the arcane? Whatever it is, there seems to be vast potential in this white stone, husband. And this valley? It's *full* of it."

There it was. A name that fit like a puzzle piece. A name that was true, that described and aspired and founded this city upon the rock that would mark it in history's many books.

Truth be told, Darius, Frida, their children, the Sunfather, many of the survivors . . . they had been thinking of it for a while. As green came on, as my light warmed them, as they saw the promise of spring in my valley, they began to see a future, too.

A future where they stayed. Where they built. Where they cared and took care, as best they could, free to choose the life they wished. And with a strange, dizzying new resource and a tree they saw was sent by one of their beloved gods, it took only a few days to agree on it.

Whitestone—a city, a resource, a burgeoning soul—was born.

Generations came and went, and I learned to mourn each. As Whitestone grew, sprawling as the vine creeps ever out and up toward the sun, I saw each life as a precious leaf, from bud to full to withering—and to the eventual fall.

Across the expanse of the city, I felt life arriving like sudden sunrays, adding to the warmth of Whitestone—squalls of newborns, coming into Exandria with the suddenness of a summer storm, exuberant and loud. I could feel each and every heartbeat thrumming through the ground, at first a humble rhythm that grew with each passing year. Every scout who went afield returned with messages from communities hundreds of miles north and south and west, bringing with them a merchant here, a priestess there, and so forth. The pace of life in Whitestone began to grow. And every year ended with more heartbeats than when it began.

But the opposite was true as well. Though the number of dead couldn't match the pace of new life appearing across the city, death also had its time in Whitestone. It took a very trained ear to know when a certain heart left the chorus of life. But eventually, I learned how.

The old. The infirm. Catastrophes, accidents, purposeful violence. I knew them all, in one way or another, and learned how to grieve for each. I did not have a heart in the mortal sense, and yet, whatever mechanism I grew to care for these brief lives broke at their leaving all the same.

The first that I knew deeply, terribly, was the Sunfather, who arrived under my boughs only a handful of years after he had first appeared. He'd already been an elderly halfling, and that last winter sank into his bones with a hunger that healing could not stave off.

He died with his hand on my trunk, whispering to me, "I go now to our father, Sun Tree. And in this way, I—I have always f-felt us . . . kindred. Siblings. I . . . I will give . . . give him your love."

When his heart finally stopped, I knew what it was to grieve.

I would hope to say I have gotten better over the centuries, but I cannot claim so. Each loss makes my branches shudder and shake with fury, causes the little animals who clamber about me to scatter, to make my golden leaves fall in a rain like tears.

Is this how my father feels each time he loses a follower to the long night of death? No, he does not mourn, for his faithful join him in celestial rest. But maybe, I think, this is how he felt leaving me on this side of the divine gate. Left behind. An earthen promise as he rose skyward. Surely the sun's heart ached, too, leaving his child alone. In this is the only consolation. That whether you're fated to remain or destined to go, pain awaits. But it is pain shared by both parties, and maybe more bearable because of it.

Maybe loss will always hurt, no matter who you are—god, mortal, or otherwise.

And yet, life, beautiful and precious, would not be either if it lasted forever. As the old man's successor said at his funeral, "Sunrise would not be so sweet if we did not endure the cold night before it. Sunset would not be so heartbreaking if it lingered forever on the horizon."

As Whitestone grew, stretching up and outward with every generation, mourning became as natural as my leaves and light. The castle rose higher and higher, even as Darius de Rolo took his last breath, with Frida following only a scant few years after. They were the first to be interred within the family crypts, and a statue of them was built in the center of town, made of brilliant whitestone.

Their walls and parapets grew to match as their children—now adults themselves, married, each with children of their own—eventually fell to the flux. Gardens were planned, planted, and pruned as a marriage brought the von Musels into the family line, blood becoming rich with history, heavy with names.

Despite disaster and conflict, great fires and calamities of the everyday, Whitestone flourished. It seemed every other generation brought more houses, more structures, more and more and more!

It did not hurt that the studious among them had cracked the secret of that whitestone all those years ago following Frida's discovery. I could not tell you by what process the mortal mind unraveled those mysteries, but in all the vast energies of the Calamity, the valley and earth and mountains had become suffused with magic itself.

And when some great force was put to it, refining and compressing and pushing all that infused stone in on itself, something tremendous happened. What was left, residing in the emerald glass born from the process, was a potent magical material.

They called it residuum. Soon enough, word left the valley of this precious resource on offer from the Lord and Lady of Whitestone.

Trade exploded as it became known to the arcane communities of this landmass, Tal'Dorei. Dwarven royalty of far-off Kraghammer, whose halls rang with the music of metal meeting anvil, promised precious gems and ingenious contraptions. Members of a council from Emon came with chests of gold and platinum, making promise of exclusive trade, of power for power. There were even peoples from distant Syngorn, elven diplomats and long-lived merchants intent on acquisition to enhance their serious mystic studies.

Whitestone had no shortage of visitors, and so the Lord and Lady de Rolo, now with the names Frederick and Joanna, did not hesitate to welcome them. With them was their gaggle of precocious children, each of them as inquisitive and brilliant and varied as a jewel in the sun. And—

I . . .

It . . .

It pains me, knowing what came next. To look back and see it plain as day, the path so clear in hindsight, a part of me aches for what could have been done to prevent it.

But I am no warrior. No commander. I am not mortal, charged with mortal responsibility. I am of the Dawnfather. I was planted as a sign and symbol of his love, an icon of light. A witness, like the sun above.

And so I recount my terrible witnessing of the days of darkness.

When I truly learned what death was, and how cold life could be without the sun.

When you live life away from most of the world, why would you choose to live in fear? If your walls are high and your people trusted and your guards trained and their blades sharp, what use is paranoia? If all your life is spent looking out, wary for signs of danger approaching, why would you look over your shoulder to those within?

Such is how the Briarwoods took Whitestone for themselves.

Like rot, they started small and moved slowly, their terrible touch infecting everything: stone and earth, air and light, the souls of the people and populace. And like any good predator, they hid in plain sight until it was too late.

Styled as nobility, they arrived like the shadow cast by a crow in flight, a rush of darkness and distraction, insinuating themselves among the upper echelons of Whitestone society. How were the people of Whitestone to know that this woman of dark hair and pale skin, bedecked in jewels and with eyes of deep knowledge, stank like grave dirt and headstone? How were they to know this man, red-eyed and bone white, with a tailored suit and an intimidatingly regal blade at his side, reeked of blood and death, his teeth aching from the hiding of his secret?

No. They could not know.

Until it was too late.

That night . . . You couldn't imagine it. You could try. But the fire would not burn hot enough in your imagination. The screams of confused, dying children would not be loud enough. The horror and fury of their parents, powerless before these conquerors made drunk on the unleashing of their plans, would not be deep enough.

Even now I tremble when recalling that night. The song of blades arcing through the air, separating head from body. The brutal cross from ear to ear, the lifeblood of de Rolos and nobles staining rich carpets crimson, the splatter of red ruining portraits and paintings, turning the lineage of their families awful.

And while there were others in their employ, even within the castle itself, whom they had seduced and taken in, it was Lord and Lady Briarwood who led the razing.

The teacher, Anders, brought some of the de Rolo children to them.

The doctor, Ripley, caught the others.

Many of the de Rolo children were put to death, swiftly. Two were kept back for torture, to see what they knew. And even when those two escaped, tragedy followed.

The youngest, Cassandra, was filled with arrows, and she fell, red, to the snow.

The other barely managed to flee.

One of the boys. Percival, always the middle of the pack, suddenly a lone wolf cub on the run. I felt his heart, pumping like the hare's fleeing a dozen owls' talons, and with every moment, I felt him run farther and farther from me. Through the tears in his eyes and the torture they had done to his body, he ran with abandon, until finally I could feel him no more.

It was one of the last cogent thoughts I had before she tried to kill me, too.

It was near dawn, the morning following their bloody coup, and I sensed the fear throughout the city, citizens not knowing what to do.

And for a moment, I did not give a damn to be witness. The screams of those little children lived in my roots; I could hear them still. (I can *still* hear them.) I tasted the blood and tears of their mother and father, killed before them. I held little Cassandra, bleeding out in the snow. I urged Percival on, hoping he heard me shouting for him to flee from this place lest he die as well.

I did not know what I could do, but I could be what I was meant to be: a sign, a symbol, a beacon.

As the first rays of morning broke across the mountain peaks, the snow dazzling with sunrise's kiss, I made myself bright with the fury and heartbreak I held within. My golden leaves shimmered, blazing like a righteous torch across my myriad branches. My whole canopy began to shine so bright that I hoped those on the edge of the city would think me a second sun.

The Briarwoods had brought death and darkness. Why was beyond my ken; I knew the way of root and leaf, sun and moon. What drove people to commit the horror I felt keenly throughout my very being, I could not know, and even had I the capability, a part of me believes still I would refuse such knowledge.

I had to act. I had to do something to remind the people of Whitestone, my family, that death and darkness were not forever. So I greeted the morning sun with my own luminous rage.

And then she made the sun go away.

Her hand on me was cold as a corpse and yet it burned like a terrible fire. From beneath my shining canopy, her voice, wicked and gentle: "Oh, that won't do. A brave little light show, dear thing, but your god is far. And don't take this the wrong way," she said, mirth coating her words like oil, "but my husband and I aren't exactly morning people."

Light began to fade.

At her touch, my leaves dimmed, my light drained from me. The morning sunrise suddenly found clouds in front of it, gray and heavy as a funeral shroud. Thunder rumbled across the length and breadth of Whitestone, and though it was morning, the sun was a mere suggestion behind this conjured curtain.

My glow went away entirely; I watched her drink of it, the light dancing across her palm before it wilted into shadow and then nothingness. In her poison-green eyes I saw satisfaction and knew her to be a monster.

"Darling," she called behind her. "Would you help me send a message?"

"Gladly, my love," her husband said, coming to her side. In his hand was the black blade, as long as he was tall, jagged and barbed as though it were made of thorns. It was red where it wasn't black. "May I ask to whom we're addressing it?"

"Oh, Sylas. To none other than Whitestone itself."

Pain.

Sudden, burning pain! A pain I had never known because I had never had reason to know pain at all. From my trunk that blade protruded, driven into me by the might of her husband's hand. Black, oily smoke rose, and I feared bursting into flame at any moment. If I listened closely, I could almost hear a third voice, howling with hunger. I was overcome with this unbearable torment; had I the ability to scream, the Alabaster Sierras themselves would free their snowy heights with my heartbreak.

He withdrew it, leaving a mighty gash in my trunk. And before I could see what was happening, the Lady Briarwood came forward and put her hand within me.

A pulse of pure despair ran through me, from the top of my crown to the very bottom of my roots, deep beneath the city itself.

I didn't know what was happening. I felt . . . sick. Weak.

Some*thing* was within me. Waiting to leech, claw, grasp at me. A seed of pure oblivion that would kill me as surely as steel plunged into a mortal's heart.

I felt her joy at my distress, his disgust at my light. Knowing what I did of these two bringers of hate, they would not kill me quickly. They would want me to suffer as they made all else suffer.

And so, as prey flees, making itself so small as to appear absolutely gone, I remembered the smallness of my seed days. I recalled that miniscule shape I grew from and knew it to be the only place to hide my life. And as I had grown with a small part of shadow within me, I remembered how, in the fear it taught, I learned how to hide from such darkness.

They would kill all of me if they could. And so, I would not let them.

Even from that moment, my hale brown bark had begun to gray at the site of impact. I could feel light evaporating from my leaves, one by one. And I had many leaves in my crown.

"Well, that should do nicely, wouldn't you say, Sylas?"

"It will," he replied, nuzzling her neck with his lips, breathing deep of her perfume of rot and decay. "Come, my dear. Anders says the little whelp lives yet. Poor thing leaked all over the foyer."

Turning, she kissed him deeply, and then with that glint in her serpent eye she said, "Ah, interesting. Well, we'll find a way to make the girl pay us back. Let us go and see to our new ward. Patch her up and begin her new education."

They turned, leaving me to die.

And I might've, if they had known what I knew.

I knew, even this close to death, what the evil leaving my sight feared above all: no matter what they did, and no matter how hard they tried, there would be light again.

The sun would return.

And I would one day return with it.

Until then, I felt the dark poison beginning to move through me, inch by inch. I knew I had to retreat to the safety of sleep, hidden from her touch until a day when I might be healed. Around me, my once golden leaves, now white and gray and smoking with death, dropped in heavy weeping.

The last thing I remember is hands, hundreds of them, that came forward when no guard was near and lifted my leaves to their hearts. Into pockets and bags and sachets, my leaves were taken by the many of Whitestone who knew I had been afflicted.

It seemed I had enough for nearly the whole city. Craftsmen and children, rangers and loyal soldiers, nurses and tinkerers, all snuck over to me, and in my coming slumber, I could have wept to know my many children took a part of me home to safeguard, to find comfort in.

My final leaf, I could feel, found a safe place in the hands of the latest steward of the gods, a devotee to the Lawbearer. Keeper Yennen, an older man of divine renown and a kind heart, took my leaf and held it to his holy symbol, a symbol of war inlaid with a symbol of justice.

His hand on my trunk, gentle and warm. His voice, a whisper, soft and heavy with sorrow. "Justice will come. We will bring the sun back. Rest now, my friend."

And with the comforting void of sleep calling me to safety, I had no choice but to obey.

For the next five years, shadow reigned in Whitestone. And while I did my best to hide from the touch of death that spread through me, it found me. I could not help but hear the city I had been tasked to watch over cry for help.

Guards were replaced with those loyal to the Briarwoods and their assembled faction.

One by one, temples were closed, the altars to the Prime Deities bare and cold.

Soldiers began to prowl the streets at night, terrorizing citizens and barring the fearful from leaving. Any rebellion warranted terrible punishment.

The first time they hung someone from my bare and shivering branches, I cried in my sleep. I still feel the weight of those nooses, heavy with horror.

Every year or so, someone would try to organize, gather together, make plans to smuggle word out to neighboring cities, or to arm the people, but the Briarwoods had spies everywhere.

Finally, Lady Briarwood raised her hand one evening and, one by one, the dead came to her aid. Whitestone gave up the lives that had been given to it, interred into the earth or stone caverns, and they shambled outward, heeding her call. She even found a few giant corpses up in the mountains, had them pulled to the city and bid them stand.

I had never truly felt time before those miserable five years. Time, like the air, had always moved through me, invisible, barely felt. Centuries had passed for me in the blink of a mortal eye.

And yet, as I slumbered, I felt time's crawl like blood dripping down stone. I felt every scream of terror, every tear that fell from every eye. I heard every conversation in the dead of night, some grasping toward hope, others planning continued destruction.

I felt, keen as a dagger, the wispy, thin voice of Cassandra up in the castle, whispering through broken ribs and tight bandages. Were they prayers? Pleas? When you are tortured each day as she had been, could those two concepts be said to be any different?

At some point, she stopped. I can only imagine what happened to her when she did.

The hardest nights were those when the Briarwoods went below my roots, clearing out the ancient temple that had been sealed for all those years by my parent. Those evenings held fell and foul magic, thick with the rot of death, as Lady Briarwood carved dread symbols into stone, erasing the Knowing Mistress's history. Her husband ordered servants around, his sword at his side to remind them of insolence answered.

It was this excavation that truly worked death into me, the terrible magic of decay and hate, necromancy and rot worming their way ever upward into my mighty roots. With each new section of the temple converted, the Knowing Mistress's language of knowledge perverted into that of horror and undeath, it seemed my very life was being used as fuel for these dark transmutations. Even hidden, even as small and still as I remained, I could feel darkness like blades trying to end my life inside me.

The worst of it all—beyond the corruption, the sacrilege—was their love.

When alone, they spoke honeyed words to each other. He kissed her cheek when she didn't expect it, and she ran a hand along his arm in quiet moments. They told each other the little everyday nothings that are of interest only to lovers; they did not skip details, and their laughter often bounced off the ziggurat's walls and my roots above.

I could not make sense of it. I slept like a fitful child, hiding from a fact learned too young: the greatest evil could have the capacity to love, selflessly and fully, and still choose to believe the world deserved none of it. Even now I remain baffled as to how two people could love each other so deeply and yet see all other life as their enemy.

What purpose they sought, they never spoke aloud, at least never above a whisper. But in the absolute midnight of my slumber, I felt as though eyes watched me from a great and terrible distance. They were brilliant in their malice, and bright with their ambition. I had known fire's touch, and the hunger in this gaze burned hotter still. I shudder, remembering them.

To recount every atrocity that happened in Whitestone in those years . . . it is too much to bear, even for I, a witness of purpose. But there was one that shook my very roots, for after is when everything changed.

But for everything to change, seven people had to hang from my branches.

Soaked from whipping, cold rain, dragged downward by gravity's weight, necks bruised, they swayed. Who they were, I could only guess at: a young, dark-haired woman with a touch of inner magic, a little girl with white hair, a horrifying amalgamation of several men stitched together into a single massive grotesquerie.

I felt each of them go. Felt each of them hang.

Until they were cut down by hands and voices I did not know, could not place. One that was vague in its shape, but familiar.

And another that gave me hope for the first time in five years.

It had been so long since I'd known the gentleness of one versed in the way of leaf and loam. Keyleth was her name. And she knew mine.

"Sun Tree? A-Are you there? My name . . . my name is Keyleth. We're here to help. Are you there?"

How I wished I could answer! To exert the gold of my father, my inner light. But I was so diminished. So very, very small.

I could say not a thing, but I tried, as best I could, to tell her that I was here. That I was alive. That though death was in me, I remained. I had held fast.

I could only hope these newcomers did, too.

Little did I know who had returned with them. But the more I heard his voice—the cadence, the accent, the inherent nobility, the intelligence—the more I came to recognize him. Even years later, there was something of youth in him, like he had grown up too fast. And he had.

My boy.

My dear Percival had returned.

I know he's not mine, I do. But how could I see that young man who used to climb my branches and not think of him as my boy?

My boy, come home again!

I did not know whoever he had brought with him, apart from kind Keyleth. But as I felt him and his band move through the expanse of Whitestone, meeting with Keeper Yennen, relearning the city that had been his home once, and could be again, I tried to hold to that spark of hope I had found.

As they moved from one end of the city to the other, into the manors of the Briarwoods' faction, and into their own jail to free citizens, it was almost as though these heroes were sent by the gods. With their voices leading the charge, I felt through my withered roots the soul of Whitestone start to find itself once more.

Ah, but I feared for my boy. He was him, and yet as he ran through these once-familiar streets, he cast a second shadow. Whether his friends could see it, I do not know. But I *felt* it. I had become all too intimate with darkness as of late, and I tasted it on him like the choking stink of burning charcoal. It flared and it raged, whispering to him like the fire whispers to the wood that fuels it.

Come. Come and burn. Burn for me and I will burn them for you.

Oh, my boy. I only hoped he was strong enough to outpace that burning shadow behind him.

But every day, with dagger and song, arrow and axe, light and lead and the elements themselves, Percival and his band carved open Whitestone like a gangrenous wound, plunging deeper, toward the heart of the infection. Intent on ridding the city of the two who had made a plague of themselves, I watched them head into the castle in pursuit of the Briarwoods like a nightmare unspooling.

It was too much. Too frenzied. Chaos incarnate as these heroes pursued death itself, hoping to deliver justice.

The Briarwoods were not their gross lieutenants, ruling for a chance at wealth and power. They were not crafty like Dr. Anna Ripley, who served them long enough to escape their grasp and Whitestone altogether. No, the Briarwoods had what all of them lacked. Conviction and a devoted love for each other.

Together, love and conviction make a potent alchemy.

But in the end, neither was stronger than justice or vengeance.

The first to end was the Lord Briarwood. I knew why he had feared me, and feeling Keyleth call the light to her, as I used to, I felt my roots soak up the sudden radiance, warmth rushing through me, almost like blood.

The slumbering part of me could've wept. It had been so long, and yet . . .

Yes. Yes, that is how it feels.

As for the lady, Cassandra ran her through with steel. My once-sweet Cassandra, a shell of herself, but finally free.

And whatever fell ritual the lovers had spent five years working on . . . something had changed, but I was too weak, still asleep, to know what.

All I could focus on was my boy.

His second shadow had its claw gripped around his heart. It had risen and towered above him. Like in a nightmare, I could not touch the moment, could not help. I could only pray to my father that Percival, regardless of his sorrow, regardless of his grief, remembered how beautiful life could be in the sun.

Tense moments passed, and my heart broke for the boy forced to become a weapon in order to survive.

In the end, though he had been built for death, he chose life.

And so did I.

Did my life begin to return to me when he broke free of the second shadow? A part of me likes to think so. That the scion of Whitestone had to choose the future so we all could have one, too.

He might not know it, but he did more than save himself in that moment.

He made it possible for us to save ourselves, too.

And if that isn't the soul of Whitestone, I couldn't tell you what is. And I've been here for quite a while.

It was some time before I awoke, and even now, I'm not sure if I'm all the way there just yet. Most days, I feel like I am caught somewhere between dream and reality. As such, I am often drowsy; I fear Keyleth and her kin may think me a tad more laid-back than I believed I was.

But maybe I am now. These last years have been a time of great change for Whitestone. Who is to say that their Sun Tree cannot change with them?

While much of the darkness within me vanished upon Lady Briarwood's death, I know I am still recovering. My leaves have returned, and my crown of gold is brilliant again. And yet, I know my near death, my mournful slumber, is not so easily cured.

But the days are beautiful, and the people who live here are good. And isn't that enough? I will take my time to heal, for there are many days ahead to rest.

Percival and his wife, the Lady Vex'ahlia, have made a home of the castle, and watching their family welcomed into Whitestone, one child after the other, makes my leaves blush marigold from joy. Even now a gaggle of children run past, Vesper de Rolo and Juni running ahead, Wax with a nervous hand placed upon the side of noble Trinket, graying and proud, and their Ashari friend, Audra, catching up. In the distance, I hear little Leona de Rolo threaten to tattle on her twin, though her heart doesn't seem to be in it.

I'm sure mischief abounds, but if any asked, I would tell them that Whitestone has handled far worse than a few children eager for adventure.

The moments I am most present are when my boy and his wife sit here with me, and I shade them under golden boughs. Why should this simple act feel like privilege? Yet it does, giving them the gift of rest. Maybe it is because I was there with them, then, now, and always. That every day, we wake and feel keenly the pain of our losses, the weight of our grief.

These things do not leave. But they do grow with you.

I know. I know.

My favorite times are evenings, just at sunset. Percival sits with Vex'ahlia, sometimes with tea, sometimes not. There is a spot in my roots where they nestle in comfort, watching the day's light wane. Their eyes drink in each other and then sweep across Whitestone; sometimes Vex'ahlia will blow a kiss at where her brother is buried. When she does, Percival often shakes his head, as though in awe of the man, and he waves, each of them holding the other tighter.

(Even if I could speak, I don't think I'd tell them of the raven in my branches who so often visits and sits above them, head cocked, listening. Something tells me he's more comfortable when hidden.)

But every time they do this, just as the sun alights on the Alabaster Sierras, painting the sky that final shade of gold before the indigo of night, Vex'ahlia turns to her husband and says, "Isn't this just perfect, darling?"

I can feel the pain in his body. The scar in his soul. The trembling in his knuckles. The slight wheeze in his chest, the strength of his arms and legs, his stalwart heart. When he is this close, it is as though I hold Percival in an embrace. The child who survived, the fighter who came back, the man who chose to live.

His wife asks him if this is just perfect, and my boy, every time, says, "It is, darling. It really is."

And every time he says it, I believe him.

Because it is.

I am the Sun Tree, and as long as I stand, I will keep watch. I will witness. I will do my best to keep Whitestone and those who call it home safe, just as Percival and his wife do now.

Together, the three of us watch the sun set. Night falls, and, one by one, constellations begin to dot Exandria's sky.

The night has never frightened me.

It just means there will be dawn tomorrow.

THE EXPLOITS OF KAYLIE
(VOLUME 1)

Izzy Wasserstein

A list, kept in Kaylie's journal:

> *Things I've Heard About My Father*
> ~ *His name is Scanlan Shorthalt.*
> ~ *He's a traveling musician.*
> ~ *He's clever, charming, and funny (he must have been, to sweep Mom off her feet).*
>
> —*Kaylie, age 12*

Mom's been sewing for hours, mending holes in clothes, hemming, doing whatever else her clients demand for the pittance they pay. She's careful not to let me see her weariness, the pain in her fingers, but sometimes she pauses, flexes her hand, in and out, in and out, and I can see the exhaustion in her eyes. She works so hard to keep a roof over our heads, to keep us fed, and she doesn't want me to think about what it costs her.

But I do. All the time.

I'm useless with a needle and thread, my stitches clumsy and inexact, what should be precise lines looking instead like jagged scars. So I try to entertain her, keep her mind off her work. I pluck at my lute, the one my father left behind along with whatever honeyed promises he made my mother. The lute wasn't the only thing he left behind. A few months later, I arrived.

My songs aren't anything special. They're not even proper songs. Little ditties about her customers, other big folk from the neighborhood: Mrs. Dollop, with her hair like a beehive, who always "accidentally" leaves candy for me when she stops by to pick up an order; the twins, Sergei and Stomper, who are hilariously different heights and laugh at everything the other says; and Captain K'bit of the Public Defense, who is all sneers and condescension when he talks to Mom. I try out some new verses to my ever-expanding song about him.

Of all the guards in Kymal town
There's none like Captain K'bit.
He swears that he's the best around
Though he's a massive . . .

"Kaylie!" Mom interjects, trying to sound stern while laughing. That's her part in our little call-and-response. Not my finest work, but K'bit doesn't deserve my finest, and it keeps Mom entertained, which is the whole point.

"You should go out and play," Mom says between songs. "What's Lorit up to?" Mom doesn't know that Lorit is Lora now, and that she's a girl, but that's something Lora asked me to keep a secret, just between us. Just like the little street-corner hustles we run to snag a bit of coin from drunk winners staggering away from the casino. If Mom knew what we got up to, she'd worry even more than she already does.

"Lorit's busy today," I say, hating the way her old name feels on my tongue. "And anyway, I like spending time with you. I've been working on this song, 'The Many Foul Smells of Kymal.' Do you want to hear it?"

She makes a face, but I can tell she does. It's not fair, her being stuck in this nowhere town, barely hanging on, with a daughter who probably constantly reminds her of the man who left her. I can't make that right, but at least I can make her laugh.

> ~ *He's won and lost more coin than I've ever seen.*
>
> *—Kaylie, age 15*

The troubadour is terrible. I've heard mating cats that sounded more melodious. Lora laughs at me.

"What?" I demand. We're hanging out just inside the doorway of the Lucky Mutt inn, looking to make some easy coin delivering messages. The Mutt is where a lot of the out-of-towners stay, and because the only reason anyone voluntarily comes to Kymal is to gamble, it can be a profitable place to be.

"Your face," Lora replies. "You look like a gambler who just lost everything on a throw of the dice." She's about my age and tall even for a human. We look like a mismatched set: her long and gangly, with hair down to her waist, and me a gnome in a town of big folk, my hair all unruly spikes. People give us weird looks, but they usually turn away if I glare hard enough.

"Yeah," I say, "well, they only lost some coin. 'Sember the Master Lutist' is making me lose faith in music." Sember's played a handful of songs, all with the same three chords. If you asked him to play in a minor key, I bet his head would explode.

Maybe Lora sees something in my face she doesn't like. She frowns. "Don't, Kaylie."

"Don't what?" I ask, all innocent-like.

"Whatever you're thinking of," she says. "I know that look." Lora would prefer to fade into the background. Not me.

"I'll behave myself," I say, but a few minutes later Sember makes a particularly atrocious rhyme, and that's more than I can take. I boo. Loudly.

He flubs a chord, then another one, and tries to cover it by stopping mid-song, like that was always his plan. He's a human with a stylish beard, expensive, and an expression that says no one's ever suggested he might be the worst. A noble, then, slumming it down here with us. Or maybe he spent his fortune at the tables.

"Sounds like we've got a critic in the audience," he says. I feel Lora cringe back from me, so I step forward, drawing eyes to me and away from her.

"Too bad we don't have a musician onstage!" I shout back. That gets a chuckle from the room.

He finally spots me in the crowd, peering down in exaggerated fashion. "It must be hard to see true genius from way down there," he says, like he's the first person to make a joke about my size.

"Oh, don't worry," I reply. "It's easy to hear how terrible you are. Rhyming 'hornet' with 'sonnet'? Really?"

His cheeks go all red, and I almost feel bad for him. He's a full-grown man and a performer. This should be at least a *little* challenging. "I suppose you could do better than the man who earned fourth place in the Westruun talent show?" he demands.

"In my sleep," I say. "You aren't a bard, you're just a buzzing hornet. / A hack's a hack, however you adorn it."

He stares at me, furious, for a long moment. I can just about see the calculation in his eyes, the opportunity he thinks he's got to show me up, and the need to do so. He holds out his instrument. "You think you're so clever. Why don't you step up here and show us?"

I hear Lora gasp, because she knows I'm going to go through with it. How could I not?

"Gladly," I say, and the patrons part as I approach the stage, take the lute from him. It's too big for me, but I've been moving through a big folks' world my whole life. It's not a problem. I shift my grip on the neck, tilt the whole thing slightly toward me to adjust for my reach, and strum a couple chords experimentally. The sound is good, the instrument well cared for. So he's not *completely* useless.

"I think these folks deserve a decent rendition of 'The Barmaid and the Baker,'" I announce. It's a crowd-pleaser, especially if you know that the bawdy lyrics are there in service to the jokes. It helps if you can do a funny voice for the baker. I use our neighbor Mr. Tanigol as a model, with his gruff tone and voice like gravel, and it sells the song well enough.

I get a healthy round of applause, which feels great, but already I'm thinking I can do better. I can make them *love* this. Meanwhile, Sember's twitching angrily, which means I'll need to be cautious when it's time to return his lute. He doesn't strike me as the violent type, but it pays to be careful. I'll give it back to him in the middle of the crowd, so if he tries anything he'll have angry patrons to deal with while I dart between legs. I set that aside and launch into another tune. This one's a love song. I've never been a fan of love songs, since love's a sucker's bet. But they're always popular, especially late in the evening when everyone's a little drunk and more than a few are feeling a little lonely.

I play a handful of standards, the ones I'm most familiar with. I know my own songs aren't ready for a crowd, not yet, but I end "Two Moons, Two Hearts" with an improvised verse of my own, and the crowd honest-to-gods sways along.

The audience is pleased with my set, and even Sember has decided to be gracious in defeat and gives me a sardonic little bow when I hand him back his instrument. I feel light and effortless, like when you hit the high note perfectly and hold it just for the joy of the sound.

"That could have gone really bad," Lora tells me on our way home.

"I had it under control," I say, though I'm better at improv than planning.

"Everyone thinks they do until they don't," Lora says.

I hate that I've made her worried. "By the end, I had them eating out of my hand."

"I mean, you were great," she admits, her grin a little begrudging, a little amused.

"You think so?" I ask. "I think I kind of lost them partway through 'Moons.'"

"And then won them back." She shakes her head. "I'm not sure what you're better at, Kaylie: pissing people off or delighting them."

"Depends on my mood," I say, and only later I wonder if Mom ever said something similar to my father. If she did, maybe she'll tell me about it someday, and I'll add it to the list I've been keeping of things I know about him.

When Mom goes to bed, I slip the coin patrons left for me into her bag. I fall asleep dreaming of crowds chanting my name.

~ *Mom says I'm too much like him.*

—Kaylie, age 16

"I don't know, Kaylie," Lora says. We're sitting on a rooftop across from the Lucky Mutt. Well, she's on the roof and I'm perched on the chimney's edge, which makes us almost eye level. Her face is scrunched up in the way it always is when I'm about to talk her into something she knows better than to do.

"What are you so worried about?" I ask, though we'll have bigger problems than the Public Defense if we get caught. High rollers tend to take it personally when you steal their coin. "Autumn said it was a good idea, right?"

"No," she says, exasperated. "Autumn said it was 'an opportunity and a fulcrum.' That's the kind of thing they say when it's very risky." Autumn—full name, Autumn Leaves Upon Night's Threshold—is Lora's mentor. They're an elf, but they've always struck me as strange and ethereal. That makes me think of every story of fey entanglement I've ever heard, but they've taught her a lot and treat her well, so I try not to worry too much. Besides, they showed her how to shift her body so what everyone else sees when they look at her is what she sees when she thinks about herself. I love Autumn a little for that, even though I always thought Lora looked beautiful.

"They wouldn't have told you if they didn't want you to do it," I insist.

"I think they want me to make informed decisions," Lora says.

"Well, what informs my decision is that I need the coin."

She pauses, looks more closely at me, and her eyes widen with realization. "You're leaving." It's not a question, but a statement.

I nod. "If I can afford it." I hold out the letter from the College of the White Duke inviting me to audition. She reads it then looks at me, wet-eyed and smiling.

"I'm so happy for you, Kaylie!" We're hugging then, and my shoulder is wet where her cheek is pressed against it.

"But you're crying," I say.

"Out of joy. And because I'll miss you. But"—she pulls back slightly, looks into my eyes—"you need to go. This town won't ever have what you need."

An hour later I'm onstage at the Lucky Mutt. It's not hard, unless there's a big-deal traveling performer in town (never my father; he got what he wanted from this place and never looked back). I'm doing my thing, reveling in the way I can draw every eye to me, and waiting for the High Roller to arrive. Then it will be my job to keep him distracted while Lora relieves him of the coin he was about to "donate" to the casino.

It's thrilling, holding the crowd in my thrall, knowing I can make them laugh, dance, cry, whatever I want. And tonight it's more thrilling because at one table with his friends is a half-orc boy I've never seen before, with high cheekbones, big eyes, and a deeply misguided attempt at a beard. He's enraptured by me, and it feels *great*.

When I sing a tearjerker, his breath catches at the bridge. Then a love song, and he leans in and wipes his eyes. His friends notice and nudge one another, amused. But I can't focus on him, pretty though he is. The High Roller has shown up, with a couple bodyguards, but they're no problem. They're watching me, too. I switch over to something more high-energy, trying to give Lora an opportunity from where she's posted up near the bar. The High Roller seems into it, but Cheekbones loses a bit of interest.

I know Cheekbones's type. He feels things intensely, prefers tragedies to comedies, and confuses the singer with the song. Later, I imagine, he'll tell his friends that my beauty made him weep, and he'll mean it, at least until the next object of his infatuation comes along. So for the next song I switch to "The Last Ride of the Resolute," all heartbreak and regret, and the boy gratifies me with a quivering lip.

I'm well into the song before I realize that the High Roller is bored. Picking at his dinner, not touching his drink. Bored! My face flushes, and I catch Lora, who's been edging closer, looking at me incredulously. I've been playing to the wrong audience, and not because I'm into Cheekbones, but because I knew I could play him easy as a lute.

I finish the song as quickly as I can manage. Losing focus over a boy! I'd thought better of myself. I make myself think about what the High Roller, with his fancy clothes and his narrow, eager face, might want to hear, and I settle on "Throw," which uses my lyrics over an old tune. It's about a gambler who has to choose between his fortune and his love. It's nothing much, really, just a simple tune that appeals to gamblers, with a chorus that's catchy so that the drunks can sing along, but the High Roller is captivated. The boy, meanwhile, sees the song for what it is, sentimental and too easy, and I can't stand that look on his face, so I meet the High Roller's eyes, play like I'm performing just for him, and he can't look away. He's mouthing the words with me, splashing ale from his tankard as he sways his arms to and fro, like he's known this song his whole life. I don't even need to see Lora glide by to know what's happened. She was always going to be able to do her job as long as I was doing mine.

By the time I start the next song, she's long gone. I finish the set—it's my alibi, after all—and win the boy back. That's why I duck out quickly. Better for me to feel the glow of his admiration than to have an actual entanglement. I tell myself it's better for him to have the dream of me than the reality.

Lora and I meet up after, split the coin. She makes me promise to hang out with her tomorrow, before I leave town. As though I'd leave without seeing my best friend!

Mom's asleep in her chair when I get home, her sewing on her lap, needle still in her hand. I wonder how hard it will be for her when I tell her I'm leaving. We haven't exactly been getting along great. She thinks I'm reckless, and I can't imagine what there could possibly be in Kymal that would make me willing to play it safe. But that doesn't mean I want to see her suffer, and at least I can do one thing to help out. I slip half of my take into her bag.

"That's so much coin!"

I startle. Apparently she wasn't quite as asleep as I'd thought.

"Uh, yeah, someone left a big tip," I reply, not quite looking her in the eyes. Lying isn't so easy when it's to her.

Her silence stretches long enough that I look up, hoping maybe she's fallen back to sleep. No such luck. She's just staring down at me, her lips thin with concern. For the first time I'm aware that she's still young, only the depth of her dark eyes hinting at how much she's been through. "I worry about you, Kaylie," she says.

"Don't, Mom. Really. I'm fine."

I can see she doesn't buy it, and I think this is escalating to another fight, but then she says, "You're too much like your father."

That brings me up short. "What . . . what do you mean?" I manage to ask. I've never heard her speak of him except when I bugged her for scraps of information.

She stares at me, like maybe she's hoping to see something in my face, or afraid she will. Then she shakes her head. "I couldn't take it, if anything happened to you," she says, and I'm angry all over again. Where has all that caution left us?

But for once I hold my tongue.

Later, in the privacy of my room, I add "Mom says I'm too much like him" to the list of things I know about my father, even though it hurts. By sunrise, I'm on my way to Westruun. You might say Mom and I didn't leave things in the best place, though at least she stopped short of forbidding me from going. Which wouldn't have worked and would have ensured things got even uglier. Still, not great.

I forget about my promise to Lora until I'm already on the road. Crap. I'll write her from Westruun. I tell myself I'll write all the time.

You're too much like your father. The thought gnaws at my guts. I try to remember the tone she used: Accusatory? Sad? Bittersweet? Each time I remember it differently. Then I see the towers of Westruun in the distance, shining like silver, like the promise of something better.

> ~ *He could talk a dragon out of its horde but would prefer to talk a woman out of her skirts. (Ew.)*
>
> —*Kaylie, age 19*

I've got competition at the fountain. That's not unusual. I'm not the only busker looking to make some easy coin. The square has shopping and good food and draws people from all over, townies doing their thing, travelers taking in the sights. And it's far enough from school that no one there needs to know about my side hustle. Usually I like the competition. It sharpens me, makes me a better performer. Nothing like being shown up on the fiddle or flute to make me improve and to prepare me for when it's time to leave the college behind and make a name for myself.

Except this boy isn't busking, not really. He's drawn a group of young women around him, and he's strumming his lute, singing "(I'm Telling You) You're Gorgeous." He's got perfectly coiffed hair, too-bright teeth, and is oh-so-earnestly crooning:

You're rocking that bod, don't put it on the shelf,
That smile and those eyes! You're one real sexy elf.
I need all your love like this song needs a chorus,
That's why (oh yeah) I'm telling you you're gorgeous.

It's none of my damn business, but that song's a crime against music, so of course I wander over there. He glances at me before turning his focus back to a striking dwarven girl. He's staring at her intently as he sings, and she's watching the ground uncomfortably while the other girls—her friends, I'm guessing—stare, enraptured.

He's not my type, but to each their own, I guess. Except that he's put all his attention on the one of them who clearly doesn't want it. She's not blushing, not fluttering eyelashes, just staring at her feet like maybe it will make him go away.

Well, people have been running from me since before I was born.

When he starts back in on the chorus, I harmonize with him, loudly, belting out slightly altered lyrics:

You're trying too hard, put it back on the shelf,
By perving on girls, you embarrass yourself.
You sing all this crap like this song will impress her,
We know (oh no) you're thinking you'll possess her.

His audience is giving me looks like I've kicked a puppy, except for the dwarven girl. Her face is still turned to the ground, but she's smiling now. That's all the encouragement I need.

Pretty Boy sings louder in response, which isn't a great way to impress. But I guess when all you have is vibes, you work with what you've got. I drop in my own lines when he persists in not shutting up:

By all the gods, you've got it wrong,
When you go after girls with this gross-ass song.
Look at yourself! There's no excuse,
You think you're hot stuff, but you're just a douche.

The other girls are looking disgusted at both of us now, which is fine with me. We've both committed crimes against music, but mine's a minor offense, and in a just world, he'd be banished to a deserted island.

"No one asked for your opinion!" he says when it's clear I'm not about to leave. He stands up, looms over me.

"And no one asked for you to be a creep." I flash my brightest smile at him, all faux-sweetness.

It's one of the girls who fires back, which surprises me. "Come *on*!" she says. "We don't want you here." Fair enough. I am showing up the guy she clearly has a crush on. And I am being quite a prick about it. Well, some people bring that out in me.

"I'll go," I say, releasing the dagger in my pocket, the one I've been palming just in case. I turn toward the dwarven girl, who is watching me intently, and I realize her eyes are the deep green of oak leaves after the rain. "If you ask me to."

Her lovely eyes widen, and when she speaks, her low voice is barely more than a whisper. "I think you should go," she says.

How did I misread this so badly? Then, very quietly, she adds, "Maybe I'll come with you. If you don't mind the company?" She gives me a wary, hopeful smile. My heart beats staccato, and I offer her my hand.

Turns out her name is Saveen, and her laugh is musical. Later, as we're sharing shy kisses, I wonder if I'm really all that different from the busker. Or my father. I've heard, and duly recorded, stories about his, uh, prowess. But I don't want to think about that, especially right now.

So I think about the little gasps Saveen makes when our lips part.

> ~ *He's great at playing the lute.*
> ~ *He did "something unspeakable" in a nobleman's bed. Pretty sure I don't want to know.*
>
> *—Kaylie, age 20*

Sunset brings out the best in Westruun, and today's is a fine specimen. The morning rain has given way to soft, wispy clouds, and the air shimmers as the reds, oranges, and golds of evening make Saveen look lovelier than ever. This rooftop is one of my favorite spots, with a view of the city that makes it look lovely and huge (it's much larger than Kymal, but it already feels small to me). Best of all, we've got enough privacy for . . . other activities.

We've paused from those activities to wish the day goodbye, or anyway, that's the idea, but she catches me looking at her, blushes—how I can still make her blush is beyond me, but pleasantly so—and looks down.

"*Now* you're going to be shy?" I tease.

"You look at me like I'm the prettiest girl in the world," Saveen says, still looking down.

"Only a fool would look at you differently."

She's quiet for a long moment. "You're very charming," she says. "You know how to make me feel special." Something about the way she says it makes me uneasy.

"Why do I feel like there's a 'but' coming?" I ask.

She shakes her head. "No 'but,'" she says, and lifts her head just enough to look up at me through her lashes. Any other time I'd think she's flirting with me. Now I'm beginning to wonder what this is really about, and I feel a little like a hare who's suddenly realizing that she's out in the open and that shadow overhead might be a raptor.

Because I can't think of anything else, I say, "I've been working on a song about you. It's not finished, but would you like to hear it?" I reach for my lute, and she doesn't object, so I start playing. It's pretty decent, if I do say so myself. Kind of understated, because Saveen embarrasses easily, so I've omitted the lyrics that rhyme with "wit," "submit," and various other words of increasing explicitness. Just as well, as one of those rhyming words was "commit."

Instead I've gone with:

How hot's my girlfriend? Let me lay it out.
I'll tell you of her eyes, perfect sea green,

Her striking face, her nose so aquiline,
A rockin' bod? Of that there is no doubt . . .

"I'm still working on the ending," I admit after the second verse, a little apologetic. "Do you think 'lips' and 'eclipse' is too cheesy?" It's *definitely* too cheesy, but I ask because she's wearing a searching expression as she looks at me, like she's hunting for something in my face.

"You're the poet," she demurs.

"You might be one, too, and not even . . . realize it," I offer. A terrible joke, but she doesn't even groan. "You didn't like the song?" my mouth asks before my brain catches up.

"It's not that." Saveen's folding her hands back and forth over each other nervously. "It's a good song, and you're fun and brave and"—she blushes again—"you make me feel really good."

"Well, thank you, m'lady," I say in my best haughty noblewoman impersonation. I even mimic tossing my hair back like a certain kind of hot girl does, though I keep it too short to actually toss it. "You know I love making you . . . feel good."

Usually that would have earned a good-naturedly horrified "Kaylie!" from her, but she just keeps fiddling with her hands, and now I'm sure I know what she wants. I've seen it in the eyes of audience members who've chosen to forget that I'm being paid to hold their attention, who want to believe that the emotions I'm calling forth are real, that the reason I'm making long eye contact is because I've fallen for them, not because it's my freakin' job. They're clueless or possessive, and I want nothing to do with either. But Saveen's different. She has a right to that look.

But I don't want her mouth to ask the question I see in her eyes: *Who am I to you? What is this that we're doing?*

That makes me think of my father. I sometimes wonder if he's been in every inn and pub on the continent, given how often I hear stories about him (yes, I ask after him sometimes; no, I'm not proud of it).

"It's a lovely evening," I say, trying to find my way out of the thicket

I've found myself in. "And you're the hottest woman in the world, and I'm just so damned charming." I wink and slip closer to her. "Now, where were we?"

But she flinches back. Then, almost apologetically, she shakes her head. "Can we just—sit here for a bit?"

"As the lady wishes," I say in the noblewoman voice and try to do as she's suggested. But I've never been great with silence. I fidget, expending significant willpower not to pluck at the lute, whistle a tune, or put my foot in my mouth.

"I don't like the thought of being a jailer," she says, and it makes so little sense that at first I think I must have heard wrong.

"You're a librarian's apprentice," I say, feeling my way around in emotional darkness.

She meets my eyes. Hers are large, shining, on the verge of tears. I look away. "What I'm trying to say," Saveen says finally, "is that I know what I want, but I'm afraid to hope for it."

I make a slightly obscene guess as to what she might want and how I can provide it, because I'm a complete dumbass. She turns from me. Night's coming on now, the brightest stars making themselves known.

"Bad joke, sorry," I mumble. "Speaking of: Did I tell you the one about the two priests discussing their holy vows?"

"I know better than to fall for you, Kaylie," Saveen replies, and my whole face heats up. For once I can think of nothing to say. "I'd like this to be real, but I won't put you in a cage to get it."

I think of my father and the wreckage he's left behind him. Anger burns like coals in my chest cavity. "I'm not going to abandon you!" I hate the way my voice breaks.

"I know you won't." Saveen's voice is quavering, too. "But you'll come to resent me for asking for something you didn't want to give."

I'm shaking with all the fury and mindlessness of an earthquake. Later, I'll think of any number of things I could have said that were wise or true or sharp.

"I resent that implication" is what I find myself saying instead, clutching my lute and standing. "Don't worry. I'll save you from *caging* me." I turn on my heel and walk as fast as I can without running, fearing that if I hesitate, I'll turn and look at her, and if I do that, I'll be lost.

It takes me a long time to forgive her for being absolutely right.

> ~ *He was a member of Dr. Dranzel's Spectacular Traveling Troupe.*
> ~ *Women seem to love him, even the ones that hate him. Some men, too.*
>
> *—Kaylie, age 21*

WE'RE SITTING AROUND THE CAMPFIRE after practice, and Zedd's staring at me. At first I assume that this is just one of those percussionist things, like the way he says "check this out" right before he launches into some misguided solo, or his propensity to drool when concentrating. But the more he looks at me, the less I like it. It's not lecherous; I could deal with that. He's got something on his mind, and I don't care for it.

I've been with Dr. Dranzel's Spectacular Traveling Troupe a few months. When they came through Westruun, I saw an opportunity for coin, to see the world, and maybe to learn a bit more about the bastard who made me, well, a bastard. Compared to that, what was another year at college going to do for me? Besides, things there had gotten . . . messy. Music's easier than people. Music makes sense.

Not that this troupe is free from complications. Celurdor the Mellifluous (real name, he confessed after a night of drinking: Kevin), sitting to my right, has been crushing on me from the moment I joined up, and I've pretended not to notice. He's got a decent stage presence, but off it, he's all hesitation and nervous glances. I've resolved to ignore him and hope he gives up.

"You played well tonight, Kaylie," Zedd says, looking at me from behind his ragged hair.

"Uh, thanks?" I say. His tone suggested maybe he was surprised.

"No offense," he says a bit gruffly. "I just mean that it's impressive for someone new to the flute." I tense, but Dr. Dranzel's over by the cart, busy with some scheme, too far to hear that.

"Is my flute playing inadequate to your lofty standards?" I ask.

"No, not at all!" He holds his hands in front of himself like maybe my eyes could literally shoot daggers at him. "But you came from the college, and your breath control's for shit."

"Loving these compliments," I bite out.

"Stop picking on her," Celurdor says, and I'm honestly a little impressed. Even though I don't need the help, it's a sweet thought.

"Not picking. Curious," Zedd replies. "What's your first instrument?"

"The lute," I say quietly, hating how embarrassed I sound.

He nods like this makes total sense, like maybe he's more perceptive than I gave him credit for. It doesn't feel great.

I feel Celurdor staring at me, too. I like having all eyes on me during a performance, but when it's just sitting around a campfire with colleagues? No, thank you.

"What?" I snap at Celurdor. He flusters, then gathers himself.

"I play the lute," he says.

"Yeah, that's why I auditioned as a flutist. I wanted the job."

We fall silent for a while, going hard on the ale to cut the tension. But Zedd is still looking at me like there's more he wants to say. "Out with it," I say at last. "Do you want to tell me I'm off-key? That my embouchure is a mess?" The former is flat-out false, the latter too true for comfort.

"Nah." Zedd wipes some foam from his upper lip, looks at it curiously, and licks it off his finger. Then, as if that didn't just happen, he continues. "You remind me of someone, you know that?"

The hairs on the back of my neck stand all the way up. No one had remarked on it since I joined the troupe, which I'd thought—hoped—meant that I didn't look enough like him. But now.

"Someone who doesn't know how to play the flute?" I ask, seeking a way to divert this line of thought. I know immediately it's a mistake.

"Someone who is great at it, more like," he says, then shouts out, "Hey, Dranz, does Kaylie here remind you of Scanlan?"

Dr. Dranzel—I've never heard anyone else call him Dranz—stops staring at the papers for whatever new plan he's cooking up and wanders over to the fire, looking at me curiously.

"Who?" I ask, as innocently as I know how. Celurdor has tensed, too, clearly expecting this to be some new line of insult he might be able to defend me from. If only he knew.

"Scanlan Shorthalt," Dranzel replies. "One of our former members. A gnome, with eyes a lot like—"

"So all gnomes look alike to you, is that it?" I demand. Not a great thing to say to one's boss, but I don't want them to know who Scanlan is to me. Dranzel flinches—good for him—and puts up his hands like *Whoa, I didn't mean it like that.*

"Gods, Zedd," Celurdor cuts in. "You've been on her all evening. Give her a break!" He looks like he's about to cry. Not a good look.

Zedd shrugs like he didn't mean anything by it, and knowing him he probably didn't. He's a good guy, just a weird one. He throws down the last of his drink and stands. Dranzel watches the whole thing with narrowed eyes, but the two of them head off together, probably to talk about kids these days.

"Thanks," I say softly to Celurdor.

"No problem," he replies. "I don't like to see people getting picked on."

I don't quite know why I say "And you really don't like people picking on me."

He cringes slightly, rubs his hands together, and nods an admission.

"Here's a free tip," I say. "If you like someone, let them know it. Even if they aren't interested, they'll respect you for being honest."

There's quiet then, except for the slurping sounds of each of us getting a bit more tipsy.

"I like you, Kaylie," he says at last, much to my surprise. "I think maybe we'd be good together . . . um, if you're interested, I mean."

I'm not all that interested, but now I'm also wondering if maybe there's more to Kevin than I thought. Why not give the kid a chance? Aside from the fact that I'm manifestly bad at these things. But he's cute, and maybe I'm a little lonely. So:

"I tell you what," I say. "If you can outduel me with a lute, you can take me out on a date."

His eyes light up. As well they should. I'm a freakin' *catch.* And I'm going to let him win, because if we're going to date, I'm going to need to cultivate a little bit of confidence in him.

"You're on," he says, and grabs his lute. He's good, but I've known I was better since my first week with the troupe. He lays down a melody, and I riff off of it, careful not to show him up too badly, as the other troupe members are starting to take notice. He steps his game up—good for him—pushing me harder. We go back and forth a bit, now with genuine applause from our colleagues as our little showdown intensifies.

I'm not thrilled to have everyone's attention, not with them thinking of Scanlan, but since I have it, I go on the offensive and jab a finger in Zedd's direction. "Here to critique my fingering?" I ask him pointedly. "My rhythm?" I know both are excellent. He looks at me wide-eyed, like he doesn't understand why I'd ask such a thing. Nor would he: his observations about my work as a flutist were scrupulously fair.

"No, you're good," he says, making me feel like a dork fishing for a compliment.

Annoyed at myself, I step up my performance. See, it's not that no one's better than me. But not too many people are, and that includes most of the ones who are confident they can outplay me. Maybe that's why I've always felt the need to put people like that in their place. Or maybe it's that I see my father in them. Or maybe—

Maybe I don't want to think too much about what it says about me. And just like that, I'm sliding in at the end of one of Celurdor's riffs and layering in the melody from "Victory March (Sing of the Fallen)," either to show that I can or just because I'm an ass. It's too much for him, and I know it.

When I'm finished, he applauds with the rest and bows, acknowledging defeat. It's dignified of him, and I like to think that I'm the only one close enough to him to see the sadness in his expression. It doesn't feel great.

"Tough luck, Celurdor," I say softly.

"Now *that's* fingering!" Zedd drunkenly announces.

> ~ *He solved an "unsolvable" riddle with a dirty pun.*
>
> *—Kaylie, age 22*

Around me, the Laughing Lamia is full almost to bursting. There's laughter and shouting and lots of drinks. Tonight is going to be either a great show or a disaster, depending on whether, when our set starts, the crowd (and some members of my troupe) are way too drunk or just drunk enough. I'm nursing a cider, because I've never performed in Emon before, and I intend to be impressive. I can always get wasted later, if I want. I'm deep in my own thoughts, wondering if my father ever played here and if I'm as talented as he is, then imagining some future where I'm known across the continent, a famous and beloved musician—famous enough that I don't have to put up with much bullshit, beloved enough that I can pretend I've never hurt anyone.

"Kaylie?"

I do a double take. "Lora!" I feel myself smiling ear to ear and hug my friend fiercely. She hugs me back, and when she sits down with me, she's smiling, too, though not quite so fiercely as I am.

"Gods," I say. "It's good to see you! What are you doing all the way in Emon?"

"Autumn and I had some business here." Lora's always been willowy, but now it's more pronounced. Her hair moves in some wind I can't feel, and there's a depth in her eyes that makes it hard to believe we're the same age. I've never fully understood the terms of her partnership with Autumn, but clearly they're good for each other. "And I heard that Dr.

Dranzel would be in town, so we figured this was a good time to be here."

"I didn't realize my comings and goings were so kept track of," I say, meaning it as a gentle tease, but she doesn't quite smile.

"I looked for you at the college a few months ago." She shifts her weight uncomfortably. "They said you'd joined up, so I figured maybe you were still traveling with the troupe."

"Oh," I say, flushing, "yeah. I'm sorry I didn't write to you about that. It all happened so quickly, and then we've always been on the road. . . ." I stop myself. "What I mean is, I should have told you."

"You don't owe me that," she says. "Though I know your mom would have appreciated it."

Ouch. I can't think of anything to say to that. We both sip drinks in silence.

"I'm sorry, I'm not trying to make you feel bad." She sighs. "I didn't want the conversation to go this way. I'm so glad you got out, Kaylie. Kymal was eating you up, and you deserve to find something better for yourself. But that doesn't mean we don't miss you, me and your mom, and even Autumn in their way." Something in the way she says that last bit lets me know it's a big-deal compliment.

"I miss you, too, Lora," I say. "How are you and Autumn? How's Mom?"

But life, unlike music, refuses to be bound by my rhythm, and from the stage someone shouts that it's time to welcome Dr. Dranzel's Spectacular Traveling Troupe, and I grab my instruments. "I'm sorry," I shout to Lora over the drunken cheers. "Let's talk afterward?"

Next thing I know we're onstage, and the crowd isn't too drunk, and I even get to do lead vocals on "Mandy of the Many Mountains." I've got them eating out of my hand, all of them drunk enough to think, for an evening, that maybe they're in love with me, and they'll go back to their partners or meet a stranger in the crowd, and there will be some extra spice in their night that they'll know, and I'll know, was my doing, because music is its own kind of magic.

By the time we step offstage, my hair is going every direction—what's not stuck to my sweaty forehead, anyway—and lots of people want to shake my hand, shoot their (unsuccessful) shot at me, or buy me a drink. It's all a haze of pleasure, and minutes become hours as I savor the kind of power that I've loved from the first time I played, way back at the Lucky Mutt—

Crap. I fight my way through the crowd, which is clearing out a little after the show, but only a little, because it's drunk o'clock, and it will be until the tavern kicks us out. I take a clumsy foot to the knee but manage to get back to the table otherwise uninjured.

No sign of Lora. How long did she wait for me before giving up? The answer is obvious: too long.

From behind me, Zedd is shouting, "Kaylie! Kaylie! Where are you? I heard the *best* joke. . . ."

But the cider has soured in my gut, and I slip out into the night, where the bustle of the promenade's open-air market has been replaced by long shadows and occasional clusters of drunken revelers.

Music is magic, but even magic can't fix me.

~ A mighty lover (of himself)
~ An (in)famous performer
~ Someone who doesn't stick around for a fight (or for people who care about him)

—Kaylie, age 22

I stand outside for a long time. Winter is on the doorstep, but I barely notice the rain and sharp wind. Paint peels on the old, familiar door, and a single light burns inside. Mom is home, no doubt working. I'm a coward, lurking outside because each year that's passed has made returning home that much more unthinkable. Time has done nothing to endear Kymal to me. It's a town that survives by taking gold from the rich (fine by me) and the desperate (much less fine), with casinos, inns, and taverns shined up because no one wants to think of poverty while they try to win coin. Then you turn a corner and there's everyone else, folks who keep the coin flowing but are themselves scrambling to get by. A gilded dungheap, Kymal. How I loathe it.

And I'm its truest daughter, someone who has made good by ignoring where I came from and the people who helped me get here. Sure, I sent Mom letters for a while, and coin more often. But I was fooling myself thinking that was enough.

"Just do the damn thing," I say to myself for the dozenth time, and this time I do. I hurry to the door so fast that I stumble, afraid that if I lose momentum I'll turn around and never come back. I knock and hear slow steps coming.

"We're closed—" Mom starts, then her eyes widen. "Kaylie!" She breaks out in a huge smile and pulls me into a hug.

"Mom!" I say, hearing my adolescent self in my tone but unable to adjust it. "You're gonna get all wet!" Maybe getting soaked through before this reunion wasn't my smartest idea.

She *pfffts* dismissively and pulls me inside. Then she insists that I get into dry clothes while she makes some hot tea.

That's how I end up sitting at the old kitchen table, in clothes that my sixteen-year-old self thought were the height of (scavenged) fashion but that look to me now like a clown's vomit.

There are pleasantries, then long stretches of silence. I'm torn between avoiding her gaze and studying the lines of her face that seem deeper, even more careworn, than they did when I left. How could she have changed so much in six years?

"Gods be good, Kaylie," she says, maybe thinking something similar, "you're all grown up."

Sitting in my mother's kitchen, wearing the castoffs of my younger self, I don't feel particularly adult. I pick at my fingernails. "I guess time will do that," I say, and regret it at once, a reminder of the gulf between us. "How's the tailoring business?"

She laughs. It's not unkind, but there's no joy in it, either. "Same as ever. I'm thinking of bringing on help, with some of the extra money that *someone's* been sending."

My face burns, and I mumble something that doesn't quite acknowledge that lately when I've sent coin, it's been without a signed note, because everything I tried to say sounded trite or false.

I'm a songwriter, improviser, performer; you'd think that would mean I could find the words. This isn't romance or bawdy lyrics or tales of heroes saving the world. It's my life, and I'm finally realizing I've never known how to live it.

In a kindness I don't deserve, she moves the conversation on. "Life here is as it ever was, Kaylie. I want to know about what you've been up to! Lora says you've joined a traveling troupe?"

Speaking of undeserved kindnesses, Lora not telling Mom that I joined up with Scanlan's old troupe means she has one less thing to worry about. I promised myself that, if I was going to come home, have this conversation, I'd be honest with Mom and with myself. But "honest" doesn't mean I'm going to tell her about what I've decided to do after I leave Kymal. After all, Mom doesn't approve of violence.

"That's right," I say instead. "We're pretty good, I think. We mostly play the standards, you know, but some of the songs I've written are in our regular repertoire."

Her face lights up like it hasn't since this conversation began. "Of course! You've always been so talented, sweetheart. I always knew you'd do great things."

I'm not sure a jaunty tune full of double entendres about self-pleasure is *precisely* what she had in mind, but I keep that to myself. "It's nice," I say instead. "The pay's pretty good, and I get to see the world."

"And is there a, um, special someone in your life?" she asks, and I can't quite parse whether this is just a mother's curiosity, she's worried for me, or she's worried for this hypothetical someone.

It was in this very room that she'd said that I was too much like my father.

"Nope," I say. "For now I'm just enjoying being single." And I've always been careful, but that's another conversation I'm not about to have with my mother. The one "talk" we had was plenty, thankyouverymuch.

I eventually break the ensuing silence. "I'm sorry I didn't write more often," I find myself saying. The dregs of my tea clump sadly at the bottom of the cup. "I, uh, have lots of excuses, but the truth is I never knew what to say."

"Maybe," Mom says carefully, "something like, 'Hi, Mom, I'm doing fine. We're in some far-flung place you've never heard of, but I'm thinking of you'?" This would have been a lot easier to take if she were the type to be passive-aggressive, but she's entirely sincere as always, my mom.

"Yeah, um, that would have been a good start," I admit. "I hate this place, Mom. *Hate* it. I hate that you're here, and I'd fix that if I knew how, but I don't, and it eats me up. . . ." I don't expect to say that, and I really don't expect to start crying, but I guess I do because the next thing I know she's by my side, holding me tightly, and I'm soaking her shoulder, even though my clothes are now dry.

"Oh, dear one," she says. "You don't need to worry about me. I'm doing fine. I do have a life, you know. Friends and everything. We go to the lake and feed the ducks, and Mrs. Lamberg's kid knows how to talk to them. I know it's not the life you want, but it makes me happy."

I pull back, wipe at my eyes, and stare at her to be sure she's not just trying to make me feel better. (I've once again made this all about me, haven't I?) But she was never the type to lie.

"From the time you were little, I knew you'd leave someday," she goes on as she pulls down a couple shot glasses and a bottle of some dark liquor from the shelf. "All these big folk in town, but I knew early on that Kymal was too small for you."

She sets a glass before me and takes one herself, raises them into the air. "To you, Kaylie," she says, and I have to fight off tears.

I raise a glass. "To both of us," I say. "I never thought I'd be having a drink in this house."

Mom laughs with obvious delight. "You mean, you never thought *I'd know* about the drinks you had here."

I laugh, too, embarrassed and somehow pleased. Our conversation turns lighter for a while, but a drink and a half in, I say, "You're right, I did need to get out of here. But I should have stayed in touch. Running to something doesn't mean I needed to run away from anything."

Her eyes are a little glassy—she doesn't have my tolerance for booze—and maybe someday I'll be able to process this moment, this conversation that I never wanted to have but desperately needed. But for now I'm just glad to see the corners of her eyes crinkle with happiness.

"You have a good heart, Kaylie. You always have. Your father hurt me, but I should never have put those fears on you."

I'm not sure I entirely believe her about my heart, but maybe wanting to live up to her vision of me is enough.

"The goodness in me came from you, Mom." It's the truest thing I've ever said. Being vulnerable with her feels terrible. But also kind of great? Maybe I'm a little more buzzed than I thought. Or maybe this is just what facing up to myself feels like.

We talk late into the night. I even tell her a little about my exes, because it turns out this vulnerability thing can be hard to turn off. There's only one thing I don't tell her: that I have a pretty good idea where Scanlan's at, and I've talked the troupe into heading that way (though I haven't told them why). When I'm done in Kymal, I'm going to find him and there's going to be a reckoning. Because my mom, who is kind and brave and wise, deserved so much better than my asshole father. So I'm going to hear his explanation from his own lips and then I'm going to make him bleed.

First, though, is more talking, and then I play some music for her—my mom, my first and best audience.

Sometime tomorrow I'll go to Lora's place, and if I'm lucky she'll be in town and I'll get to apologize and promise to do better if she'll give me the chance. She probably will, because that's the kind of person she is. Then comes the hard part: living up to my promises.

The sky's already turning gray with predawn as I drift toward sleep, staring again at my list of things I know about Scanlan, about my father.

But I'm beginning to realize that maybe there's another list I should be keeping, a more important one.

I find a blank page and write at the top in big, tipsy letters: THE PERSON I WILL BE. Most of what will be on that list is a mystery to me, but the first entry is easy:

~ Someone who never runs from the people who love her.

LIAR

Rory Power

It finds her first in dreams.

Nightmares, you might call them. Raishan does not. She hardly even remembers them at first. Just clouds of light, of bursting color—draped vines and white flowers, a woman's voice in the distance, someone weeping—until she wakes, unafraid. If there is pain, it fades before the sun is up.

Is this your curse, Wildmother? she asks, the mountains standing proud behind her, the trees bowing at her feet. *Is this all a god can do?*

"Raishan. Wake up."

A dream ends; Raishan's eyes open. Stone walls hemming in close, fire-glow flickering through the slitted windows, and the dark silhouette of a familiar figure.

"Well?" Talya asks. "Are you coming?"

Raishan sits up, bed creaking beneath her. "Yes. Yes, of course."

"Then get up. Meet me outside."

The door shuts, and Raishan lets out a sigh of relief. Just a moment's company amongst these creatures is almost more than she can stand. But today she will endure anything. Today it'll all be worth it, as long as Talya keeps her promise.

Raishan smiles. Runs her tongue over her too-sharp teeth. There's no time to waste, is there?

She climbs out of bed, winces as a bone in her spine clicks into place. Her muscles spasm under her skin. A flash of green scales covers her for an instant before vanishing. Every day, the temptation calls to her—abandon this human body and return to her true form, a green dragon slicing through the sky, power and poison hers to wield.

But she knows too well what waits for her if she does. Wounds that never heal, blood that burns in her veins. A curse she did nothing to earn, rotting through her dragonflesh, leaving her weak and vulnerable.

Not for much longer, she reminds herself. This business with the Ashari is how she fixes it.

Dressed in a clean tunic, her human form perfectly in place, Raishan takes a final look around the room the Ashari have assigned to her. It's tiny, but at least she has it to herself; the tribe shares most everything here in Pyrah, something she's had to pretend to admire. If everything goes to plan today, she'll never have to sleep here again.

"Good riddance," she says to the little stone chamber, and heads out to find Talya.

It's early still as Raishan reaches the street, the sky black enough that she can make out a golden glow in the distance, an aura over the treetops. Light from the portal to the Fire Plane, a rift guarded by these Fire Ashari for generations. Today is the day Raishan sees it for herself.

"There you are," Talya says, pushing off from the dormitory's roughhewn wall. "You took your time."

Talya is a tall woman, her skin marked with dozens of burns from as many years guarding the portal. She is not, Raishan has found over the course of her apprenticeship here, someone easily intimidated.

"I'm sorry," Raishan says sweetly, though the words taste as bitter as any poison. "I won't slow you down again."

"Very well." Talya nods toward the empty street. "Let's go."

Their route winds between stone houses, past outcroppings of black rock and a stand of dead trees, and through the center of Pyrah. Most everyone is sleeping still, but those they pass offer Raishan a nod of greeting, each one bringing her a rush of satisfaction.

She chose her form carefully when she arrived here. Sculpted herself into a girl just at the edge of childhood, her body small and hollowed out with hunger. And for all their caution, all their vigilance, these Ashari opened their doors to her without a second thought. They fed her from their table. Tended to her in their house of healing.

Fools, the lot of them. Every day they teach her something they should not, too charmed by her frailty to wonder how she could've wandered down from the mountains all alone.

Sweat is already beading on Raishan's forehead by the time she and Talya have reached the village's edge. She wipes it away, disgusted. This body feels the heat in ways she hadn't anticipated. Pain she understands—can even appreciate—but discomfort like this? It is so deeply beneath her. And yet, here she is.

Raishan grimaces. Needs must.

With the village behind them, the path winds up the mountain and into the trees. Here the trunks are blackened, burned through to the core wherein some embers still smolder. The ground is blanketed in ash as though it were new snow. The Cindergrove forest, they call it. Raishan shudders, shying away from the reach of the broken branches. To call it a forest is an insult to the lands she left behind. There is no life here, no breath. Nothing to claim or conquer when it's all already dead.

"Here," Talya says when they've reached a small plateau, the ground studded with obsidian shrapnel. The trees press close against the path's edge. "This is far enough."

It isn't, really. The portal to the Fire Plane is still out of sight, deeper into the forest and closer to the mountain's volcanic peak. But Raishan nods, stopping short. In the year that she's been apprenticed to Talya, she's learned how fond her mentor is of a stern lecture before the start of any lesson.

"You haven't been to the portal yet," Talya says, setting down her pack. It isn't a question; Raishan nods anyway. "Do you know what it is that lives on the other side?"

I know more than you ever will, Raishan thinks. "Fire elementals?" she says instead.

"Yes. Others, too. Flame giants, messengers from the Hells." Talya kneels by the side of the path. From her pack she pulls out a small black stone and a stick of incense. "All manner of great creatures, from which we must protect Pyrah."

"Creatures?" Raishan echoes. Here is her opening. "Like what?"

Talya does not answer. She remains focused on the ground before her, where she's used the stone to draw a series of runes in the ash. Surprised, Raishan casts her eyes over them quickly. *Peace,* reads one. *Help,* reads another. And the third—

Wildmother.

Unease churns in Raishan's stomach. Draped vines, white flowers. A beautiful, terrible dream.

She doesn't recognize this particular ritual. But she can imagine what it might be for.

"You pray?" she asks. "I didn't know."

If she had, she would've chosen someone else to train under. Only some of the Ashari worship the Wildmother, and she's made a point to avoid them when she can.

"I don't often." Talya props the stick of incense upright in a small mound of ash and murmurs a quiet word. Fire catches the incense, sends smoke billowing into the air before winking out. "But it's quite meaningful to see the portal for the first time. A reminder that so much of our survival is a gift from those more powerful than we are. We'll offer the Wildmother our respect, you and I."

Raishan clenches her fists, anger lancing through her. She's survived this long because of her own intelligence, her own will. All the Wildmother will ever get from her is pure spite.

"Will the portal be open when we get there?" she asks, drawing closer to the line of runes. If she can break Talya's focus, surely the Wildmother's gaze will not find them.

"Perhaps." Talya sets the black stone aside and takes a slow, deep breath.

"Have you ever seen anything come through?" Silence, egging Raishan on. "How often have you been through the portal yourself?"

Talya makes a noncommittal sound but does not stop her ritual. Her hands draw circles in the incense smoke. With every breath, the air seems to thicken. Still and heavy, pressing on the nape of Raishan's neck.

She has spent a year in Pyrah holding tightly to caution, to a keen, cutting care. Every word chosen just so. Every lie perfectly told, every day lived within the bounds of what these Ashari expect. And it will crumble to dust if the Wildmother answers Talya's call. The goddess will know Raishan for what she is; all her sacrifice will be for nothing.

"What about dragons?" she asks. Reckless, desperate. "Are there dragons beyond the portal?"

Talya freezes. Looks up after a heartbeat, her gaze intent. "Excuse me?"

"I've heard one lives somewhere beyond."

"Who told you that?"

There. Raishan can feel it. The charge is gone from the air, the spell interrupted. The cloud of incense dissipates as Talya waits for her answer.

"A woman," she says. "I think I met her before I came here."

Talya gets to her feet, expression turning even more grave. Raishan savors a rush of satisfaction. As much as she likes to lie, sometimes a little sliver of the truth feels even better.

"Where was this?" Talya asks. "Who was she?"

"I don't remember her name."

"But what did she say to you? You must tell me everything."

Must I? Raishan thinks, looking up at Talya's imposing figure. If she had worn some other form when she'd come to Pyrah—if she'd made herself an ancient wild mage, perhaps, and not a child—it would be Talya kneeling at her feet. Talya telling her everything and begging for her mercy.

It could be that way even now, if she chose.

But there is more, still, that Raishan needs from these people. Information she cannot get through sheer might alone.

Trust that you chose wisely, she reminds herself. *You have never failed before.*

"The woman told me a story," she says. "She said somewhere in the beyond, a great red dragon waits for the end of the world."

A twitch pulls at the corner of Talya's mouth. For a moment, Raishan can see it plainly in her eyes—a bone-breaking fear, strong enough to shake the foundations of the mountain beneath their feet. Then it's gone, and Talya is shaking her head.

"She was wrong," she says. "There is no such beast beyond that portal."

Beast? A dragon is no *beast.* Oh, how Raishan longs to make her regret ever using that word. But she has better things to do. A victory to revel in, because a liar knows a lie when she hears it, and Talya has just told one.

Thordak is here. The great red dragon who promised a cure to the curse that plagues her in exchange for her service. He is within her reach at long last, after so many years of searching.

"Do you hear me?" Talya presses. "Whoever that woman was, she was mistaken."

Raishan hides a smile. "Of course. I'm sorry to have brought it up."

"Think nothing of it." Talya shoulders her pack and clears her throat. "Let's return to the village. You'll visit the portal another time."

It's a disappointment—another night with the curse unbroken, not to mention another night's sleep in that wretched little Ashari bed—but Talya is rattled, her hackles raised. If Raishan insists they continue, she might start asking exactly the sort of questions she shouldn't.

And besides, Raishan has won a victory in her search. Yesterday, she had only the word of others to rely on. Now she has her own. Thordak is here; she is as close to freeing him as she has ever been.

Raishan follows Talya back down the mountain without protest. She'll be back here on her own soon enough.

THERE IS ONLY ONE SAGE still living: the Wildmother's favorite, the architect of this blasphemous temple. Her body is sprawled over the altar. Her blood pools on the stone floor, and Raishan can hear the labored rattle of her breath echoing off what's left of the walls.

With this last kill, the Rifenmist Jungle will be Raishan's once more. None of the Wildmother's worshippers will ever dare return.

She furls her wings. Stretches her long dragon's neck and approaches the altar, careless of the corpses that break beneath her feet, of the way her scales scrape and tear against the wreckage. It's a pitiful thing, really—just an arch of twined wood protected by some of the Wildmother's magic. Raishan will destroy it after this last sage is gone.

The dying woman stares up at her from beneath the arch. One of her eyes has burst; the other is steady, and oddly unafraid.

"Well," Raishan growls. "Do you understand now?"

Leave these lands, she told them when they arrived. *Build no temple; say no prayers. This place is not yours.*

The sage's mouth opens. Yes, Raishan thinks, now is the time to beg.

"I call upon the Wildmother," the sage says instead. Blood burbles down her chin. "I call upon the hunger of her sea, upon the heat of her fire. I call upon the wisdom of her ancient oaks to curse you, monster. Let the death of every innocent here be wreaked upon you tenfold."

Raishan cannot help it. She laughs, the sound guttural, as if ripped from the rock itself. These will be the sage's last words, her last breaths ever taken, and she uses them for what? Some nonsense curse?

Oh, but this kill will be the sweetest of them all. Poison spittle drips from Raishan's teeth and lands on the sage's cheek.

"Innocent?" she says. "You think you all died innocent?"

The sage shuts her remaining eye. Her palm is pressed to the wooden arch and her mouth is moving silently. Perhaps she is praying.

Raishan does not care.

"Tell your god you died a liar," she growls, and crushes the sage's skull, and—

Raishan sits bolt upright. The dream has broken; she's in Pyrah, in her small, rickety bed, but that's all she has time to realize before a bolt of pain ricochets through her human body. Building, flickering, surging until she crumples. Tumbles onto the floor and vomits. Stinging green liquid spatters across the stones, the smell of it sour and spoiled.

Raishan spits. Wipes her mouth on the back of her hand.

It's getting worse. She can feel it, knows that despite this body's unblemished skin, the Wildmother's curse is still somewhere inside: a weakness burrowing through her. A rot eating away at her flesh. Who knows how much of her will be left when she returns to her dragon form?

She gets to her feet. She can no longer afford to be so cautious. She needs the help Thordak promised her, and she needs it now.

She keeps the dark wrapped tightly around her. Climbs the path to the portal with steps made lighter by a spell of Talya's teaching and stays out of sight, even from the Firetamers on their midnight patrols. This is higher than she has ever climbed. Closer than she has ever been to achieving her goal at last.

So many years have passed since that day in the sages' temple. And every time she's buckled beneath the strain of this curse, she's risen again. The Wildmother will not win; Thordak will break this curse, and Raishan will survive, just as she always has.

Warmth begins to gather in the air, rippling like water as she slips between the charred trees. On her way up, the path was covered in soft black ash; now the mountain rock beneath shows through in long, winding tracks, tracing where gusts of hot air have barreled down from the portal. And at the edge of her sight, she can make out something strange—a line, almost, of pure light, as if some distant river has caught fire.

She must be nearly there. And as easy as it's been to avoid the guards so far, surely the Ashari will have more protections at the portal itself. Better to take a little extra care.

She stops, mutters a short phrase, and carves a handful of air out of the shadows. Molds it in her palms as though it were clay to shape, until she's holding a translucent orb the size of a dragon's eye.

"Go on, then," she whispers to it, and nudges it into midair. After hovering in place for a moment, it drifts off up the mountain, leaving her to follow at a distance.

It's practical, she reminds herself. Invisible to everyone but her, and quite long-lasting. Yes, it would have been more elegant to scry, but this sort of magic is less taxing, and she will need every bit of strength she can spare once she's at the portal.

From the safety of the shadows, Raishan focuses her own sight through the roving eye, steering it through the thinning trees. She was right—there are more guards at this altitude, and wards, too, shining symbols etched into trees scattered throughout the forest. She could simply kill them all, of course. Set the wards off to draw them in, leave a pile of corpses behind. But there is another way. A safer way, where nobody knows anything has happened until long after she and Thordak have disappeared.

She keeps to the shadows, holding her breath when a pair of Firetamers pass by on their way back to the village. If not for the distraction of their own idle conversation, Raishan is sure they would've seen her; the air is growing brighter with every step she takes, light streaming over a rise that's only just ahead. *Not much farther now,* Raishan tells herself, *not much farther at all,* and then—then the forest is breaking open at her feet, laying bare a great span of the mountain rock. And cutting through it like a fresh wound, a chasm of molten lava. The portal itself.

Raishan stands in the shelter of the tree line and fights to catch her breath. It is so much bigger than she expected. So much more alive. Lava writhes in a pool at the center of the crevasse. Bubbles form and burst, spray landing high along its banks, where strange formations have built up as the lava cools and melts and cools again. Above it all hangs a red haze of heat that warps the whole clearing.

Raishan can hardly hear her own heart beating over the roar of it. But she can feel it thundering, her pulse frantic.

Thordak is a red dragon. He was made for this, for fire, but she was not. How is she meant to—

Enough, she tells herself. She cannot afford to be afraid. She's here, at the portal's edge; she knows what comes next.

One Firetamer across the path to the right. Another just visible through the shifting air, emerging from the forest near the portal's far end. They are close enough, Raishan thinks as she draws a deep, burning breath and reaches for the deepest part of her power.

"Stop," she says, in her true, dragon's voice.

The guards obey; more than that, time itself obeys. The lava still simmers, and the scorching breeze still blows, but for now it is as though Raishan is the only creature left alive.

She steps out of the tree line. The roving eye has fallen away, but she has no need of it anymore. In fact, what comes next requires almost no magic at all.

Closer, then, closer to the portal. Raishan wills herself through the blistering heat, ignoring the instinct to flee.

It was a stray remark of Talya's that first caught her interest, a reference to something called an Aramenté. As far as she could find out from the Ashari elders, it's a primitive sort of ritual, undertaken by a tribe leader and involving passage through each of the portals guarded by the

Ashari. And though there were no descriptions of it in Pyrah's library of scrolls, Raishan found everything she needed elsewhere: in the memories of Pyrah's headmaster, Cerkonos.

He is wise for a human, Raishan thinks. But not enough to keep her from reaching into his mind. And not enough to keep her from altering what she found there, so that he might never know she'd intruded at all.

She kneels at the portal's edge, just as she watched a much younger Cerkonos do in one particular stolen memory. This ritual he performed—it's almost offensively rudimentary, and unbearably slow. But it will put her exactly where she needs to be on the Fire Plane, without the risk of ending up stranded in the middle of a sunburned desert or trapped in a forgotten dungeon in the City of Brass.

Besides, there's something particularly satisfying about using the Ashari's own tricks against them. Just this once.

Raishan closes her eyes and presses her hands to the portal's rock edge. Cries out as the heat scalds her skin, but the agony of it fades just as quickly as it came. Left behind is only a pleasant warmth. It gathers, humming against her palms, before spreading up her arms. Down her spine. Up the back of her neck. A sense, almost, of something waking. She opens her eyes.

Ah, yes, the portal seems to say. *I see you now.*

Raishan could not bear it when Talya's prayer threatened to draw the Wildmother's attention. This is different. It is not a god looking back at her but a deeper essence—the very stuff the world is made of. She can respect a power like this.

And I see you, she answers. *So let me pass.*

The portal's response comes without words. Instead, a current begins to spiral through the lava. Circling the center, faster and faster, deepening by the second until the bottom has dropped out of sight.

Raishan stares into the whirlpool's gaping maw. She can feel the pull of it. Of the heat-shimmer, of the endless drop.

There is only one thing to do. With Thordak's name etched into her mind, she leaps. Plummets through the portal's center with a rush of sparks, and hardly has time to scream—to fear, to wish for her dragon wings—before a strange new gravity takes hold of her, yanking her to the side.

Her feet hit rock. She stumbles forward, catching herself on the wall of what seems to be a long tunnel. Darkness around her, tinted with a ruby glow, but at the far end, a light beckons; a breeze at her back urges her toward it.

Raishan grits her teeth, musters every scrap of pride and strength she's sacrificed since the Wildmother's curse took hold of her. She will not let Thordak see how far she's fallen.

She is standing tall as she finally crosses the threshold and steps onto the Fire Plane. Charred desert flats stretch toward an ocean ablaze, the horizon beyond dotted with cyclones of ash. The air is punishingly dry, the sun too close and too bright.

But she cares for none of that, because looming over her is a colossal red dragon. Scales gleaming, his head crowned by a set of gnarled horns, and his hulking, spiked body familiar save for one new addition: a crystal glowing crimson, housed in the center of his chest.

"Raishan," Thordak says. His voice shakes the ground, resonates through the roots of the world. "I've been waiting for you."

If Raishan never sees this plane again, it will be too soon. She is sick of it to her very bones, sick of the sun and the heat and the brute force required to survive it. Fire rolling across the sky like fog, rising from the ashen desert like mountain peaks, leaving nowhere to hide. Strength measured in muscle, in pure endurance, rather than wit and cunning. Painful *and* boring, Raishan thinks. What could possibly be worse?

Right here, right now—the waiting. Raishan stares up at the stone walls surrounding the courtyard she was brought to, searching the windows for any sign of movement. Surely there must be someone keeping watch, but then, she doesn't know how many flame giants live here at this fort. Or, in fact, how many are left alive. For centuries, this stronghold stood empty; now it houses those giants who managed to escape the City of Brass after being betrayed there by one of their own.

Raishan can still remember the delicious anticipation she'd felt upon hearing of it. Oh, the things she might build from a bit of strife.

And she has. Or rather, she will, as soon as her escort returns to lead her inside.

She tries to tamp down on her impatience, but it's been such slow going getting here already. Her allies in the mortal world are no help. She thought having other dragons on her side would make a difference and spent considerable energy and time roping three others into an official alliance with herself and Thordak. But Vorugal and Umbrasyl seem more concerned with their own lives, especially since Brimscythe's death. So far, the Chroma Conclave is more a hindrance than anything else.

Even the simple task of learning the name of the device in Thordak's chest has been a chore. With nothing useful to be found in her own collection of arcane texts, she snuck off to Emon, where the right lie told to the right scholar led her to a craftsman favored by the Arcana Pansophical. And when he wouldn't talk, she found people who would. Customers, rivals. Each one offering her another thread of rumor until she had enough to follow, from the City of Brass across the burning desert and right to the forge under this very fort.

It's a soul anchor, the giants' blacksmith told her once her gold was tucked safely in his pocket. Of arcanist make, designed to bind a soul to the Fire Plane. It would have to be destroyed for its prisoner to leave the plane, he said, but he didn't think that was possible.

Raishan thought of her own curse, of the Wildmother's poison rooted inside her, and smiled. Why destroy what you can make yours?

The bargain they struck then was simple. Gold in exchange for a tool crafted by flame giants, something capable of infecting the soul anchor with the essence of the Fire Plane itself. Thordak can escape this plane, the blacksmith explained, and all the while it will be to the soul anchor as though he never left.

The Ember Seed, the flame giants have begun to call it. They're quite proud of their work, which is all very well and good, except Raishan was supposed to have it in her hands a fortnight ago, and now she's stuck here waiting.

She begins to pace, eddies of ash swirling around her ankles as the breeze kicks up. Her escort, a young giant still taller than twice her human form, said he would return shortly, but she doesn't have time to waste like this. Not when everything is so close to coming together.

At last, heavy footsteps behind her. Raishan turns, expecting her escort, only to find a pair of massive guards poised at the entrance to the courtyard.

"Well?" she says. These giants are so tall it's difficult to make out their expressions, and though it's her own doing—she could've come here in dragon form, but she prefers appearing weaker than she is—she can't help but be annoyed by it. "Did you bring the Ember Seed?"

The guards don't acknowledge her question. "Our captain requests your presence," one says.

"Your captain?" Raishan has never heard any mention of such a person from these giants. Her dealings have all been with the blacksmith at the forge or with the fort's leader, a guard lieutenant too shaken by her eviction from the City of Brass to be any hindrance. "Who, exactly?"

"She is waiting," the second guard says, his arm extended toward the door as if to hurry Raishan along.

"Yes," she says, "I've been doing a bit of that myself."

But this captain is a stranger; Raishan doesn't know yet what sort of power will be most effective. Better to go along with it for now.

Her pride set aside, she lets herself be ushered through a pair of scarred stone doors and into the fort's great hall. In here the air is cooler, darker. The torches are few and far between, and the windows house obsidian panes to deflect the sun. Raishan is grateful for the shadows—for the break they offer from the heat, yes, but mostly for the way they obscure the true scale of this place. She doesn't need any more reminders of how fragile this human form is.

The guards lead her down the center of the room, between two long wooden tables that tower over her head. Other giants are seated, eating some sort of meal that smells absolutely atrocious. They eye Raishan as she passes, and she stares back. Many of these faces are new. Perhaps they arrived with the captain, whoever she is.

"Here," one of the guards says. He's holding open a door set into the room's back wall. Past the threshold, she can see a stone hallway, sunlight at the other end. "Down the hall. The captain waits."

"So you said." Raishan sneers up at him. His heavy armor, the mace strapped to his back—she could still break his body in a heartbeat, and he has no idea. "Lead the way."

The guard shakes his head. "The captain needs no protection. You go alone."

That suits Raishan well enough, but still, she's wary as she starts down the hallway. A new player in this game could be quite dangerous. Not to her own survival—if she needs to escape, she can do so handily—but to that of her plan. If this arrangement with the flame giants falls apart, she might never find another way to break Thordak's imprisonment—and, thereby, the Wildmother's curse.

The hallway leads to a broad balcony overlooking what must have once been the fort's parade grounds. A cloth canopy casts shade over one side, under which two ornately etched stone benches have been placed. Between them, a table holds a pair of mismatched goblets, one small enough to suit Raishan, and a bottle of dark wine. And standing in front of it all is a giant, a woman with hair like fire and skin like ash, dressed in full armor.

"Welcome," she says. "You must be Raishan."

"I am. And you must be Captain . . ." Raishan trails off, waiting for the woman to supply the rest.

"Ordis. Please, sit." The captain gestures to the table. "Will you drink with me? I'm sorry I can't offer more. We don't have much here in the way of luxury."

Ah—now that she's closer, Raishan can smell the wine's rancid bouquet, and she can see that the canopy is actually a threadbare banner propped up on splintered spears. Even the benches are cracked, the stone chipped and broken.

Is this meant to be an insult? A trick? She doesn't think so; she has a dragon's sense for that sort of thing.

Raishan smiles and takes a seat on the sturdier of the two benches. "I've never cared much for wine anyway."

"I am glad to hear it." Ordis's armor clanks as she sits down opposite Raishan. "And I suppose you've seen the fort in a much worse state than this."

Bait laid out before her. Raishan will not bite. "Have I?" she says, tilting her head.

"Yes. I hear you've been visiting for quite some time."

"And yet you and I have never met."

"You've heard of what happened in the City of Brass, yes?" Ordis asks. "My guard and I were away on patrol when it happened. We returned to find everything overturned, with no way to reach those who had left the city." She leans in, her forearms braced on her knees. Raishan does not retreat. "We searched this whole plane for our kin. And now we've found them here, only to be told that someone else found them first."

The scent of fear on the wind, like metal and blood. What is it that the captain is afraid of losing? Her kin, or her authority over them? Raishan will simply have to find a way to assuage both.

"I'm quite grateful to them," she says. "I'm sure they've told you what they've crafted for me. The gold I have paid for their work is well earned."

"Gold," Ordis repeats. "I'm glad you mentioned that. You see, we have no need of it."

"Is that so? Your kinsmen seemed more than happy to accept it."

Let the bargain stand, Raishan thinks, willing Ordis to hear her warning. Let me leave with the Ember Seed; do not force my hand, or you will walk your people to the edge of ruin.

"I'm sure they were." The giant's expression turns grave. "But they don't know who it is they're working for."

"And you do?" Raishan says, her tone light even as she considers which spell to kill Ordis with.

The captain nods. "I heard his name often as I searched for my people. The Cinder King. I am an admirer."

There's a gleam in Ordis's eyes, a thirst that Raishan recognizes—ambition. The captain means not to break this bargain, but to remake it on new terms.

A loose ease drapes itself over Raishan, relief that quickly turns predatory and sharp. Nobody is ever made quite so reckless as they are by ambition. "If you have no need for gold, what is it I can offer you instead?"

Ordis smiles. An ember-glow shines through the cracks in her blackened teeth. "A promise. From you on behalf of your Cinder King. We will give you your Ember Seed. We will even fight under your command. In exchange, you will help me take back the City of Brass, and give me a position of power in your king's new world."

"You and your kin, you mean?"

Ordis blinks, as if she's only just realized her omission. "Yes. Of course. But perhaps . . ." She lowers her voice. "Your king needs a general."

"Perhaps he does," Raishan says. Yes, this will do. "I think that can be arranged."

Thordak might very well honor this promise. He also might burn Ordis to bones the moment he's free. He was already changeable, mercurial, but there's been a particularly strange air to him of late, a ragged laughter that's made her wonder—

Nothing.

Raishan seals the bargain, her own bloodied palm pressed to Ordis's. Thordak can do whatever he likes, as long as she still gets what she needs.

Some hours later, the portal closes behind Raishan as she starts back down the mountain path toward Pyrah. She will return to the Fire Plane eventually, but in the meantime, instructions have been left with Ordis and the giants, and if all goes to plan, the Ember Seed will have been planted in Thordak's soul anchor by the time she sees him again.

So more of that interminable waiting through the winter, yes, but then the celestial solstice, when the barriers between the planes are thinnest, and when she will break him free at last.

Raishan stops on the path and stares up at the gray sweep of the sky. She can see snow falling, but this close to the portal, the flakes melt in midair, leaving a fine mist of rain across her skin. For a moment, she can think only of her home. Her jungle, her mountains, her—

Draped vines and white flowers and the death of every innocent wreaked upon her tenfold—

No. Thordak will cure her. When she returns to the Rifenmist, the curse will not come with her.

Her resolve bolsters her, forms to her body like armor as she leaves the ember-crackle hush of the Cindergrove behind and re-enters Pyrah proper. This part of the village is always less busy than the rest—few but Firetamers have business with the portal itself—but today she's startled to find it entirely empty. No children hurrying to their lessons. Nobody browsing at the herbalist's stall; no herbalist, in fact, selling anything whatsoever. And in the distance she can hear voices nearer to the village center growing louder by the minute. It's more commotion than Pyrah's ever seen, at least during her time here.

Raishan rolls her eyes. These Ashari will make a fuss over anything. Likely she will reach the main square and be told that Cerkonos has invented a new method for steeping tea. Three minutes instead of two, he'll announce to the gathered crowd, and as they all wail and swoon, Raishan will consider letting the curse kill her, if only for an excuse to not be here in this backwater any longer.

But she has to pass by the square on her way back to her bed, where she plans to sleep for at least a day and a half, so she braces herself and continues on. Down narrow streets pockmarked with obsidian, past stone buildings worn smooth by the wind. Looming over it all, the mountain, its volcanic summit hidden in the clouds.

Soon, she reaches the edge of Pyrah's market and finds she is no longer alone. Though most of the stalls have been left empty, a handful of shopkeepers have doggedly remained at their posts despite the lack of customers. Raishan stops at the nearest one, where a dwarf she faintly recognizes is selling an array of painfully ugly jewelry.

"Excuse me," she says. "Where is everyone? Has something happened?"

The dwarf—what is his name? Barkin? Larkin?—nods vigorously. "Visitors," he says. "One of them's an Air Ashari sage."

Something at the back of Raishan's mind twitches. That's familiar. Why is that familiar?

"From Zephrah?" she asks. Has she been there? She doesn't think so, but she's lived many years, and if she were to forget anything, it would certainly be more of these Ashari. "What've they come here for?"

The dwarven shopkeeper shrugs. "Couldn't tell you." He leans in, beckoning for her to do the same. "But what I can do is offer you a onetime-only deal on one of these fine . . ."

Raishan leaves without waiting to hear the rest, anxiety prickling at the back of her neck. What is she forgetting? Perhaps she researched the Air Ashari before finding Thordak here under the Firetamers' guard. Or perhaps simply the mention of another sage is enough to conjure up that temple in the Rifenmist and set her teeth on edge.

Whatever the case, the square is right on the other side of the market. She'll cut through it on her way back to her room, see what all the fuss is about. Just to ease her mind; she'll sleep better that way.

But it reaches her before she's even gotten to the market's edge. Rumor, gossip, idle chatter—blades she has honed and wielded for a hundred years, turned against her now. The Air Ashari wears a crown of antlers, the crowd whispers. Her hair is like fire, and she walks in the company of heroes.

Brimscythe's lair, viewed through the black distortion of an obsidian orb. Collapsing rock, the corpse of the young blue dragon sprawled beneath, and, most important, a group of intruders, one wearing an antlered crown.

They are here. The ones who killed Brimscythe, whom Raishan thought hardly warranted any further attention. Insects, she called them, and now they're in Pyrah. Have they followed her? Discovered her, and come to destroy all the work she's done?

She cannot allow that.

Raishan breaks from the crowd, a plan already forming in her mind. She told the giants and the others in the Conclave to prepare for Thordak's release on the solstice, when Exandria's magic is heightened, pliable and powerful.

Now, knowing that there are enemies on her trail, she can no longer afford to wait that long. It will have to be sooner. Winter's Crest, in a little more than a month's time. It's lacking the arcane power of the solstice, but the planes are closest during Winter's Crest; Raishan will still have an advantage.

She just has to convince the others to help. The flame giants will obey whatever orders she gives. The rest of the Conclave is another matter, but even though Vorugal and Umbrasyl have yet to prove themselves capable of any meaningful intelligence, she is sure they will see reason here.

Back in her little stone room, Raishan sends messages across continents, across planes, a stubborn fury running through her veins. Everything must happen as she wills it to. There is no other choice.

Raishan does not sleep that night.

The dreams find her anyway.

For the first time, Raishan finds herself wishing Brimscythe weren't dead. He was, of course, insufferable, and too smart to be manipulated in the way she generally prefers to work, but at least he understood the value of using other faces, other bodies, instead of a dragon's imposing might. If he were still alive, Vorugal and Umbrasyl might have been convinced to have this meeting elsewhere. Humans seated around a table in the corner of some ramshackle tavern, perhaps—assuming her allies are even capable of transforming at all.

As it is, Raishan prowls the edge of a large clearing in the Cindergrove, her withered muscles aching in protest. The other dragons know of her curse, yes, but she still would rather they not see her like this. Even the weakness of a human's body is preferable, if it's one they would all share.

Vorugal is the first to arrive, his white form briefly blotting out the sun before he lands in the clearing so heavily that two trees shudder and topple. Raishan tolerates the rush of air, holding back an annoyed sigh. Of her two allies, Vorugal is the more eager, the more reckless. It was he who insisted they meet this close to the portal, as if being near to Thordak's prison is the same thing as setting him free.

Umbrasyl will be more careful, certainly. He understands the danger of being found out.

"Raishan," Vorugal says, by way of greeting, even as another tree is knocked over by the thrash of his tail.

She's spent too much time in Thordak's company to be impressed by Vorugal's size, but the difference between his bulk and hers is still startling. Even at her full height, Raishan does not reach the forest canopy; meanwhile, every turn of Vorugal's head sends another burned-out branch crashing to the ground.

Wherever he's been since joining the Conclave, it's suited him well. His scales are mottled silver and white, the healthy ice-shine of them almost as bright as that of his blue eyes. Icicles hang from his jaws and from the spines along the crest of his head; Raishan can see that already they've started to melt in the Cindergrove's uncomfortable warmth.

His jaws open, dislodging the remaining icicles as he breathes in deeply. "Your scent. It worsens." A smile, and then, "You're starting to rot."

Raishan would perhaps be more impressed by this if she weren't well aware of the scars crossing her body, the sores weeping along the underside of her neck. The disease itself is no secret—only its cause.

Suddenly, a breeze buffets her, and before she can answer Vorugal, the air over the clearing shimmers. Out of the emptiness appears a large black dragon, his wings beating slowly as he drifts down toward them. Raishan maneuvers out of the way, keeps her wings furled and her neck in a neat coil.

If Vorugal's surroundings have been treating him well, Umbrasyl's have been doing the opposite. He looks almost as diminished as Raishan herself. Black scales dull, even flaking off in spots. Jagged teeth dripping not acid but clear bile. And there is something in the way Umbrasyl keeps his tail curled around his body, something about the bitterness of his scent that suggests a deep, potent exhaustion.

"Welcome," she says, pushing down a surge of envy. All Umbrasyl needs is a bit of rest. He'll recover whether they free Thordak or not; meanwhile, she remains at the mercy of a curse she never deserved in the first place.

"Spare me your pleasantries," Umbrasyl says, his tail twitching with annoyance. "Why have you called us, Raishan? The solstice is still a ways off yet, and I have matters to tend to of my own."

"Are you hunted, still?" Vorugal sneers. "Some of us do not allow ourselves to become prey."

"Some of us do not hide in the north," Umbrasyl replies, and Raishan knows that if she does not intervene, these two will never cease arguing.

"Please," she says, drawing their attention. "You have traveled far, I know. I am grateful. Let me waste no more of your time."

Vorugal is mollified by this small touch of flattery. Umbrasyl seems less swayed; for a moment his wings shift, as if he's considering taking flight.

She explains it as simply as she can. The group from Brimscythe's lair, the threat of being discovered. She leaves out what she's read in Ordis's latest report from the Fire Plane—the descriptions of Thordak's mutating body, of the madness in his eyes. Things are complicated enough already.

"I don't understand," Vorugal says when she's finished.

Of course you don't, she thinks.

"Raishan suggests that this group of travelers is reason enough to change our plans," Umbrasyl says, turning entirely toward Vorugal. "She considers them a threat."

Vorugal meets Raishan's gaze and cocks his head, looking for a moment more like a dog than a dragon.

"A threat?" His eyes narrow. "They are nothing. They are insects."

Yes, she wants to tell him. They are, which makes it all the more intolerable that they could prevent her from getting her cure.

"I would not care," she says instead, "if our goal were not so important. Thordak—"

"Have you told him of this plan?" Umbrasyl interrupts.

"He charged me with freeing him."

"That is not an answer." He stalks toward her, forcing her to retreat against the trees crowding the clearing's edge. "You have not told him. You must know he would not agree."

Raishan knows no such thing. The Thordak trapped on the Fire Plane now is not the same dragon trapped there some fifteen years ago; given what she hears from Ordis, she doubts he is even the same dragon he was fifteen days ago. Where once he might have dismissed Raishan's plea, now he might insist she try to free him immediately, without waiting even for Winter's Crest.

"I have told him what he needs to know," she says. "He trusts me, as you should."

Umbrasyl lets out a gurgling bubble of laughter. Acid sprays across the ground at his feet. "First you tell us these fools pose a threat to us, and now you ask us for our trust. I think your time with these Ashari has dulled your mind."

"I am not *with* the—" She snaps her jaws shut. Swallows the rest of her protest, banishes the image of the Wildmother's altar from behind her eyes. "These fools, as you call them, may be only the first arrow to be fired by our enemies. If we do not act now, we might not have another chance before others follow."

As soon as she's finished, she can tell it was a mistake. Too much, said too passionately. She's forgotten what it's like to speak to creatures whose power equals her own.

Only it isn't equal, is it? Another mistake, to forget the curse written across her skin when the other two dragons certainly haven't.

"Listen to her," Vorugal says. "She begs us."

Umbrasyl's muscles tense. His wings rustle. "She does, doesn't she?"

"Yes. As if for mercy." Icy breath billows out from between Vorugal's jaws, coating Raishan's talons with frost. "As if for her life."

His meaning is all too clear. She can hear it in his voice, see it written in the way he's drawn closer so he dominates the clearing. If she tried now to take to the sky, she wouldn't have room to spread her wings.

Vorugal has no intention of letting her leave alive.

And from the way Umbrasyl is looking on with idle interest, he seems to have no objection to that.

For a moment, Raishan feels everything coming down on her. The Ashari with her crown of antlers, the mad spark in Thordak's eyes. The sheer agony of her curse, waiting to swallow her whole, and now this—two fellow dragons, each with the strength to grind her brittle body to dust, turning on the alliance she forged among them.

It wasn't supposed to go like this.

She bares her teeth, draws her magic to her until the air hums with power. It wasn't supposed to go like this, and so it won't. She has survived worse; what she knows better than anyone else is that there is always, always another way out.

Without a word, Raishan transforms. Her dragon hide disintegrates, revealing pale skin that bubbles as the bones beneath break and rearrange themselves. Muscles split and tear. Nerves and tendons slithering, squirming, until her human form takes its shape, too powerfully cast to be dispelled or undone by anyone but her.

A word tumbles from her lips, calling up a lilac glow around her. She blinks—vanishes in an instant—appears again in a copse of dead trees. Still in the Cindergrove, but closer now to Pyrah.

She sags with relief. The other two dragons will not follow her today. This is too easy a hunt to appeal to Vorugal, and she is too weak in Umbrasyl's eyes to be dangerous if left on her own. But if she's bought herself time, it isn't much. This alliance will shatter, and soon. Perhaps it already has.

She has to speak to Thordak as soon as possible.

Raishan begins the walk back to Pyrah, her eyes trained to the sky for any glimpse of the other Conclave members. It's as she's reaching the outskirts of the village that their farewell reaches her. Umbrasyl's contemptuous voice, whispered in her ear with a spell of his own.

"Cowardly," he says. "Foolish. Stay with your Ashari, Raishan. You are right where you belong."

Umbrasyl's words echo in her head without end. *Your Ashari,* as she arrives back in her bedroom, intent on resting until her magic has recovered its full strength. *Your Ashari,* as she ignores Talya's knocks on the door and as the time for her regular lesson with Cerkonos comes and goes.

He was wrong, of course. These people are not hers. They are not her equals, and no time spent with them could drag her down that far.

But still.

Still.

Draped vines on fire, white flowers crumbled to ash and scattered across the temple ruins. Raishan roars as a sage's spell finds the gap between her scales. Behind her, people fleeing—she will catch them all before this is over—and on his knees at her feet, another sage, this one drowning in a noxious cloud. He was halfway through transforming into some animal when her poison hit him; now his body writhes uncontrollably, flickering grotesquely between one form and the next.

"End it," he wails. "Kill me, I beg you."

Raishan turns away. There is no one here whom she will spare an ounce of pain. Not even—

She wakes. Weeping, this time. Blood pours from her mouth, leaving streaks all down her shirt. When she tries to reach a hand up to wipe it away, she cannot move. Cannot look down at her body and recognize it as her own, and for a moment, it isn't. It's something else instead, something *between.* Talons breaking through her skin. Green scales sprouting, growing inward until they pierce human muscle.

No, Raishan thinks, even as the moment passes. *No, no. It cannot take me now.*

She has served Thordak well, done everything he's asked of her. If he doesn't cure her now, she might die before he ever can.

There isn't any strength left in her. She rises anyway, carried by the force of her own will. Out into the clutch of midnight. Through Pyrah, quiet and still, and back up the mountain.

Her rest was interrupted, and her magic is still depleted, but she has enough left to make do. The portal's guards fall asleep with a murmured word. Nobody sees her stagger toward the pool of lava. Nobody but the portal itself hears her plea to be let through.

The whirlpool opens. Raishan throws herself into it and hears herself scream; the fire hurts as it never has before. It scorches through her skin as she falls. Burning deeper and deeper until it reaches the very knit-weave of her magic. She is too weak to hold on; the pull of the portal unravels the spell binding her body into human form.

She lands heavily on the Fire Plane, a dragon once more. The air hums with the heat of an approaching firestorm; red clouds roil in the sky, and an inferno pushes across the ashen desert, drawing nearer and nearer with every second.

Raishan flinches as the wind scours the tender patches on her hide where the curse has set in deep. She has never been here before as her true self. It would've drawn too much attention—that's what she's always told herself, but there is more, too. The fear that if Thordak sees just what this curse has done to her, he will tell her his cure can no longer work. A fear she can't avoid facing anymore.

Overhead, a silhouette takes form amidst the firestorm, drawing closer with every second. Soon Raishan can make out the span of its great wings and the red shine of its scales. Thordak, approaching. Nothing happens on this plane without his notice.

She will not fly to meet him; she cannot withstand the fire like he can, and her wings have been too long out of use to be trusted right now. Instead, she lets herself feel everything, every stab of strain in her muscles, every ache, every excruciating heartbeat. This is what she's survived. This impossible pain. Empires have broken, and she's endured. Mountains have crumbled, cities fallen, and all the while, she has borne the unbearable.

She doesn't want to anymore. More than that, she's not sure if she can.

Thordak lands nearby, the beat of his wings creating a gust of air that nearly knocks Raishan over. The glow off the soul anchor in his chest is stronger than when she saw it last. Veins of fiery light radiate from it. They wind between Thordak's scales, spreading almost to his neck before they fade. If Raishan tilts her head, the veins almost seem to pulse, too, as if in time with Thordak's heart.

That must be the effect of the Ember Seed, she thinks. At least one thing has gone to plan.

"You," Thordak says, and lumbers closer. "Good. You've come."

"I—" Raishan breaks off. "Did you call? I received no message."

He doesn't answer, only stares at her with eyes like fresh coals. At his back, the plane's eternal sun seems dulled, its power put to shame by the sheer might of the Cinder King.

"I wanted to speak with you," Raishan says. "To discuss our bargain. The one we struck so many years ago."

Thordak's wings shift, but his silence remains unbroken. Raishan suppresses a shudder of unease. Strange, to see so large a creature so still, so quiet. More than that, this is unlike him. Has he spoken to Vorugal? To Umbrasyl?

Is this when she finds herself betrayed?

Caution would have her retreat. It would have her wait for him to comment, to give some sign of his state of mind. But Raishan has no time for caution. The curse moves too quickly; her enemies are too close.

"In that bargain, I promised you my service," she says. "In exchange, you promised me a cure for my disease."

"I did," Thordak answers at last. Slowly, each word carrying the weight of an avalanche.

Raishan is so relieved she can hardly breathe. If he's willing to acknowledge what he owes her, she's already halfway to getting it.

"As I promised, I have served you for many years," she says. "It was I who found you here, I who devised this plan for your escape. And there is so much more to be done, of course, but this curse . . . it ruins me."

The admission hurts as much as any wound. Raishan grimaces. The Wildmother and her cult must be so pleased.

"I know our task isn't yet complete," she continues, gathering her nerve. "But you will be back in Exandria soon, ruling over your rightful territory, and I cannot serve you there if I am dead."

Thordak snorts, twin curls of smoke rising from his nostrils. The soul anchor flares bright. A wave of hope crests in Raishan's heart as she readies herself for the curing touch of his magic; it breaks when he simply says, "My kingdom waits. Yes, soon I will return."

"But I might not." She has no patience anymore, no tact. "Please, Thordak. I need your help now. Break this curse, or tell me how I can break it myself. I have been loyal. I have been faithful. I have—"

"You have served me. I know. You said." He lowers his head, his shadow falling across her, anger simmering in his eyes. "I have many servants."

Raishan can't help feeling a sliver of fear, but she's been afraid before. It can't stop her now. "You do, but only I found you. Only I laid the path for your freedom."

"You think too much of yourself, little wyrm," he warns. "I will be free whether you live or die."

She gnashes her teeth, rising to her full height. Without her work, he would still be lost to time, with no hope of ever escaping.

"That's a lie," she snarls, "and you very well know it."

"Do I?" Thordak shakes his head. "You sound like her." Before she can ask who he means, he spits out the name as though it offends him. "Raishan."

It roots her to the spot. Freezes her blood to ice, melts her fury into confusion. "What?"

Thordak's attention seems to drift. His tail twitching restlessly, talons clenching against the ground. "Raishan. She thinks I cannot see her ambition," he says, seething. "She thinks we are all fools, that there is no one who can see her lies for what they are."

"Thordak. I'm—"

She falls silent as his gaze swings back to her. It is intent. Feverish, and sparking, and empty of recognition. All Raishan can find is a well of hate, burning for someone he thinks is not here. Burning for her.

"I am no fool," he says. "I can see her lies. I know what she is and what she means to take from me." He slams the tip of one wing down into the ground beside Raishan, blocking her retreat. "I will make you another bargain, little wyrm. I will cure your curse when you bring me Raishan's head."

IT ALWAYS GOES LIKE THIS. They call Raishan a deceiver—she knows, she's heard the names they whisper in the dark—but it's always her who ends up betrayed. The sages in the Rifenmist. Vorugal, Umbrasyl. And now this.

She agreed to Thordak's bargain, of course. What else was there to do if she wanted to survive? She promised to slaughter his enemy, told him anything he wanted to hear. Likely he'll have forgotten all about this the next time they meet, or he'll recognize her as Raishan and not some stranger. Likely, his madness means that none of what happened will ever matter.

Which almost makes it worse, doesn't it? Lied to, betrayed, and for what?

At least the sages had a reason. They wanted something from her she wasn't willing to give.

Raishan never dreams about that part of it. The last of the sages called herself an innocent, so of course the curse only ever tells that story. Death after death, night after night, dealing back the damage she did.

But Raishan remembers how everything started. How the sages arrived in the jungle, searching for somewhere to build their temple. How she left them to their peace, even as they ventured farther in, closer to her lair. The Rifenmist is not a kind place; she was sure they would turn back of their own accord. And if they didn't, well, she would do what had to be done.

She remembers what came next, too. The attack at her lair, without warning, without negotiation. She can still feel the sting of their weapons. She can still hear their voices, calling her very existence a desecration of the Wildmother's grace.

And yes, they paid for it in the end, but so did she. So, much as she might want to destroy Thordak—much as it might be for the best, given the mercurial slip of his mind—she must allow him to live on. He is, after all, still the only thing that can save her.

Winter's Crest, she tells herself. The gap between the Planes of Existence will be thinnest; she can free him then. It will be more difficult without Vorugal and Umbrasyl, but it's possible, and that's all the chance she needs. Then, once Thordak's free, she can put more distance between the two of them. Provide him and the rest of the Conclave with new problems, new targets, and while they're looking the other way, she'll find some other route to her survival.

That's what she does best.

THIS TIME, SHE DOESN'T BOTHER to stay out of sight. When she arrives at the portal on Winter's Crest, she stands in plain view, the full might of her magic crackling at her human fingertips. Two Firetamers are stationed at the top of the path; one is a stranger, but Raishan recognizes the other as Talya.

Good, she thinks. *That takes care of that.* The guards hardly have time to open their mouths before Talya collapses, dead in an instant, while the other disintegrates to dust.

Raishan can hear someone yelling—a witness, perhaps, running to tell everyone what they've seen. She doesn't care. The whole tribe can march against her if they like; her allies will be here soon enough.

She approaches the lava's edge, anticipation fizzing in her bones. Every time she's used the portal, it's been with the method she learned from Cerkonos's memories. Asking the portal's permission and traveling through almost as its equal.

Tonight she will be its master instead. From the shaft of her boot, she removes a forked piece of metal and a small obsidian shard from the Fire Plane. Both were given to her by the giants. Ordis even said the obsidian came from the rock they used to forge the Ember Seed. It should help, according to what she knows of this ritual, but then, Raishan will see this done regardless.

She clutches the forked metal to her chest and holds the obsidian shard out over the lava. Welcomes a rush of magic so powerful that for a moment she sees only red, flame and blood and crystal shine.

Do not, the portal seems to whisper. *You know this is unwise.*

Maybe so, but what choice is there? If she frees Thordak, thousands will die. If she doesn't, she will.

No, there is no choice at all.

Open, she whispers back. *I command it.*

The ritual is finished; the obsidian glows molten. Below it, a whirlpool takes shape, the current moving with an unusual violence. The portal is open like this, but only for a moment. Not long enough to draw Thordak across.

She takes a deep breath and drops the obsidian into the lava. A wave of gold ripples out as it hits the surface, gilding the rocks, the trees, before fading into a faint shimmer. Raishan can feel the tug of it, like a thread tied between her heart and the portal, where the very energy of her spell has begun to slow the whirlpool's spin.

"Now," she calls out, triumphant. She will hold this rift open as long as she can. "The portal is clear! Thordak, can you hear me?"

Her cry will carry across the plane. Others will hear it—elementals, Ordis and her giants—and they'll answer. They will come through the portal, bringing chaos with them.

Good, she thinks as a gout of fire bursts from the portal's surface. Pyrah should burn for all the indignity she's suffered here.

"Raishan," comes Thordak's answer, echoing strangely in the air. "Is it time?"

She opens her mouth only to find her words stolen. Doubt is left behind in their place, stronger for all its suddenness.

The Ember Seed could fail. It might need more time to properly take root; Thordak could be destroyed if he crosses now, and how is she meant to break her curse without him? Besides, if she waits, if the Ember Seed acclimates, the tide of Thordak's madness might ebb.

She shakes her head. It might very well rise, too. Even just one more day could cost her everything. Hasn't she learned her lesson? Strike now, strike quick, before the opportunity passes. Trust yourself and no others.

"Yes," she tells Thordak. "It's time. Come home to Exandria."

The lava begins to bubble, the earth underfoot rumbling from some deep, seismic quake. A crack like lightning—chunks of the stone rim surrounding the portal topple down into the whirlpool, which stretches, pulls. Rips as though it were fabric, bringing Raishan to her knees. She thought she understood pain, but this is beyond. This is unmaking. Her control in tatters, the burn off the portal shredding the edges of her sanity.

But Thordak is coming. She has to hold on. She can see him now, his body breaking through the rock tunnel below the portal. There are creatures with him, skittering, chattering, crowing with joy at their newfound freedom.

Faster, she thinks. *Hurry.*

Finally, Thordak's horns breach the whirlpool. Sheets of lava pour from his wings as he claws his way back into the mortal world with an earsplitting roar. His fire swallows the forest, so hot it seems to burn the air itself. Already, sprites and elementals are following him, spilling through the open portal in droves.

Raishan tries to watch, tries to memorize the sight of the Cindergrove's annihilation. But all she can see is the soul anchor in Thordak's chest, the Ember Seed within blazing like a falling star.

It had to be done, she tells herself. He had to be freed. And now his debt to her has come due at last.

Shouting in the distance, voices she faintly recognizes. The Ashari must be readying their defenses. Fools. Thordak will destroy them. He will turn their bodies to ash, split their souls in two.

A fitting fate for lesser creatures. Only, she does hope at least one soul survives. One sage's soul, to seek out the Wildmother's embrace beyond the veil. They will tell her what has happened; she will weep to know it's all her fault.

Draped vines and white flowers. Innocent, the temple sage called herself as she lay dying.

Raishan smiles, poison-sweet. "Liar," she says, and laughs until the world ends.

THE EDGE OF GORY

Kendra Wells

I AM THE DEVOURER OF BLOOD.
THE RAVENER OF BATTLEFIELDS.
WIELDED IN THE HAND OF THE MAN WHO COULD MAKE GODS TREMBLE.

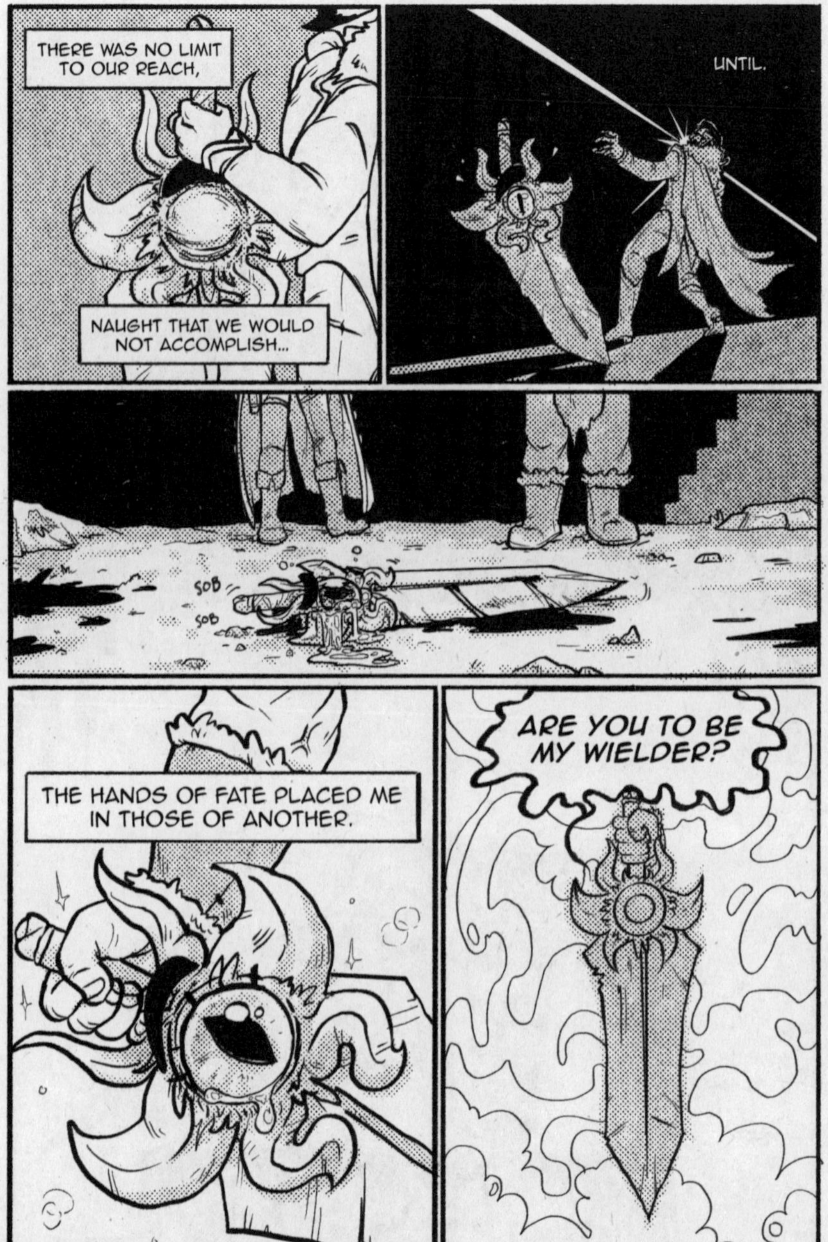
THERE WAS NO LIMIT TO OUR REACH,
NAUGHT THAT WE WOULD NOT ACCOMPLISH...
UNTIL.
SOB
SOB
THE HANDS OF FATE PLACED ME IN THOSE OF ANOTHER.
ARE YOU TO BE MY WIELDER?

WHAT THE SHIT.
DO YOU ACCEPT MY POWER?
OKAY!
FOR A BRIEF, BEAUTIFUL MOMENT, I BELIEVED THAT EVEN GREATER POWER WAS WITHIN MY GRASP IN THE HANDS OF THIS BALD LUMMOX.
WIFF
WIFF
WIFF
WIFF
ALAS...

THIS "GROG" WAS NOTHING COMPARED TO THE WICKED ELEGANCE OF MY FORMER MASTER.
CRUDE,
DISTRACTED,

DETERMINED TO CONVERSE IN OUTHOUSES
BEFOULED BY THE MOST WRETCHED OF MORTAL ASSES.
BUT BLOOD IS BLOOD.
DEATH IS DEATH.
HA
HA
HA
AND THAT MALODOROUS OAF COULD DELIVER *THAT* IN KIND.

YO. SWORD GUY. WE NEED TO TALK.
I AM CALLED CRAVEN EDGE, FOOL!!
AND WILL BE ADDRESSED AS-
WAIT, ARE WE IN AN OUTHOUSE AGAIN?
YEH. IT'S THE MOST PRIVATE PLACE I CAN THINK OF.

THAT IS NOT-
LISTEN, WE'VE GOT A REALLY BIG FIGHT COMING UP THAT I-
THAT WE CAN'T LOSE.
WHAT DID YOUR FORMER MASTER DO TO MAKE YOU MORE POWERFUL?
...
HE KEPT ME FED.
THE MORE YOU KILL, THE MORE BLOOD IS SPILLED AGAINST MY BLADE, THE STRONGER I BECOME.
THE STRONGER WE BECOME.

HELL YEAH!!!
KRAK
FUCK YOU, KEVDAK!!
?
THE INDIGNITIES WILL BE WORTH IT...
MY POWER WILL BE IMMEASURABLE... OOOUGH.
HELLOOO? UHH, WHAT'S ITS NAME AGAIN. "BACON"?

ROOOAAR!!
YES... YES... YES!!!
VISCERA... CARNAGE... BLOOD!!
WHOOPSIE!
SMACK
GET... US... BACK TO THE BATTLE... YOU DUMB OX!!
STOP... YELLING... AT... ME!!

WHAT ARE YOU-
MAKE YOURSELF USEFUL!
WAIT WAIT *WAIT*!!
AAAAAAAH
AA

WHUD
PIKEY!!
YES!! MORE BLOOD! MORE POWER!!
oww...
HEY!
WE DO NOT EAT FRIENDS, CRAZY EDGE!
YOU AGREED TO FEED ME AND I AGREED TO GIVE YOU POWER UNTOLD!

AND WHAT ISN'T GIVEN FREELY,
I WILL TAKE!!
SMACK
GROG!!
WIFF
PUNCH
WIFF

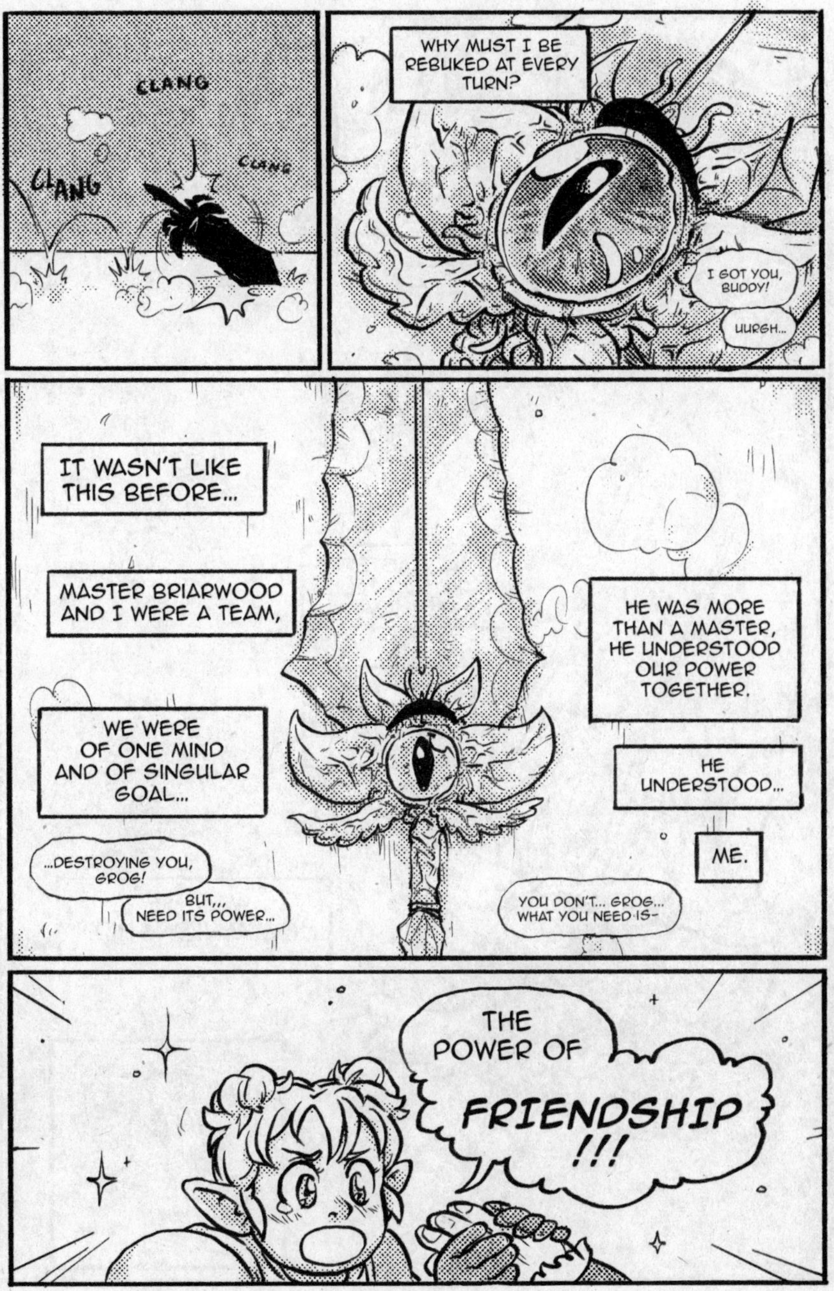
CLANG
CLANG
CLANG
WHY MUST I BE REBUKED AT EVERY TURN?
I GOT YOU, BUDDY!
UURGH...
IT WASN'T LIKE THIS BEFORE...
MASTER BRIARWOOD AND I WERE A TEAM,
WE WERE OF ONE MIND AND OF SINGULAR GOAL...
HE WAS MORE THAN A MASTER, HE UNDERSTOOD OUR POWER TOGETHER.
HE UNDERSTOOD...
ME.
...DESTROYING YOU, GROG!
BUT,,, NEED ITS POWER...
YOU DON'T... GROG... WHAT YOU NEED IS-
THE POWER OF FRIENDSHIP !!!

FRIENDSHIP...?
COULD IT BE...
WHAT MASTER BRIARWOOD TRULY OFFERED ME,
WHAT MATTERED MOST...
Z
Z
WAS HIS COMPANIONSHIP?
YOINK

SEE YA!!
NOOOOOOOOOOoooo

HM, GETTING SUCKED DRY MAKES YOU HUNGRY.
I COULDA TOLD YOU THAT...
I COULD DO LUNCH.

TAKE THIS DOWN:

BEING AN ACCURATE ACCOUNTING OF DOTY AND TARYON DARRINGTON IN THE BASILISK'S DEN

Jess Barber

Doty! Take this down.

Expert—no. *Seasoned*—no. Intrepid! Yes, good, let's go with that. *Intrepid adventurer seeks same. Sort of.*

Oh, I do like the alliteration there. But perhaps it muddies the waters a bit. No, let's try:

Intrepid Adventurer Seeks Equally Intrepid Adventuring Party.

Yes, that's better, I like that very much. Bigger than that, though, please, Doty. We want this to be readable from a distance. Perhaps a little more flourish on the lettering? Oh yes. That's looking very smart indeed.

Internationally ~~famed~~ ~~renowned~~ celebrated inventor and author Sir Taryon Gary Darrington seeks companions for a series of quests, including, but not limited to:

- *Dragon slaying*
- *Manticore slaying*
- *Basilisk slaying*
- *Any other kind of monster slaying, really*
- *Maiden rescuing*
- *Dungeon crawling*
- *Et cetera*

Travel Exandria! Experience enchanting new locales!

*Encounter exotic beasts! Fame and fortune guaranteed!**

Adventurers of all persuasions will be considered; merchandizing potential a plus. Compensation: one thousand gold per mission (negotiable). Interviews conducted Miresen next at the Mincing Mongoose Tavern, noon bells until sundown. Check in with the automaton upon arrival.

Adventure awaits!

*Fame and fortune not actually guaranteed.

"Right, then," said Tary. "We've covered favorite spells, preferred weapons, educational background . . . What else? Oh!" Doty watched as Tary implemented **Expression: Inquisitive, Yet Receptive**: fingers steepled, head tilted fifteen degrees to the right. **Subroutine: Encouraging Smile** in place. "What," asked Tary, "would you say is your biggest weakness?"

Doty's own servos were whirring furiously as Tary talked, his quill racing across the parchment to capture everything that was happening. The mage sitting across from Tary seemed to be mostly implementing **Expression: Nervous.**

Doty had already taken down the most pertinent information about the candidate upon his arrival: **Ancestry: Human. Age: Twenties. Spectacles: Smudged. Goatee: Ill-Considered.** At the "biggest weakness" question the mage brightened considerably. "Oh, that one's easy," he said. "Definitely blades of any kind. Hate blood, you see. Absolutely faint at the sight of it."

Inquisitive, Yet Receptive faltered for zero-point-six seconds. "I see," said Tary. "And that's not a concern, in this line of work?"

The mage blinked twice. "Sorry? I don't follow."

Inquisitive, Yet Receptive faltered for one-point-eight additional seconds. "You know what," said Tary. "Never you mind. I'd say we actually have just about everything we need for today! Doty, if you'd be so kind?"

Doty set down The Book, Tary's as-of-yet-untitled autobiography. Writing The Book was Doty's primary function, even before ensuring Tary's safety or distributing pre-written rejections to their would-be traveling companions. He presented one such rejection to the mage now. ***We greatly appreciate your interest in the Taryon Darrington Adventuring Party. We know how valuable your time is, and we're honored that you would meet with us today! We want you to know that positions within the Taryon Darrington Adventuring Party are extremely competitive–***

"Brilliant," said the mage, spectacles slipping down his nose as he squinted to read the card. "So you'll be in touch via—what, post? Telepathy? Or if you want to leave a message at the inn where I'm staying—"

"Yes, precisely, all that," said Tary, giving Doty the wrap-it-up gesture they'd agreed upon. Doty stood and implemented **Subroutine: Menacing Loom** until the mage stood as well.

"Please do be sure to take a closer look at my résumé before making any decisions," said the mage, awkwardly trying to collect his staff and robe as Doty herded him away from the table. "We didn't even get a chance to discuss my semester abroad before attending the Alabaster Lyceum—" He was still talking as Doty ushered him into the sunlight of the Beaded Alley and pulled the tavern door shut behind him.

"The depressing part, Doty," Tary said with a sigh, rubbing his eyes, "is that he was honestly one of the better candidates so far."

Creak.

Tary stopped rubbing his eyes. "Oh, I know, you're right. The last thing I need is to give myself premature crow's-feet."

Creak.

Tary laughed, patting Doty's uppermost rotational limb motor. "Oh, Doty. You always know just what to say to cheer me up."

Current location: The Mincing Mongoose Tavern, Beaded Alley, Port Damali, Menagerie Coast, Wildemount, Exandria, Mortal Plane. Recommended maximum occupancy: Seventy-five medium-sized creatures. Current occupancy: Six.

The tavern where I established myself to commence the search for questing partners was a squalid little affair in the most dangerous part of town, absolutely teeming with cutthroats and villains. Risky, yes, but a necessary evil if I wanted to find like-minded compatriots willing to brave the trials and hardships of adventuring life. As I swilled rotgut whiskey, the only thing the tavern had on offer, I returned the steely-eyed glares of the other patrons and wondered whether I would manage to escape with my life.

"Are you still working on your wine there, m'dear?"

Name: Hilda Thurgood. Occupation: Tavern proprietress. Ancestry: Gnomish. Apron: Blue gingham. Cheeks: Rosy.

"Oh dear, is it not to your liking?" Hilda's brow furrowed in concern as she noted Tary's mostly full glass. "It's one of my favorite vintages, but I suppose it is a little on the sweet side. Shall I bring you something else to try?"

"Oh! No, no, it's quite delightful, actually." Tary turned on his most sparkling smile. "The perfect terroir for my palate. In fact, I was just about to ask if you had any additional recommendations. It's so difficult to find a good sommelier these days, one must cherish the opportunity when one can."

Hilda's cheeks grew even rosier. "Well, that's awfully kind of you to say. I was actually just sampling from a new vineyard in Kamordah—" She was cut off by the bell on the tavern door jingling cheerfully.

New occupant analysis: Ancestry: Human. Age: Early thirties. Hair: Close-cropped black curls. Eyes: Dark, with a roguish sparkle. Lips: Full, with the slightest smiling tilt, hinting at shared secrets. Shoulders: Broad. Jawline: Chiseled.

Tary was no longer looking at Hilda, his attention having shifted fully to the new patron. His heart rate had increased approximately 10 percent. Doty recalled the protagonists from Tary's favorite romance novels, and Lawrence, and in general the sort of faces that tended to lead to Tary making bad decisions.

This was concerning.

The human lifted a hand in Tary and Doty's general direction, smiling. He had a tiny, fetching gap between his front teeth. "Afternoon!" he said. "You wouldn't happen to be Sir Darrington, would you? The one looking for a new adventuring party?"

"Wh—" said Tary. "I'm—was I—oh! Sir Darrington. Yes. Yes! Indeed, that's me. Please, do sit. All of you."

Analyzing additional party members. One: Larger-than-average half-orc. Long tusks, rough-spun clothing, significant tattoo coverage. Analysis: Intimidating. Two: Smaller-than-average eisfuura. Fluffy feathers, jaunty cap, leather vest with elaborate stitching. Analysis: Adorable.

It took a little doing to replace two of the chairs with a bench capable of supporting the half-orc's weight, but eventually the newcomers got settled in around the table, with the concerningly handsome human sitting catty-corner to Tary—a little closer to Tary, in fact, than Doty would like. "I'm Clarke," he said, extending a hand, which Tary shook warmly.

"Charmed, I'm sure," said Tary. "And your friends?"

"This is Dayner." The small eisfuura. "And Bex." The half-orc.

"Pleasure," chirped Dayner, extending a wing to Tary.

Tary took careful hold of the longest primary feathers. "The pleasure is all mine."

Bex lifted one large hand in a wave. "Hope you don't mind if I don't shake your hand," she said. Her voice was much quieter than Doty expected, and a little shy. Up close, he could see she had an assortment of twigs and dried leaves carefully woven into the unkempt reddish-brown curls of her hair. "Sometimes I accidentally, uh." She made a crushing gesture with both hands that very effectively conveyed broken bones, snapped ligaments, and general agony.

"When you put it like that, I certainly don't mind at all," said Tary. "And while we're at it, let me introduce my traveling companion, Doty. Say hello, Doty."

Creak, said Doty.

"*Fascinating,*" said Clarke. "Your flyer mentioned an automaton, but I'll admit this isn't what I was expecting. Where did you get it?"

"Well," said Tary, "I built him."

"Built! Well, damn." Clarke sat back, looking impressed. "You really are an inventor *and* an adventurer, huh. I figured that was an exaggeration, but I see now it wasn't one bit."

"Oh, well." Tary's cheeks pinked. "I like to stay busy, I suppose. You mentioned you saw my flyer . . . ?"

"Right, your flyer. We saw it down by the waterway this morning, and as soon as I read it I thought maybe we could help you. Or, more accurately, we thought maybe *you* could help *us.*"

"Please," said Tary, leaning forward and balancing his chin on his hand. "Say more."

Body angle: Fifteen-degree incline toward conversational partner. Blink ratio: One-point-seven times standard. Currently remaining below threshold for "fluttering eyelashes."

Clarke smiled, leaning forward, too, until the angle of his body matched Tary's. When he braced his elbows on the table, the swell of his biceps strained the fabric of his shirt.

This was very concerning.

"Let me start at the beginning," said Clarke. "There's a small fishing village about a day's ride from here, name of Lichenvel. They've been having trouble lately with a basilisk. It's just been a general nuisance so far: getting into the storehouses, interfering with the catch, that sort of business. So far, nobody's been hurt, but, well." His expression grew somber. "I'm sure a seasoned adventurer such as yourself is familiar with basilisks. You know as well as I do that it's only a matter of time."

Tary went from **Expression: Enchanted** to **Expression: Serious** one-point-one seconds too late. "Ah, yes. Yes, I certainly do."

If Clarke noticed the delay, he didn't show it. He continued, "They put out a call for help, and we answered. The three of us have traveled together a long time, doing this sort of work. For coin, of course, but we also try to do some good in the world, and we're no strangers to monster-hunting. We felt we were well equipped to take the beast on. And we would have been—"

"We would have been!" cut in Bex. **Tone: Distressed.** "If it weren't for Swink being a rotten little—"

Clarke winced, and Bex stopped, frowning. "Sorry," said Clarke. "There's been some . . . interteam conflict—"

"We got ditched," interrupted Dayner.

Clarke sighed, rubbing his forehead. "One of our members abandoned us. It's *not* that the three of us aren't capable—we've taken on plenty of challenges on our own. But Swink was a skilled warrior, and to defeat a basilisk, you need someone who knows how to handle a sword. And that's not any of us."

"It's not?" asked Tary. Doty calculated that the natural variation in Tary's line of sight had decreased significantly, in a way that indicated Tary was trying very hard to keep his focus on Clarke's face and nowhere else. "I'm just—surprised," Tary said, when Clarke looked puzzled. "You look like you might have trained a bit, is all."

Dayner covered her beak with a wing, muffling a cough. The blood flow to Tary's cheeks doubled.

"That's kind of you to say," said Clarke. "I mean, I do carry this." He gestured to a dagger slung at his waist: fairly standard-issue adventuring gear. "But honestly that's mostly for show. Really, I'm more of an academic. Here, look—may I?"

There was a bit of spare thread clinging to the collar of Tary's cloak.

Clarke reached long, elegant fingers toward it, then looked up at Tary, waiting for permission.

Tary, holding his breath, nodded.

Clarke plucked the thread away from the fabric of Tary's cloak and made a flourishing little gesture. There was a spark, and then, instead of the thread, he was holding a sleek green feather.

"Of course," said Clarke, "I have plenty of spells in my repertoire that can hit harder in a fight; it's not all parlor tricks. But I'd barely know the pointy end of the sword from . . . the other one."

"The hilt," said Tary. **Expression: Helplessly Charmed.**

Clarke smiled. "Yes. The hilt." He held the feather out to Tary, who took it, balancing it delicately between his fingertips. "Dayner's actually a dab hand—talon—with a crossbow," Clarke continued, "and Bex does most of the work of keeping us fed and healed up. And we can all more than hold our own in a brawl, I promise you that. But we're none of us heavy hitters, and that's what we need. The reward is one thing. We could use the coin, of course. What adventurer couldn't? But—we made a commitment to the people of that village. We promised them we'd help. And I just can't stand the thought of letting them down."

Tary's eyes were retaining higher than usual moisture content. "That's . . . very admirable, Clarke," he said, a little choked up. He cleared his throat then stood, taking Doty by the wrist. "Would you mind giving us just a moment?" he asked. "I just need to confer with my compatriot."

He was already dragging Doty away to the far side of the tavern before Clarke could respond. Doty followed along amiably, allowing Tary to pull him into a little alcove by the water closets.

Neck servos: Activated. Subroutine: Inquisitive Head Tilt.

"Well, of course we're going to say yes, Doty!" whispered Tary. "I just didn't want to seem overeager, that's all. And honestly, I needed a moment to collect myself. I mean, did you see that Clarke fellow? Nearly as dashing as I am! Come, now, pretend like you're driving a hard bargain."

Doty didn't have a routine in place for that. He did his best to improvise, activating his upper limb servos so it looked like he was waving his arms emphatically. It must have worked well enough, because Tary furrowed his brow, pretending to nod thoughtfully. "Yes, yes," he said. "Watermelon watermelon. Peas and carrots, rhubarb. All right, that's probably enough."

He and Doty made their way back across the tavern to the table where the others were waiting expectantly. "I've considered your proposal," he said, "and I'm thrilled to say, I accept. I'd like to extend an official invitation to all three of you to become formal members of the Taryon Darrington Adventuring Party."

Clarke looked at Dayner and Bex.

Dayner and Bex looked at Clarke.

"Brilliant," said Clarke. "That's absolutely—brilliant. We're honored to join you, Sir Darrington."

"Please," said Tary. "Just Tary. After all, we're adventuring companions now! And—Doty, take this down. Clarke"—a slightly awkward pause as he visibly tried to recall the remaining names, then moved on—"Feathers, Big and Tall." He focused his gaze on each of them in turn, striking a bit of a pose. **Expression: Noble, Determined.** "As the leader of your party, I give you my solemn vow: We *will* emerge victorious in our quest. No matter how dangerous the road ahead, we won't abandon our duty, nor shall we back down in the face of near-certain death. The Taryon Darrington Adventuring Party is going to slay this basilisk," said Tary, clapping one gauntleted hand over his heart. "And save the people of Lichenvel—together."

Current location: Lichenvel, Vezdaweald, Menagerie Coast, Wildemount, Exandria, Mortal Plane. Population: 662. Climate: Tropical. Terrain: Rocky. Primary export: Fish.

"It's a bad time of year for this sort of thing," said Mayor Jos, her boots crunching briskly against the white chalk of the walkway. The mayor was a tall, broad woman with close-cropped gray hair and a brusque manner, and she wasted no time on pleasantries as she led them toward the site they were meant to investigate. The village was set into the cliffside, with narrow paths and precarious hanging bridges connecting the various levels, and Doty had been devoting a larger-than-usual percentage of his processing power to ambulating, bringing up the rear of the party as he tried to transcribe and walk at the same time. "Rainy season's about to set in, so everyone's working overtime at the catch, and there just aren't enough of us to post up guards for all the storehouses. And without those stores we'll have a hard time making it through the next couple months when it's a mite too dangerous to be at sea, so you understand why we need to get this all sorted before the thing can do any more damage. Right through here, if you please."

She'd led them to one of the structures closest to sea level, and they wound their way down a long, sloping ramp that zigzagged the rest of the way to the ocean. The local architecture was mostly multistory wooden structures with sharply peaked roofs, and this building was no different: on the smaller side, but painted a cheerful robin's-egg blue, freshly appointed with bright white trim. It would have looked very smart if not for the gaping hole taken out of the side of it. The broken wall held shelving that had clearly been piled high with stores of salt-cured fish, now significantly diminished and half-strewn about the floor.

"Made out like a bandit, as you see," said Mayor Jos. "This'll make the third attack like this. The only new one since the last time you lot came by." She nodded at Clarke, Dayner, and Bex. "But same pattern as last time. Left a pretty clear trail headed up toward the mountain pass."

Clarke had one hand braced against the ruined shelf and was inspecting the damage. **Expression: Grim.** "Terrible," he said. "Such waste. I'm so sorry we weren't able to help sooner, Mayor."

"Well." Mayor Jos waved a hand. "These things happen. I understand how adventuring parties are. Worked with enough of 'em, after all. But it seems you've found a capable replacement."

Tary was standing in the middle of the room, focused on keeping a one-yard minimum distance between his armor and anything that might be soggy and/or fish-scented. *Creak,* said Doty. Tary looked up, realized Mayor Jos was talking about him, and implemented **Expression: Dazzling Smile.** "Milady," he said, bowing low with an elaborate flourish. "Sir Taryon Darrington and his associates shall vanquish the beast before any more evil can befall this charming hamlet. You have my most solemn vow."

Mayor's Expression: Amused. "That's mighty thoughtful of you," she told Tary, then squinted out at the skyline. "I'd reckon you've got a few more hours of daylight if you want to set out tonight, but if that thing's too far up in the peaks, you might be looking at camping out tonight. You don't want to be attempting those mountain trails in the dark. Or I can get you settled at the inn and y'all can head out in the morning, if you'd prefer."

"We'll camp," said Clarke, at the exact same time Tary said, "The inn would certainly be preferred."

Clarke and Tary looked at each other. Clarke suppressed a smile and gestured for Tary to go ahead.

Tary took a deep breath. **Tone: Determination Masking Foreboding.** "We'll camp."

"I HAVE TO SAY," SAID Tary, "this sleeping-out-of-doors thing is really not as dreadful as I feared it would be. All the fresh air is really doing wonders for my complexion."

As predicted, they'd had only a few hours to follow the trail out of Lichenvel before dusk had started to set in. Bex had done most of the tracking, pointing out scraped tree bark here, muddy claw prints there. They'd made it into the foothills of the Hearthstar Peaks, but when the trail had taken a sharp turn up a steep, craggy footpath, the unanimous decision had been to take advantage of a likely-looking clearing and settle in for the night.

Doty knew Tary had never spent the night out of doors before, but that wasn't to say Tary wasn't prepared for the eventuality—inevitability?—as an adventurer. In the months before leaving home, Doty had helped make sure they had every bit of gear one could possibly need for life on the road, and stocking up on camping supplies in particular had been the work of almost a week entire. There was an enchanted tent that compressed to the size of a bread loaf and expanded to comfortably fit up to five people, a magical firepit that would ignite and douse with a gesture, a full set of top-of-the-line lightweight camp cookware, and a hover-hammock. As a result, Tary's side of the campfire looked a bit like it belonged to an entire traveling circus, especially alongside the other more traditional setups of bedrolls with packs for pillows.

Nobody seemed to mind the disparity too much, however. The night was clear, the fire crackled merrily, and there was a flagon of strong ale being passed around (Tary, who didn't enjoy the taste of beer, was not actually partaking, but that didn't dampen his spirits). Doty stood posted at the edge of the clearing, taking first watch, while Bex sorted through mushrooms she'd harvested during the walk and Dayner fletched crossbow bolts. Tary was keeping himself busy, too, checking the gems that studded his helm, making sure they were polished bright and ready to use, replacing the few that had been expended during experimentation. At Tary's proclamation, Clarke looked up from where he was seated on his bedroll, sharpening his dagger. "I'm glad it's not as bad as you thought it would be," he said. "I've always liked it, myself—the fresh air, the smell of the campfire. View's not bad, either." He tilted his gaze upward, where the glittering star field was putting on an impressive display.

"No," said Tary, gaze lingering solely on Clarke. "No, it isn't."

Clarke's gaze floated downward, catching on Tary's hands and the ruby he was currently adjusting in its setting. "That helmet is really something," he said. "I've never seen anything quite like it before. Am I right in guessing all those fancy stones aren't just for looks?"

"Oh!" said Tary, perking up considerably. "Very astute of you, my friend. In fact, this is a creation of my own invention. I haven't quite settled on a name for it, but I've been thinking perhaps the Gembearer's Helm." He wiggled his fingers in a flourish.

"Very evocative," agreed Clarke.

Tary beamed. "Here, let me show you how it works." He scooted closer to Clarke's bedroll, holding out the helm so Clarke could get a closer look. "You see, each of these stones is infused with a spell, which activates when you remove the stone from its setting with just the right movement. I'll demonstrate. This yellowish stone here, you see?" Tary plucked it free with a twist of the wrist, and from his fingers there bloomed a soft beam of sunshine that bathed the whole clearing in warm gold. "An illumination spell," he explained. "Very handy. Of course, the gems can hold more powerful spells, too. This blue one, for example, contains a teleportation spell; this one here releases a concussive wave of force."

"Amazing," breathed Clarke. "And you made this all yourself?"

"Well, yes." Color was rising in Tary's cheeks, clearly visible in the light from the illumination spell. "It took quite a while—I had to invent the mechanism for spell deployment essentially from whole cloth—but I've always reveled in that sort of intensive research project, honestly."

"Amazing," Clarke repeated. He was leaning in closer now, body inclined at a twenty-degree angle toward Tary. Twenty-three . . . twenty-five . . . anticipated trajectory—

There was a good-sized branch lying in the leaf litter just a few inches away from Doty's right foot; he shifted his stance with the quietest creak possible in order to put his weight on it, snapping it in two with a loud crack. The noise reported sharply around the clearing, and Tary and Clarke both startled upright, pulling away from each other and looking around guiltily.

Dayner and Bex both found renewed interest in their crossbow bolt fletching and mushroom sorting, respectively.

Clarke cleared his throat, rubbing the back of his neck. "I think," he said, "maybe we ought to try and get some sleep."

"Ah," said Tary. **Tone: Disappointed.** "We ought not to—I don't know." He looked at Dayner and Bex again, as if reminding himself of exactly how many people were in the clearing. "Play a drinking game or two to strengthen our warriors' bond? Or at least sing a few folk songs about battles past to put ourselves in the right mental space? Feathers, Big and Tall, what do you think? I actually have quite a good singing voice, if I might flatter myself to say so."

"*If* he *might,*" Dayner whispered to Bex, who shushed her.

Clarke smiled. "I bet," he said. "And I'm sure we'll have plenty of time to enjoy it in the future. But I think we'll regret it if we're underslept when we face the basilisk."

"Oh, very well," agreed Tary reluctantly. "I commend your discipline in remaining battle-ready, Clarke. In that case, Doty and I will bid you all adieu." Tary climbed to his feet, bowing extravagantly to the group. "Good night, my boon companions! Doty, with me, please."

The interior of Tary's tent was full of magicked sumptuousness: the floor overlaid with plush, intricately patterned rugs; a crystal chandelier hanging from the center of the supports, casting the room in warm, twinkling light; a full four-poster bed heaped high with pillows. Tary settled in front of the porcelain washbasin, and Doty began the nightly ritual of brushing out Tary's hair.

"So, Doty," said Tary. "What do you think of our adventure so far? More important, what do you make of our adventuring companions?" he asked. His eyes met Doty's in the mirror. **Expression: Hopeful.**

Creak, said Doty diplomatically.

Tary sighed. "I must confess, I do like him very much. Them! I mean, I like all three of them very much. You know," he said, then paused, brow slightly furrowed. (Doty was supposed to alert Tary about any facial movements that might cause wrinkles, but he dismissed that interrupt temporarily.) Tary continued, "Maybe it's a little overly optimistic to be thinking like this already. But . . . it would be something to have found an adventuring party with . . . long-term potential already, wouldn't it? What do you think, Doty? Do you think there's something there?"

One hundred brush strokes, and Tary's hair gleamed like molten gold in the low lamplight. Doty set the brush aside and waited for his next command.

Tary sighed. "All right," he said, patting Doty's arm. "That will do, my friend. You'd better go ahead and shut down yourself for a while, too. We need you just as fresh for tomorrow as the rest of us."

Doty knew Tary was right, but there was still something about the whole situation that kept setting his alert flags high, and the temptation to stay up and keep watch for the night was strong. Orders were orders, however, and it would be obvious if Doty didn't get any shutdown time at all.

As Tary settled his sleep mask over his eyes and burrowed into the nest of his comforter, Doty took up his post by the tent flap, left just one teeny tiny monitoring subroutine running, and initiated power-saving protocols. He felt his higher-level processes begin to wind down, the routines that controlled his many servos and sensors go into sleep mode. **Entering stasis in three . . . two . . .**

Monitoring subroutine interrupt trigger activated. Outside stimuli: Noise, motion. Voice identification: Dayner, Bex, Clarke.

Auditory sensors 100 percent activated. Ocular sensors 100 percent activated. Servo activation on standby. Noise suppression routines in place.

"—sleeping," whispered Dayner. "You're being paranoid—"

"No such thing as being too careful." Clarke. "Come on, we don't need to go far—"

Quiet rustling, footsteps on the path. Doty's auditory sensors were four times more sensitive than average human ears, but he still wouldn't be able to hear their conversation if they snuck too deep into the woods.

Query: So what?

Latest registered mandate from Tary: "Go ahead and shut yourself down for a while."

Most recent shutdown period: One hour and sixteen minutes. "A while,"

definition: A period of time, especially when short. Therefore, mandate completed.

Anyhow. **Primary mandate: Protect Tary.**

Ambulatory servos: Activated. Noise suppression routines: Maximum setting.

Unfortunately, even with his noise suppression routines at maximum setting, moving quietly was not really Doty's strong suit. Fortunately, the night air was full of ambient noise: the trilling, high-pitched song of some local insect, the quiet rushing of a nearby stream. Overhead, Catha loomed close to full, its light casting silvery shadows through the lush canopy, with the coppery smudge of Ruidus right beside. Doty followed the trio for about five minutes, timing his footfalls to match Bex's, until they came to a clearing not dissimilar from the one where they'd set up camp. There was a narrow, one-person tent next to the tree line. In front of it, the embers of a banked fire glowed dimly. Doty crept to a quiet halt behind the trunk of a large tree, peering out cautiously through the leaves. Above him, an owl hooted softly. Doty looked up, holding a finger to where his lips would be, if he had a mouth. The owl gave him a baleful look but settled back into itself, resuming its watch for prey.

"Swink," Clarke called quietly, and Doty watched as a diminutive man emerged from the tent, swatting irritably at what seemed to be bugs, though Doty couldn't identify any additional life-forms in the man's vicinity.

"Took you long enough," the man—Swink—grumbled. "Fuck me, but I hate camping."

"Camping's fine when you can actually *sleep,*" said Bex, dropping heavily into a drift of leaves near Swink's tent. "Come on, Clarke, I want to go back to bed."

"I know, I know," said Clarke. "Come on, we're almost through it. I just want us to go over the plan one more time."

"Hardly counts as a plan," Dayner said, fluttering to nestle down next to Bex in the leaves. "We get in there, we rough up the 'basilisk'"—air quotes. Air quotes? **Used to call attention to or *cast doubt on* a spoken word or expression**—surely Doty was misunderstanding; there had to be another definition, but his archives were coming up empty. Dayner continued, "We let Darrington ice the thing; Clarke flutters his eyelashes so Darrington stays distracted while we hustle him out of there before he notices that the basilisk he just slayed is nothing more than a bit of magical flash from Swink. It's not exactly a heist for the ages, Clarke."

"I kinda feel bad about the whole thing, honestly," said Bex. "He's not actually *so* terrible. And who knows if he'll even pay up? I know he looks rich, but . . ."

"Oh, he's rich all right," said Clarke. "Come on, Bex, don't go soft on me now! This is Howaardt Darrington's son we're talking about. I wouldn't have concocted this scheme for just anybody. If anyone deserves to get themself swindled, it's him."

"I guess," said Bex. Then, "It will be pretty nice having that thousand gold."

Doty's indignant *creak!* was unintentional but more than loud enough to attract attention. Everyone in the clearing froze, looking around for the source of the noise.

Thinking quickly, Doty gave the tree he was hiding behind a firm shake, just enough to jostle the owl settled in its branches. The owl roused obligingly, taking off and swooping through the clearing with a loud, irritated *hoot.* Swink's fingertips crackled with the beginnings of a spell, and Clarke had his dagger in his hand in an instant, wielding it like a man who knew how to use it. When they realized it was just an owl, though, everyone visibly relaxed, letting their hands and weapons drop.

Clarke shook his head, re-sheathing his knife. "All right, so we're a little on edge. That's understandable. Let's just finish this run-through as quickly as possible, and then we can all get back to sleep. Okay?"

The rest of the group murmured agreement. Doty would've sighed in relief, if he'd been able to breathe. Instead, he focused on staying very, very still and quiet.

"Great," said Clarke. "In that case, Bex, you'll look for the signal, which is . . . ?"

"Stones stacked by the tenth mile marker," Bex recited dutifully.

"Excellent. And then you'll say?"

Bex cleared her throat and struck an awkward pose. "'Wait!'" she said loudly. "'See the way this bush is damaged? This is fresh. We're getting close!'"

"Right, maybe bring down the volume a bit, but otherwise perfect. And then, Swink, you're up after that . . ."

The rehearsal took seven and a half minutes. Notes were given, then they ran through the whole thing again. This run-through was deemed acceptable. "Good nights" were exchanged. Swink went back into his tent, and the other three headed back in the direction of the campsite.

Doty's hiding place remained undisturbed. Clarke, Dayner, and Bex didn't come anywhere close to noticing him as they left the clearing, and Swink's breathing pattern indicated deep, peaceful sleep within five minutes of re-entering his tent. All that, and Doty's calculations indicated an extremely high degree of certainty in his understanding of the situation. There was no need for him to stay there in the woods for another half hour, replaying the conversation over and over, looking for where anything that would increase his margin of error might have crept in.

He did anyway.

Morning weather conditions: Overcast and damp, sun barely visible as a patch of lighter gray through the thick cover of clouds.

Tary wasn't an early riser at the best of times, never mind when he'd spent the previous day hiking and the previous night in a tent, but Doty was prepared for this. He'd made a pot of Tary's favorite tea, imported from the Oderan Wilds, and made sure to have it fresh-brewed and fragrant (he was pretty sure—Tary hadn't fitted him with any olfactory sensors) before tapping the little hanging chime Tary had packed to use as an alarm. The sound of it tinkled brightly through the tent, and Tary half shoved his sleep mask up, cracking one begrudging eye. "Surely not yet," he said blearily. "Doty, we've only just gone to bed."

Doty jingled the chime again, more insistently.

"Eurgh," said Tary, flopping back down onto the bed. Doty was about to implement **Subroutine: Really Go to Town** on the chimes when the tent flap peeled back and Clarke poked his head through, implementing **Expression: Shy Smile.** No, that wasn't right. **Expression:** ***Artificial*** **Shy Smile.**

"Morning, Tary," Clarke said. "Sorry to wake you, but we figured you'd want to get a move on bright and early. I brought coffee, if you want."

Even without any olfactory sensors, Doty could tell the coffee Clarke had brought was *not* imported from the Oderan Wilds.

Tary, meanwhile, had sat bolt upright in bed the moment Clarke appeared and was doing his best to surreptitiously smooth his hair and check his breath. "Oh! Goodness, Clarke, that's so kind. Please, come in. Doty, clear some space, won't you?"

Clear some space. Doty could do that. He picked up the tray that held all of Tary's nighttime cosmetics from the folding nightstand, calculated his trajectory, and moved it in a slow and careful arc until it collided with the two mugs of coffee that Clarke was holding.

Clarke yelped, jumping back as coffee splashed all over the front of his clothes. Tary leapt out of bed with **Expression: Mortified.** "Doty! Oh, Clarke, your jacket, I'm so sorry. I don't know what's happened, he's usually much more precise in his movements—"

"No, it's fine, don't worry about it at all, I'll just—" Clarke looked around for something to clean up with. After a moment Tary joined him, but pretty much every textile in Tary's tent was high-quality silk, heavily embroidered, or both. Eventually they both gave up and looked at Doty.

Doty halted **Automatic Subroutine: Tidy** and stood motionless.

"I'll just go change," said Clarke. "Um, we're going to break camp in about ten minutes, if you can be ready by then. Sorry about the coffee." He ducked back through the tent flap, which fell shut behind him.

With Clarke gone, there was approximately 3.3 cubic feet more empty space in the tent than before. **Mandate: Clear Some Space** completed.

"Doty, what in the name of the Dawnfather was that? Are you feeling all right?" Tary pressed the back of his hand to Doty's forehead, frowning. "Doesn't *seem* like anything's overheating in there. What's going on, my friend? Are you nervous about the hunt?"

Creak.

"Well, you don't have to put on a brave face for me, Doty, I know you better than anyone. Truth be told, I'm the tiniest bit anxious myself."

Tary's heart rate had been elevated by fifteen beats per minute over average for the last twenty-four hours. Doty was kind enough not to inform him.

Tary pushed the covers away, patting the mattress beside him to indicate Doty should sit as well. Sitting versus standing had no material difference on Doty's power consumption, but he understood the importance of body positioning in social signaling and bonding rituals. He sat.

"I know that what we're planning to do today is dangerous," said Tary. "And that this is our first time taking on a real-life, flesh-and-blood foe. So it's understandable if you feel a little bit . . . uncertain, or unprepared. But let me remind you that we are, in fact, highly prepared! How many hundreds of hours have we spent, Doty, working toward this precise moment? Training, sparring, studying tactics. We're in peak physical condition." This one wasn't entirely true; Tary was in slightly better-than-average physical condition for a male human of his age; Doty didn't really have a basis of comparison for himself. "We've studied basilisks! We know their weaknesses, we know how they behave in the wild. And what's more, Doty—all the books we've read, all the famous battles we've reenacted? We've *visualized* this moment. We've *ideated* victory. And I truly believe we're ready for this fight where it matters: in our minds, and in our hearts. Or, in your case, I suppose: in your processing unit, and in your arcane core. All right?"

Oddly enough, Tary's speech had reduced Doty's anxiety levels considerably. He ducked his head in a nod. *Creak.*

Tary took a deep breath, then pasted on a smile, clapping Doty on the shoulder. "Come on, then, Doty. It's time to write a thrilling new chapter in the book of Sir Taryon Darrington's heroic adventures."

Though the previous day's trek through the Vezdaweald and the foothills hadn't exactly been easy, it was nothing compared to today's path, which ascended sharply into the Hearthstar Peaks. Doty's design was not well suited for navigating steep, mountainous terrain—and honestly, neither was Tary's, especially in full plate armor. Doty was doing his best to keep as many threat monitoring subroutines running as possible in order to be alert for treachery, but with so much of his focus taken up by path navigation, he was finding it a little difficult to focus on anything else.

"Trail seems like it's gonna keep going straight up," said Bex, pointing out the ostensible path with one large green finger. "Guessing it about follows that ridge there. Makes sense. Lots of caves and things up there. That's where basilisks like to live."

"Straight up," repeated Tary, winded. "Yes. Excellent. No problem whatsoever. Do you know what's a bit odd? I haven't seen any statues this whole trek. Isn't that strange?"

Clarke blinked. "Statues?"

"You know, local flora and fauna that the basilisk's turned to stone and then had a little nibble on. I remember reading that was a good way to tell when one was nearing a basilisk lair. Or—I mean, um." **Expression: Embarrassed.** "In *my* experience, that is, the presence of masticated statuary can often be an initial indicator of the presence of a basilisk habitat—"

"Wait!" interrupted Bex. **Tone: A Bit Desperate.** And still too loud. "See the way this bush is damaged, right here? This is fresh. We're getting cl—"

An auditory-sensor-damaging roar split the air, and a terrifying creature burst from the bushes and leapt into the middle of the road. The basilisk was big—much bigger than Doty was expecting, with far too many limbs, and far too many *teeth,* every one of them bared. It was under Swink's control—Doty knew it was under Swink's control, but for a moment that knowledge was barely enough to send halt commands to the dozens of emergency interrupts telling him to grab Tary and run for both of their lives.

The thing roared again, and then one of its massive forelimbs swung out toward Tary, the spread of its claws as big as a dinner plate. Doty's servos flung him forward, but Clarke got there first, leaping in front of Tary. The basilisk caught Clarke full across the ribs, sending him crashing to one side, skidding hard against the packed dirt of the path.

"Clarke!" Tary cried. Clarke, sprawled out dramatically on the ground, groaned weakly. All of Doty's processes were throwing out interrupt requests at once as he swung his ocular sensors back and forth wildly, trying to figure out where the transformation spell was coming from and how to disrupt it. Not the least of those processes was the one that monitored Tary's vital signs, which was panickedly informing him that Tary's heart rate and respiration were both elevated far above normal and kept trying to start useless subroutines such as **Offer a Sandwich** or **Suggest a Nap**.

Tary, meanwhile, was fumbling with his Gembearer's Helm, trying to prise out a stone. The one he'd been working on came free with a pop, and Tary gave a triumphant cry, brandishing it at the basilisk. The gem sparkled briefly then bloomed into a soft beam of sunshine that bathed the whole passageway in warm gold—a harmless light spell.

Doty halted **Subroutine: Face-palm** just in time.

There was a beat of confused silence, during which everyone stared at each other, including the basilisk. Then the basilisk collapsed to the ground, screwing its eyes shut and thrashing side to side in apparent agony.

"Great work, Darrington!" said Dayner, only a second or two too late.

"You've, uh, disabled its stone gaze! Now it's got no chance!" She loosed a bolt from her crossbow, just barely nicking the crown of the basilisk's head. The basilisk made a disgruntled sound.

"Oh!" said Tary. "Yes! Thank you, Feathers, just as planned!"

Clarke, meanwhile, had managed to drag himself up next to the basilisk, looking fetchingly disheveled and bloody. The basilisk continued thrashing, scrabbling to get its feet under itself. Clarke threw himself bodily on top of it, getting an arm around its neck and wrestling it onto its back. "Now, Tary!" he said, holding the thing in place as it twisted and writhed, the broad expanse of its underbelly vulnerable and exposed.

Tary froze. "Wh—" he began. "Now?"

The basilisk grunted a little, flopping back and forth half-heartedly. Clarke looked exasperated for just half a second before schooling the expression away. "Now!" he repeated. "Come on, Tary, finish the bastard off! Isn't that what you came here for?"

"Right," said Tary. "Right, yes, of course." He gripped the hilt of his Rod of Mercurial Form and pulled it free from its scabbard at his waist. "Sword!"

The metal of the rod shimmered, liquid-like, before sharpening into a longsword. Tary brandished it above his head, where it glinted threateningly in the remnants of the light spell. Tary hefted it higher—and then let it droop. "Or," he said, "maybe sword isn't quite right, really? Axe? Would battle-axe be better?"

Clarke groaned. "Tary!"

Tary was looking distinctly green. "No," he said. "Of course, you're right, I'll just—I'll just stab it. I'll just go ahead and stab it, right in its—its stomach, with my sword—"

Anomaly: Unanticipated life-form, six-point-two yards to the northeast. Visual confirmation occluded by foliage. Finally, *finally* a useful ping from one of Doty's threat detection routines.

Ambulatory servos: Activated. Maximum speed.

Doty dashed across the clearing, slamming himself bodily against whatever it was that had been hiding in the bush. Whatever it was that had been hiding in the bush said, "Augh!," and then Doty was lying prone on top of a very unhappy Swink.

"Motherfucking—what in the hell are you? Get the hell off me, you big hunk of scrap metal!" Swink tried to shove Doty off him, but it didn't have much effect. Doty made sure he had a good grip on Swink by the scruff of his neck, then stood, dragged Swink into the clearing, and dropped him at Tary's feet.

In the clearing, there was no longer a basilisk. Instead, Tary, looking very confused, stood brandishing his sword over Clarke, who was holding on to a very small vole.

"What," said Tary, "in the world—"

"Oh boy," said Dayner.

Bex said, "We can explain—"

"Sorcery!" broke in Clarke. **Tone: Kind of Desperate, Actually.** He brandished the vole. "That must be it! How—how dastardly! He must have transfigured this vole to—wreak havoc on the townspeople! How cruel, a true practitioner of the dark arts—"

Swink opened his mouth as if to protest, then seemed to change his mind. He scrambled to his feet and began sprinting for the edge of the clearing.

"Oh no, you don't," said Tary, and yanked another gem free from his helm. This one transformed into a sturdy rope, which burst forth from Tary's hands to wrap around Swink's ankle, yanking him to the ground at Doty's feet.

"Entrapment spell," said Clarke. He was starting to sound a bit hysterical. "Great. Brilliant! Just—brilliant thinking, wouldn't have wanted him to get away—"

The rope continued wending its way up Swink's body, securing his arms tightly to his sides. Swink made an expression at Clarke that Doty couldn't find an exact match for in his archives, but it involved very wide eyes and his mouth in a very thin line. "Yes," Swink finally said. "Blast you, Darrington. You've foiled my evil plan."

There were enough sideways glances being exchanged among Swink, Clarke, Dayner, and Bex that even Tary was starting to pick up on the odd energy. He clapped his hands together, putting on a broad smile, but there was something uncertain in it. "Well, then," he said. "A great victory, is it not? We can deliver this villain to the mayor and let the townsfolk know the evil has been vanquished and they're safe in their homes once more!"

Bex was frowning, looking from Swink to Tary and back again. "And . . . collect the reward?" she asked hopefully.

"Right, yes, of course, collect the reward," said Clarke. "Actually—speaking of. Our, uh, our payment from you, Tary, ought we to just . . . square that away now, so we don't need to bother with it when we're all back in town celebrating?"

Doty had never been so desperate for a voice box as he was in this moment. He opened his ocular sensors to their fullest aperture and stared meaningfully at Tary.

Tary stared back. "Ah," he said, slowly. "Well. Hm. The thing is." He scrubbed thoughtful fingers through his goatee. "The thing is, we didn't *technically* fulfill the terms of the bargain, did we? Seeing as, after all, I didn't actually *slay* the basilisk. . . ."

There was a long silence. "Defeated," said Clarke. "You *defeated* a basilisk, though—"

"Well," said Tary. "Yes, but I believe if you check the precise wording—Doty, if you'd be so kind?"

Doty was more than happy to retrieve The Book from its compartment. He shuffled the pages back to a copy of the original for-hire posting, then held it out, keeping one fingertip aligned with the relevant portion. ***Dragon slaying. Manticore slaying. Basilisk slaying. Any other kind of monster slaying, really . . .***

"You see that the *slaying* tidbit is emphasized multiple times, no getting around it, really. And we even verified it conversationally—"

Doty flipped forward a few pages to the transcript of their first conversation with Clarke and the others and held it out for everyone to see:

"'The Taryon Darrington Adventuring Party is going to slay this basilisk. And,' I said, seeing hope stirring in the faces of my new companions for the first time in gods knew how long, 'save the people of Lichenvel—together.'"

There was a long silence. Then Clarke shook his head, his hand going to the hilt of his dagger as he took a threatening step forward. "Gods-dammit, Darrington, now look here—"

Doty didn't have a dagger, but he didn't need one. He took a threatening step forward, too.

"All right, now, everyone just wait a moment," said Tary. "There's no need to get so worked up about this. We've emerged victorious! We've captured the villain, we've freed the townspeople from their strife. Can't we all just—take the win?"

Clarke threw his head back in frustration. "Come on, Darrington. You can't really be this stupid! Look—we gave you your adventure, didn't we? Isn't that what you wanted? So why don't you just pay up and—"

Implementing Subroutine: Menacing Loom.

Clarke took a step back, gaze darting from Doty to Tary and back again. Then his expression hardened. "Fine," he said. "You know what? Fuck it. It's not worth the trouble. Fine." And he lunged at Tary.

Doty moved as fast as he could to block, but Clarke was faster. Instead of attacking Tary, however, his hand went for Tary's helm. His fingers brushed the blue teleportation stone—closed around it, and twisted it free.

"Clarke," cried Tary despondently, reaching for him, but it was too late. Clarke fell back toward Bex, Dayner, and Swink, and a magical wind began to kick up, blurring the four of them around the edges.

According to the many, many adventure novels Tary had read to Doty over the past year, this was the moment when someone would say something bittersweet and heartfelt, like, *I'm sorry it had to end this way,* or at least try for a clever one-liner that would get cut off halfway through. Instead, the wind just grew stronger, pulling up a swirl of dirt and twigs and leaves that obscured the fading forms of Dayner, Bex, Swink, and Clarke, until there was nothing but a howling column of air—which collapsed as suddenly as it had formed, leaving only silence and eddying dust in its wake.

And Tary and Doty were alone on the mountain.

"My goodness," said Tary, back pressed firmly against the cliff face as he edged his way across a narrow ledge, determinedly not looking at the yawning chasm below. "It really is shocking how much more difficult it is going *down* than going *up,* isn't it?" Rainwater dripped from the bedraggled crest of his helmet down into his eyes, which was surely not making the descent any easier.

Doty desperately wanted to implement **Routine: Style Tary**, but he was once again too busy devoting every bit of processing to keeping his own footing. All of his joints were too waterlogged to even creak encouragingly.

"You'd really think it ought to be the other way around," Tary continued. "But really, the exertion is nothing compared to the precariousness. One is just constantly aware of how very far they have to fall."

The rain had started up nearly as soon as they'd left the clearing—which had admittedly taken a while after the desertion by Clarke and the others. Tary had been loath to leave at first, convinced there had been some sort of misunderstanding and that the rest of the party would be back any minute to retrieve him—or, at least, trying to convince himself he was convinced. It was only when the possibility of spending another night on the cliffside, this time without any camaraderie around a fire, started to set in that Tary had reluctantly suggested it might be time to get a move on.

"I wonder if perhaps I wouldn't be better off without this armor," continued Tary. "I know it looks fetching, but it's certainly not doing anything to help me keep my footing. But then again, what if something attacks us? There are all manner of nasty creatures up here, even if the basilisk didn't happen to be real—Augh!"

Tary yelped, pitching forward toward the abyss as a bit of the pathway crumbled out from beneath him. Doty surged forward, sending all his servos to maximum extension at maximum speed, and managed to yank Tary onto a wider, more stable bit of the pathway, momentum carrying Doty along with him just in time. It was hardly an easy landing for either of them, though: they tumbled end over end together through the gravel and mud until they fetched up against a boulder and clanged to a halt.

Damage assessment, self: All systems normal. Minor cosmetic flaws incurred. Damage assessment, Tary: Vital signs normal. Heart rate and respiration slightly elevated. No sign of fluid leakage, internal or external. Audio sensors reporting–laughter?

Tary had come to a stop in a severely undignified, almost upside-down position, back against the boulder and feet dangling in front of his face, and he was laughing.

Cranial trauma suspected. Implement examination routine immediately.

Doty crouched down in front of Tary and started trying to assess the damage to his skull, but Tary batted Doty's hands away. "I'm fine, Doty, I'm fine." He righted himself awkwardly but stayed sitting, slumped against the boulder. "I was just thinking—" He started giggling again. "I was just thinking how funny it would be if we got attacked by a basilisk right now. A real one, I mean. Wouldn't that be—" He was laughing harder now. "Wouldn't that be hilarious? Wouldn't there be a sort of—" And now he was laughing so hard he could barely speak. "A sort of poetic justice to it all?"

Doty's audio processing wasn't refined enough to identify the precise moment that laughter turned into tears, but turn into tears it did. And then Tary was sobbing—great, ugly, guttural sobs that echoed tragically all around the cliff walls.

"Oh, Doty," Tary wailed. "How could I be so stupid? Oh, Father was right, I'll never amount to anything—what am I even doing out here, playing dress-up and pretending like I'm some sort of knight in shining armor? It's ridiculous. I'm a *joke.* I ought to just go back home, let Mary-anne take over the business, and live out the rest of my days as exactly what I am—a pathetic, useless disappointment of a son."

Tary.

The rain was sheeting down heavily now, so it took some doing for Doty to flip to the right section of The Book without risking water damage to the pages. Using his free arm as a barely effectual umbrella, he extended The Book toward Tary, nudging it gently against his hand.

Creak.

Tary sniffled. "What's this?" He wiped his nose and began reading aloud. "'As the dastardly mage began to make his escape, I snatched an opal from my helm. The flash of light that ensued dazzled the scallywag, causing his teleportation spell to fizzle as he stood. "Oh no, you don't!" I exclaimed. The scoundrel wouldn't dash away without accounting for his crimes on my watch—' Oh." Tary sniffled again. "Well. I suppose, when you put it that way." The rain pattered down heavily on the cloak as Tary continued reading, silently now. "This is beautiful, Doty," he said at length. "I think—I think you really managed to capture the emotion of the moment. The adrenaline, the split-second decisions, the betrayal—" His voice cracked a little, but he covered it with a cough and continued reading. "Beautiful," he repeated after a moment. "Although—"

Creak?

"Oh, don't worry, Doty, it's nothing major," Tary reassured Doty, pointing at the relevant section of the manuscript as he climbed to his feet. "Just this one bit here, is all. You describe my cloak as 'sapphire-colored,' but I'd really say it's closer to azure, wouldn't you? And technically, it's a robe, not a cloak—due to the presence of sleeves; you see the distinction?"

The rain was starting to let up, lightening enough that Tary was able to hold The Book without risking too much damp as he and Doty began picking their way back down the mountain path. "Now, this is the part I want to focus in on here," said Tary, stumbling over his feet just a little as he tried to make annotations while they walked. "Just at the very end of the section. You've written, 'That was one villain vanquished, but the poor souls across Exandria who required my aid remained innumerable. I turned to the sunset and began the journey toward my next big adventure.' Let's try instead—" Tary scratched out the line and narrated aloud as he rewrote: "'*My most trusted companion, Doty, and I* turned to the sunset and began the journey toward *our* next big adventure.'"

Creak, said Doty.

"Yes," said Tary. "I think it's much better like that, too."

BEND THE KNEE

Nibedita Sen

They take the caravan on the Silvercut Roadway, just south of the big city. Meager pickings: bolts of silk, hats, other such fancy-folk fripperies. Some serviceable jerkins, a smattering of gold and iron, but precious fuck-all else they can put to use.

And this is a problem, because they have too many fucking mouths to feed, and too many fucking hands grasping for loot.

The sky is blue. The day is warm. The tallgrass of the Dividing Plains stretches as far as the eye can see to either side of the road, and Kevdak, Thunderlord of the Herd of Storms, is discontent.

He sits on an overturned crate, wiping blood off his axe with a silk shirt, and watches with a jaundiced eye as his warriors turn into a pack of feral dogs. The last caravan guard isn't even done gurgling his lifeblood into the road-dust before Veskin and Mortar are having a stone-cursed literal *tug-of-war* over his sword and armor. A female elf and some human broad—former Rivermaw folk, he can't be arsed to learn their names—are bickering over how best to strip the horses' tack for straps and leather. Others dig through the smashed remnants of cargo, paw at stiffening corpses, pry up the wagon's baseboards in, he doesn't even fucking know what, some storm-forsaken hope of treasure underneath? Horace and Cole have each seized one of the driver's arms and are playing wishbone.

And then there's his idiot offspring. Zanroar. Strutting about the company like a peacock, crooked jaw jutted out as he barks orders. *Grab this. Leave that. You, lookout, don't take your eyes off the road.*

Worse—Kevdak's men are listening to him. *His* men, not his idiot son's, though some of them seem to have forgotten this fact ever since Zanroar took the Rivermaw chieftain's head. He should get up. Remind them. He will, in a moment.

For now he looks at the bloated, belching, farting thing his once-proud Herd of Storms has become. A hundred-odd brigands in scavenged leathers, wielding battered blades. More half-men and short-folk and puny humans than actual stoneborn at this point. Flinching their eyes at the horizon every other second for sight of the godsdamned death cultists who haunt these plains.

And he thinks, not for the first time, *Is this all there fucking is?*

"Pathetic," someone says.

Kevdak needn't turn to know the speaker. The stench of turned milk and tree sap precedes Greenbeard wherever he goes, consequence of the eye that's been rotting in its socket as long as Kevdak's known the old fuck. Why it hasn't killed him yet, he can't say. Witch shit. Probably.

"Hm," he grunts in response.

The old, half-blind seer leans on his knotted staff and curls his lips at the men. A fresh rivulet of pus runs from his weeping eye, soaking the lichenous crust along his throat and neck that gives him his name.

"Pathetic," he repeats. "Look at 'em, fighting each other for scraps. Your Herd is hungry, Thunderlord. Too fucking hungry. You best feed 'em soon, if you don't want 'em eating each other next."

Stoneborn tend not to live long. Least not *real* stoneborn like the kind in his Herd. City-dwelling sellouts might survive to toothlessness and decrepitude, who the fuck knows. Kevdak keeps the old ways, as do the men who follow him. Live by the strength of your fists and the edge of your steel. Give no quarter, take no shit.

Greenbeard, like most seers, is an exception. Oldest stoneborn Kevdak has ever seen. Limbs like bundles of skinny branches wrapped in boiled leather, gray skin gone almost white where it isn't blotched green with moss. Age didn't soften Greenbeard, though. It just made him tough as a tree root in winter. He can call lightning from the sky and make the earth pull apart to swallow their foes whole. He advised Kevdak's old man before him, watched both Kevdak and Zanroar slide birth-sticky and bawling into this world. He's the only reason they've survived as many fucking Ravager attacks as they have.

All of which means Kevdak must tread lightly around him, for all he sometimes yearns to knock out the mossy fuck's last few teeth. So he takes a moment to ponder a reply.

And that's when the dragons fly overhead.

He feels them before he sees or hears them. A change in the wind. A prickle at the nape of his neck. The ancient instinct of meat that walks on land and learns to fear death from the sky.

And then—wingbeats. Dull as a headache at first, then hammer-booms up in the blue. Wind whistling over scales like a kettle on boil.

Kevdak is on his feet before he knows it, fists clenched around the haft of his Bloodaxe. Panicked cries rise around him. Dirt and gravel and torn grass become a storm that stings his tattooed skin, and the Titanstone Knuckles crackle, but he doesn't have time to call up their banked power.

Doesn't need to. It's over that fast.

Scarred reptile bellies big as battlements sail overhead. Tooth and claw and scale. Dragons. *Three* of them: snow white, rot black, and a poisonous green. Bigger than any he's ever seen before.

One moment in the dark. One moment of terror as great wings blot out the sun. Then they're blinking in the light again and the dragons are leaving them behind, streaking away across the plains, flattening the tallgrass with the force of their passage. No relief. Only shock.

Three godsdamned massive fucking dragons. Headed for Westruun.

"*Run,*" someone howls. Others are already doing just that, falling over themselves to scramble into the tallgrass like frightened curs. Scattering. Dropping weapons and loot. The horses wrench free of fear-slackened hands and bolt, eyes rolling every which way with terror.

Kevdak brings his fists together.

Again, he holds back the full power of the gauntlets. For now. The crack of god-blessed heartstone still splits the air like the Stormlord himself has spoken, stalling his men in their tracks.

"*Enough!*" he thunders loud enough to shake the earth. "*Hold your fucking ground, maggots!*"

They stare up at him, bulge-eyed and green-faced. Cowards and piss-bellied curs the lot of them—particularly those Rivermaw fucks. He notes with grim satisfaction that Zanroar, at least, has held his ground. Next to him, Greenbeard is wrapped around his staff with a look Kevdak has never seen on his leathered mug: part horror, part *hunger.*

"We have to *hide,*" Zanroar babbles, gray skin gone pale under his tattoos. "If those things come back—"

"Use your fucking head, boy," Kevdak growls. "Look!"

He points across the miles of tallgrass to where Westruun sits, lumpen and resplendent, on the horizon. Even from here, they can see the dragons flare their great wings and pull up as they reach the city walls. Fan out around it like the prongs of some terrible trident. Preparing to strike.

Even from here, they can see ice shimmer in the sun as the white dragon opens its massive jaws and breathes a blizzard down on its prey. See the big black beast go careening into one of the city's great towers and crack it clean in half. See the green one slink lizard-like along the battlements, surrounded by a poisonous mist.

Even from here, they can hear the screams begin.

Moans and mewls spread through the Herd as the slaughter they're witnessing sinks in. Kevdak feels them surge against his authority once more. Preparing to break. Give in to panic.

"We're going to fall back to the Bramblewood," he grinds out. "But we're going to do it low and slow, you hear me? Which means *shut the fuck up with that stone-cursed bleating!* Mortar, Veskin, Tress—keep these idiots on track. The rest of you maggots, stick together and follow 'em if you know what's good for you. If you run off into the grass and get snatched up, or go too deep in those cursed woods and get eaten by a fucking wight, we're leaving you to rot! As for you, and you."

Here, he pauses to jab a finger at two of the Rivermaw folk he knows to be good trackers. Good at getting low to the ground and going unseen. One shifty elf with braided hair, one swarthy halfling.

After a moment's thought, 'cause he'll be damned if he trusts the fish-fuckers enough to send 'em off alone, he also points at one of the stoneborn under his command. Wiry kid named Shuthmil, young enough that she hasn't grown into her girth yet. Protégé of Greenbeard's, or getting there.

"You three—get close to the city and see what the fuck's happening over there. Don't let the overgrown lizards spot you. Meet us at the woods when you got something to report. Now, *move* your fucking arses, maggots! What are you waiting for? *Go!*"

THEY MAKE IT TO THE woods, find a rise in the land and watch from the tree line as the carnage unfolds. Westruun is a man-sized lump from this distance, the dragons' scaly forms like carrion crows as they swoop, rise, and bank over the city's bleeding corpse. The sight stiffens the shit in Kevdak's bowels, though he'll sooner gut himself than admit it. Bursts of ice and acid. Fat, stinking curls of smoke. The explosive hiss of dissolving stone and the crash of toppled masonry blow their way on the wind, together with a stench so acrid it threatens to fry his nostril hairs.

And the screaming—the screaming never fucking stops. Not when the city gates burst open and people scatter into the countryside like black ants. Not even when, after an hour-odd of slaughter, the dragons depart as swiftly as they came, great wings and swishing tails carrying them off into the blue. It thins to a gurgling, like the last gasps of a man having his neck wrung, but it keeps on. On and fucking on.

He's still standing there, gauntleted hands planted on the haft of his Bloodaxe, when he hears the stump and shuffle of Greenbeard's approach. "What the fuck am I looking at?" he grinds out.

The seer eyes him balefully and shakes his head.

"Don't know," he says. "Dragons aren't exactly given to *working together.* Three of 'em banding up like this? Never heard of it."

He turns both eyes—one intact, one weeping and milky—to the smoking wreckage of the city. Looks it up and down, pursing his shriveled old lips.

"Might be an opportunity for us, though."

Kevdak grunts. "Oh?"

"Gates are open. City watch either dead or eaten, if I had to guess." Greenbeard gestures with his staff. "Could be easy pickings for an ambitious Thunderlord and his mighty Herd."

"You got moss growing on your *brain* now, old man?" says Zanroar, incredulous. Kevdak grinds his teeth as his son emerges from the twisted trees, other stoneborn treading heavy in his wake. "You want us to assault a fucking *city*? Do we look like an army to you? You got a siege breaker hidden in your britches I don't know about? 'Cause I've seen your shriveled cock, and it's not knocking down any walls."

"Quiet," Kevdak growls. "Let him speak."

The contempt in the old half-giant's rheumy eyes is clear as Greenbeard looks at Zanroar and the men behind him. "Siege breakers?" he says slowly. "We're stoneborn, aren't we? Blood of the mountain? *We* are the siege breakers."

He thumps the butt of his gnarled wooden staff on the ground. The wind picks up, the earth rumbles under their feet, and Kevdak scoffs to himself. Party tricks.

Can't deny it works, though. The Herd is listening. And Greenbeard's next words hit all the harder for being backed by the crunch of shifting rock.

"The city is an egg that's been cracked open," the seer hisses. "You think the Ravagers won't come lapping at that yolk? You think they won't take all the gold and good steel and fancy plate they find and then turn 'em on us? But if we get there first—*we* can be the ones to feed. Grow strong. Hold our own. We, the mightiest Herd on these plains."

And here he points a withered finger at Kevdak. "The Herd led by a man who wields the power of the *gods*!"

All eyes turn to Kevdak. He rubs his jaw with one massive, gauntleted hand as he looks at the smoking wreck of Westruun in the distance. Partly to buy himself time to think. Partly 'cause he knows the silence will get Zanroar all the more steamed, and it pleases him to see the pup fume and gnash his teeth.

Unlike his idiot offspring, Kevdak has brain to match his brawn. He knows better than to let everyone see how good Greenbeard's words taste. For now.

"Any of you fuckers been inside that city?" he says at last. A chorus of grunts and *ayes*. "And I don't mean popped in for an evening to whet your whistle—or your wick." Appreciative hoots. "I mean really *been* in there. Know the streets. What kind of fighting force they got. Huh?"

Fewer voices this time—mostly former Rivermaw, he notices. Figures those fish-fuckers would be the kind to lick the boots of city folk.

"Right, then." Kevdak gestures. "Get over here and tell me everything you know while we wait for those scouts to get back."

THE SCOUTS, WHEN THEY RETURN, prove Greenbeard right. What they describe is chaos. Ice encasing half the city, acid eating holes in the rest. Streets awash in blood and shit and terror. City watch running around trying to douse poison-fumed flames and dig people free of the rubble.

Gaps grinning in the great stone walls, like a man with half his teeth knocked out by a punch to the face.

Even better: the gates are *open.* All of them. Thrown wide to let a river of bleeding, shrieking, cowardly pissants flee for their lives. Most streaming into the Foramere Basin, say the scouts, others scrambling toward Turst Fields. A few unlucky bastards even ran east, toward the Bramblewood, till they spotted the Herd massing on its border and decided they'd take their chances elsewhere.

Do they think they'll find refuge? If those overgrown lizards come back, there's not a damned tree or rock or blade of grass on these plains that'll be safe. Kevdak would rather stand his ground and look his death in the eye. Under the sky, weapon in hand.

Not that he means to die today. Oh no. Greenbeard can fawn and flatter all he likes, but Kevdak doesn't need that festering corpse to tell him what he already knows. Has known since the day he took the Titanstone Knuckles from that old orc's corpse and felt the power of the Stormlord himself surge through his fists.

He is meant for *more.* Banditry and brigandry may be where Kevdak began, but it will not be where he ends.

So, this? This is just fate. Delicious fucking providence, waiting to be seized.

Greenbeard, victory secured, retreats into smug silence while Kevdak questions the scouts. Zanroar pouts and paces some more. Worra stands impassive at her mate's side, one hand on her swollen belly.

Ah, Worra. Now *there's* a stoneborn woman. Carved from the bones of the mountain, as his old man would have said. Near as tall as Zanroar, black hair shaved close above the ears and streaming wild down her back. Heavy with child and ready to spill blood all the same. Kevdak knows she'll be in the thick of it when they take the city, a hatchet in each hand. Who's going to stop her? There's not a man here with the stones to tell her she can't have her share of glory, least of all his lily-livered son.

Worra's the only good decision Zanroar ever made. Picking her. Putting that baby in her belly. Guess he's not *quite* as limp-dicked as he seems.

A grandchild, though. Now there's a notion. Kevdak can't put a name to how that makes him feel, other than *odd.*

"Right," he says again once the sun is sinking in the sky and he's gotten all he needs to know. "Here's how we're going to do this."

"Stormlord's balls, Father!" Zanroar bursts out. "This is madness."

"What's wrong, pebble?" He smirks at his offspring's fury. "Too chickenshit to take on a challenge?"

"I told you *not to fucking call me that—*"

"Quiet, boy." Like a loathsome statue coming to life, Greenbeard uncurls himself from around his staff. "Your elders and betters are speaking. Shut your mouth and listen, and you may live to match them, someday."

Kevdak holds his son's gaze. Lets his gauntleted fists hang loose by his sides, doesn't bother to lift his chin. Doesn't fucking need to. The boy's grown, he'll give him that. Gotten enough kills to mark his skin with a respectable bit of ink. But Kevdak stands a head taller and is half as wide again in the shoulders. Kevdak wields a god-touched weapon, and fate smiles on him today, and this mewling brat he has the misfortune to share blood with is no better than shit on the sole of his boot.

Come on, whelp, he silently taunts. *Maybe someday you'll grow the stones to challenge me. But today is not that day. You know it. I know it. That pretty bitch of yours knows it.*

That familiar hatred reddens Zanroar's eyes. His once-broken jaw pushes to the side as he grinds his teeth. For a moment, Kevdak thinks he might actually do it. Take a swing at him right here, before the whole Herd's eyes.

But then Worra places a hand on Zanroar's shoulder, and his son subsides, swinging his head reluctantly away.

"Fine," he spits. "But you'd better have a good fucking plan to not get us all killed."

Not even the outlying farmsteads escaped the dragon onslaught. As the Herd closes in on the city, their boots crunch shards of ice underfoot. The fields stink and sizzle where great swaths of acid have cut through the wheat and potato crop. Looks like at least one of the beasts did a spite loop as a final *fuck you* on its way out, flinging bile in ever-widening arcs.

Gonna be lean times ahead for Westruun. If they make it through this at all.

Behind them, the sun skims the tops of the Bramblewood's black trees. They walk beneath a sky blushing red in their wake. Like a bashful maid—or an open wound. Either fits. This city's about to be their bitch, whether or not it knows it yet.

The air fairly crackles with excitement, like the tickle on your tongue when you breathe in a coming storm. Greenbeard was right. His Herd is hungry. They've been hungry too godsdamned long, and by all the gods known and unknown, they're ready to *feast.* Their faces are marked with pitch and paint. They hoot and holler as they march. Bang the butts of their swords and spears against their shields. The stoneborn set up the old battle chant in the guttural giant tongue.

"Spread out," Kevdak growls.

The bulk of his men break away to either side, as they planned. Headed to the north and south. Ten stoneborn, including Greenbeard, stay with Kevdak as he continues forward.

Straight shot, as the crow flies, from the twisted edge of the Bramblewood to Westruun's smoking walls brings them to the great western gate. Something called the Scholar Ward lies just beyond, he's learned. Home of fancy book learning and smart folk. Too bad their big brains couldn't save them from dragon-bile and falling rocks, huh?

People scatter out of their way, squealing like stuck pigs, as they come to the gate. Bleeding, hobbling, pissing themselves. Clutching their brats and salvaged geegaws. Some of the men lunge at them for fun, snarl and snap their teeth to see them shriek. Kevdak doesn't stop them.

Let the vermin fear them. Let them flee.

The city lies before them. Every bit as fucked as the scouts described, smoke and rubble and sunset washing over it all. He halts right on the threshold. Takes in the sight of the battered buildings, the bodies, the long cobbled street. Hears the cries of alarm and the crackling flames.

Then he brings his fists together.

And this time, he doesn't hold back.

The hammer boom of the Titanstone Knuckles coming together deafens the whole world. Lightning and thunder, rolled into one. The power roils through his veins and electrifies them. He drinks it all up and demands *more.*

And more comes. Kevdak's shadow, red sun at his back, unfolds along the road into the city as he goes from eight feet tall to ten, eleven, *twelve.* He feels his bones crack and lengthen, his muscles tear and re-form. The pain is the best thing he's ever felt. He luxuriates in it, letting the fire-ant itch eating along his limbs sink deep enough that it awakens that old ancestral *rage.* The fury that always sleeps just beneath his skin.

A red gleam burns across his tattooed chest. One tattoo for every life he has taken. The blood-light briefly outlines the shape of a bear hidden within the markings.

Everything is red. The wounded sun. The edges of his vision. The gore-spattered streets. The wide-eyed faces of the hapless sheep scrambling away from the gate.

The ground shakes under his boot when he takes a step forward. The Titanstone Knuckles, already massive, have grown with him to become blue-veined boulders. He pulls his Bloodaxe from his back, and its wicked edge shines red, too.

Kevdak throws his arms wide, plants his feet, and *roars,* baring spit-ribboned teeth. His warriors roar with him, echoing his rage.

"*Herd of Storms,*" he bellows. "*Show these fools the meaning of fear!*"

THE HERD AS KEVDAK INHERITED it was some forty-odd men and women, mostly giantkin. Gained some and lost some over the years but never broke fifty.

Then they took the Rivermaw.

Seemed like a good idea at first. More boots to raise a mighty dust in their wake as they prowled the Dividing Plains. More strong arms to wield spears and swords as they raided hamlets and caravans. Even had a few stoneborn among 'em, like Worra and the sorry sack of shit who used to be their leader.

The rest, though? *Soft.* Fish-fuckers, the lot of them, living out their lives on the fertile banks and fens of the rivers draining into the Foramere Basin. Weaving their nets, caulking their boats, singing their songs. Not domesticated folk like what live in the big city, Kevdak will grant them that, but not real nomads, neither. Not like the Herd of Storms.

Stoneborn can march a day on no food and little sleep. Stoneborn hides can endure rain and shine. Stoneborn feet can eat up miles of fen and farm and prairie, squat in the muck or under a tree for the night, and then be ready to go again when the sun comes up. They're hard as the bones of the land, like the giants who spawned them, and their strongest children are born with lightning in their veins.

Fish-fuckers, on the other hand, will whine about needing *rest* and *shelter.* Want to haul around the canvas tents and stools and puny plains ponies they used when they lived along the riverbank. Don't much like being reminded of their place, neither. Might even get to muttering among themselves about how *the damn half-giants think they're better than us* and *how come they get to keep all the best loot for themselves?*

Turns out doubling in size overnight makes you *slow.* Go from fifty men to a hundred, and suddenly, it's not just that you have a bunch of extra mouths to feed and a bunch of extra voices yammering to be heard. Suddenly, the ass end of your Herd can still be hanging out your britches by the time the head's made it to its destination.

Now, this don't matter if you're getting in position to ambush a line of wagons loaded with grain and steel. But when bloodcurdling shrieks split the air and you realize a roving band of Ravagers have caught your scent?

Being slow means *death.*

The fucking cultists don't fight fair. Don't fight rational. They don't want loot, nor hostages, nor land. Don't want nothing at all but to please that mad god of theirs, and the only offering that'll do for the Ruiner is blood. Yours—or theirs.

All the battle experience in the world don't do shit against an enemy that will let you run a spear through its heart so it can get close enough to sink teeth in your throat. Their shamans dope them up to the gills with foul magic. Their bloated Slaughter Lords will rip your entrails out and eat 'em while you're still alive and screaming.

The Herd has lost more men than Kevdak likes to count to those insane fucks over the last year. Would have lost far more if not for Greenbeard flinging fire and calling up magic fog. The old fuck *knows* it, too, though being their saving grace doesn't seem to please him none. If anything, the seer's temper gets more rancid with every close call.

So, this? Pounding through a battlefield with a few hand-chosen stoneborn at his back? This feels like coming *home.* This feels like the good old days. No shambling curs to keep in line. Just him and his axe and the joy of the kill.

The first couple barely register. Civilians, like as not. Too soft. Kevdak shatters a rib cage with a swing of his axe, pulls back and drives the butt end of the haft into someone's nose hard enough that their sinuses mate with their brain matter.

Number three is a soldier. Or so he's guessing from the black tabard and half plate. Oh, and the greatsword. The man actually tries to *parry* his axe—so Kevdak just takes both his hands off at the wrist. The idiot's still staring dumbfounded at his gushing stumps when Kevdak wraps his gauntleted fingers all the way around his head and neck and crushes him like an overripe plum.

There's a howl of pain behind him as Thulla, one of his finest warmongers, drives her spear through another soldier's gut. Old one-eyed

Eudon puts a hatchet in a woman's skull and then seizes her wailing, snot-nosed brat by its collar.

"*Atrix,*" he snarls. "Tell Atrix to show himself, or I feed this little shit his own spleen!"

Kevdak feels his grin broaden. It flickers as sulfur-stink fills the air and green fire detonates overhead. Seems like some of the fancy magic types of the Scholar Ward haven't kicked the bucket yet.

Greenbeard is already moving, ripping briar and bramble from the cobblestones to shield them from the blast. He sends vines darting into the sobbing, stumbling, fleeing crowd. A shriek erupts as the vines return, dragging a robed fucker by the ankle and hoisting him up into the air.

"No," he snaps when Eudon makes to throw another hatchet at the trapped man. "Leave him to me. Focus on the plan!"

And they do. Thulla guts another guard. Another of his warmongers seizes a towheaded gnome and drags her with them, sword against her throat.

"*Atrix!*" The cry goes up again. "You! And you! Tell every useless cunt you find that Atrix better show himself!"

Kevdak shoulders onward, crushing debris underfoot. Smashes a couple more skulls together, puts the edge of his axe right through a man's jaw. Splashes through an acid puddle one of the dragons left behind. He doesn't even feel his flesh sizzle when it flecks his thighs. Doesn't even feel the arrows that bounce off his tattooed skin, toughened by god-lightning and sheer rage.

"You hear that, Margrave?" he roars. "We're gonna gut your people! String 'em up in the streets! How many's it gonna take before you crawl out of your hole? How many of their lives for yours?"

His strategy was simple, in the end. Kevdak's led enough raids to know elaborate plans are a waste of time. All you really gotta remember is that everyone bleeds, and if you hit a thing hard enough, it dies.

So, part one: strike fast. Hit 'em while they're reeling. Can't give the fuckers time to regroup—or the Ravagers time to scent blood in the water.

Part two: make use of the chaos. That's why he's got the Herd splitting up and encircling the city. Coming in through every single gate at once, breaking up into smaller bands to go war-whooping and ululating and splashing blood all through the streets like the Hells themselves spat them up to claim Westruun's soul. One stormborn with every group, so they can show any city watch they run into why it's a real bad idea to wear metal armor around the children of the mountain.

And finally, part three: go for the leader. The big man in charge is apparently one margrave, name of Atrix. Good leader, and well respected, as one of the Rivermaw fucks—greasy little man with a bald, scarred scalp—eagerly tells him. If the dragons didn't already get this Atrix, he'll probably be in the Opal Ward, at the city's center.

Every fighting force that thinks itself hot shit is really just a chicken at heart. Cut off the head and watch the body dance till it dies. It's what they did when they absorbed the Rivermaw Herd.

Well. What his idiot offspring, Zanroar, did. Went and challenged the stoneborn leader to single combat. Split him from neck to nuts then hacked off his head, held it up gushing and gaping for the man's horrified folk to see and proclaimed, *You belong to the Herd of Storms now.*

All well and good, except he didn't think to consult Kevdak before he did it. Not even so much as a fucking by-your-leave, an oh-by-the-way, to his own *father.* His *Thunderlord.*

Should've beat his ass for the disrespect. Kevdak was real tempted, seeing the little shit grinning at him all gore-caked and smug-toothed. But there they were. His own men hollering with savage joy. The brats like Horace and Cole, who grew up alongside Zanroar, with their arms in the air cheering him like he was the fucking Stormlord himself come down from the sky. The Rivermaw seething and cringing, on the knife-edge of indecision: Bend the knee, or strike back?

And he knew—by the lord of lightning's blasted cock, he *knew* that if he struck down his son in his moment of triumph, it would all come apart.

So he didn't. Because unlike his idiot offspring, he knows what it means to be a godsdamned *leader.* To look beyond the next skull that needs splitting. The next bit of meat that needs chewing. He's proud to be giantkin. But his people, like his son, lack vision. Foresight.

History won't remember a blood smear on anyone's boot. But *no one* will ever fucking forget Kevdak by the time he is done.

It's almost too easy, in the end. The sun hasn't even sunk all the way behind Westruun's cracked stone walls when they find the man. Margrave Atrix has a mustache that was probably impressive in better times. It's looking a little limp right now. So's the man himself. Face gray, fancy tunic all caked with blood and grime. Must be hard work trying to get your city back in order after dragons shat all over it. Boo-fucking-hoo.

Still, there he stands. Blocking their path. A half dozen equally battered city watch behind him. He's gotta know he's a dead man, but he came out to meet 'em all the same. Kevdak can respect that.

"You wanted to see me, ogre?" Atrix says dryly. "Here I am. Now release my citizens, if you would."

Kevdak crooks a finger at his warmongers, who drag forward all the sniveling pieces of shit they've collected along their way.

"Since you asked so nicely," he says, grinning, "I'll do you one better. Tell your men to drop their weapons—and I'll let 'em keep their heads. Not you, of course. *You,* I'm gonna kill. But the rest of your folk? They're under new management now. Way I see it, you can make the handover nice and smooth, or you can go down kicking and screaming and shitting your pants. Sound fair?"

Atrix does not, it turns out, think that sounds fair. Kevdak supposes he can respect that, too.

He kills him anyway. Not right away, of course. First, they cut down the men at his back. Kevdak beheads a couple, Greenbeard turns into a fucking dire wolf and rips out another's throat, and his warmongers disembowel the rest.

Kevdak seizes Atrix's head, like he has so many others this evening, but doesn't squash it—just squeezes hard enough to get the man shrieking bloody murder. Then he drags him, hollering and bleeding, all the way through the ruined city streets. All the way to the town square right at the heart of the fancy Opal Ward where the bigwigs live. Holds him up nice and high so his weeping citizens can get a good look, then grabs his torso in his other massive hand and twists his head off like he's popping the cork on a bottle of wine.

And with that, it's done. A couple city watch still put up a fight, but the Herd stomps them into pulp. The rest bend the knee.

Westruun is theirs. To ransack, to rule. Whatever they fucking want. *Theirs.*

No—it's *his.*

THAT NIGHT, THEY FEAST.

The dragons smashed the city up pretty good. But there's good, dark beer to be salvaged from taverns, and mead and ale besides—kegs and kegs of the stuff, enough to slake even throats as parched as theirs. Butcher shops and slaughterhouses yield meat aplenty, and there's dead plainscows in the outlying fields that shouldn't go to waste. The margrave's own stores provide salt pork and venison, soft white bread, and toothsome wheels of cheese.

The Herd leave Westruun's fallen to rot where they lie but burn the five warriors they lost while taking the city—only five! Hah!—as is the stoneborn way, sending their spirits back to the sky and the mountaintops in curls of white smoke. The town square becomes the center of their celebration. They build a giant bonfire and roast a whole cow. Build an equally large pile of loot that soon dwarfs the fire. Gold coins and gems. Swords of fine steel forged by master smiths. Adamantine plate and leather cuirasses with dwarven tooling, oiled and buffed to a fine shine, stripped from the corpses of the city's defenders. Tower shields and sturdy bucklers. Enough to outfit every warrior in the Herd twice over.

That night, every finger gleams with rings, and every throat is strewn with gold chains. His men strut around draped in torn silks and velvets, pretending to bow to one another and doff imaginary hats. Some of the Rivermaw find instruments and strike up a tune. Sounds like cats in heat to Kevdak's ears, but his men must like it well enough, 'cause there's clapping and stomping and eventually words being bellowed along.

Zanroar is the fucking life of the party, prancing around the bonfire. Teeth bared in a grin, clapping this man and that on the shoulder, shouting abuse and encouragement in equal measure. Little shit was real quick to forget he tried to shout this whole idea down, huh?

Horace, Suda, Cole, and some of the other young'uns have made a game out of offering ridiculous trinkets to Worra: Here a silver fork, there a broken music box. A single beribboned slipper, a cracked porcelain plate. She turns each one down with a shake of her head, but Kevdak sees a smile touch her usually stoic face.

The margrave's house—identifiable by the big-ass fancy crest above the doorway—occupies pride of place in the town square. Which makes it the perfect spot to oversee the festivities. Just him and the house's previous occupant, decapitated and stuck on a wooden pike lashed to the balcony.

Kevdak gives Atrix's blood-matted ginger dome a companionable pat before raising a goblet of wine to his lips. The dead man's kitchens had more than meat and cheese to offer. Fucker had a whole *wine cellar.* Bottle on bottle on bottle of delectable ruby and purple and blue-black delight. Didn't pass *those* out for the men to share. Call it a Thunderlord's privilege.

The reek of spoiled milk reaches his nose. Well. Thunderlord and his inner circle, maybe.

"Could get used to this," Greenbeard grunts. The old half-giant stands just inside the doors that open onto the balcony, clutching a bottle of wine in one gnarled hand. The squat, toad-like stretch to his lips is so foreign it takes Kevdak a moment to tell he's smiling, too.

Huh. Guess this really is a night of fucking firsts.

Down in the square, someone has noticed him standing on the balcony. There's cheers, and pointing, and then fists pumped in the air.

"*Thunderlord!*" someone cries. Another someone takes up the shout. "*Thunderlord! Thunderlord!*"

Night lays light on Westruun, veined by the glowing, smoldering wreckage in its streets. Its people weep, and its conquerors feast. Kevdak's people praise his name, and it sounds sweet. Deserved. Fucking *overdue.*

He raises one gauntleted fist over his head in response to the cheers, making them redouble in volume.

"Aye," he says to Greenbeard. "So could I."

HE SLEEPS IN THE MARGRAVE's bed that night. Silk sheets and cushioned eiderdowns cradling his massive form. It's like spooning with a godsdamned *cloud.* Just the one night is enough to make him feel years younger. Rich city fucks live like this all the time?

Of course, his idiot offspring can't let his father have some well-deserved peace. Kevdak is enjoying a restful breakfast of cured meats and preserves purloined from the margrave's kitchens the next morning when Zanroar comes barging into the parlor. All dressed up in brand-new armor, Kevdak notes balefully.

"Why are we still here?" Zanroar demands. Not so much as a *good day, Father,* or even a *Thunderlord.* "Sun's been up for hours. We should be moving out."

"Hasty," drawls Greenbeard, who sits slouched in a chair with a pipe in hand. They found good tobacco in old Atrix's stores this morning, and the seer has been contentedly wreathed in smoke ever since. "Always so hasty, pup. Why the rush? Loot not to your liking? You seem to have made out well enough."

"Says the man sitting on his wrinkled arse while I actually try to keep some order around here," Zanroar snarls. "Did you know our scouts saw the black dragon? It's roosting up on Gatshadow. What do you plan to do if it—"

Kevdak brings a fist down on the table, silencing him. The crockery jolts and shivers. Glass and silver set to tinkling.

"You sent out scouts?" he says.

His voice is calm. Reasonable. A danger sign, as Zanroar well knows. His son stops to think before he answers, thereby proving he's not *completely* fucking devoid of sense.

"Ravagers are still out there," he says eventually. "And maybe the margrave called for help before you tore his head off. Maybe reinforcements from Emon or Kymal or some-fucking-where are gonna show up any day now. I don't fucking know! My point is, we *have to go.* Grab what loot we can and get packing."

"*Grab what loot we can,*" Greenbeard mocks. "Ah, Zanroar. Shortsighted as ever. Do you know the riches this city holds? We—"

"Are sitting ducks as long as we squat here. Might as well paint a target on your arse and bend over!"

"Safer in here than on those blasted plains—"

"Coward," Zanroar jeers. "You don't think I know what you're doing, old man? I see the fear of death in your eyes. I see you pouring poison in my father's ears. You would have us *domesticated.* You would sit in craven comfort while we—"

"*Enough!*"

Kevdak rises, knocking over his chair. He strides across the room and takes his idiot offspring by his once-broken jaw. Squeezes hard enough that Zanroar momentarily chokes on his own spit, pulls him in so he's looking him directly in those eyes the color of old blood. Just like his own.

Whatever happened to the clumsy-footed brat who dogged his every move and would have shamed himself for a single word of Kevdak's approval? All he sees when he looks at his son now is insolence. Sedition. Disappointment. A worm in the apple-core of the Herd he has built.

"I am Thunderlord of this Herd," he says, every word taut with fury. "Not you. Not that pustulant old fuck over there. We leave when *I* say we're good and ready, and not one fucking second earlier. If I hear you sent out scouts without my say-so again? I won't just break your fucking jaw. I'll break your *back.* Make it so you never walk again. So that woman of yours has to carry you around. You hear me?"

He tightens his grip, gauntleted fingers pressing into the soft flesh beneath Zanroar's jaw. Just long enough that his son's eyes begin to bulge and his face takes on a mottled hue. Then he shoves him away so the boy staggers and falls on his ass.

"If you're so worried about our *safety,*" Kevdak growls, "go make yourself fucking useful and set up some godsdamned barricades. Don't let me see your ugly mug back here until every one of the city gates is secured. Go!"

Zanroar doesn't argue. The hate in his red eyes is a striking snake, but he stumbles to his feet and flees, rubbing his neck.

Greenbeard coughs out a cloud of smoke as he goes, cackle-wheezing to himself.

Possibly there are stoneborn chieftains in this world who would rejoice to be unseated by a son of their blood, a worthy successor. Not Kevdak. All his blood has ever done is disappoint. His half-wit brother Stonejaw, chewed up by a wight. His traitor nephew Grog, who had the stones to make Kevdak think he showed *promise*—only to turn on his people to protect a dribbling weakling of a gnome.

And then there's Zanroar. Shit-for-brains Zanroar, who talked a big game and then got his jaw broken by the traitor in single combat. Ass in the dirt for the whole Herd to see, and his father's shame. And did he stop there? Bones of the mountain, no. Tried to feed them a fat fib about meeting his dead traitor cousin up north, like they didn't all see that whoreson lying smashed and bleeding on the ground with their own eyes. Like *Kevdak* wasn't the one who staved in his skull.

The Herd beat him for a liar, but the whelp stuck to his story. Only when Kevdak threatened to shatter his jaw a second time did Zanroar fold. Went surly and quiet for a time after that, keeping to himself, casting Kevdak hateful glares.

Good, Kevdak thought at the time. Maybe that last beating finally knocked something into place. Maybe the boy's finally ready to become a man.

If hating Kevdak's what it takes, so be it. Hate does a man good. Makes him strong. His own pa was a piece of shit. Best thing he ever did for Kevdak was go get wound-rot from an infected stump. Made killing him real easy, and not just 'cause he couldn't even pick up his axe to defend himself by the end. Was just the smartest thing to do for the Herd at that point. Cull the weak. Lead the strong forward.

A father's job isn't to coddle his son. It's to make him tough enough to take all the shit the world will throw at him. For a time, it seemed like he'd succeeded. Zanroar quit bellyaching, got serious about killing. Found himself a stoneborn woman, even if she was from another tribe. Got a child in her and everything.

Why couldn't the little shit have stopped there? Didn't need to get too big for his britches. Didn't need to start yearning to take what he hadn't earned. But maybe that's all a son is, in the end. A hungry thing that takes and takes and takes until it has grown enough that it must eat you, unseat you next. Unless you eat it first. Take back the life it has only because *you* gave it the gift of breath and seed, brought it mewling into this world and allowed it to get big enough to get ideas above its station.

Fuck family. All family does is disappoint. Even the soft, unknown little thing growing in Worra's womb is just the promise of a lie. *Stay yolked and unformed, little one,* he thinks. *Stay a dream. A dream can't disappoint.*

Flesh, though? Flesh always fails in the end. Fate can't be found in blood and womb-water. Fate is what you make, what you *take,* reaching into the ribs of the world and wrenching out its still-steaming heart.

HE'LL NEVER FORGET THE DAY he found these gauntlets. The day his destiny became clear to him.

They were roaming the plains at dusk when they came upon the remains of a Ravager cell, maybe two. All dead. Ribs crushed, heads split open, guts leaking onto the grass. Even a storm-forsaken Slaughter Lord, all four of its arms ripped off its body and its neck broken.

At the center of this circle of death stood an old orc. Spattered with Ravager blood from head to toe. Bull-chested, thick-necked, tall as any stoneborn.

And dying. Kevdak knew it just from looking at him. The orc knew it, too, for there was resignation in his eyes as he lifted them to meet Kevdak's.

Then those eyes flashed the pure white of a lightning strike. The scent of ozone filled the air. The great gore-caked gauntlets that sheathed the orc's fists—that pulled Kevdak's gaze like lodestones—came alive with light once more.

And the dying man opened his lifeblood-stained lips to speak with the weight of prophecy.

"No, tyrant," he rasped in a voice that came from the heart of the storm. A voice of broken shields and shattered swords, of thunderclap and crunching bone. "These weapons of the gods are not meant for you. But through you, they shall find their way to the hands they were meant for."

The light faded from the old orc's eyes. He placed his feet well apart. Raised his gauntleted fists before him.

"Now come," he said, and was just a man once more. Tired. Hoarse. "Let us finish this. Send me to my god and claim your temporary prize."

To this day, Kevdak doesn't know why he fought the bastard one-on-one. Maybe it was the taunts sliding under his tattooed skin: *not meant for you, temporary prize.* Maybe it was that he felt the presence of the gods on the plains that evening. The unspoken call of destiny.

But fight him he did, and, half-dead or not, the old orc almost killed him. Cracked half Kevdak's ribs, punctured a lung, concussed him to the Hells and back before Kevdak, raging and bloodied and bellowing, finally got an elbow around the fucker's throat and crushed his windpipe. He was hacking up bone fragments himself for a week after. Might have gone the way of his pa if not for Greenbeard's magic patching him up.

It was all worth it for the moment he peeled the Titanstone Knuckles from the old orc's stiffening fingers and slid them on. When he first felt the Stormlord's lightning crackle through his veins, it was like the scales fell from Kevdak's eyes. He understood at last that he hadn't been denied his stormborn destiny, as he'd thought for all those years. The gods just had something greater in store for him. Not stormborn, but lightning-touched, thunder-blessed. Thunder*lord.*

Fuck that dying fool for daring to say the gauntlets would not be his for long. The Ravagers must've pounded him hard enough to addle his brains before he killed them all. The Titanstone Knuckles are *Kevdak's.* Bought and paid for in blood. Taken by might and right, as is the old way of the giantkin.

Survival through strength. Strength through power. Behold how his Herd continues to grow! Behold how the Dividing Plains quake at Kevdak's name!

"Your men deserve this," Greenbeard says to him in Atrix's parlor. "Let 'em enjoy their wine and women. Let 'em rest and grow strong."

"We have to go," Zanroar says. "We can't stay here."

"Shitting in the woods," the seer hisses. "Wiping your arse with leaves. Don't you want more, Thunderlord? Don't you want to be a *king*?"

"*Father,*" his son pleads, standing behind him on the dead margrave's balcony. "Father—*da*—please. This isn't the stoneborn way!"

Kevdak places his massive hands on the railing and watches his men carouse in the square below. Hears them cheer for him and raise tankards to his health.

"You'll understand someday, pebble," he says. "Someday, if I've done my job right. Until then—get the fuck out of my sight."

THEY GET ONE MORE DAY before it all goes to shit. One more day of lording it over the ruined city, thinking themselves kings, before it all comes crashing down.

It starts with screaming this time, too. Hollering, more like. Not the caterwauling of pampered city folk, but the full-throated rage of fighting men. Kevdak has that much warning at least. Ten seconds of *what the fuck* before he can go bolting out onto the balcony where Atrix's head is now beginning to melt down the wooden spike.

It should be midday. Should be brighter than this. *A cloud?* he thinks for a moment before the shadow resolves into a *falling elf.* Kevdak leaps out of the way with a curse as the man bounces off the railing and hits the floor by his feet. *Crack.* Brains and blood absolutely fucking everywhere.

A couple more bodies come windmilling out of the sky. These two go *splat* on the cobblestones of the square.

Then something blots out the sun.

And the dragon descends.

It's the black one. The one the scouts said was roosting up in that cursed mountain. None of the reports did the monster's sheer fucking *size* justice. It's like Gatshadow itself came to life and decided to take flight. Talons the length of a man's forearm, poison-green eyes as big around as Kevdak's skull. Miles on miles on miles of black scales. They have a strange swampy sheen in motion but resolve into scarred and tarry dullness when the creature stills.

When it lands in the town square, the whole city shakes. The dragon gives its tail a lazy swish, scattering the charred remnants of their bonfire. It places one great clawed foot possessively over the pile of loot his men have made in the square.

"Tribute," it says in a voice like piss and swamp water. Like how

Greenbeard smells at the height of summer, made sound instead of stink. "That was very wise. Maybe I *won't* eat you all and use your bones to pick my teeth."

"That loot is not for you, wyrm," Kevdak growls. "It belongs to the Herd of Storms."

"Fool!" hisses Greenbeard, who joined him on the balcony at some point. "What are you doing?"

The dragon's awful eyes turn his way. It lifts its great, jagged black head.

"Herd of Storms." It sounds almost *amused.* "I do not know this name."

"Guess you'd better fucking learn it, huh?"

Greenbeard mutters an oath and tries to seize at the back of Kevdak's furred cape. Kevdak steps away. He props one booted foot on the railing and pushes up to stand on it. Out of the corner of one eye, he sees his warriors slowly filling the town square. Reaching for weapons. Zanroar cautiously skirts around the beast's tail, drawing his sword.

Three days ago, they whimpered and pissed themselves at the sight of dragons flying overhead. Today, they look to him. Their motherfucking *Thunderlord.* They stand ready to fight on his command.

Stone and storm, he is fed up to the back teeth with fuckers trying to muscle in and take what's his. What he bled and butchered for. His Herd may be no match for three dragons, but one? While they're fed and rested and kitted out in the best gear and armor they've seen in a decade? With the Titanstone Knuckles on their side?

They took a godsdamned *city*! Mighty Westruun, jewel of the Dividing Plains! What is one storm-forsaken lizard to that?

"If you wanted this city for your own," he spits, "you should've stayed put. Go back to your mountain, wyrm. Westruun is mine! I, Kevdak, Thunderlord of the Herd of Storms and wielder of the Titanstone Knuckles, claim it for my own. That loot you so crave was bought by the blood of me and mine. You want it? Then let us add your skull to the heap!"

The dragon coughs. Least that's what it sounds like at first. Hacking noises, like it's trying to work free a knot of phlegm or got a chicken bone stuck in its throat.

Then it hits him. The beast is *laughing.*

"So be it," it says. "Well met, Kevdak, Thunderlord of the Herd of Storms. I am Umbrasyl, the Hope Devourer—and it will please me greatly to teach you the folly of your ways."

It pulls its head down into its shoulders and gurgles. Juts out its lower jaw. Inflates its cheeks and chest.

When the acid comes, it is inescapable. A torrent of corrosive slime with death in every droplet. The only thing that saves Kevdak is Greenbeard, who turns into a giant eagle, one final curse morphing mid-syllable into a ringing avian shriek. The seer sinks talons into the meat of Kevdak's shoulders and bears him bodily off the balcony as dragon-bile eats through stone where they stood seconds ago.

He should have known right then how fucked they all were. What a godsdamned colossal fucking mistake he'd made. But he is too occupied by hitting the cobblestones and rolling upright, bleeding and furious. Bringing the Titanstone Knuckles together to drink down their god-born power. Feeling his form stretch and expand.

Bellowing, with a rage unlike any he's known before, "*Kill the fucking wyrm!*"

Maybe it would've been better if the beast had toyed with them. Dragged it out. Maybe then he could have fooled himself they put up a fight.

Instead, it just slaughters them.

Thulla and Eudon are among the first to die. Felled by a hail of acid rain, screaming until their lips melt off their teeth and the bile runs in to dissolve their vocal cords. The dragon—Umbrasyl—devours his men by the mouthful, crunching plate armor like crispy pork skin. It launches warriors into the air with claw and tail and beat of mighty wing, laughing its sandpaper laugh, and then steps on the maimed and moaning survivors. Zanroar manages to wedge a sword between two of the scales on its ankle and gets a tail-whip to the gut for his trouble, knocking him clean through the nearest brick wall. Others just find their blades bouncing off. Spent arrows and spears litter the ground like straw.

Kevdak doesn't even remember when it gets him. Insult to injury, that. He remembers seizing the creature's tail in his gauntleted fists. Remembers a maw like the end of the world turning on him. Indescribable pressure. Being shaken like a rat in a dog's jaws.

And then he comes to, fetched up on a doorstep with Greenbeard healing his wounds. The gauntlets are inert, his body shrunken to its usual size. The ground quakes under him as the dragon churns through the square, tail shattering windows and knocking shingles off roofs.

"Imbecile," Greenbeard rages, spraying him with pus and spittle. "Cocksure fool! Make it right! You still have a chance. Tell the beast you surrender!"

Kevdak swallows the blood filling his mouth. "No," he slurs. "We can still . . ."

The seer finishes closing up his caved-in chest and yanks his hands away. "Half your Herd is dead, *Thunderlord.* Half! The rest wait to be devoured. If you don't fucking surrender, you will die with them!"

Half? No. Surely not. And yet . . . the cobblestones he lies on are awash in a trembling inch of gore. Everywhere he looks, bodies slag together in steaming heaps. The fumes of the dragon's acid breath turn the sky green and burn his throat.

He can hear his men screaming. Full-throated terror, now. No more rage. He can hear the townsfolk wail and the dragon laugh. And still, Kevdak hesitates.

Until somehow, through all the din and death, he hears Zanroar make a terrible sound. Sees Worra in the square, sheltering behind a hunk of fallen masonry. Curled in around her swollen belly to protect the precious thing within.

The end of his line and everything he's built. His Herd destroyed. His name forgotten. His Titanstone Knuckles taken—not by his disappointment of a son, as he feared, but by someone even worse. A gods-damned *stranger.* An unworthy fuck who happens to stumble on his corpse, the way he once stumbled on the gauntlets' dying former wielder.

All because of one stone-cursed *lizard.*

The hate is stronger than the shame. The hate is what drives him to his feet and across blood-slick cobblestones toward the beast.

"*Umbrasyl!*" he bellows.

One sickly green eye swivels toward him.

"You want tribute?" Kevdak spreads his arms wide. "This city's full of it. Gold and magic shit as far as the eye can see. Gonna be hard for you to get at it, though, isn't it? Big scaly fuck like you? Can't exactly go creeping through people's houses like a sneak-thief. Not unless you want to melt down half of what you're looking for and crush the rest."

A long, swamp-green tongue slides across the dragon's toothy maw. Umbrasyl crawls closer, belly pressed to the ground like a cat. Acid seeps between its teeth. Mingles with the blood of his Herd to drip in long, curdled streaks to the cobblestones.

"Go on," it rasps.

"Let us get it for you. We'll hunt down every last fucking copper and trinket, pile it up nice and convenient-like. In return? You leave us the city. You let *us* rule for you."

There's that hacking laugh again. The dragon lifts its mountain of a head and peers down at him.

"You amuse me," it says. "Kevdak, Thunderlord of the Herd of Storms. And because you amuse me—and because you may yet be of use—I will consider your offer."

It pauses. There *is* amusement in those burning-bog eyes, and a cruel intelligence, too. Up close like this, he can see the countless dents of blade and spell upon the creature's weathered scales. The beast is *old.* Old enough to know how to wound with more than fang and claw.

"*If,*" the Hope Devourer continues, drawing out the words with relish, "you kneel before me and swear to serve."

Shortsighted. Lacking vision. All the curses he has heaped on Zanroar's head. He will not let them apply to him, too.

This dragon will not be his end. It will be his *stage.* His stepping stone to glory. All he needs is *time.* Let the beast turn its back. Let it think him tame. They will regroup. They will survive, as they have always done.

"So be it," Kevdak grinds out.

And there, in the blood and bile and melted flesh, he does it. Among the moans of the dying and the wreck of his once-proud Herd, he bends the knee.

THE TIDES

Sam Maggs

Kima had always known how she would die.

Well, not *exactly,* but as an exemplar dedicated to the god of justice, she had a pretty good idea. Moving just a little too slow; feinting in the wrong direction. Outwitted by a foe, even for the briefest of moments? Bam. Mace to the face, greatsword through the chest, riddled with arrows while slowly bleeding out on the wildflowers thinking about all the things you regret not doing.

Kima spent too much of her time swinging a sword far too large for her around some dangerous folks. Eventually, inevitably, the evil she struck down would strike back. She'd accepted it, and she'd moved on.

Which is all by way of saying that Lady Kima of Vord did not expect her untimely end to come in the middle of the Lucidian Ocean, with the only visible weapon for miles around strapped to her own back. Her blade was useless here.

"Allie, are—?!" Kima's cry was cut short by another swell. The water was so dark it was nearly black, reflecting an overcast sky. Whitecaps foamed around her like the Lucidian was frothing at the mouth to swallow her and her heavy golden armor whole, ravenous for halfling blood.

"Kima . . . !" Allura's accent was carried by the wind over the buffeting waves, and Kima held on to it like a life preserver.

She'd never liked the open sea—she was so small, and only the gods knew what hideous creatures roamed beneath the surface; frankly, better to never find out, thank you very much—but now here she was, faced with becoming little more than a stone that would sink through the depths to the sandy bottom, where she would never, ever see Allura again.

Allie—with eyes bluer than any ocean, her voice so calming, her fingers so capable and sure—was in this damned water with her, facing the same horrifying fate. And Kima couldn't save her.

You had one job. And you failed.

Kima desperately searched for a glimpse of Allura through the turbulence, and her failure was the last thing on her mind before she was swallowed and everything, everything went dark.

Kima woke to nothing of note.

The streets of Westruun were dismal as usual, the upper stories of buildings tilting precariously inward toward one another, but that night, it felt like she was surrounded by them, drowning in a teeming sea of people and crime and refuse. She clawed at her throat for a moment, struggling to breathe.

At her side, Ghenn's snores mixed with the occasional rumble of a carriage rolling by.

It was the middle of the night, and there was nothing happening.

But that wasn't true. There was an arcane blue light approaching; Kima could see it through the slats of the wooden fence to their back. Kima scrambled to her knees, reaching for her knife, grumpy that she was going to have to break the nose of yet another jerk who made the mistake of thinking they were easy prey. It wasn't the first time, and it certainly wouldn't be the last.

Still, you'd think she'd have gained enough of a reputation in town by now.

"I'm not here to hurt you!" came a weathered and weary voice from a few feet away. The light stopped moving abruptly. "Will you let me speak with you?"

"Who's asking?" Kima found herself saying, against her better judgment. There was just something about the man's voice that was . . . calming? Sweet?

So, probably a trap. She kept hold of her knife.

"I am called Highbearer Vord," the man said, and Kima snorted.

"Damn, you come up with that yourself?"

A long-suffering sigh.

"Come out, child, let me look at you."

And, for reasons it would take her many years to fully understand, Kima did.

Highbearer Vord was a kindly-looking older elven man, a blue tinge to his skin from the magical light bobbing softly next to him, illuminating pitying, pupilless eyes.

He shook his head with another sigh, and Kima wanted to punch him in the nose. "No parents? Early teens? On the street your whole life?"

Kima blinked. "No. Not that it's any of your business." She shrugged, looking down at the easy rise and fall of Ghenn's wide stomach. Years on the streets, and he still lacked any sense of self-preservation.

"And him?"

"The same."

"And that makes you angry," Highbearer Vord asked in a way that sounded less like a question and more like an answer, looking pointedly at her knife.

"Yes," Kima said, without hesitating.

The Highbearer cleared his throat, and Kima suddenly felt that pressure around her neck again. It was so hard to breathe. But then he was asking, "I've helped many urchins find their way to the dragon's fold—all are quick to help, but also quick to cut. I've been attempting to find their friends from the streets and offer them . . . purpose. Do you have a conduit for all that anger, or is it just like a live edge swung by an unsteady hand?" Vord's eyes flashed—but not with malice.

With compassion.

That memory stayed with Kima through her years at the temple of the Platinum Dragon. Nearly the entirety of her second decade passed behind those kindly stone walls, where her rage at the world took shape on the training courts. She trained twice as hard and twice as long as any other adept, weighting down her practice weapons so that she would one day be able to wield the massive greatswords she admired in the armory.

Vord had been right; she'd been aimless. It had made her feel helpless and small.

Here, though. Here she had *reason.*

She'd never been the religious sort; she imagined the violent things she'd had to do to survive precluded her from a life of piousness. She was also a huge fan of kissing in all ways, at all times. A nun, she was not.

But the exemplars of the temple didn't expect her to be a saint. They just expected her to defend what the Platinum Dragon stood for: infinite empathy for those this cruel and unforgiving world had left behind, those who weren't lucky enough to be born into privilege or magic or wealth or status. The helpless, the unhoused, the dispossessed. And that, she had no problem with. When the time came to commit herself to their oaths, she did so gladly.

And then Kima became what she had always been meant to be: Lady Kima of Vord. Her life was no longer about her. She was a weapon, a sword with a purpose, and she would be honed to flawlessness, no matter how much work or how many years it took.

Of course, the more you sharpen a sword, the weaker it becomes.

The next time Kima's head crested the waves, she found she'd come to a section of calm on the otherwise roiling ocean. For a moment, Kima almost laughed; the gifts from her god, the greatsword and armor that had saved her time and time again from certain death, were now going to be her cursed anchors.

She hated irony.

"Kima!" This time, she could place the direction of Allura's voice.

Taking as deep a breath as she could without inhaling too much brine, Kima shouted back, "Allie! I'm coming!"

Lifting one of her arms to stroke felt like plowing through molten gold; kicking her legs made the muscles in her thighs *scream.* But there was Allura's voice again, and there, just ahead, there—was that a blond head? Was that a pale hand?

"Kima, here!"

Kima heard Allura's ragged sigh of relief as she finally paddled up next to her. "Don't you *ever*—"

And then Allura was choking on salt water and then so was Kima and she was gulping water before she knew what was happening and this wasn't supposed to be happening, and—

Drowning was neither peaceful nor easy. No, instead, it was violent, vicious, all-consuming. It was an ugly death, and not even a fast one, to keep it civilized. It was the only thing Kima could think about, if you could even call being bullied by the animal force of her mind "thinking." It was almost more than she could bear, but bear it she did.

Kima stroked and stroked and kicked and kicked and still the waves rose higher around her, and all she could taste was salt and her eyes burned and she was under again, under and couldn't tell which way was up, and it was so dark, and worst of all, she couldn't hear Allura's voice.

Kima was *NOT* supposed to be here.

"We need help," Ghenn said, far too cheerfully. "You'll like them. I promise."

As Ghenn knew very well, Kima did not like many people. She spent most of her time on her own, aside from Tulip, a great, slobbering beast of a shepherd whose soft brown fur blended into a nearly black muzzle in a way Kima found extremely charming. Anyone who wanted to tag along had to be better company than Tulip, and, frankly, that was hard to find.

But she'd known Ghenn for as long as she could remember. He was different; he understood her duty. And he was so large and so damn *earnest* that she couldn't turn him down when he asked for her assistance in clearing the raiders out of a temple, and here they were. And if Ghenn now came with the friends he'd made in Kima's absence, she would have to take it, mostly, in stride.

Drake was the worst of them; already he'd gone ruddy with drink and was all but screaming a raucous battle hymn. You'd expect an elementalist to take better care of himself. Dohla, the juggernaut of a dragonkin with a huge personality, had managed to win Kima over by coming prepared with treats for Tulip, at least. And Sirus she just couldn't crack; the charming-looking swashbuckler hadn't said a word since their arrival, instead simply taking a stein and sipping it in a manner that she'd almost call contemplative.

Also, you're not supposed to be here. Something else is happening. Why won't you remember?

"We took out the raiders on our own," grumbled Kima. Tulip panted at her in response, and Kima reached over to scritch her under her chin. She'd considered using the pup as a battle mount in the past, but Tulip was far more valuable in combat if she was fast and unburdened, able to leap at an exposed throat or disarm an opponent at a moment's notice.

"We did do that," agreed Ghenn with all of his usual enthusiasm. He stuck out a hand and Tulip licked it with equal enthusiasm—traitor. Ghenn's eyes crinkled in both disgust and mirth as Tulip got him all slobbery. "But there were maybe twenty of them, all untrained. This is more than that."

"This is *two.*"

"Yeeess," Ghenn conceded slowly. "The two being a drakerider and their colossal wyvern."

"Yeah," Kima said. "*Two.* But fine."

He laughed. "Honestly, we could still use another—"

"Hello?"

Kima whipped around. A woman stood in the doorway of the tavern's grimy little back room. Long, willowy, and dripping in silks far too fancy for this garbage mountain road and this garbage mountain bar. She wore light blue traveler's robes under a deep navy cloak that Kima thought matched her eyes, though it was hard to tell in the general gloom. Her hair was kept in two short braids the color of corn silk.

She was the most beautiful person Kima had ever seen, and that immediately made Kima assume she was useless. Pretty people never really had to develop any useful traits; they just got by on their looks.

"Oh, we're good, thanks, we're not buying—"

"No, I'm not selling anything. I'm *not* selling anything," the woman interrupted, her voice accented with the annoying lilt of the well bred and well read. So she was rich to boot; pretty *and* rich made for the most useless combination of all. "I heard you were hiring? I was hoping you were hiring."

Before Kima could stop her, Tulip had already bounded over, her giant paws flinging into the air and onto the woman's shoulders. She laughed, craning her face away from an overzealous tongue.

"I'm Lady Allura Vysoren," the woman said. "And I want to help." Strapped to one of two belts at her waist was a large and apparently well-loved tome; in her hand was a short staff topped with what might have been, for all Kima knew, an icicle.

"We already have an arcanist," Kima said gruffly. Tulip wasn't usually quite so trusting of strangers.

"That's all right," she said, more to Tulip than to anyone else. "I specialize in protective magic, which it seems like you desperately need."

She was eyeing Kima's beat-up armor in a way Kima wasn't sure that she loved. "I heard you're going after a drakerider. You're going to need all the assistance you can get."

When Kima looked to him for support, Ghenn shrugged in a universal gesture of *Your call.*

"I'm our magical protector, thanks. What's someone like you doing up in the Cliffkeeps?" Kima questioned, watching as her giant hound fell and rolled onto her back with her tongue lolling out of her mouth, begging for belly rubs.

The woman—Allura—dropped to her knees to give the pup a proper scratch. "Oh, you know," Allura said vaguely. "Out of school, looking to do good in the world. And, uh . . ." She paused for a second, her hand on Tulip's tummy. Tulip whined, and Allura got right back to it with a muttered apology. "My previous party left this morning. Without me."

Right, Kima thought to herself. *Useless.*

But the gal had a point. If she wanted to throw herself into the maw of a wyvern, who was Kima to stop her?

"D'you like dogs?" asked Kima.

"Ah." Allura smiled apologetically. "I have a cat."

Kima rolled her eyes. "Blech."

With the most strength she'd ever mustered, Kima reached an arm above the waves, her steel gauntlets long since lost to the tumultuous waters—and finally, *finally* grabbed Allura's outstretched hand.

"I've got you!" yelled Allura. "I've got you, hold on!"

"I'm holding!"

Kima felt Allura *yank* with all her delicate might and some perfect bit of spellcraft, and the two of them were together, body to body.

"What do we do?!"

"I'm thinking!" Allura clearly had no better ideas than Kima. Kicking extra hard to keep afloat, she attempted to unbuckle Kima's armor—but finding purchase on the slippery fastenings was impossible.

Kima would have attempted to turn in the water to potentially give Allura better access to the straps of her armor, willing to lose even her greatsword to the vast black if it meant she would live—*they* would live—but there was no hope for it. Turning meant possibly losing Allura's already tenuous grip on her, and now that they'd been reunited, Kima wasn't about to let her go. Not without a fight.

Still, Kima didn't know how many times she could take the up and down, feeling like she was being tossed around the hold of a ship without the walls to protect her. Kima's stomach roiled, but she barely took notice; all of her precious time and energy was taken up by trying not to drag herself and Allura down to the ocean floor.

Kima clung to Allura as they bobbed under yet again, and the world became muted and cold, but at least this time she wasn't completely alone.

"Kima," she heard Allura say, "Kima, you're bleeding. Can you—"

Oh; and so she was. And fairly rapidly, it seemed; Kima watched the water stain red around her, the idea that it might draw some apex predator toward them barely a blip in her mind.

"Someone should heal that," Kima said stupidly, before she passed out.

KIMA NEVER, NOT IN AN eternity, could have guessed where life would take her, Ghenn, Tulip, and the weirdos she'd met in the mountains. It had been the six of them for pushing a year now. Once they'd defeated the wyvern and its rider, and started calling themselves "Mors Draconis"—not because they were actually that pretentious, but because they found that people took them more seriously if they had a pretentious-sounding *name,* so they just leaned in to it—word got around that they were the drake-killing squad, and suddenly the moneyed and problem'd were coming out of the woodwork to hire their band of good-guy mercs.

So that's how their group had gotten along, and things had been going pretty well. Ghenn kept the Mors in good shape with his healing.

Sirus whipped through the darkness like a shade. Allura and Drake brought up the rear, slinging their spells. And Dohla and Kima took hits the others couldn't—not if they wanted to walk away in one piece. It was a good system. It could have been perfect.

But Allura was terrible at *listening*. She never wanted to follow a single damn order Kima laid out for her. So every fight had gone similarly: Kima would tell Allura to stay back, Allura would ignore her, and Kima would grudgingly plant herself directly in front of the stubborn arcanist with her silly, shoulder-length braids. Kima had started wearing two little pigtails, too, but there was nothing unusual about that. It kept her hair out of her face.

"You ready?" Kima would ask with grim confidence.

"For this?" Allura would reach her hands out in front of her, prepping her first spell, her answer the same each time. "*Always.*"

And fine, she was willing to admit it. Kima might have initially thought Allura was a privileged rich kid who never had to work for anything, but she was a *force;* Kima would watch with awe in her eyes as the woman shot spell after spell at their foes, pausing for nothing, like a hurricane, her skirts flying up around her. No one fought like Allura did without some baggage behind it, and there was a determination in Allura's eyes—a desire to prove herself.

It was a look Kima recognized, mostly from the mirror.

And that turned protecting Allura from a chore into a godsdamned pleasure. It was more than a little exhausting, and Kima still found herself wishing on more than one occasion that they hadn't decided to run around with such a dainty waif of a mage. But it *did* allow Kima to do more than simply serve; it was, like her work for her god, an act of complete *devotion,* and she appreciated that, despite having constantly to save her arcanist from imminent danger.

At least Coriander, her ridiculous orange cat, was pretty cute, Kima supposed. Even if Tulip *did* keep trying to eat him.

But the worst thing about Allura by far was the *questions.* Every night they'd sit around their fire and Kima would flop down with whatever piece of leather needed to be repaired or sword sharpened or tack cleaned and there would be Allura, right next to her, *asking* her things. About *herself.*

It was infuriating.

"Why do you do what you do?" *What else would I be doing?* "Why do you follow the Platinum Dragon?" *How else will I mete out justice in an unjust world?* "Who do you do it for?" *The people who need help.*

It was like an inescapable vortex—and it wasn't limited to fireside chats. Allura's irritating ability to make Kima question even her most base programming came up in battle, too: chastising Kima for placing herself in harm's way too often; demanding she heal herself as often as she healed others; looking out for her when Allura knew very well that it was Kima's job to look out for everyone else. She was fine. Her own well-being was meaningless in the face of fulfilling her role.

Finally, during one such interrogation at their camp outside of some small town, Kima had to blurt out:

"Why do you want to know all these things about me?"

It was a late night, and the fire was already banked. They lay next to each other in their bedrolls, talking quietly so as not to disturb the rest of their crew. They were close enough together that it was still fairly easy to hear, but not so close that Kima had to feel weird about it.

She reached a hand forward to brush a lock of blond hair out of Allura's face and away from her mouth, so Kima could read her lips better when she talked. Her blue eyes blinked slowly as Kima tucked the hair back behind her ear.

Allura had answered, and she hadn't been listening.

"Say again?" she asked.

"Because I want to know what drives you," Allura answered, as completely earnest as she always was. "I have a family legacy to uphold. Sirus has her children; Drake will never stop hunting the man who took away his father. That's one thing. But you're another beast entirely. I've never once heard you say that you're doing something for *yourself.* It's always for someone else; always for the dragon, or for justice, or to protect me, or whomever we're fighting for. But what about *you,* Kima?" She paused. "What do you want for *you*?"

The question was so ridiculous it didn't even bear answering. Not that that was going to stop Allura.

"Don't you want to ask me anything about me?"

Kima squinted into the darkness. Those blue eyes were gigantic, reflecting the last embers of light from the fire, making them look even more alive than when she was in the heat of battle.

She must have been just staring in silence for a while, because finally Allura said, "All right. My last party left me in the mountains because I refused to listen to the leader. He was an idiot, and I knew better. But there was absolutely no getting him to understand that his decisions were stupid and were getting people killed. So I—well, I didn't choose to leave, but . . . it was for the best.

"But somehow, against all my better judgment . . . with you all, I know that would never happen. I know it in my soul." Allura paused for a moment and looked Kima straight in the eyes. "You know?"

Kima swallowed, suddenly feeling like it was hard to breathe. "Yeah," she choked out. "I know."

And then everyone they gave a shit about died.

Sirus, scattered across the rocks. Dohla, reduced to ashes. And Ghenn . . .

She'd almost lost Allura, too. The mage had been gravely injured—a shot to the heart—and in the moment, Kima had been certain she'd lost her. In the end, she and Drake had to drag Allura's unconscious body off the battlefield. Thanks to the healer's quick thinking, Allura had lived to fight another day.

And that was good. But it simply wasn't enough.

"You are never, ever allowed to get hurt like that again," said Kima, clinging tightly, desperately, to Allura's belt, her arms wrapped around her middle. In the safety of their rooms in the Laughing Lamia, they held each other like their lives depended on it.

"I don't take your orders, remember?" Allura mock-scolded, but her voice betrayed the depth of emotion she was feeling, and her arms closed tightly around Kima's back from above, holding her tighter than she ever had.

They'd won, in the end.

But at what cost?

Dohla, the sweetest person Kima had ever met. Her smile was contagious; her laughter, feral, interrupted only by the crack of her hammer against bone. Sirus, with her easy charm, her ruddy brown cheeks always just as ready to blush at a compliment as she was ready to give one.

And Ghenn. Ghenn, with his perfect peachy smile and unwavering, deeply annoying cheer. Ghenn, her first friend. The first of the Mors Draconis, and the last to die.

They lay buried in the graveyard behind the temple.

Kima hadn't been able to save them. It was her job, and she had failed.

She squeezed Allura tighter around her waist and then let go abruptly, aware that she was staining her beautiful blue silk robes with her salty tears. Turning her head away quickly, she attempted to wipe the tears off her face before Allura could see—

But then they were gone, as though they'd never even been there. Kima looked up, and one of Allura's hands was glowing. Magicked. Disappeared. Cleaned.

"I'm sorry," Kima said, embarrassed at her outburst of emotion. She was supposed to be the strong one here, the armored shoulder for Allura to cry on. The exemplar. The light. "I shouldn't be—"

"Don't be stupid," Allura said, far more gently than Kima had ever heard her before. Suddenly, Kima felt a finger under her chin, and she followed its slight pressure, tilting her head up toward Allura's. Allura looked down at her like an actual angel, a blessing from the Platinum

Dragon himself, her hair backlit by candlelight, her eyes just as filled with tears as Kima's. "You're allowed to grieve however you need to."

Kima reached up, slowly, to grab Allura's hand by the wrist, pulling her fingers away from her chin—and then placing them upon her cheek. She leaned into the touch, pressing Allura's palm into what, moments ago, had been tear-soaked skin, savoring the warmth and the *realness* of her.

Ghenn might be gone. Sirus and Dohla might be gone. Drake was so deep in his drink he was unreachable.

But they still had each other. The person each of them needed most. Their protector. Right here, right now—they still had this.

Kima had defended her arcanist. And they stood here together, after the fight, able to piece each other back together in whatever way they needed to.

That was enough. It was going to have to be enough.

Without speaking, without even looking up to see Allura's expression, Kima pulled Allura's palm to her lips and pressed a soft kiss to Allura's most dangerous weapon. She heard an intake of breath, but Allura didn't pull away—and that was all Kima needed right now.

"Don't ever," she mouthed into Allura's palm, "get hurt like that," Kima pressed another kiss to the pulse point at Allura's wrist, feeling her heart beat through the thin skin, imagining she could see it pulse through veins as blue as her magic, "*again.*"

Until Allura touched her thigh gently, Kima hadn't even realized she'd been doing it—grasping her own leg with her nails so tightly she had drawn blood. She heard Allura suck in air through her teeth at the sudden gruesomeness of it; but just as quickly, Kima loosened her grip, softly tracing over Allura's kind and empathetic hand with her own fingertips, over and over, the comforting heat of her healing magic flowing between them both, out and through and in, sealing up the wounds on her thighs but not coming close to touching the ones in her heart.

"I make no promises," Allura said, her voice tender but firm. Kima finally allowed herself to look up at her arcanist—and was not at all prepared for what she saw there in her eyes. "And I'm sick of watching you recklessly risk your life for others, even when they haven't asked it of you. It will only end in heartbreak."

Kima didn't want to think about any of that, not even for a moment. "You're still injured," she said gruffly.

"I am," agreed Allura. "Will you help me?"

Kima nodded, slowly, and reached out toward Allura, preparing for the laying on of hands. To her surprise, Allura dropped to her knees, her robes billowing out around her, putting her eye to eye with Kima.

Kima had knelt before, to honor her god. She saved the gesture for moments of true devotion.

There was no denying what she saw in Allura's face then. And there was no time for Kima to wonder if her desire to worship Allura in turn would destroy her pact with her god.

She found, in that moment, she did not care.

Slowly, carefully, Kima placed one hand on Allura's cheek. She watched as the angelic figure leaned in slightly to her touch. The other hand went directly to the center of Allura's chest, right over her heart. Kima could feel it pounding through her robes, the blue offsetting her eyes in the way Kima knew, now, that Allura did on purpose. She held her hands still and closed her eyes, just for a moment, listening to and feeling Allura's breath come quicker and quicker.

Finally, she let her magic loose, unraveling it from her chest like a knot, feeling its warmth spread through her chest, down her arms, and finally through her hands, where it flowed over Allura's chest and neck in waves. Putting her will into it, Kima forced the magic through Allura's skin with a gentle thrust, pushing it to where it needed to be, finding all the spots that wanted her touch, her healing—the places that hurt, the places that ached, the places that demanded attention and the ones that asked for it more quietly still. They were all equally important.

To Kima, every part of Allura was important.

Kima opened her eyes and found Allura staring right back, on an even keel, for once, from her vantage point on her knees. She noticed that one of Allura's hands was twitching, but it wasn't random; she was absentmindedly tracing some sort of sigils in the air, a matter of habit, muscle memory when she was in an overwhelming situation.

"We were lucky today," she said, still staring into Kima's dark eyes.

Kima shook her head in response, not moving her hands from Allura's body. "No," she said quietly. "We had each other."

And then Allura's lips were on her lips, and they were immediately lost in each other, in the moment, in the comfort of solid bodies and wild heartbeats. Kima ran her hands across Allura's soft curves, so the opposite of her own sturdy build, and found herself reveling in the realness of it all. They were here, and they had lived, and they would continue to live, even through the grief and heartache of it all.

This was far from the first time Kima had kissed a woman. She'd been on the road for years, and she was hot, and the work was stressful, and stress needed dealing with, and drink wasn't always the answer.

But something here—something today—was different. Something was—

Suddenly, Allura grasped Kima's hands, her hold stronger than Kima thought it would be, blessedly shaking Kima from her reverie before she could get much further. Allura looked up at Kima with seriousness—not faux-seriousness, but actual concern. "I won't leave marks. We have to be respectable after this."

Kima laughed, shaking her hands out of Allura's grip. "Please," she said, hoping the break in her voice didn't betray anything she wasn't ready to admit.

"They'll heal," Kima continued with more confidence, a wicked gleam in her eyes, "when I say so."

Blue light flared, and Kima came to, groggy but alive. She was relieved to find that Allura was still clinging tightly to her, and that there seemed to be less blood in the water. But her relief once again turned to devastation just as quickly when her brain caught up with their current circumstances: Allura wasn't strong enough to keep them both afloat for much longer. Hells, not even Kima was strong enough for that.

But they were here, and they were holding hands, and Allura was saying something to her, and Kima was trying to concentrate on exactly what it was.

"It's all right," she was repeating. "It's all right. We're alive. I—I don't know where we are. But . . . we'll figure this out. We'll figure this out."

Whenever Allura got flustered, she started doing this, saying phrases over and over again like a chant or a mantra, trying to make it as real as she would a spell she brought to life with her hands and with her words. Kima rarely heard it; Allura's whole thing was that she was calm, cool, and collected in even the direst of circumstances.

All at once, the crushing pressure of the water receded in her mind, replaced by the familiar, bizarrely comforting pressure that was the typical background radiation of her daily life: her duty.

Kima would not be responsible for Allura's mental state sinking as quickly as her poor gauntlets and boots. Hanging on to her for dear life, Kima strained her neck, squinting over the white swells to try to find the location of the sun.

"North!" She pointed with one of her fingers while still keeping her grip around Allura's neck. "Our best shot at getting back to the beach," she clarified—then was cut off abruptly as they were caught up in a huge wave.

"You're sure?!" Allura spluttered when they resurfaced.

"No!" Kima shouted back. "But it's the best I've got!"

Allura nodded, keeping one hand secure around Kima's shoulders and freeing the other to help them swim forward together as a unit. They made it—a couple of minutes? Maybe less? It was so hard to tell out here, and the swells kept blotting out the light—before:

"Hold your breath!"

And the next wave tore them apart.

Kima had let Allura go. She might never find her again. She might be dead already—

And the thought of it suffocated her almost as much as the sea-foam in her lungs.

Kima sat in the kitchen with Allura, eating her breakfast with uneasy contentment. Allura smiled at her over her teacup, still in her worn housecoat. She looked so beautiful in the mornings. And the afternoons, Kima supposed. And also the evenings. And the middle of the night, of course.

Ugh. She was really *in it.*

It had been nearly a year since they'd lost the Mors. And it had been a difficult one, to be sure—first came memorial services, then a move to the city, and a refactoring of everything Kima had been building for herself until now. She and Allura found rooms above a bookshop, subsidized by funds from Allura's wealthy father, who was just happy she'd given up the adventuring life (for now, anyway). Allura and Kima had mourned together, but Drake had pushed them away—though they still made time to see him when they could. Tulip and Coriander slowly came to a truce that included Tulip chasing him around their apartment only very occasionally.

And, of course, the grief and guilt. The crushing weight of it all. When she woke up, Kima would forget for a moment, before it would all come rushing back. And then there was no escaping it.

"Whatever stupid thing you're going to say," advised Allura, sipping on her tea, "I wouldn't."

Kima looked over at her lover in surprise. "How did you—?"

Allura raised an eyebrow that might as well have contained the entirety of several volumes of text.

Every day, Kima would get up and make sure her armor was in fighting shape. She kept it polished and oiled, cleaned and sparkling. She kept a live edge on her swords, and solid bolts on her hammers. She saved and invested in new boots, and for her birthday, Allura surprised her by absconding with her armor one night while Kima was at the pub and getting it washed in a subtle and gorgeous shade of gold. "For my fiercest warrior," she said. "My protector. My lion."

Kima had never felt less like a lion. She loved her life with Allura—they made for good roommates, and they brought each other so much comfort.

Plus, Allura made a mean sunny-side up egg.

"There's too much out there, Allura," Kima said, already dreading the rest of the conversation and yet knowing it was inevitable. "I took an oath."

"And you're not fulfilling it here?" Allura demanded, pausing to crunch with barely disguised frustration on a piece of toast.

"I've told you, Allura, the dragon has been—" Kima stopped. It was too hard to see Allura's beautiful, perfect mouth twisted into hurt like that.

"Yes, you have. And you have to risk it all—for what? Some unclear visions?"

Kima looked away from the now-familiar conversation. They had come to a standstill on this issue many times, and she was torn. She wasn't entirely sure if she was in love. Kima had never been in love in her life, and how does a person even know when it's true? Everyone says you just *know.* But Kima was no arcanist; her biceps had always been more reliable than her brain. She had her sword and her god and her devotion—split though they felt these days.

"I can't stay," Kima said plaintively, and it was the truest thing she had to offer. "I can't. I don't see a path forward for me in the city. There are so many out there that the dragon's gift could touch, lives I could change . . . How can I stay here, knowing that there's something out there and I'm the one responsible for stopping it?"

When Allura didn't speak for several moments, Kima was finally forced to look at her again. She expected anger; what she found was much, much worse.

"Is there really nothing for you here?" Allura asked quietly. "Is this a gilded cage?"

No. The problem was not that she was a lion imprisoned by the city. The problem was that she was a divine sword, and her purpose could not and would not be limited to patrolling the city streets. The Platinum Dragon had plenty of devoted followers who did the good work in Emon every single day, and they were far better suited to it than Kima. Unable to fulfill her role here in the city, Kima would chafe and fall into resentment. Emon was Allura's dream: settled and happy and safe in one place, helping people on a scale that was impossible for individual adventurers on the road. But there was something so empty about it, so monotonous.

Not Allura, of course. She was glorious, every day. But Allura couldn't make up for everything. Nor should she. No one person should be responsible for all that.

"Does your oath really not include looking after your own heart, Lady Kima of Vord?"

Allura's question landed heavy at Kima's feet.

The Platinum Dragon had always taken care of her, always called on her to put others first. And that call had never been more urgent.

Lately, Kima had been receiving dark visions from the dragon: There was a rot spreading in Tal'Dorei. A hideousness; a blight. It had to be fixed, and she was the one chosen to fix it. She knew it in her soul—and following her faith, Kima feared, was even more important than following her heart.

And it was going to tear them apart for good.

"We're a team, Kima, and you are not invincible. You are more than a protector; you're a person, whole and real. You're *my* person. And if you go—if you go out there, on your own, without me," said Allura, and Kima could hear the pain and the realization in her voice, "I'm afraid you may never come back. And I don't know how to handle that."

When there was no light—when it was all darkness—there was no way to tell time.

That was probably for the best. Kima could not—*would* not—think about how many sunrises and sunsets she had missed chained to a rack underground, her skin flayed and her bones shattered, trying desperately to ignore the many different kinds of agony.

She existed to help those in need. That was what made her Lady Kima of Vord. Her dedication to the dragon, and her dedication to others.

So why was she here, strapped to a table, naked and screaming into the darkness?

Why was she here, when the one person who had ever bothered to wonder who she was sat an eternity away, thinking that Kima had abandoned her?

What was she when she had nothing to give?

Lying there, it was all Kima could consider. How poor of a decision she had made in facing the darkness under Tal'Dorei alone. Allura had warned her, all those years ago, and again weeks before Kima set off for the darkness. The letter she'd sent, the one begging Kima to reconsider, had been taken from its place in the pocket nearest her heart and burned in an opening salvo of cruelty. Kima had thought she was touched by the gods, and that was enough to justify any and all of her choices, no matter how reckless.

But Allura had been right, like she so often was. They were a team. Kima had been good, before, but no one exemplar is an island. The truth was that Kima was *better* with Allura—better with someone reminding her that she didn't always have to be the one to stick her neck out. When her arcanist was at her back, Kima had more than a purpose—she had a *partner.* And a constant reminder that she was of more use alive than buried underground.

Though, Kima thought, it was better to be buried underground than to be alive underground.

And then her tormentors were back; and the hooks, and the cutting, and the screaming.

She lived without hope or logic. But when she closed her eyes to float away from all of it, she saw blond braids and blue eyes. A slobbering shepherd and a little orange cat. And that was enough to keep her going.

It had to be, when everything else was black.

And it was black, it was lightless and fathomless, and her lungs were filled not with blood but with brine, and there was nowhere to go but back down into the darkness.

But was that, above her, a pinprick of light?

It was sunlight. Sunlight bouncing off Allura's golden hair and lighting up her blue eyes so brightly that she had to shield them from the sun, Kima noticed, watching Allura open the door to her gleaming white tower. Just like Kima, she had more lines etched onto her beautiful face than she had when they'd met; a touch of white in her blonde. She was all the more perfect for it.

"My lord, you've all arrived!" Allura said to her escort, and, fair enough, the Vox Machina crew were pretty distracting with all their . . . everything, going on. Allura hadn't noticed her in the back, not yet, and she would wait patiently through a round of hugs and platitudes and pleasantries until finally, *finally* one of them said, "We've brought you a present."

And then there—the full force of her attention was on Kima, and it was all worth it. The pain and the brutality and the nights where she might have died but didn't, all to find herself here, looking back at Allura—at the one person who knew her, *truly* knew her, in a world where no one else did, and few people ever, ever cared to ask.

There were certainly fewer people still that Kima would care to answer.

And then they were flying into each other's arms, and Kima could barely breathe with the weight of it, her arcanist—the smell of her, of her at *home,* the fragrances she wore and the tea she loved to drink still hot on her breath, and oh gods, her *breath* on Kima's neck, and she could hear her whispering something but wasn't sure what it was, and when she finally asked, Allura just said, "Oh, you know," and Kima laughed and said, "I know," and that was that.

Well, not entirely.

Allura had been furious. After they'd been reunited for several hours—days? Hard to keep track, sometimes, honestly—she had laid into Kima like no one ever had, not even in the most difficult days of her training in the temple.

"Selfish," Allura listed off, counting on Kima's own fingers. "Foolhardy. Wasteful. *Stupid.*"

Kima had taken a breath to respond, but Allura wasn't yet finished.

"Cruel," Allura added softly, and it broke Kima's heart.

Still, Kima thought she remembered what happened after their reunion in Emon—she knew there'd been a meeting and then the council and then a million other things, but apparently memory while dying doesn't quite work like that, and instead she found herself with her arms around Allura another time, after a bastard had bespelled the brilliance out of Allura and Kima had found her curled up in a corner, terrified, hardly sure of where or who she was, lashing out at anyone who came close to her—

But not Kima. Even under the dark psychic hold of an evil mage, something inside of Allura had known Kima, and Kima had been able to calm her, convincing her to stay alive, that it would all be okay, because Kima's job was to make it okay.

But everything wasn't okay. Not quite yet—they still agreed to take things slowly, to go back to being friends until they were sure there was trust again, to ignore all the other things they felt about each other, to ignore the fact that she was drowning, right now, oh gods—

THERE WAS A MOMENT, UNDER the waves, alone, where Kima began to think about stopping.

She'd been fighting her entire adult life. It would be so, so easy to just . . . not. Her armor was so heavy, and her legs were so tired, and she felt as though even the muscles moving her lungs were getting ready to give out. It would be so much easier to just let herself succumb to the water's icy embrace. Perhaps this was the dragon's vengeance for letting his loyal devotee Ghenn be taken. She could have done more to save him.

It was her job to save people. Especially—

Kima's legs started to kick almost of their own volition as her brain finally snapped back on, and when she broke the surface, Allura was only a few feet away. There was no keeping them apart, it seemed.

"Still head north?" Kima gasped out, her exhausted body starting to betray her.

Allura held fast to Kima with one hand while treading water with the other, peering toward the horizon at the peak of a swell. "I . . ." She shook her head in despair. There was nothing but ocean in every direction, and they both knew it. The search was pointless. "I don't know. I don't know how we get out of this, Kima."

"Together," Kima said firmly, shaking water out of her eyes.

And that was true. They could do anything together. Kima held her breath at the top of a swell to keep the brine out of her lungs as she peered around the surface one last time, a small part of her still holding out hope . . . but there was nothing. Water, and more water. It hardly mattered; her extremities were so numb from the cold that she couldn't feel it anyway.

Kima would not let Allura die. Her mission was to uphold justice. And holding on to Kima, her heavy armor and all, was putting Allura directly *in* the path of an unjust death, not out of it.

There was little hope of both of them lasting long enough for help to arrive, and Kima knew that Allura would put herself into the path of danger over and over again if it meant possibly saving Kima.

So there was only one thing to do.

Kima looked at Allura's panicked face, occasionally obscured by foamy waves, and knew what she had known for years, really, without wanting to admit it: that she loved this woman, more than she had ever loved anyone. That she was *in* love with her. Her arcanist.

And now might not have been the moment to say it. But she could *show* it. In the best way she knew how.

"Let go of me," Kima said, knowing Allura could hear her even over the crash of the ocean.

Allura looked over, bewildered. "What?"

"I'm too heavy."

She would mourn Kima. But she would recover, like they had before.

Kima heard Allura's fierce protests as she shoved herself away from her arcanist, and finally, *finally,* stilled her aching legs.

And then she let herself sink beneath the surface, saving Allura one last time.

"THAT WAS *SO* STUPID."

Kima opened her eyes with a gasp and was shocked to find that her lungs did not fill with water as she expected them to. Instead, she noted first that she was seated, and then that she was seated on extremely solid ground. In a forest, it looked like, with dirt under her hands and thick tree cover overhead, light piercing through the canopy in the places it was thinnest. It looked . . . *wrong,* but not in a bad way; it was difficult for Kima to process exactly what she was experiencing. It was all just a little *too* real.

"I think I was drowning," she said.

"You *are* drowning."

"Ah," Kima said. "Well, that's all right, then. As long as Allura's okay."

"*Ugh.*" There was a grunt, and a figure stepped out of the trees. It was a priest, clearly, barefooted even on the sharp sticks and fallen pine needles. He had blond hair and deeply tanned skin. He wore traditional black-and-silver priest's robes, wrapped with red string, and held a well-worn staff.

"Even for one of mine, you're absolutely hopeless." The priest plucked a blade of grass, still covered in morning dew, from the forest floor, and licked the moisture clean off the stem. He closed his eyes in delight, savoring the taste of the dew for just a moment before letting the blade drop back down to the ground, which absorbed it whole. "I like that about you, Lady Kima," he finished. When he looked toward her, she saw that his eyes glowed a deep, golden yellow.

She scrambled up from her cross-legged position, landing on her knees and dropping her forehead to the mossy forest floor.

"My lord," she breathed. There was no mistaking him, not even in this form, not now that Kima had her faculties about her once again.

This was the champion of the downtrodden, the dispossessed, the helpless. This was the Lord of the North Wind, the world's only Platinum Dragon.

And this was her god.

Kima felt a gentle finger under her chin, and it tilted her head upward to stare directly into her patron's eyes. She tried to avert her gaze in humility and found that she couldn't.

"I have to save her," Kima said plainly. She couldn't do anything else but be honest. "It's the only thing I can think of. No one is coming to save us; she'll drown if she tries to hang on to me."

The golden priest—her *god*—smiled at her the way one might look at a child trying their very best to draw something that turns out looking like a three-necked bear on drugs. "You don't know that. It's an awfully great risk to take."

"It's worth it." Kima didn't even hesitate. "For her, anything is worth it."

"And why is that?" asked the God of Dragons, with absolutely none of the urgency that the situation demanded. For some reason, Kima found that she couldn't feel stress anymore either—nor fear, nor despair. Just . . . peace.

"Because," she answered slowly. "Because I'm in love with her."

He made a sound with his tongue like a *tsk.* "So close. Do you want to try again?"

Kima frowned. "But I *am* in love with her."

The Platinum Dragon rolled his golden eyes. "I know *that,* child, I've known that *far* longer than you. I'm asking you *why.*"

"I just—"

Her god sighed, cutting her off. "*Yes,* dying helps your arcanist. But does it help *you*? Listen to me, Lady Kima of Vord." And suddenly, Kima found she could do nothing else. "You have spent your life in service to others: to me, first, and then to those in need. But hear me when I say this, little lion: Your rage is worthy. Your anger at the injustices of this world is *worthy.* You do not have to do anything for *me,* Lady Kima. Your existence is devotion enough. Your truest power comes from your faith in *yourself,* not in me."

He paused, then hastily added, "Well, most of it comes from me. I'm using a metaphor. Regardless, tell me again."

Kima found her throat suddenly worked again. "Because . . ." Lady Kima said slowly, contemplating what she had just heard. She had the vague feeling that she would be processing all of this for years to come, but the part of her brain that usually held higher-functioning thoughts like that simply wasn't working right now. "Because there are people who love me. *Me.* Not just what I can do for them. And that is worth living for."

"Ah." Her god dropped her chin and stepped backward, sticking his hands into his pockets. "Good. Then you can go."

Kima just knelt there. "I can go?"

"Yes." The dragon nodded. "It took you long enough, but we don't judge people who are late to the truth. We are just happy when they find it at all."

Kima swallowed. "So am . . . am I dead? I'm going to the underworld?"

Her god laughed. "No, Lady Kima of Vord. You're not. You are, perhaps, the most alive you've ever been."

Did dragons ever not talk in code?

"But there's one problem: Are you prepared to name it?"

The exemplar sat for a moment, thinking. She had stayed true to her oath for years. She felt powerful to remember it . . . and yet, somehow, disconnected from it.

Kima had once decided to become a creature devoted solely to fighting for others. It was the path she had seen, coming out of that difficult and destitute life she'd lived as a child, that would allow her to return everything she had been given by her god. She had fought for the downtrodden; for Ghenn; for her team.

And she had never, ever fought harder than she had fought for one Allura Vysoren, the love of her life.

But she felt something else, even stronger, in the back of her mind. In her *soul.* Perhaps . . . perhaps there was something the Platinum Dragon was trying to say to her—something that, Kima hated to admit even now, she recognized Allura had been gently pushing her toward for years. That there was something else worth fighting for, even more than love. Even more than *the* love.

Herself.

"How could you ever hope to care for those around you if you leave care for yourself by the wayside entirely?" said her god. "You have fought well. I was right to choose you as my champion. But that's the key, I fear: I chose *you.* I trust *you.* Will you not take that trust and use it to make yourself whole? To provide love, care, and protection not only for others, but for *yourself*—and, in doing so, allow yourself to help make those around you whole?"

When he put it like that, she realized how simple it could be.

"Yes," the Platinum Dragon said with a nod, though Kima had not spoken a word. "Then I will return you home." He held out a hand. "Bow, my golden lion."

So Kima bowed her head, and she was surrounded by light, and she bathed in the loving glow of her god—

And then she woke up.

"Kima, hold on!"

Kima crested the surface of the waves one last time, coughing up so much water she didn't think she should have been alive; and yet here she was. Allura floated in the air above her, a hand wrapped around Kima's forearm.

"Keep holding on!" someone shouted. If Kima squinted, she could just make out a silhouette perched on a broomstick, their hair whipping in the fierce winds. Vex'ahlia?

"I'm—trying—" Allura gritted out in response.

"I have them!" Vex yelled. She grasped Allura's free hand.

And suddenly, Kima was being hoisted out of the water, Allura's grip stronger than it had *any* right to be.

Almost as though she had been blessed by a god himself.

"We're almost close enough." Kima could hear the clench in Allura's teeth. Hanging on took all of her effort—and then her arcanist shouted: "*Now!*"

All she saw, for the briefest of moments, was blue.

Kima had not meant to find herself in the middle of the sea, but that was where protecting Allura had taken her. She had nearly drowned; she had met her god. She wondered, for a brief and delirious moment: Was she supposed to feel different? Was it the rush of endorphins and adrenaline and oxygen into her bloodstream that was making her head spin, was making her armor feel weightless, her sense of purpose renewed and more certain than ever?

And, more than that . . . new?

It was all too much for right now. And when she blinked the light of Allura's spellwork away, Kima wasn't in the ocean; nor was she suspended from a broomstick in the air.

Instead, she was on a magic carpet.

"Agh!" came another well-bred voice from behind her. Kima swung around—Percy, looking the worst she'd ever seen him. "Oh," he said, smiling at her in exhaustion. "I'm so tired."

And then arms wrapped around her from behind, and Kima spun, and she knew before she even knew that the arms were Allura's, and that they were both alive, and they were soaked to their cores, and frozen, and sapped of all strength—

But Kima buried her face into Allura's shoulder, and she hugged her as tight as she ever had, and she allowed herself to cry.

"Oh, my dear," Allura said into Kima's ear, quiet enough that Percy couldn't hear them over the wind—he was too busy keeping the carpet aloft and aimed at the shore to notice, anyway. "My darling. My little lion. I thought I'd lost you."

"Not for lack of trying," Kima muttered. "I won't do that to you again. I promise. Allura—" Kima craned her head back. Nothing felt more important than this, at this very second. Not even breathing. "I love you. I can't believe I haven't said it sooner. I've been an idiot. I'm so sorry. I love you. I've always loved you. Please tell me you feel the same. I couldn't bear it if—"

And then she couldn't say anything else because Allura's mouth was on hers, and she was whispering "I love you, too" through their kiss, and not even Percy's silent proximity could ruin the moment. They sat there, wet and half-dead, holding each other, as they sped back to the beach.

And they would never, ever be apart again. Kima would make certain of it.

THE LIVES WE MAKE

Rebecca Coffindaffer

Kynan Leore only smelled gunpowder in his nightmares.

There had been months, not so long ago, when the acrid tang of it had been his constant companion, hanging in the air in a haze, burrowing into his clothes. He had slept with it surrounding him, embedded in the blankets of his bedroll.

But not anymore. Not since he came to Whitestone.

Which was how he knew this had to be a nightmare.

He knelt in the middle of Greyfield cemetery, the lumpy, indistinct shapes of headstones crowding around him like pale ghosts, the Zenith looming tall against the dark horizon. Dew and damp earth soaked into the knees of his woolen pants, and a cold, sharp breeze cut through the night, making him shiver. Some kind of wet, sticky substance covered his hands and fingers and the front of his clothes.

Another gust of wind, carrying a familiar scent—dark and metallic underneath the gunpowder smoke.

Blood.

Kynan rubbed frantically at the gunk coating his fingers, but all he did was spread it around more until it was all over his wrists and his forearms. It was just mud, it *had* to be mud.

But it was too dark to know for sure. Or maybe he didn't want to know for sure.

Something moved in the deep shadows. He couldn't see it, but he could hear it. The creaking of branches and a soft sucking sound, like when you pull your boot out of marshy ground. And a sibilant hiss, barely audible on the breeze.

Kynan shot to his feet, heart pounding—

And suddenly, he wasn't in the middle of the Greyfield anymore. He was standing on the street, just outside the iron cemetery gates, the Eastern Ruins sitting mist-shrouded and silent off to his left. Gone were his woolen pants and shirt, replaced by his thin nightclothes. Gone were his boots; he stood barefoot now.

Gone was the gun smoke and the blood. As if they had never been there at all.

"Move your feet!"

Kynan shifted his weight back, slanting his sword down across his body to block an incoming blow. He braced himself for the jarring clash of metal on metal—but it never came. His opponent feinted, swept low, and, a moment later, Kynan's back hit the ground hard enough to raise a little cloud of dust.

Dammit. He struggled to sit up, groaning at the bruised and battered muscles all over his body. Every move he made today felt off—wrong and sluggish—and his head was muddled. Full of cobwebs.

Probably because you woke up outside the cemetery with no idea how or why.

A shadow fell across him, and he looked up into the narrowed dark eyes and unimpressed expression of Captain Jarett Howarth. Jarett cut the perfect heroic figure in the dark grays and yellows of the Pale Guard, Whitestone's city watch, the blunted training sword loose in his grip and bright sunlight arrayed around him like a halo. Even the fresh, angry red scars on the side of his neck managed to somehow make him look more dashing, a symbol of how he'd gallantly defended Tal'Dorei from an evil, tyrannical dragon.

Kynan glanced down at his own clothes, streaked with dust and dirt, the muted brown marking him as a mere trainee. A hot flush of embarrassment rose in his cheeks, and he dropped his head so Jarett wouldn't see. The last thing he needed was to give the captain another reason to critique him.

Jarett held out his free hand, offering to help Kynan up. "You're slower than usual today."

Kynan grimaced. *Slower than usual.* Implying that he was already slow as it was.

"I'm just a little off," Kynan said. "I didn't sleep well last night." He climbed to his feet on his own, pretending not to see the proffered hand. *Shit.* His back really hurt. He'd hit the ground harder than he'd realized.

Jarett snorted and reached out, poking Kynan hard right in the middle of his forehead. "You think you can use that as an excuse? You have to be able to fight in any circumstances or you'll end up with a sword in your belly." He strode off toward the weapons rack on the side of the training pitch, adding over his shoulder, "It's not as if your enemy is going to check if you need a nap before attacking you, pup."

Kynan never knew how he felt about that nickname: "pup." Jarett always said it lightheartedly, but part of Kynan bristled against it. Wanted to scream that he wasn't a *pup,* he wasn't a *kid,* he couldn't be *pushed around anymore—*

"I'm trying, okay?" Kynan picked up his own training sword from the dirt, wiping it clean on the hem of his shirt as he followed Jarett off the pitch. "I've made a lot of progress. . . ." He hesitated, stretching the silence out, hoping Jarett would hear the question Kynan wasn't asking.

But he didn't. So Kynan was forced to add, "Haven't I?"

Jarett grabbed a clean rag hanging from the rack, swiping at the dust and sweat on his face. "Haven't you what?"

Of course Jarett wouldn't get it, of course Kynan would have to spell it out for him. The man probably hadn't had a single moment of self-doubt in his entire life. "Have I made progress? Am I doing all right, I mean? Do you think . . . I'm going to be *good* at this?"

Jarett shrugged, tossing the rag back onto the rack. "You're doing fine. Coming along as well as anyone else I've trained."

Anyone else.

You're no different from anyone else.

Anger opened up in Kynan's chest—twisted, thorny snarls of it, an old, familiar friend. He couldn't remember a day of his life when it hadn't been there, digging deep roots into his belly, whispering and snapping in the back of his head, telling him that he was going to be lost, forgotten, less than a footnote in history. Just another poor kid from the Upper Slums who was born from nothing and became nothing.

He'd left Emon on a journey to try to cut it out of himself. He'd followed Ripley, thinking she was his answer, doing everything she'd asked because her lies had sounded like promises. And look how all that had ended.

"Let's call it a day, eh?" Jarett scooped his dark gray cape off the ground, patting the dust off before slinging it over his shoulder. "Come get some food with me and stop all your worrying for a bit. It gives you bad posture, makes you slouch."

Kynan stepped away, shaking his head. The thought of going into the mess hall where there were always people around was . . . too much. "No. I'm not really that hungry."

Jarett paused, frowning at him, and for a moment, Kynan thought—*hoped*—he might insist on him coming. He might make it clear that Kynan wasn't just conveniently nearby, but that Jarett actually wanted his company.

But then it passed, and he just shrugged and clapped Kynan on his shoulder. "Suit yourself. Make sure you get some sleep tonight. We'll be running those drills again tomorrow." He headed off down the hill toward the mess hall, calling back as he went, "I want to see you moving quicker, easier. No more excuses."

No room in the barracks could really be called opulent, but Kynan's was sparser than most. He'd arrived in Whitestone in a fog of blood and guilt with even fewer possessions than when he'd fled Emon. Vax'ildan had given him daggers, which he kept tucked securely into sheaths on his body, and the snake belt—Simon—but all he'd added since then were two sets of trainee uniforms . . .

And the long wooden box half-hidden in the shadows under his bed.

Kynan knelt down on the rough slats of the floor, slipping a small silver key out of his pocket and unlocking the box with a soft click. Nestled inside on folds of dark cloth was the rifle Lord de Rolo had given him.

One of Ripley's.

He'd promised Lord de Rolo he'd be responsible with it, keep it safe, make sure it didn't fall into the wrong hands. He'd also promised that he'd build on what Lord de Rolo had shown him, what Ripley had taught him . . .

Kynan let the lid fall shut with a snap. He couldn't do it. He wasn't touching that thing, let alone firing it.

Jamming the key back into the lock, Kynan twisted it closed and then stood, kicking the box deeper underneath his bed.

Out of sight.

The cold wind cut through the skinny trunks of young spruce trees, its voice harsh and hissing. Even with layers on underneath his overcoat and a balaclava wrapped around his head and neck, Kynan shivered. But he kept creeping silently forward, his footsteps not even making a whisper of sound on the carpet of dead needles. Just ahead of him, he saw his targets–a woman and a man, wrapped in their own winter clothes, seated on logs around a campfire. Beyond them, three tents sat huddled together, dusted with frost.

In one silent blur of movement, Kynan surged forward, grabbing the back of the man's hood. The man cried out, startled, but went very still at the feel of a pin-sharp dagger point against his neck.

Kynan grinned. "And just like that, Brath? You're dead."

The woman–Sardel–looked at Kynan with wide eyes, awestruck. "That was incredible!"

"So impressive." Brath swallowed nervously. "Would love to not have a knife to my neck anymore, though?"

Laughing a little, Kynan sheathed his dagger, clapping Brath on the back. He hadn't been sure, at first, when Ripley had added the brother and sister to the group. They were older than him; he thought they might outshine him or treat him like a little kid. But they'd shown a lot of appreciation for what he could do.

Crossing to the other side of camp, Kynan dropped down onto the hard ground next to Ripley, who was sitting cross-legged outside her tent, carefully polishing and cleaning the pieces of her pepper-box pistol, Animus. As far as Kynan could tell, Issylra seemed constantly socked in by low, brooding gray clouds, but even in this dim form of daylight, the deep gray metal and brass of Animus seemed to gleam.

"That was impressive, Leore," Ripley said without looking up.

Kynan flushed–not that anyone could really tell given how pink his cheeks already were from the cold. He liked how she called him by his surname. It made him feel older for some reason. She didn't call anyone else by their surname. Just Kynan. Like he'd earned a level of respect from her the others had not.

He flipped one of his daggers in his hand, shrugging off the compliment. "It's not much. Just a few tricks I've picked up."

Ripley shook her head as she clicked the last piece of Animus into place and slipped it back into its holster. "Don't shortchange yourself. You've got real talent. Trust me, I don't waste my time with mediocre people." She tilted her head, eyeing Brath and Sardel, who were alternating trying to take each other down just like Kynan had shown them. "Don't you notice how they look at you? They see it, too."

Kynan followed her gaze, frowning. "See what?"

Ripley turned to him, and even though, in his head, she was always sharp and calculating, the cold edge of a knife, there were times when she looked at him that Kynan thought he saw her soften a little. "That you're going to be something special. A leader. All you need is a little guidance."

The warm, glowing feeling in Kynan's chest flickered a little. "Like from a mentor?"

"Exactly."

He could still see it, as clearly as if it had happened yesterday and not weeks ago. Vax'ildan in front of Greyskull Keep, somehow so much taller, stronger, more intimidating than Kynan had even imagined. *Come back when you're ready. Come back again. Train yourself, and I, personally, will be your mentor.*

Kynan's gaze dropped to his lap. "He promised me that. That he'd be my mentor."

"And you believed him?" Ripley's tone was incredulous, and Kynan burned with embarrassment all over again. How stupid he'd been, camping outside that castle, and for what? A bruise on his skull, and a wound in his pride. A headache for days afterward, a bitter taste lingering in his mouth.

Things move very fast with us. I don't think you understand what you're asking for.

So much for heroes.

Ripley sighed, leaning back on her hands, watching Brath and Sardel spar without really seeing them. "You can't trust people like him, Leore. They're only ever looking out for themselves, their own reputation, their own greatness. He probably looked at you and saw someone who could eclipse him."

Kynan's eyes widened. That... seemed a little impossible. But then again, Ripley was one of the smartest people he'd ever met, and she'd seen a lot more of the world than he had. "You really think so?"

"It wouldn't surprise me in the slightest. That'd be just like one of *them.*" For one flickering moment, her face twisted with disgust, and then it was gone and she was looking at him with that almost soft expression. "You were never meant to live in his shadow, though. You were meant to be here, with me. My right hand." She reached out and set a hand on his shoulder, warm and steady through the layers of his coat. "And together? Together, you and I are going to do great things."

The crossbow sat heavy and awkward in Kynan's hands, and he shifted it around, clumsily adjusting to get it into a better position. The polished wood stock dug into the front of his shoulder as he sighted down the bolt. On the other side of the training pitch, stacks of hay bales had been set up with concentric circles painted on them.

Kynan tried to steady his aim on the center mark, but his body didn't seem to want to listen. He was too tense—he knew that. Every muscle was bunched and knotted, his insides a writhing mess, his jaw clenched so tight he could hear his teeth grind.

"Remember to exhale as you squeeze the trigger," Jarett said from his spot a few steps away.

Easy for the *Captain Jarett Howarth to say.* "I will," he grumbled.

Jarett scoffed, which only made Kynan even tenser than before. "Are you sure? Because I'm not even sure you're breathing at all at this point—"

"I've *got* it."

Gripping the crossbow as tight as he could, Kynan pulled the trigger. The weapon jerked upward in his grip—because of its own momentum or because of some unconscious movement on Kynan's end, he didn't know. And it didn't matter. All that mattered was the crossbow bolt, sailing in an arc far up over the targets and into the woodland beyond.

A moment later, there was a squawk from some poor bird that was in the wrong place at the wrong time.

Anger ricocheted down Kynan's body, and he threw the crossbow down onto the dirt. "Shit!"

Jarett chuckled, seemingly unfazed. "Well. On the bright side, now we know what we're having for dinner."

"It's not funny!" Snatching the crossbow back up, Kynan marched off the training pitch and threw it toward the weapons rack, still cursing. "Shit, shit, shit!"

"Hey, easy now," Jarett said, ambling up behind him, brow furrowed. "If you break a bow, you're going to have to pay for it. It's just one missed shot."

Kynan scrubbed roughly at his face. Everything inside him felt all snarled up, anger hot in his stomach, anxiety creeping along his skin, and he couldn't tell which one had shown up first or whether they were always together. Twin roots, wrapped and twisted around his insides, slowly strangling him.

"It's my *sixth* missed shot, though, and I'm just getting worse and worse."

"Sometimes you get worse before you get better."

"Helpful advice from the *hero of Whitestone*!" He spun around and gestured furiously at Jarett, standing there looking as cool and polished as ever, like he'd just sprung to life one day fully formed with a crossbow in his hands. "You have no idea what this feels like! You never even have to try!"

Tilting his head back, Jarett laughed, sounding genuinely amused, and it was only when he looked back at Kynan and noticed his expression that the smile dropped off Jarett's face. "Oh, you're serious."

"Of course I am! Look at you!" Kynan held up a hand, ticking his reasonings off one finger at a time. "You're good with every weapon you pick up and blend in with everyone you meet. You never seem to make a mistake or even just have a bad day. You might as well be a member of Vox Machina, for fuck's sake! You just make moving through life look so . . . simple."

Every hint of amusement and good humor faded from Jarett's face. He shifted his weight back, and his eyes got a distant, closed-off look in them. "Not that I owe you any explanation, but I didn't have a choice. I had to fit in everywhere or I'd survive nowhere."

Kynan pulled up short, not quite sure how to respond to that, but before his mouth could catch up to his head, Jarett was already waving him away.

"I don't want to get into it right now," he said. "Lessons are over for today." And with that, he turned and strode off down the hill, his cape billowing softly behind him.

Kynan watched him go, an empty feeling splitting his chest, opening between those angry, vining roots. He knew that closed-off look in Jarett's eyes; he'd seen it before, lots of times. Jarett was giving up on him. Had obviously realized he wasn't worth the time or effort.

Kynan glanced over at the crossbow he'd thrown into the weapons rack. The impact had snapped its string and dented part of its bow. Damaged now. Worthless.

Just like him.

Kynan was in the Greyfield again.

Again.

Every night for the past week he'd found himself kneeling amidst the gravestones, something dark and sticky coating his hands, the scents of blood and gunpowder in his nostrils. And then coming back to himself with a jerk in some random part of Whitestone in his nightclothes, not remembering how he'd gotten there. Not knowing what else to do except drag himself back to bed, where he lay awake, staring through the dark until dawn finally came to rescue him from himself.

Not wanting to say anything, to anyone, because then they might see the rot deep inside him.

But it was different this time. There was a dagger in his hand.

For a moment, he thought it was one of the daggers Vax'ildan had given him, but it was too light in his fingers, and the material of the hilt didn't feel quite right. And then he noticed how the curved blade caught the spare amounts of starlight, dancing and shifting along the metal, and he remembered.

Whisper.

He'd wielded it only briefly, on Glintshore, but it was too unique to ever forget. The way it had felt alive and humming and powerful in his grasp.

The way it had sunk into flesh . . .

He looked closer at the blade, and it wasn't shining anymore. It was covered in something dark and dripping, and he knew it was blood. He knew it. Because there was a body at his feet, sprawled on the damp ground, limbs twisted unnaturally around them. Blood soaked into their clothes and their bright red hair—

Keyleth.

Kynan shut his eyes, digging his knuckles into the sockets, shaking all over. No, no, Keyleth was alive. The others had healed her on Glintshore. This had to be a trick. An illusion of some kind.

He opened his eyes.

The body had changed. Smaller build. Dark brown hair cropped short, with streaks of white at her temples.

You know the white-haired guy I travel with? He's got a sister.

This wasn't happening. . . .

Keep an eye on her and keep her safe.

No! No, he didn't—he couldn't have—

Kynan dropped Whisper, turned his back on the still, small form of Lady de Rolo, and ran.

He pelted, full speed, toward the Zenith and the exit just beyond, heedless of the uneven ground, of how many times he rolled his ankle as he pushed faster and faster.

If he could just get out, if he could just get back to the barracks and into his bed, then it would all disappear and everything would be fine, he would be fine—

A shadow loomed suddenly in front of him.

Kynan skidded to a stop, crashing into a gravestone and clinging to it to keep his feet, even as the shadow began to take shape.

A human, but only partly. Their chest split open along the breastbone, and from out of the hole there sprouted a tree sapling, its twisting trunk half-fused into the person's flesh as it grew up past their shoulder. Thick roots spilled out of their stomach, some dangling loose, others wrapping tight around their legs. Branches from the sapling's trunk curled around their neck and along their horrible, familiar face.

Ripley.

Her skin was gray and sagging on her bones, her sharp eyes dulled by a misty white haze. Black blood dribbled from the corner of her mouth as her lips split wide in a smile, revealing rotting teeth and a swollen purple tongue.

My right hand . . .

Her mouth didn't move, but Kynan heard her voice all the same, echoing around him and inside of him.

My great disappointment . . .

Ripley shambled toward him, her movements stiff and jerky, like a puppet. Kynan pushed off the gravestone and inched backward, unable to tear his eyes from her.

Never good enough. Never strong enough. Never . . . enough . . .

And then she rushed at him, her tree-ravaged corpse suddenly surging forward at an impossible speed. With a shout of alarm, Kynan lurched backward, wrenching his body around to flee, to get away—

—and slammed into the enormous trunk of the Sun Tree, his right shoulder taking most of the impact in a bright burst of pain.

Slowly, his heart still rabbiting inside his chest, Kynan turned, putting his back against the rough bark. All around him were the quiet, empty streets of Whitestone, slumbering under the star-strewn sky.

No gravestones.

No monstrous Ripley reaching for him.

Kynan's legs shook, muscles softened by exhaustion and fear, and he slid down to the ground between the Sun Tree's towering, twisted roots, his head tilted back to stare at the cloud of white flowers above.

He stayed there, underneath those branches, until the pale gray light of dawn.

"Kynan!"

Kynan hit the ground face-first with a thud that knocked the wind from his stomach, dirt and dust filling his mouth. Spluttering, he pushed up onto his hands and knees, rubbing grit from his eyes as he looked around. All around him on the training pitch, other guards and trainees were paired up, blunted swords in hand, but it felt like every single one of them paused what they were doing to watch Kynan climb awkwardly back onto his feet.

Overhead, the sun burned clear and bright, warm for early Dualahei, as if giving everyone a taste of the coming spring.

But *was* it still Dualahei? Time felt so slippery to Kynan right now. He was so exhausted that it sat like an ache in his bones. The appearance of Ripley and then sitting up all night beneath the Sun Tree, unable to even think about closing his eyes—it had left him even more drained than usual. Frankly, it was a miracle that he'd managed to make it out to the training pitch.

"You okay, Kynan?" His training partner for today—Nai—was staring at him in concern. She had hazel-green eyes.

Like Sardel.

Before he could answer, a hand gripped his back collar, spinning him around until he was looking up into Jarett's frowning face. The captain of the Pale Guard stared at Kynan as if he might suddenly sprout fur or antlers.

Or a tree from his chest.

"What in the Hells was that?" Jarett reached out and patted some of the dust from Kynan's uniform, making him cough. "You just stood there watching as she swept your legs out from under you!"

Kynan shivered even in the warm sunlight. "I'm just a little—"

"Off, yes, I know. So you've been saying." Jarett's scowl deepened. "That excuse is getting pretty old, pup."

Irritation prickled down Kynan's spine, and he clenched his jaw against it. "Don't call me pup."

Jarett shook his head, glaring. "You stop acting like one and I'll stop calling you one. How am I supposed to sharpen you into a fighter if this is all you're giving me?"

Supposed to. Because this was just a job to him. Because the only reason he even gave a shit about Kynan was because Vax'ildan was paying him to. "I told you, I'm doing my best."

"And I told you"—Jarett poked him hard in the chest—"there are no points for effort on a battlefield. You either do the work here or you get yourself impaled out there!"

"Maybe I'm just a lost cause, then!" Kynan hadn't actually meant to say that aloud, but it just came spilling out. "Maybe this is a waste of time!"

"Maybe it is!"

Kynan's shoulders sagged, the weight of Jarett's words settling on his chest so naturally it was like they'd always been there. *A lost cause. A waste of time.* Maybe it would be better if he could just sink into the ground, return to the dirt like a worm. Surely that had to be a better option than existing in this tired, aching body for one second longer, waiting for the other shoe to drop.

If Jarett noticed any of this, any change in Kynan's expression or posture, it didn't show. He just stared down at him with that same closed-off look on his face.

"Go," he said in a short, sharp tone. "Get off my training pitch. Don't come back till you have your head on straight."

Kynan felt the eyes of every guard and trainee burning into his back as he threw his sword into the dirt and stalked away.

THE SILVERY ASPEN SHIVERED AS a dagger whistled through the air and buried itself into its trunk.

Twenty feet away, Kynan pinched the tip of another dagger, sighted his target, and threw, feeling a bitter prick of satisfaction as the blade thunked into the living wood.

He'd been at it for hours, hidden in the shadows of the forest around Whitestone, throwing his daggers over and over and over. Trying to drive out all the noisy thoughts and images crowding into his brain.

The cluster of blankets in an impossible mansion, huddled around the cold, pale body of Percival de Rolo.

Keyleth wiping blood from her chin, staring him down as the battle raged all around them, the accusation in her eyes cutting deeper than any knife.

Ripley's face lit by the campfire. The compliments that fell from her mouth, rare and priceless as jewels. The unnatural hunger in her eyes that he didn't really see until it was too late.

His father, reeking of alcohol, face flushed red as he kicked over their spindly kitchen table, sending dishes flying. How Kynan had flinched and then hated himself for flinching. Wished he could be strong enough, dangerous enough, to not have to flinch anymore.

The words of their last fight. Kynan had told his father that he was leaving, he was going to make himself a hero, and his father had hit him, big meaty knuckles meeting the side of Kynan's face.

You think you're above me? Above this house that I provide for you? You're nothing special, boy, trust me. You're no different from anyone else.

Kynan threw another of his daggers, this one hard enough that he heard wood splinter, saw a shard go flying.

He'd left the Upper Slums, swore he would never lay eyes on that place again.

But somehow, the Upper Slums followed him anyway.

"Ripley, I . . . I'm so sorry."

Kynan stood nervously in the middle of the room in a run-down inn on the outskirts of the port city of Shammel. Ripley sat on the bed in front of him, eyes shuttered and closed off, back ramrod straight, hands in her lap, metal fingers laced together with ones of bone and flesh. Sardel and Brath stood off to his left, huddled together up against the wall, diligently looking anywhere except at Kynan. Behind Ripley, standing with her enormous, muscled arms crossed, was Luska, the female half-giant who had joined them not long after Brath and Sardel. Over in the far corner was Giffard, a mage who'd just joined them a couple weeks ago and who was staring at him now with flat gray eyes.

Kynan felt the weight of the stares, the icy chill of disapproval coming off of Ripley. They'd had to scramble to get out of Ank'Harel, and it was all his fault. Ripley had given him an enormous responsibility–to slip into Mistress Asharru's dwelling and assassinate her, quickly and quietly–but he'd failed at the last moment, unable to slit her throat like he'd been instructed.

Instead, Ripley and the others had had to step in and finish the job with guns and knives and magic, making a lot more noise than had been the plan, and then they'd booked it double time over the sands to make sure they were well away by the time Asharru's body was found.

Kynan cleared his throat, balling his fists so tight that his fingernails cut into his palms. "I know I made a mistake–"

"Is that what you would call it? A mistake?" Ripley's voice was so calm, so cold. He'd never heard her use that tone with him before. Other people, maybe, but not him. "Luska," she called, and the half-giant straightened a little. "What would you call it?"

Luska leveled a glare at Kynan and growled, "A royal fuckup."

"Sardel? Brath?"

Kynan looked over at the siblings, who both looked deeply uncomfortable but also weren't about to disagree with Ripley.

"He put us all at risk," Brath said, his eyes still on his boots.

"He put Boss's plans at risk most of all," added Sardel, and she was rewarded with a little smile and a nod from Ripley. She visibly brightened, apparently much less uncomfortable now that she'd received some slight praise.

Ripley stood slowly, clasping her hands behind her back as she stalked forward. She stepped right up to Kynan, but she didn't look at him. She looked past him, as if he weren't there.

"I'll tell you what I would call it," she said in a voice for only his ears. "A *disappointment.* I expect a blunder like this from the rest of these fools, but you? Who I saw so much promise in? Who had me believing I had a true partner in my plans?" She sighed, and the disillusionment in it was so palpable that Kynan felt a little piece of himself shatter. "I thought you were special...."

"I am," he insisted.

"Are you?" She frowned, pensive, shaking her head. "The path I walk is not an easy one. Maybe you're just not ready. Maybe you aren't strong enough to walk it with me."

Kynan couldn't help himself. He seized her arm with both hands, gripping it desperately. "I'm strong enough, I swear I'm strong enough." He knew he was begging and didn't really care in that moment. "I won't mess up again, I promise."

Ripley held the silence for a long, long moment, but then, finally—*finally*—she looked at him and nodded.

"One last chance, Leore. We sail in two days." She leaned in even closer, voice low and dark as a storm. "I don't travel with nobodies. Prove to me that you're somebody."

POTATO SOUP AND BANNOCKS WERE one of Kynan's least favorite meals, so of course that was what the mess hall served that night. He sat in his customary back corner, poking at the thick soup and the crumbling barley biscuit. It wasn't like he was hungry anyway. The fight with Jarett, the nights in the graveyard, the lingering memories—all of it had long since stolen his appetite.

There was a shout and a gust of laughter on the far end of the mess hall, where almost all the other Pale Guard and their trainees were clustered, and Kynan glanced up.

Jarett. Of course. Welcomed and popular, winging through the door to a chorus of *hellos* and calls to join them.

Kynan looked quickly back down at his dinner. Maybe . . . maybe Jarett would still see him back here. Maybe he'd come sit down and apologize for what he'd said earlier that day. And then, Kynan imagined, maybe he would apologize, too. He might even try to tell him what was going on, see if he knew any way to help Kynan put a stop to it.

For a few, breathless minutes, that all seemed perfectly possible.

But then Kynan looked up and saw the captain of the Pale Guard sitting in the middle of one of the tables, laughing at a story that another guard was telling. All around Jarett, in fact, were people talking, hollering, ribbing one another—bonding and blowing off steam after a long day.

They all fit together, Kynan realized. *They belong.*

Jarett had been right back on the training pitch. The problem here was him. It had always been him.

And that, at least, was a problem he could solve.

THAT NIGHT, KYNAN DIDN'T BOTHER going to sleep. He sat on the edge of his bed, folded over his knees, his face in his hands, and counted the passing minutes and hours, listening to the movements outside his room. Footsteps in the hallway, voices chatting and calling to one another, doors slamming shut as members of the Pale Guard slowly filtered to their own beds for the night.

And then, when all had been quiet for a while, Kynan got to his feet.

Stepping over to the little desk tucked against the wall, he took off Simon, replacing it with another, standard-issue belt. He sheathed two of his regular daggers on his body, but the ones Vax'ildan gave him—those he put on the desk next to Simon. His rucksack was already packed with the few extra clothes he had and a spare blanket. He'd sneak into the mess hall on his way out of town to grab some food. Not much, just enough to get him by until he could get to another town.

He couldn't stay. It didn't matter anymore what he'd told Vax'ildan or how much he wanted to start over. How many times had he messed up and told himself he'd do things different, just to mess up *again*? How many times had someone said they saw something special in him only to realize he was a screwup and wasn't worth the effort? And all these past nights, waking up in the graveyard . . .

It was a sign. Just a matter of time before he made the wrong choice and hurt someone else.

As he moved toward the door, Kynan's gaze caught on the long wooden box under his bed, and he hesitated. Should he take it? Lord de Rolo was so adamant, so worried about this technology getting into the wrong hands.

But whose hands were more wrong to wield it than his?

He'd leave it. Jarett would ensure that it was returned to the de Rolos, and they'd take care of it from there.

Kynan made it two steps into the streets outside the barracks, heading for the back door of the nearby mess hall, when he heard a voice behind him.

"Finally. What took you so long?"

Kynan whirled around, drawing one of his daggers, but it turned out to just be Jarett, half sitting, half leaning against a stump not far from the barracks door, his arms crossed over his chest, the hint of a smile on his face.

"I've been sitting out here for forever. My back is getting stiff."

"What . . ." Kynan stared at him, incredulous. "How are . . . How did you know?"

"It wasn't that hard to figure out." Jarett pushed himself off the stump he'd been perching on and stepped out into the street, circling around until he was in between Kynan and the mess hall. "I was on the run from trouble once, too."

He said it so coolly, like they were the same, like he knew exactly what Kynan was dealing with. But Kynan was a mess, a mistake, a nobody, and Jarett was *Jarett.* One of them seemed to make every place he went better, and one of them was better off gone.

"It's not the same thing." Kynan adjusted the straps tighter on his rucksack and stepped around Jarett, heading off down the street again. "You wouldn't understand."

Jarett was right on Kynan's heels, *tsk*ing in disapproval. "See, now you sound like a petulant child—"

Hot anger flared in Kynan's belly, and he whipped around. "I'm not a—"

But he wasn't in the streets of Whitestone anymore. He was back in Greyfield, surrounded by ghosts.

Ripley, standing in front of him, the black blood now seeping down her chest and dripping from the ends of the protruding tree roots.

Behind her, Luska, gaunt and decomposing, covered in deep slashes from an enormous great axe.

Next to Kynan, Sardel, grinning with blackened teeth and no eyes, her skin charred almost beyond recognition, and Brath, hanging limply in midair, a mass of bleeding flesh that didn't even look like there were any bones left inside to hold him up.

I knew you were special, Ripley's voice crooned all around him.

You finally got him. Sardel's voice this time, excited, her empty sockets staring down at the ground in front of Kynan. At the body in front of Kynan. Not Keyleth this time or Lady Cassandra.

It was Vax'ildan, crumpled like a fallen raven, glassy eyes staring up at the night sky. And his blood—his blood was all over Whisper, flowing down the blade onto Kynan's hands.

What have I done?

Someone clapped him on the shoulder, and Kynan reacted instantly, rounding on them, slicing his blade in an upward arc—

A hand gripped his wrist, staying his attack, and Kynan was once more looking up at Jarett, the dark, silent buildings of Whitestone all around him, the solid cobblestones beneath his boots. Kynan's dagger—a regular one, not Whisper—was a hairbreadth from Jarett's throat, but you wouldn't know it by the calm, steady look on the man's face.

"You asked me a week or so ago," Jarett said quietly, "why everything comes so easily for me."

"Because you're just that talented." Despite Kynan's best efforts, the words came out harsh, rank with barely concealed jealousy.

Jarett snorted a deeply bitter laugh. "Because I was just that desperate. When I lost Ank'Harel, I lost *everything.* All I had left was my sword . . . and fear. Fear of dying, fear of failing . . ." He narrowed his dark eyes, staring Kynan down with a hard look. "But for people like you and me, fear is not our enemy. It's not something we have to run from. It's our constant companion, and it will make you strong—"

Kynan's head spun, dizzying, and everything around him flickered from the cemetery to the town street and back again, and he couldn't keep it straight.

He was standing in front of Jarett.

He was standing over Vax'ildan's body.

He was outside the barracks.

He was in the middle of the cemetery and the blood was flowing down his arms now, over his shoulders and chest, and up into his throat, and it was all his fault, everything was his fault—

Someone tugged on his wrist, shaking his dagger arm hard.

"Look at me!"

Kynan blinked, and the world around him steadied. Cobblestones under his feet. Sleepy Whitestone all around him. Jarett's hard grip on him, holding him still.

"I know what you want to hear," Jarett said. There was no casualness in his voice anymore, no easy, devil-may-care tone. Just an undercurrent of flint and fire. "You want me to give you a reason to stay. You want me to tell you that fate brought you here, it's your destiny, you're going to do incredible things here. But I'm not going to do that. What happens now has to come from you, and only from you."

Slowly, Jarett pushed Kynan's dagger down, away from his throat. "Survival is a choice. Making something of yourself is a choice. And you can't just do it once and be done with it. Every morning you have to wake up and choose it again." He stood back, squaring his shoulders and opening his arms wide. "So, Kynan. What choice are you going to make?"

Kynan stood, trembling, in the street. The exhaustion in him felt like a river pulling him down underneath its surface, and he wanted to let it. He didn't want to go back to the Greyfield. But the other path Jarett offered—choosing day after day, again and again, to get out of bed and be better—that felt insurmountable.

"What if I can't do it?" he whispered. "What if I fuck up again?"

"You almost certainly will," said Jarett, but the way he said it didn't feel like a blow. It was comforting, in a way. "We all do. You can't grow unless you fuck up. Just like you can't be brave without first knowing fear."

Kynan swallowed. "And if you have . . . a *lot* of fear?"

Jarett reached out and put a hand on his shoulder. "Then you have an even greater opportunity to rise above it."

Kynan looked up at Jarett—the effortless, easygoing warrior who seemed to take everything in stride. But also the banished boy who fled his home, who pieced himself back together from nothing, who woke up every morning and chose to survive.

Taking a deep breath, Kynan closed his eyes and turned around.

He opened them again to darkness and pale gray gravestones and the corpses of his former comrades waiting for him. Vax'ildan's body on the ground. Slick, sticky blood all over Kynan's hands.

Ripley grinned wide, reaching for him.

I always knew you were special.

Kynan smiled back grimly, flipping Whisper over in his fingers. Then, whip-fast, he grabbed it by its deadly point and flung it straight at Ripley's face. As soon as it left his hand, he was following it, disappearing and then reappearing directly in front of her even as Whisper was still flying toward its target. His hand was on the hilt the instant it hit Ripley, right in one of her misty eyes, and he slammed it in even deeper, driving it straight through to her brain.

For a moment, the scene hung suspended—Kynan and Ripley and the grinning corpses.

And then Kynan blinked, and he was back on the street and no one else was there except Jarett. The dagger in his hand was just a regular dagger, and his hands were clean. He spun in a slow circle, his heart still hammering hard enough that he felt it in his throat, but everything looked exactly as it was supposed to.

"I don't understand," he said, partly to Jarett, partly to himself. "Was any of that real?"

Later, Kynan was extremely grateful that Jarett hadn't asked what Kynan had been talking about or what exactly Kynan had thought he'd seen. That he hadn't grilled Kynan or tried to get answers that Kynan didn't even know himself.

Instead, the only thing Jarett asked was, "Did it feel real to you?" And when Kynan nodded, Jarett just patted him on the back and said, "Then it was real enough."

THE LONG BLACK BARREL GLINTED in the sunlight, sharp against Kynan's eyes, but he kept the butt of the rifle tucked tight against his shoulder, the cheekpiece pressing into the side of his face, his gaze steady down the sights to the target set up beyond. Reaching a thumb up, he cocked the rifle, the scent of flint biting at his nose. Then, on his next exhale, Kynan squeezed the trigger.

Fifty yards away, the target rocked at the impact, the bullet shredding a hole almost exactly in the middle.

"Nice shot."

Kynan dropped the rifle barrel, pointing it at the ground, and looked over his shoulder. Jarett stood several feet back, his arms crossed over his chest, the hint of a smile on his face.

Kynan glanced back at the target, and for one moment—just one—he let himself notice it. The smoky scent of gunpowder and hot metal all around him. The heavy weight of the rifle in his hand. But there he was, steady, holding his ground. With a near-perfect bull's-eye, too.

And that was something.

"Keep your elbow up, though," Jarett added, stepping up next to him and tapping his right arm. "You dropped it just before you pulled the trigger."

Kynan nodded. Yeah, he could do that. "You want to try it?" he asked, holding the rifle out.

Jarett made a face, waving the gun away. "Absolutely not. Those things are too loud for my taste. There's no . . . *elegance* to it." He hesitated and then added, "How did you sleep?"

"Better." Jarett raised a skeptical eyebrow, and Kynan ducked his head, sheepish. "Well, a little better, anyway. Still some bad dreams." *Keyleth bloody on the ground, Lord de Rolo still and cold in death, Vax'ildan's grieving face.* Maybe those dreams, those images, would fade eventually. Maybe they'd always be with him. He'd have to just keep moving and find out. "But I didn't wake up in a random part of town, so . . . that's an improvement."

Jarett studied him for a long moment, his eyes narrowed and shrewd, like he saw past the casual front Kynan was trying to put on. The same one Jarett probably wore. One damaged fighter recognizing another, seeing them for all their patched-up spiderweb cracks. Layers of hurt and guilt and fear that were slowly healing, even if they would never truly be gone.

Jarett finally nodded and reached out a hand, clapping Kynan on the back hard enough that Kynan nearly stumbled a bit. "Come eat with me, Kynan. The others keep asking questions about this contraption of yours, and I have no idea what to tell them. Maybe you can get them off my back."

Kynan hesitated for a second, almost ready to say no. But he did have that promise he made—to Vax'ildan, to Lord de Rolo, to himself. He flipped the rifle over his head, slipping it into the scabbard-style holster strapped to his back.

"Yeah," he said. "That sounds good."

SHAUN

Aabria Iyengar

Shaun Gilmore is a beautiful man. He is warm bronze skin, glossy black locks, and a broad, proud figure wrapped in the finest of garments. Where he walks, the tinkling of exquisite metal jewelry heralds his approach. Where he lingers, the perfumed scent of woodsmoke and ripe red fruit remains. He dazzles as a simple fact of himself, like the sunlight that usually dances through the airy rainbow silks and dapples the pristinely polished and faceted treasures of his shop. Today, though, the only light in this trove of glorious goods comes from the brass oil lamps and candelabras burning throughout the shop. As Shaun himself emerges from the gloomy dark of the storage cellar, he finds a stout young dwarf with wide brown eyes lost in contemplation of one of the lamps sitting beside the till.

Shaun pauses, resisting the urge to adjust the heavy box in his arms, and watches the mage study. Ingvie Greenthatch, a student of the Alabaster Lyceum, scratches their auburn stubble, muttering to themself.

Narrowing their eyes, they blink, and suddenly the flame flickers from pale yellow to bright pink. The squawk of surprise sends Shaun into a peal of laughter, and Ingvie blushes furiously as they are joined at the counter by the shopkeeper.

"What do you think, Master Ingvie?"

"You don't have to call me that, Mr. Gilmore. I'm still in my first year, and I'm not some third-born lordling like the other students. . . ." The tinge of spite in their voice is unmistakable, but Shaun lets it pass without remark as the student digs through their bag for the Lyceum bursar's note. Gilmore is one of several arcanists in Abdar's Promenade who provides supplies to the college, and though the task of enchanting sands and inks for spellwork is a bit beneath him, the coin is good and steady. With the Westruun expansion going over budget already, every silver helps.

"Well, then, Ingvie, what do you think?" The young dwarf's bright brown eyes lock with Shaun's as he gestures with a nod toward the lamp.

"I don't—I didn't think there was anything to it," Ingvie stammers. "But then I noticed the residue by the edge of the burner. It's blue. I've never seen . . . and then when I cast a spell of detection, the flame changed."

Shaun gives a little hum of affirmation and gestures for the note as Ingvie lapses into thoughtful silence once more. He scans the parchment before adding it to the pile of this month's requests in the bottom of the till and makes a mental note to send Sherri up to the Erudite Quarter later today to settle accounts. Peering past the dwarf and out through the heavy gold beading of his front doorway, Shaun sees the ominous gray clouds of this late Duscar morning giving over fully to an unpleasant, sleety squall. Tomorrow, then.

"That's it, isn't it?" Ingvie mutters. Shaun looks back to the student as their deeply knitted brows begin to relax with dawning realization. Gilmore quirks an eyebrow in return. "It detects magic being cast!"

"Correct, young master! But do keep going. Why?"

Ingvie's face lights up, and Shaun can almost hear the gears turning in their mind. What a delight, to find such joy in small puzzles. The mage grins, nodding to themself as their thoughts pick up steam.

"Well, the wares you sell here are very expensive. No, not that. Not just that. Your customers are not just mages in the city. They are adventurers, too. People that might try to use magic to trick you. To take advantage?"

"Mostly they're just trying to get a better deal!" Shaun laughs and claps the youth on the shoulder. Ingvie beams, almost a little dazed by the full force of Gilmore's attention and praise. Though Ingvie has supplemented the steep tuition of the Lyceum by being an errand-runner to Gilmore's for months, the two of them have never exchanged more than vague pleasantries. Ingvie didn't even know he knew their name.

"But the lamp itself isn't magic?"

"Just the oil. Harder to detect. Especially if the reservoir is—"

"Lined with lead! Which is why I couldn't tell what was happening. And lining a font with lead is much easier than making the whole lamp a magical item."

"Precisely, Master Ingvie. Work smarter, not harder. You've a bright future ahead of you at the Alabaster Lyceum. I can tell." Shaun gives them a nod and a wink, and the hope-filled grin he receives in return warms him through the wintry chill in the air. "You'd better get going before the storm worsens, but I look forward to your return."

Ingvie's round cheeks go rosy for a second time as they nod enthusiastically and grab the box of components. For all the simple pleasure of that transaction, Shaun's mind has already wandered to other matters by the time he hears the beads rattle with the errand-runner's egress. He feels his attention brush up against the memory of last night's conversation, and pity in a pair of sad, dark eyes. He closes his own and tries to attribute the ache he feels to a well-earned hangover from Howarth's swill.

He hears a distant roll of thunder, and suddenly in his mind he is a child again, the young son of Opesa and Soren Geddmore and a child of the Rumedam Desert. He lies across a long, flat stone still warm from a sun currently hiding behind a high and roiling gray sky. He holds his little brown arm aloft, trying to envision how far away the thundering clouds must be, until he gets distracted by the newly emerging rune on the back of his hand. It isn't visible yet, not like the one on his forehead, but he can feel it just beneath the surface of his skin.

Little Shaun hears his mother's voice calling to him, but he is transfixed by the warmth of the stone and the itch of new magic beneath his skin and the smell of a storm on the wind. It isn't until he can hear the sandy crunch of her footsteps approaching that he even remembers to blink, and his eyes sting and blur with tears as he looks over to her.

"Mama," he whispers, wiping the tears from his cheeks. "Why doesn't the sky rain every time the storm clouds come?"

"My sweet boy. Do you weep every time you feel sad or mad or scared? Maybe"—and here she sits beside his head and wipes the dusty tear streak from his face—"the sky only rains when it's sad enough. Or perhaps, just when you're sad enough."

"I'm too brave to cry, Mama."

Here, Opesa sweeps him up into her arms, and Shaun remembers with perfect clarity the cool, sweet melon scent of her. She rocks him gently, and he is happy to be held. There is a long beat before she speaks again, and it is only with the lens of adulthood that Shaun recognizes the thoughtfulness in her pause.

"Then the Rumedam remains a desert, my love."

There is a mystery to his mother's lessons that Shaun has never quite solved. How does one raise a child whose first rune appeared as their milk teeth began to fall? Perhaps a sterner hand or straighter answers would have made his sorcerous adolescence less maddening. But then again, how could the Geddmores have known what it felt like for Shaun to push an unfriendly breeze away from himself as easily as shutting a door? Sweet, serene Opesa did her best to guide her son toward an understanding that magic is a conversation with the world, just as growing up is a conversation with oneself.

Shaun, comforted only momentarily by the memory of his mother's soft and subtle guidance, blinks. A pair of tears drip down onto a sheaf of parchment full of accounting tables, two of which are now blurred and barely legible. He sighs and tuts, walking two gold-dipped fingers across the page toward the blotches as gentle wisps of the arcane issue from the faint rune embossed on his hand. The wisps poke at the teary smears, which reconstitute into round little droplets tinged violet with ink. They obediently roll up his fingertips, leaving pristine parchment behind.

"Not so fast, darlings. I still need those masonry numbers."

The inky teardrops drip back down, redepositing their pigment as crisp figures on the page before traveling back up his fingers to be flicked away harmlessly. Shaun smiles at the charm of his magic as the more serious parts of his mind track the progress of his Westruun expansion across the ones and zeros of his ledgers. He feels something, an internal tension like the beginning of a headache behind his eyes.

The Rumedam remains a desert, my love.

Shaun's eyes flick up, searching not for the source of the voice in the storm-darkened shop, but for a mirrored surface. If he knows anything, it's the sound of his own voice. Some have said it's his favorite sound, and he's never bothered to correct them. He spots it—his reflection—in a polished gold disk used for planar travel forbiddance. He's there for just a moment, sad and tired and a touch hungover, before Gilmore appears. Gilmore, the larger-than-life persona made of smirks and winks and intoxicating confidence. Gilmore smirks, shaking his head slightly at the sorry state of himself.

We're a mess.

"I think I'm handling things quite well, all things considered." His headache sharpens just as (or maybe just before) an angry peal of thunder rolls across the sky. He feels something similar rattle through the hollow of his chest; it makes the delicate fractures of wanting etched across his ribs flare painfully. His breaths grow a little more shallow as he thinks of last night's conversation. As he thinks of Vax'ildan. The sadness in his eyes as he resigned himself to a difficult conversation. The softness of his voice as he confessed his love for another. The gentleness of a kiss flavored with goodbye.

Of course we did well—we're glorious.

"Don't you ever get tired?"

Shaun hears the growl in his throat hitch onto the edges of his Marquesian lilt. It makes the words he spits aloud to no one scrape across the roof of his mouth like a blade sharpened over a strop. He runs his hands through his dark curls and averts his gaze from the golden mirror, looking to the storm-battered banners outside his window. The rain picks up steam, and Shaun takes its cue as he confronts his reflection once again.

"It's exhausting! The *mask* of you. Always easy, always gracious. Nothing gets under the skin of a man almost larger than life! The Rumedam remains a cool and beautiful desert, and you remain here on the sidelines—ready to help him with a tip and a quip. No wonder Vax moved on. You? You're not even *real.*"

Shaun yells, and yet his voice barely carries above the din of the storm's bluster. He's grateful that Sherri's errands this morning will keep her from intruding on whatever delightful little breakdown this has turned into. He's grateful for the storm. For his part, Gilmore simply watches with a glint of smug delight in his mirrored eye.

"What?"

You're not mad at Vax'ildan?

"Of course not."

You're not mad at me, either.

"No, I'm definitely mad at you."

You'd blame the armor of your own creation for doing its job. Were you so in love with him? But it's you who never dared to show him the tender flesh and feelings beneath it. You never even told him how you really felt. You let him walk away from the dance without a word.

"The bravery of admitting you're in love with someone who might not love you back is a quality I admire in Vax'ildan but clearly do not share."

That's not my fault.

"You make it easy. Easier."

That's my job.

"That doesn't make it right."

So then, what is it that you actually want?

"I just want—"

No, show me.

Shaun feels his runes before he sees their pale purple glow across his forearms and below his palms. He imagines, and the power of his imagination spreads like a haze throughout the room as he wraps himself and his little slice of Exandria up in a dream.

Shaun imagines the end of weeks of treacherous travel across the southern reaches of the continent that's led them—Vox Machina and himself—down into the fetid bowels of an ancient dungeon. Pike's divine magic lights the way, but even the Everlight's gifts flicker and balk in the domain of such overwhelming evil.

He scouts ahead with Vax, eyes blazing to detect any magical traps that Vax's roguish cunning might miss. There is nothing in their body language to suggest romance here in the midst of lurking danger, but their wordless synchronicity is its own intimacy.

Vax's ears twitch, straining to hear beyond the drip of the damp dungeon walls and the low shuffling of their party behind them. The rogue turns his head, and Gilmore's eyes follow, catching the arcane flare of an activated glyph. He shouts a warning, but it's drowned out by the scraping of heavy, ancient stone as the hallway shifts and reconfigures, a cramped and claustrophobic tunnel widening impossibly into a massive ritual chamber. The space is lit with a poisonous green glow emanating from a strange structure on the ceiling—like a hardened drop of tree resin containing a skeletal humanoid figure.

There's a part in the back of Gilmore's mind that wonders what they'd say. Who would crack a joke? Who would strike first? For all the stories of their exploits shared over meals and ales, he doesn't know quite how to imagine Vox Machina in battle. To be honest, he doesn't know how to imagine himself, either. In the face of true danger, would he still carry his smirking bravado? Strangely, he feels the ache again; it shakes along the fault lines inside him.

The green cocoon shatters overhead, and all eight of them scatter across the cavern as the entombed figure drops to the cave floor. What stands is a jagged onyx skeleton, easily fifteen feet tall, with bony wings protruding from its back and a simple spiky onyx crown floating a foot above its skull. The rain of glowing resin fragments around it reflect off its glassy surface, and the surge of fear in Gilmore's gut is dampened by the squeeze of Vax's hand as he pulls them behind a massive stalagmite.

"We have to get to the crown," Vax whispers, and the brush of his breath on Shaun's ear feels so real he begins to forget it's all an illusion. "Can you keep its eye sockets on you so I can sneak up and get a shot?"

Shaun nods, turning to face Vax. He parts his lips to speak, but a sudden roar steals the moment as Grog sprints across the cavern, axe in hand.

"Let's go!"

Vax melts into the shadows as Vox Machina launches their assault. Magic and arrows fly, and the crash of metal on stone rings out as physical blows are traded between the monster and heroes. They keep their foe frustrated and focused but cannot manage to crack its shining bones.

What more could he do?

And then Gilmore thinks of Ingvie and their wonder at the lead-lined lamp. Working smarter, not harder. If the crown is its point of vulnerability, then trying to injure it otherwise is a waste of energy. He steps out from his hiding space, the runes across his skin almost sizzling with potential. He reaches toward the earth, feeling it within the grip of his magic as familiar as holding his mother's hand. With a flick of his wrist, he beckons the stone up from the ground to loop through the space between the bones of its lower leg like thread through a needle before rejoining the solid cave floor. It attempts to raise its other leg to kick at Pike and Keyleth, but it cannot shift itself enough to keep balance and crashes to the ground.

Rushing forward to stand beside Percy, Gilmore coaxes the stone once more, this time through the gap between its ribs. Scanlan reinforces it with his own wards, bolstering the stone holding the creature in a bent posture reminiscent of prayer. He feels a surge of joy at turning the tide of the battle, even as a distant part of his mind reminds him this is no different from a dream. A flutter of motion in the darkness over the skeleton's head pulls his attention back, and he holds his breath as Vax moves on the crown.

"Look out!"

Gilmore's brow furrows with confusion at Vex's shout. Who was she yelling at? The monster isn't even looking at Vax. Gilmore looks at the skull, and even though it has no eyes or expression, he understands it is focused on him. The one who pinned it down. The one standing close enough to reach. Shaun follows the lines of its anatomy from head to shoulder to arm extended out with the tips of its spiky fingers buried into his torso. The pain hits him as he sees the blood stain his beautiful purple robes, but he is too stunned to cry out. He staggers back, unimpaling himself and sinking to the ground.

A massive crash fills the cavern as Vax'ildan shatters the crown in a single strike of his dagger. Gilmore sees the others throw their hands over their ears, but he doesn't seem to hear the sound over the thud of his own heartbeat. The creature slumps completely to the ground, defeated and inert. It all seems so distant all of a sudden.

There is only his breath and his heartbeat and the cold cavern floor. He starts to close his eyes.

"No, no, you don't."

Vax is suddenly over him, filling Gilmore's slowly blurring vision. He's vaguely aware of being held in the half-elf's arms. If the others are here, too, he cannot see or hear them. There is only Vax'ildan.

"You did it." Shaun's voice is soft and shaky. Vax looks afraid, so very afraid.

But why? They won the day!

"I couldn't have done it without you, Shaun. Clever work, pinning it to the ground with stone."

Vax looks away for a moment, shouting something that Shaun cannot hear.

He's so tired; it's hard to keep his eyes open. He could drift off to sleep right now, looking at the man he loves. Wouldn't that be nice? His breathing slows, and the heartbeat in his ears does likewise.

"No, Shaun, stay with me." Vax leans closer, and his eyes are filled with tears. "I love you. You cannot leave me like this."

Shaun opens his mouth to speak, but instead of words of love and hope he can find only the taste of blood on his tongue.

Well, didn't this take a turn for the melodramatic?

Shaun looks away from his lover's tear-filled eyes to the golden ghost of himself barely holding back laughter as it leans over Vax's shoulder. The dream doesn't freeze, but it waits, ignoring the interruption of Shaun's other imagining.

"Oh, I'm not looking for notes here. You wanted to see my fantasy. Well"—Shaun reaches a bloody but gentle hand up to stroke Vax's cheek—"here it is."

Our fantasy.

"To be fair, you're also a figment. No need to quibble over terms."

Shaun's eyes remain locked with Vax's as he continues to savor this charged moment, but the spell is broken. He scrabbles desperately against his own mind to find the note to pick the dream up again, but self-consciousness has won out. His thoughts meander away from the fantasy to pick it apart: *Why this? Why not some romantic stroll through Azalea Street Park as the sun sets a fiery orange over the Ozmit Waterways? Why not a breathless but inevitable kiss as they exchange heartfelt gifts on Winter's Crest?*

This time, he doesn't hear Gilmore's voice in his doubts; but, then again, that voice was always his. He leans in, and the illusion of Vax does the same. Something in the strangeness of Vax's expression piques Shaun, and it takes him a long while to find the root of it in the lack of tension around the half-elf's eyes and mouth.

Shaun's imaginings lack the real Vax's guardedness, and in the moment when he realizes just how much they both wear their respective masks, the storm breaks loose.

Shaun slams his eyes shut, but the tears flow unabated. The dream dissipates around him, and the conjured sounds of the dungeon give way to the torrential downpour outside his doors. Some part of him, perhaps the bit he thinks of as Gilmore, is grateful that the noise of the world is drowning out his sorrow.

The Rumedam finally receives its rain, and it threatens a flood.

He weeps now, well and truly. He weeps for what was lost in Vax's confession—a chance to really know Vax'ildan, and to be known by him in turn. To look into his eyes and see care, perhaps even love, without guile or guard. He weeps for the doorway to adventure that closes along with his hopes for Vax's heart. To fight alongside him against monsters and magics that he knows a great deal about but has never seen for himself. He weeps for the person he might be—the rune-wrapped man that loves and fights and truly lives—as he tucks his boundless potential away into his stores brick by brick. He thinks of the success he chases—outposts across the map outfitting the adventurers and heroes of Exandria with arcane workings crafted by his clever, restless hands—and he weeps harder.

Here, on the polished wood floor of his storm-darkened store, Shaun Gilmore meets the bottom rung of his grief. There is no hazy illusion or imagined self to soothe him. There's only the truth: he longs for *change.* It makes perfect sense; Shaun crossed the world and changed his name in pursuit of his dreams. He built Gilmore's Glorious Goods into the jewel of the Promenade and will no doubt dazzle Westruun in time. From there, to Whitestone and Wildemount and anywhere else in the wide, wild world. But with every success, a part of him is rooted down, like the monster in his fantasy. Shops need wares, and they require clerks and bookkeepers and a thousand other things that would keep Shaun tied to a desk for the rest of his extremely stately and prosperous days.

The winds of change that blew him to Emon are no match for strong bricks and deep roots. It is a comfort known acutely and intimately by

Gilmore in this moment of shelter from the tempest. But for all the safety and security of strong walls, there is a trade-off in not seeing the high gray sky or feeling the sun-warmed earth. He continues to lie on the pristine and polished wooden floor of his shop, looking up and imagining. He dreams of adventure and romance. He dreams of unknown dangers through doors that will close with every new wall he builds. He dreams of feeling the curiosity and surprise he saw in Ingvie's eyes this morning. He dreams of something new.

And that's when he places the aching grief that has thundered in his ribs; it's not just the sting of thwarted romance, but the hope that somehow love—this love—could save him from the fear of a *known* future. A road of safety and softness that he's still too young to settle down for.

Gilmore thinks again of Vax, and though his eyes twinge with the exhaustion of summoning more tears, he does not feel any of his longing or affection turn to bitterness. In the tempest of emotions he's wrestled all morning, anger toward Vax or *her* has yet to appear among them. He thinks of her, the object of Vax's unrequited affections. Gilmore reaches toward the thought of Keyleth like a tongue feeling the jagged edge of a chipped tooth. Will there be pain? Blood? To his great surprise and relief: neither.

The sound of a chuckle in the silence startles him. He searches the room but finds he is alone with his thoughts. The chuckle was his. He feels himself smirk—a tiny, lopsided thing—at his resumed thoughts of Keyleth and Vax'ildan. In their drunken conversation the night before, no name was mentioned, but Gilmore is a quick reader of people in general. Vax he knows better than most, and the way the two half-elves orbit each other, subtle but steady, feels almost natural. There is a correctness to it, like the paths of the stars or the moons at night. And, of course, she is lovely, if a bit anxious.

Gilmore runs his fingertips over a lucky coin displayed on a lush velvet pillow as he considers Vax's chances of getting through to the Ashari woman. He wonders absently when he finally stood back up, and how long he's drifted around the shop lost in thought. The whinny of a horse turns his attention outward, where the storm seems to have exhausted itself enough to bring the market streets back to life and trade despite the lingering drizzle.

The world moves along, even if it's still a bit of a mess.

Gilmore sighs at the truth of it. He enjoyed the dance, of course, but his partner is still out there. And with any luck, finding him will be an adventure of its own. The beads tinkle, and a slightly bedraggled Sherri enters with an apology for her lateness on her lips.

"Your timing couldn't be more perfect, my dear!" Gilmore laughs, hearty and sincere, even as he sends his magic on a warm breeze to dry her off. "It's been quite a morning."

She narrows her eyes with disbelief as she looks around the quiet shop. "Sure. Now, I know I'm running behind today, but aren't you supposed to be in Westruun? I thought you were going to check on things before Sovereign Uriel's meeting this evening?"

Shaun nods, his thoughts on Uriel and the whispers he's heard about the announcement tonight. Abdication. The creation of a council. The world truly does keep moving along, and the wise know the best course is often to move right along with it. Even when it hurts. Especially when it hurts. Uriel Tal'Dorei, last sovereign of the land. The only person Gilmore can think of who might be having a tougher day than him. That last thought makes him smile, at least until he looks back at Sherri to see her scowling at him from her perch behind the counter.

"GO TO WESTRUUN, SIR."

Shaun barks a laugh and scurries through the front door. Looking back, he takes in the little building that is both his store and his home with pride and longing in equal measure. He has made something wonderful here, and even still, he yearns for more. He acknowledges the fact without guilt or castigation. He is Shaun Gilmore, and he can and will have a life just as glorious as his dreams.

He takes in the drab and sodden silks bunched unattractively in snarls on their poles and reaches out with his many-ringed fingers to begin a series of spells to restore his storefront to splendor. But past his fingertips, he sees the heavy gray clouds of the passing storm breaking up just enough to limn them in silvery sunlight. The storm has passed, yes. But there's no need to pretend it never happened. It rained. And things might look a little rough right now, but the sun always returns. The silks will dry, in time, and Abdar's Promenade will be vibrant once more.

Shaun lowers his hands, though his eyes remain aloft. The little rune-child, far from home, looks at the silver lining of the clouds that wept with him all morning and sees a benevolent omen: the worst of the day is behind him. The storm has passed, as they all do. He returns to himself well and truly as a misty gust of wind cuts through his gauzy robes and robs him of warmth. There are only a few hours to see to things in Westruun before he must return for Sovereign Uriel's speech in the Cloudtop at sunset. Perhaps tomorrow there will be time enough to find an adventure worthy of him. He smirks at the thought.

Shaun takes one last look at his decidedly unhumble shop before calling on great magic that will move him across the face of Tal'Dorei in mere moments. His runes flare, his spirit filling with the wild heat of the arcane as his body glows, then it fades to nothing, and Gilmore walks away.

GOING ON A BEAR HUNT

Sarah Glenn Marsh

As Vesper de Rolo ran a fine-tooth comb through a particularly stubborn snarl of his fur, Trinket gave an involuntary grumble of protest low in his chest and realized it was about time he started examining all the life choices and thorny paths taken that had led him to this moment, a new low. Only there wasn't any time for that, because Juniper Shorthalt was sticking little silk bows into his newly braided fur with a maniacal grin on her sweet face while her brother, Wax, frowned thoughtfully as he tied a bell around Trinket's collar, and it was taking all the grizzly's focus not to accidentally bare his teeth when small fingers tugged too hard.

Vex'ahlia never would have allowed this; she knew exactly how he felt about being groomed and decorated like some kind of show bear. But what Vex would have allowed didn't matter right now, because she wasn't home at the castle tonight to witness Trinket's humiliation at the hands of these unruly cubs, which was giving him flashbacks to the one and only time Vax and Keyleth had dressed him up in bows years ago.

Parenting was the most exhausting sort of work; someone really should have warned him, and probably Vex, too, before she went and had three cubs with Percy. After the way this evening was shaping up, thanks to his first real taste of being a parent, Trinket at least knew better than to ever consider having a cub himself.

After all, that's technically what he was tonight, even if Vesper had made it clear from the moment her parents took off for the festivities that she thought being newly thirteen made her an Adult, and therefore too old to look to Trinket for guidance on everything the way she once had; she had already attempted to assert her dominance by eating double dessert for dinner, which Trinket let slide only because she slipped him an entire rooster pie in exchange, making them partners in crime once again.

His current predicament was all Keyleth's fault, really, Trinket decided as his back paw thumped against the drawing room's plush burgundy carpet; Vesper had just hit his favorite spot to be scratched, above his right shoulder. That must have been on purpose, an apology of sorts, since Vesper could tell in a single dark-eyed glance that Trinket wasn't enjoying himself in the slightest, no words or growls ever needed between them to know what the other was thinking. It was simply second nature.

Anyway, Keyleth was the one who had brought Audra with her to the castle. Again. The ash-blond half-elf was currently sitting by the warm hearth in Percy's favorite leather chair with her feet up, weaving a flower crown for Trinket (since when did pink-and-white blossoms smell like menace and defeat?). The dreamy look in her gray eyes didn't at all match her nefarious intentions to make Trinket *pretty* rather than appreciating his natural majesty.

Audra was a favored trainee of Keyleth's, a druid in the making, and only a few months older than Vesper, which meant the eldest of the de Rolo cubs had been desperate to impress her at every opportunity since the girls first met on one of Keyleth's visits to Whitestone. It had been Audra's idea to "get Trinket ready to attract all the lady-bears at the party," even though they weren't supposed to be going anywhere near the Renewal Festival to welcome the spring season with the rest of the crew tonight.

Vex'ahlia had given Trinket specific instructions to keep these four cubs—her eldest, plus Juni and Wax, and Keyleth's young protégé—safely contained within the confines of Whitestone Castle while she and Percy had a long-overdue night of catching up with their friends. There would, Trinket guessed, be no shortage of drinking, reminiscing, and probably singing. Just like old times. Scanlan and Pike had traveled all the way from Westruun with their family to kick off the new season with the de Rolos and Keyleth, who had agreed to this rare break from her duties among the Ashari only after a few months of persuading from the others.

At least Vex had hired a proper nanny for her young twins while she was at the party. Trinket loved Leona and Wolfe like they were his own, but he drew the line at being outnumbered by cubs six-to-one. Those were terrible odds.

Audra nestled the flower crown gently on Trinket's head, then stepped back to admire her handiwork and frowned. "Something's still missing," she declared.

"A big bear smile?" Vesper murmured slyly as she ran a hand down her bone-pale braid, grinning when she earned the expected groan from Trinket. He was so going to make her pay for that later.

"Well, that, and . . . perfume, I think. The flowers aren't enough," Audra said, delicately sniffing the air around him, which Trinket found wildly offensive. She glanced hopefully at Juniper, who was finishing up with the last of the bows. They had all seen the gnome make the flames in the hearth change colors earlier just to make her brother laugh, which meant she had already started studying magic at home in Westruun. "Juni, can you do anything with this, or—?"

"How about we all go sneak some more dessert out of the kitchen?"

Vesper quickly cut in, clearly sensing that Trinket had hit his limit without even having to glance at her old friend this time. "It's late enough, the place should be practically empty."

Wax, who had been studying some of the thick, dusty volumes on the bookshelves like he actually wanted to know what was in them, turned to look at her, his auburn brows drawn together with great concern. "Won't the cook mind? Or your mom?" he asked cautiously. "We already had plenty, but . . . I could eat. . . ."

Trinket still found himself perplexed every time he studied the youngest of these cubs. Wax had his father's face, so many similarities it was startling, but Trinket couldn't recall Scanlan ever looking that worried about anything. Not even when a fight seemed unwinnable.

"C'mon, Wax. Where's your sense of adventure?" Juniper prodded cheerfully, slinging an arm around her brother's shoulders and guiding him toward the drawing room doors ahead of the older girls. She looked so much like Pike before her resurrection, with her black hair and pale blue eyes. "That reminds me: I heard a great song about pie the other day. Want to hear it?"

Over everyone's collective groans—Juni favored her mother in looks, but she certainly had her father's talent, and his taste for songs with dubious lyrics—Trinket noticed the way Vesper drew in a breath and her steps subtly slowed, falling behind the others. A tiny line had appeared between her brows, one that was halfway between deep thought and worry.

She had to be hearing something in another part of the castle.

But when Trinket nudged her in the side (to get her attention, of course. It was only a happy side effect that the flower crown fell off in the process), she shook her head and muttered quietly to him, "Thought I heard—I don't know, somebody falling or something. We should keep an eye out on our way, in case somebody's hurt." Pressing her lips together for another moment's thought, she then added, "No need to tell the others yet, though. It could've been anything."

Trinket bobbed his head in agreement. He could tell that the way he stuck close to Vesper's side as they left the drawing room helped her to stand a little taller, even if she was an Adult now. He hummed to himself low in his chest, pleased to still be needed somehow.

They crept down the first of a few long halls that would take them to the other side of the castle where the kitchen was, sticking to the shadows as if they were performing some kind of heist, which made Juni giggle with purpose and Wax look like he was headed off to his doom. Just behind them, Audra waved serenely at every small spider they passed, and smiled at each creature scuttling unseen within the walls.

Trinket and Vesper brought up the rear. That tiny line between her brows hadn't gone away, and she canted her head to the side as they reached the lofty central foyer where the front staircases were, listening again. "Something isn't where it's supposed to be," she declared at last, quietly, but sounding sure of herself.

It couldn't hurt to check in with the castle staff, Trinket decided. After all, he was in charge here. And he had been Vesper's constant companion long enough to know that when she had an unshakable feeling, it was always something worth listening to.

While Vesper moved ahead to join the others, who were glancing curiously back at the pair now, the grizzly lumbered over to the enchanted button mat on the floor against the far wall that let him quickly and easily communicate with the Whitestone staff. There was one on each level of the castle, with options he could press like "bathroom break," "snack time," and "service please," which would send a magically magnified voice echoing through the halls with his request. It was an invention of Percy's, with buttons just the right size for his enormous paws, since not everyone understood him like Vex and Vesper. He'd even had to use the buttons with Percy on occasion when the man was too deep into a project to see past the end of his nose and Trinket really needed someone to let him outside.

He pushed the button for service and waited, which was easier than Vesper having to shout through the corridors to get someone to answer her summons.

"What's going on?" Juni whispered curiously to Vesper, wide-eyed, as words suddenly boomed through the castle in a low, pleasant voice.

Hey, have you ever done it with a bear?

Trinket stared down at the button beneath his paw. He was sure he had hit "service please," but all the same, he tried again with the button beside it, which should have simply said "help requested."

Hey, have you ever done it with a bear?

He tried them all, and they all said the same damn thing.

Trinket and Vesper locked eyes, and he watched her fight not to giggle as a realization swept over him: Scanlan had been in the foyer earlier that afternoon, asking Vex all about what the buttons on the floor did.

Well, that was useless. He'd have words for Scanlan later. Or at least, Vex would.

Across the foyer, Vesper shrugged and motioned for him to hurry up, that tiny line of thinking-worry still stubbornly in place.

"I thought I heard something earlier, like a crash somewhere else in the castle, maybe," the pale-haired girl finally confessed to the others where they huddled in the gloom under a large, winding staircase, and she put a hand on Trinket's braided fur as he returned to her side.

"It's just the mice in the walls. You've got quite an infestation," Audra reported with a dreamy smile.

Vesper shook her head. "No, this sounded too big to be mice. But everything's quiet now."

Still, that worry line persisted, and Trinket kept a wary eye out for anything out of place as they roamed the halls. The few guards and others they passed didn't seem to be injured or in bad spirits, especially not once Juniper's beautiful voice started echoing through the drafty corridors. The song she had been bursting to share with them wasn't really about pie, but rather was full of innuendos that left Trinket in no doubt as to where she'd learned it.

For his part, Trinket had surprised himself by finding that over the years, he'd rather developed a taste for the real deal, pies both sweet and savory, despite having once made himself sick on it in a ridiculous pie-eating contest many moons ago. When they reached the kitchen and found that Chef Varon had closed the place down for the night, he sniffed the high counters hopefully while Audra and Vesper started lowering all the cakes and treats they could find to a small worktable so that everyone could take their pick.

Whoever said there were no prizes for suffering, like staying behind for the good of the team when the rest of your friends were enjoying an overdue catch-up, clearly hadn't tasted strawberry rhubarb in a buttery, flaky, still-warm shell. It was handed over with a wink by one determined de Rolo cub who was, even Trinket had to admit, on the way to being grown-up.

"Ooh, fairy cake," Juniper cheered, picking up a pastry dusted with sugar and berries and showing it to her brother. "Your favorite, Wax."

The dessert coaxed a reluctant smile onto the boy's face. Unlike Audra, he didn't appear to be excited about the idea of mice in the walls, or the secrecy involved in their mission to the kitchen.

"Anyone else want a cookie? These are chocolate charms—an Ashari specialty. They'll give you good dreams," Audra said thickly through a mouthful as she offered the plate out. Vex'ahlia must have asked the cooks to make them for Keyleth's visit. "Or maybe they give you good luck. . . ."

Trinket, however, already had his snout buried in his pie. Vesper, leaning against him, was eating some kind of custard cream puff.

This parenting thing wasn't so bad, really. Was it tiring? Sure, but so was being Lord Trinket, the Wonder Bear. Maybe this wasn't Trinket's ideal way to spend the evening, but everyone was eating, everyone seemed happy, and no one had yelled at anyone or broken anything—the worst that had happened so far had been playing dress-up, but if it kept everyone out of trouble, Trinket could tolerate the bows and the braids until Vex came home to rescue him and told him what a fantastic job he had done of walking in her boots for the night. He had everything under control.

Or, at least, he did until they started making their way with the rest of their bounty back to the drawing room, where they'd left their books and games scattered around the rug, and Audra decided they should take a different path after crossing the foyer again.

As they wandered a narrow hall that wasn't often used—a servants' corridor barely wide enough for Trinket—Audra pointed with her half-eaten plate of cookies at a small door that crouched in the shadows like it was trying to avoid notice. It was rounded at the top, a little shorter than most of the other doors here, and made of solid oak. There were some deep grooves in its surface, as if, at some point, someone had tried to claw their way through (or perhaps had been fighting to keep something contained on the other side). The handle was a dark iron ring, and faintly, as Trinket's sensitive nose lifted toward it, he detected a hint of cool air escaping from the bottom.

"Where does that go?" the Ashari asked, her storm-gray eyes flashing with interest.

The door was one of the least remarkable things about the castle, something that Trinket had never given any amount of thought to, really, as it was usually concealed by some kind of enchantment. He knew it was Off-Limits, and that was reason enough not to dwell on it.

"That," Vesper said, drawing herself up to her full height and beaming at knowing something that the ever-so-slightly-older girl did not, "leads down to the dungeons. There used to be another way in, over in the west wing, but it's been boarded up for years." She rolled her eyes, and Trinket supposed she was thinking of the message scrawled across those wooden planks, the one that began: *Clever as you are, there is nothing for you here.* "Percy thinks I don't know about this one just because it's got some concealment spell on it—or it did. Like anything stays secret around here."

She smirked, her dark eyes dancing, and Trinket quickly swallowed the rumble of laughter that stirred deep in his chest. Ever since Vesper had figured out how to make herself a pop gun last year (only for Percy to swiftly confiscate it in the name of safety, but with a thoughtful look that made Trinket think they might see it again once he made some adjustments), she had started calling her father by his name as if to assert her dominance over him, too. But judging by the gleam that entered Percy's eyes whenever she said it, he seemed to respect her independence, if anything.

"What do you think is down there?" Juniper asked with as much curiosity as Audra, taking a bold step toward the door. Her brother quickly grabbed her hand and tried to pull her back, like just touching the handle would cause the castle to come crumbling down around them.

Vesper shrugged. "Dunno. I've never been. It's always locked, and probably covered in wards. Definitely a trap or two of Percy's as well, if I know anything about this place by now. . . ."

She was still trying to show off, Trinket guessed.

"Besides," she added with a sharp grin that was all her mother's, "I've always had more important things to do."

"Well, you're free tonight," Audra pointed out, her face shining eagerly.

Juni grinned and nodded, making clear what she thought of this plan, too. "I bet you can figure out how to break a couple wards," she added to Vesper. "I mean, it's *your* castle, too. All the doors should open for you."

"We're supposed to stay in the castle with Trinket," Wax pointed out in the loudest voice he had used all evening.

Vesper strode over to the door and grinned at the young gnome. "And we will be," she said, to little cheers and whoops of excitement from her friends. "The dungeons are technically still part of the castle. Just a different floor than we're on now. Nobody will get in any trouble."

"Forget trouble. We could get *eaten,*" Wax said through gritted teeth, again with Scanlan's face scrunched up in an expression of concern unlike anything Trinket could imagine on the musician himself.

"Eaten?" Vesper arched a delicate brow. "If there was anything serious down there, don't you think my mom and dad would have taken care of it by now?" They had, at some point before she came along, cleared out the old chambers down there, scoured and destroyed all the evidence of the Briarwoods' occupation.

But before she tested the door, she looked for a long moment at Trinket.

He had no idea what lurked beneath the castle these days. He hadn't been down there since before Vesper was born, and he suspected the girl herself had no idea what awaited them, either, even if she did know where both entrances were. Those tunnels, from what he remembered, stretched on for miles beneath Whitestone. Some even connected out in the Parchwood Timberlands. Any number of things could have wandered in if they found an opening, or made one.

He also wouldn't have any bear buttons down there, no way to call for backup if things got out of hand. Even the button labeled "Vex," the one that could directly connect him to her from anywhere, was likely currently out of service, as he suspected every button in the castle now simply asked, "Have you ever done it with a bear?"

Still, he could see how badly Vesper wanted to explore, wanted to impress her friends with a spooky stroll through some cobwebby tunnels and whatever debris remained that hadn't been important enough for her parents to clear away. Her dark eyes shone with the desire to adventure on her own, to be brave and strong. He knew that look right away, because he'd seen it on Vex many times over the years.

Then Vesper blinked, and her eyes shone with a question for Trinket instead.

He gave a low grunt of permission, and a smile broke across Vesper's face like the sun appearing unexpectedly from behind the clouds.

They were still partners in crime. Vesper might take the lead from here on out, but Trinket was her right-hand man, her muscle if anything went sideways. Not that it would. Spiders and mice or even some errant undead that had crawled up from the depths were nothing he couldn't handle. The cubs would get a little thrill, maybe a chill, and come back to warm up in front of the drawing room fire before their parents rolled in at some unholy hour, hazy-eyed but happy they had spent the time together.

He had this cub-rearing thing completely figured out.

Wrapping her fingers around the iron handle, Vesper tugged, and the door gave with little resistance. As she staggered back, surprised, Trinket noticed a swath of dust on the floor had been displaced like they weren't the first ones to try this door in recent days.

The four cubs crowded around the entrance, gazing down a set of wooden stairs that led into inky darkness so thick Trinket could almost taste the years of decay and neglect.

"That was easy," Juni squeaked, a little in awe for once.

Vesper put on a brave grin, and only Trinket saw it waver for half a second. "Well, it's like you said. This is my castle, too. I guess the door just . . . knew."

Trinket gave a quiet rumble of contemplation. Something wasn't right here; it wasn't at all like Percy or Vex to leave a door so potentially dangerous unattended like this. But the grizzly had already agreed to Vesper's plan, so all he could do was keep his eyes open despite being rather full of pie.

"Just give me a second. Trinket, you stay with the others until I get back," Vesper instructed, her blue skirt swishing around her ankles as she started hurrying back toward the foyer and the staircases there. Tossing a grin over her shoulder at the group, she added, "I'm going to get my crossbow."

Trinket wasn't at all surprised by that. Vesper's crossbow was her only real defense. Still, she wouldn't need it to do more than bolster her confidence while he was around. His claws were much sharper than bolts.

"If we get eaten, my ghost gets to tell Mom every day that it was your fault for dragging me down there," Wax muttered to his sister.

"And if we don't?" Audra prodded, with a wink at Juni.

Wax had to consider that for a moment. "Then . . . I'll do your chores for a month," he said to his sister, confident they were going to meet their untimely end descending into the cold, dark earth beneath the castle.

Juni narrowed her eyes at him, stuck out a hand, and said, "Deal, *Wilhand'ildan.* Because nothing's going to happen. Not when you're with me."

"And me and Vesper," Audra added with an encouraging smile. "Keyleth has been teaching me *everything*."

Trinket shrugged to himself. Sure, forget the overly decorated bear in the room. Besides, if anything did go wrong, he preferred having the element of surprise on his side.

It was only after the tall girl with hair like a winter's moon had breezed past, head held high and steps quick with purpose, that three shadows separated themselves from the narrow alcove at the top of the stairs. They were all sick of holding their breath, grateful to get some space from one another at last.

"That's the de Rolo girl," a lithe half-elven woman with long scarlet hair mouthed quietly to the others. "We could just take her now and go. We'll make a killing on her ransom alone."

"Losing your nerve already, Gilly?" a sallow-faced, dark-haired dwarf asked as he rubbed his lower leg. It was already swelling from a brush with the nasty trap he and his companions had dismantled in a back hallway on the lower floor. Not his finest moment, triggering that. Now the others would be irritated with him for the rest of the night.

At least the guards on duty had been too drunk to come running at the sound. They had also been too rosy-cheeked and reeking of mead to notice the small band of thieves slipping past them on the heels of a couple workers making a kitchen supply delivery earlier that evening. It gave the wayward trio easier access to explore the castle than they could have hoped for.

While Gilly rolled her eyes at the dwarf, the black-and-white-striped katari beside her stroked his whiskers thoughtfully. They had watched from on high as the small group crossed the foyer and returned to it some long minutes later with hands full of sweets before disappearing from view again, counting four targets in all. One de Rolo heir—clearly touched by some higher light—an Ashari, and two young gnomes.

Of course, they had also seen the bear. Heard him, too, thanks to that jingling bell around his neck. He was impossible to miss, all things considered, even without being covered in bows.

"I think," the katari said slowly, keeping his voice low as he listened for the faintest sounds of the girl's return, "that four children means four times *more* payout from their worried parents. And if they're staying here, that means they must have something close to de Rolo money."

The gleam of a sharp tooth followed as he grinned at his fellow conspirators: this wasn't his first stint at stealing babies from a castle, such as they were, even if he and his partners had only snuck into Whitestone tonight with the aim of relieving the de Rolos of a few of their treasures, not their darling daughter and her precious little friends. That was pure opportunity, and, as always, he would seize it.

"The girl could scream and alert the others if we do anything now," the katari continued, almost purring as he considered the possibilities. "We should wait, surprise them all at once . . . after we take out the bear, of course."

Narya, the dwarf with the smarting, bloodied leg, pulled a slim case from his belt and popped the latch. The darts inside glistened in the lamplight, their tips a faint, eerie green that meant he'd laced them with some sort of poison. Toxins were his specialty. He looked between the half-elf, Gilly, and the katari, Sparks, and showed every one of his broken teeth as he laughed softly and said, "Sounds like we're going on a bear hunt. I'm game."

Moments later, the de Rolo girl swept back through the hall, skirt exchanged for trousers, crossbow and lantern in hand. By then, the three burglars had folded themselves back into their alcove, molding themselves into the shadows behind a statue of someone's long-forgotten ancestor.

Sparks and Narya exchanged a glance at the sight of the weapon. It was a surprise, like the grizzly, but not a total deterrent when so much coin was at stake. Life-changing amounts, for the likes of them.

The girl's steps paused for the briefest moment, as if she could sense the shadows holding a collective breath. But then she shook her head to herself and was gone, back to her friends. Down below somewhere, one of them wolf-whistled. They were no doubt impressed at seeing the wicked-looking crossbow in the girl's hands.

Gilly, once again, looked uncertain.

Sparks nudged her in the shoulder. "C'mon," he growled. "It's just kids. Much simpler than any of your spellwork. This is easy pickings."

They waited, listening as a heavy door groaned slowly outward a few more inches. The bear huffed what sounded like a sigh. The boy whined, "I can't believe we're doing this," and a girl giggled.

Then all was calm, quiet, and still.

They stole down the stairs, swift and silent, moving in the direction from which they were almost certain they had heard the whistle and the bear's grumblings, and found themselves in a back service hallway they had already explored once this evening.

Beside the plain oak door at the end, just before the hall curved, sat a plate of cookies and half-eaten pastries. The snacks the children had taken from the kitchen.

Noticing Narya eyeing them with a glimmer of interest, Sparks kicked the plate aside with a scornful swipe of his boot, scattering crumbs.

The old door had been a difficult one even for three accomplished burglars to crack with magic and tools alike. Gilly had worked up a sweat breaking the enchantments that kept it locked and hidden, not to mention the clever trap that had bitten into Narya's leg and clamped down like the jaws of a grizzly until Sparks freed him. All this made them certain there was bound to be something incredible waiting behind it, like a small de Rolo fortune—only to see a set of rickety wooden stairs plummeting down into deeper darkness.

Sparks pulled the door wider, releasing a burst of cooler air that smelled slightly stale. A few loose bear hairs floated gently along in their own current, and a small silk bow had fallen on one of the top steps.

Their quarry was now down *there.* In the dungeons beneath the castle.

But while Narya frowned irritably at this new obstacle and Gilly took a cautious step back, Sparks looked like he'd just swallowed some delicious, rare bird. "It's better this way," he purred, his voice silky with persuasion. "Let the dungeons tire them out; surely you've heard the rumors of what's still down there. We'll go slow, let them have their fun, and sweep in just when they're all ready for bedtime."

He eventually took the lead, as usual, once they had given the girl and her friends enough of a head start, glancing back at the others with luminous, coin-bright eyes as he dared in a hiss, "Where's your sense of adventure?"

THE DUNGEON WAS, JUST AS Trinket expected, still cold, dirty, and damp. Shoving his bulk down the long flight of stairs ahead of the cubs had been arguably the worst part, even if he had the bright glow that Juni held in her cupped hands. It was a gift from the Everlight, just like her mother's, and clearly a powerful one despite her youth and inexperience. Vesper, he knew, didn't need any light at all to see by; she was just born that way. Still, she had remembered to give Wax a lantern to help guide his steps as well in case they got separated.

"Well, we've seen it. We're officially cool. And this place is officially boring. We can go back now, right?" Wax asked hopefully as they gathered in what appeared to be a central chamber at the bottom of the steps. The ceilings were high, bare in places with roots poking through, and several doorways offered them different ways forward, each watched over by a pair of what looked to Trinket like waving stone imps. The statues were covered in a thick layer of gritty dust and cobwebs, obviously undisturbed for some time; a small spider scuttled in and out of one imp's open mouth, weaving a new web over its carven teeth.

Vesper wandered up to each of the four open doorways, peering through them but not quite choosing a particular path just yet, crossbow held at the ready all the while. Trinket guessed that she was remembering what her parents had told her of this place: that somewhere down here in the pervasive chill, the rulers of Whitestone past rested in the walls. That the Briarwoods had once done terrible, unspeakable things in some of these chambers, though all evidence of them and their magic had long since been erased.

Which left . . .

Empty rooms. Scorch marks. The occasional indecipherable bloody scrawl staining the stones, where there were any stones in the walls left at all. A vague, foul stench. Trinket took it all in as he whuffed a heavy breath at Vesper's side and assured himself that, while unpleasant, there was nothing in this warren of rooms that was a cause for concern.

The pair turned back to the others. Audra seemed to be hunting for mice with the lantern she had borrowed from Wax, while Juni held her light up to some dark graffiti that read *I'm sorry.*

Wax glanced pointedly from the chilling words to his sister and muttered, "That's the kind of thing your ghost is going to be writing to my ghost if we don't get out of here soon."

"Don't you want a souvenir, Wax?" Vesper called, an edge of excitement in her voice. Trinket had noticed the quiet was giving her new confidence. "We've got to at least find something to take back, so we can prove we were down here. Otherwise, no one's going to believe us."

Wax narrowed his copper eyes at her. But he apparently couldn't argue with her logic, or thought doing so would be a waste of breath, so he simply nodded.

"Not even the mice seem to like this part of the dungeon," Audra said in a hushed voice as she rejoined the others, the lantern light bouncing off the walls in time with her steps. "I think we'll have to go deeper. Which way, Vesper?" She looked to the pale-haired girl as if she would have some innate sense of which path to take, much like the door had opened so easily at her touch. Trinket still didn't trust that.

Vesper indicated an entryway leading into an empty chamber. At the back of it, Trinket supposed, she could see another doorway, though even Juni's light didn't fully illuminate their surroundings enough for him to check for himself.

The darkness down here was a living, breathing thing crawling into Trinket's fur and making itself at home. Despite the distraction, he could sense that Vesper was bluffing, simply guessing where she wanted to lead them next, but it all seemed relatively safe—until she charged confidently through the entryway ahead of the others and fire gusted along Trinket's right side, nearly scorching him.

He leapt out of the way just in time, glancing up to see smoke curling from the mouth of one of the stone imps. The others hung behind him, fidgeting with their clothes or staring at their feet, each trying to act less startled than they were.

Likely confused as to why no one had followed, Vesper poked her head back through the open doorway and followed Trinket's gaze upward.

"What, no one's in the mood for a roast tonight after all that dessert?" she asked, her pale cheeks flushing scarlet despite her words as she surely realized what she had almost done, triggering an old trap.

Glancing back up to the statues, she seemed to see right away what Trinket was also noticing: the cobwebs between the statues' little arms were now broken, the dust over their fingers disturbed.

"I think," she said slowly, "those things want a greeting in return before we pass through. One of them definitely waved to me just before it shot fire out of its mouth."

Trinket eyed her warily. This whole adventure was getting more questionable by the second. But Vesper stared right back, unblinking and still determined—and he relented, although with a deep sigh.

Before the door, he lowered his shaggy head toward his paws and then plodded cautiously forward. He trusted Vesper's instincts, even if he didn't trust those statues. And sure enough, nothing happened this time. Either she was right or the trap was spent.

Wax went up to the door next and bowed to the imps.

Audra blew them kisses.

And Juni and her bright light, bringing up the rear, sang them a little song of welcome.

Finally, they were all on the other side. The cubs grinned at one another while Trinket tried to unclench his jaw, realizing he'd been grinding his teeth the whole time each of his young charges was passing through the doorway.

There were more entryways ahead to cross through, as he expected. More pairs of waving stone imps above each of them to greet, though Vesper's idea, at least, seemed to prevent them from setting off any more traps. Then there was the occasional mark on the stones that Trinket started to *hope* was blood and not something worse, like lasting residue from one of the Briarwoods' dark rituals. But the rooms were all empty, the tunnels quiet and lonely, evidence of Percy and Vex's thorough cleansing of the place years ago.

"We could just cut a couple of roots to take back as our proof. Or pull one of these stones out of the walls. No one will miss them," Wax suggested at one point when they were faced with another long tunnel and the promise of more distance yet to cover on aching feet. The slight curve to the walls seemed to suggest that they formed concentric rings.

Vesper turned to him, the lantern in Audra's hand casting dancing shadows over her face, a glint of mischief in her dark eyes. "If you're tired of walking, you can always ride Trinket."

Trinket and Wax stared at each other for a long moment until Audra broke the silence.

"Juni, is now really the time for the pie song?" she whispered, sounding annoyed.

"What?" the young gnome asked, her cheeks flushing pink in the glow of the Everlight as she looped her arm through Wax's, pulling him along to get him moving again. "I wasn't singing."

"No, but you were humming it," Vesper agreed softly, her eyes searching Juniper's face. "Weren't you . . . ?"

"I didn't hear anything," Wax offered, but he didn't sound certain.

Vesper turned to Trinket, and he slowly shook his head. He hadn't heard anything that sounded like singing, though as he focused his senses, he found there *was* a sound of some kind echoing down the smaller passageway to their right. It was a scraping like long, hairy limbs rubbing together, like many feet scrabbling along the floor. And it was getting louder. It reminded Trinket of insects—only, for a bug to make that much noise, it would have to be almost as big as he was.

He glanced at the cubs, using his own bulk to crowd them into the tunnel ahead, to put distance between them and whatever was now rushing toward them from the other opening, hissing and clicking as it gained speed.

Vesper took a few steps backward as she readied her crossbow, having been taught never to turn her back on a fight, only to collide with a giant spiderweb completely closing off the tunnel and blocking their escape. She struggled against its stickiness, trying to take aim even while stuck.

"Go," Vesper commanded the others calmly, so that once again only Trinket recognized the tiny tremor in her voice. "Run. Back the way we came. Trinket and I will handle this."

To the cubs' credit, not one of them listened. Juni closed her eyes, already chanting something under her breath, while Audra readied the lantern like a missile, prepared to launch it at whatever was now rushing toward them before calling on her own magic. Wax raised his fists, and Trinket was sure he heard the littlest cub muttering something about "being strong like Grog." Of course, strength would do only so much if the creature or creatures coming at them had any poison.

As the first of many long black limbs poked out of the opening, someone swore colorfully—Wax again, Trinket realized, unable to stop a snort of amusement. He had a feeling he knew what was coming, as he could think of just one creature that made webs that big and sticky, but he still had a few seconds to hope for something easier to handle before Audra gasped and said, "Oh. It's like an eight-legged pony."

A spider almost as big as himself crawled out of the opening, its many eyes blinking and squinting against the glare of Juni's light, which she had tossed up into the air to free her hands.

Trinket bared all of his many impressive teeth; there was, after all, a chance that the spider would take one look at him and decide to crawl back into its hole. But it charged forward anyway, either bold or stupid or not afraid of bears wearing bows.

Most of all, Trinket suspected, it was desperately hungry.

Vesper let out a frustrated cry. The first of her bolts, aimed at a tender spot just behind the enormous, glistening carapace of the creature trying to corner Trinket, had just flown wider than any of her shots ever did during training.

"When we get back, I'm asking Mom for a dagger," she panted, struggling against the web's restraints. She stopped trying to aim the crossbow for a moment, instead using one of her bolts in an attempt to cut herself free, but it was no use. The bolt wasn't sharp enough to stab through a web this strong.

Boldly scuttling past Trinket, the spider pressed forward like it wanted to back Audra into the web with Vesper, but the Ashari's eyes gleamed with some secret knowledge for a moment before weeds and vines erupted from the dirt floor, a garden growing before their eyes that wrapped around the spider's many limbs and Trinket's legs alike, missing the four cubs by only a few inches.

At least the spider was now captured, even if Trinket was stuck along with it. He was determined to be the first to break free so he could pounce and end this.

But before he could exhaust himself thrashing against the vines, a flash of blazing light illuminated the whole tunnel for a moment, making even Trinket's breath catch: the powerful glare of Juni's spell.

Whatever she had done completely blinded the spider, allowing Vesper to get a few shots off with one of her bolts even in her weakened state. The first only seemed to anger their attacker, making it thrash so hard that it broke the vines restraining it. But her next quick shot into its tender abdomen took it down to the ground and popped it like a balloon full of water, spraying them all with guts and gore. The creature lay unmoving atop the weeds and vines that began to wither as Audra's spell ended, and the Ashari sank to her knees, relieved.

"Everyone okay?" Vesper asked on a ragged breath as her crossbow fell from her limp hand despite her efforts to hold on.

Audra, still on the ground, ran a hand through her mussed blond hair and nodded. It was hard to tell against the brilliant glow of Juni's light, but Trinket thought the Ashari looked paler than before, perhaps a little dizzy. Giant spider goo flecked her cheeks like dark freckles.

"Apparently spider blood *stinks.* And I'm covered in cobwebs," Wax observed bitterly. "Plus, we nearly all got covered in bites."

"But we didn't, brother-dear," Juni countered with a wide grin. "Just a little blood."

The knowledge seemed to raise their spirits as they collected themselves as best they could, fixing their clothes and hair, wiping their faces clean, and rubbing their hands over little sore spots that were, Trinket gathered from their giggles and grins, worn as proudly as battle scars.

"You know, these cobwebs would be a great souvenir. Impressive stuff, and hard to get rid of, too," Wax tried to argue, just once, before apparently realizing it was absolutely useless.

Audra swiped a finger over some of the sticky residue on his shoulder and popped it into her mouth. "Tastes like . . . cotton candy," she declared, but no one else was in the mood to try it, even if they were energized to press on.

"Trinket, think your claws can cut me out of this mess? I want to see where this tunnel goes while we still have time. I see some kind of light up ahead, and . . . what looks like a cave," Vesper said, her gaze effortlessly piercing the darkness beyond the web as she glanced over her shoulder.

Trinket was about ready to turn around. The warm spot in front of the drawing room hearth sounded better by the second, and he needed time to figure out how to explain any of the cubs' new little bruises to Vex, but he knew there was no stopping Vesper now.

Oh, to be young, eager, and invincible.

She clearly had adrenaline coursing through her veins and a new fire in her eyes as Trinket cut her free of the webbing. She was even singing—a high, lilting song that had a pleasant melody but no words Trinket could quite understand.

He stopped trying to clear the rest of the web from their path as he realized that wasn't Vesper's voice at all.

Nor was it Juni, whose singing was more polished and less raspy than this.

Something was down here with them, something besides spiders and other worshippers of the dark that had taken up residence in the echoing, loveless tunnels. Something that perhaps had been here all along. Even Trinket could sense it as he breathed in, the taste of something ancient crawling into his throat.

It was fouler than giant spider blood.

Before he could growl a warning, something swooped through the torn web.

Juni screamed as a bloodbat collided with her, drawn by the scent of the fresh kill that was still oozing in a wide, spreading stain across the tunnel floor.

"Incoming!" Vesper gasped, suddenly angling her crossbow through the torn webbing, eyes going wide as she caught a glimpse of what was now speeding toward them.

It was a whole swarm of bloodbats, Trinket realized as he prepared to dart between the cubs and the oncoming dark cloud of rustling wings. Hopefully, he could draw most of them onto himself instead.

But before he could dive through the tattered web, two more giant spiders spilled out of the hole behind them, one of them leaping onto Trinket's back.

The cubs' shrieks and gasps filled the tunnel as the bloodbats descended, seeking a taste of warmer blood than the dead spider's, since it was being offered.

Trinket roared at the irritatingly strong creature on his back, trying to toss it off.

At least the other spider hadn't advanced, though Trinket didn't feel any better when he realized why that was: she was apparently busy having cubs of her own. The carpet of tiny, writhing bodies—hundreds of little spiders, Trinket guessed—swiftly advanced toward Vesper and the others as they swatted bloodbats off one another, already bleeding all over from tiny bites on their arms, necks, and faces.

Even with a bloodbat stuck to his back, Wax managed to grab their lantern and throw it at the spider doing all the spawning. The resulting explosion was large enough to engulf the giant creature in flames but too late to stop the advancing tide of tiny spiders.

The mother spider hissed and shrieked as her carapace melted away while her army of babies darted through the fray. They crawled up Juni's legs, scuttled along Wax's arms, and tickled Vesper's cheek as she shot at a bloodbat that would have landed on Juni's neck.

Audra kept apologizing as she frantically brushed off the baby spiders, interrupting herself while she began a familiar spell that Trinket knew would douse the fire before they all had burning alive to worry about, too.

At least they would still have Juni's bright light to see by, though not for long if the bloodbats kept attacking before Trinket reached the cubs.

Furious with the spider writhing on top of him, he bit into one of its grasping legs—big mistake—and coughed on a mouthful of bitter blood as the creature shook him off and redoubled its efforts to stab him with its pointy, venomous teeth.

The spider made a screeching noise as it suddenly tugged on a snarl of Trinket's fur. A few of its legs were now stuck in his braids, and Trinket took the opportunity to bite down on another mouthful of the creature, this time showering himself in dark blood that sizzled unpleasantly where it soaked him.

He would be the first to admit he needed a bath tonight before Vex got an eyeful of him, but at least the spider had stopped struggling. It curled up and collapsed beside him as the life quietly drained out of it, soaking more of the ground around them while the smaller spiders tried to flee the chaos.

The bloodbats, however, were either too hungry or too stubborn to retreat when there was so much fresh carnage, and so many warm bodies still standing.

As the vampiric creatures kept diving at them with purpose, Juni finally shielded herself, trying to draw Wax into the protection of her magic as well. He dodged her grasping hand, attempting to run through the web toward the faint light and supposed cavern Vesper had glimpsed as if that might provide some better shelter.

But he made it only a few feet before four of the creatures managed to attach themselves to him. Screaming and tearing at them with his hands didn't seem to deter them much, not when they had already stuck their proboscises deep into his neck and shoulders.

His sister ran toward him while Audra tried, unsuccessfully, to keep the furry little bloodsuckers off the dark-haired gnome, though whatever spell the Ashari was conjuring did seem to have confused the cloud of bats, a flurry of stars now twinkling around the tunnel as Audra continued to add power to her enchantment. The sight of the glimmering stars made Trinket slightly giddy; he finally understood why Keyleth was so proud of the girl.

"Ouch!" Audra yelped as one of the bloodbats attached itself to her arm, breaking her concentration. "Sorry, little guy," she murmured as she tried hard to pry the fuzzy body off of herself and get the awful suckers out. But without the deterrent of her dizzying stars, the bloodbats called to one another with clicks and chirps, reorganizing for a stronger attack.

Trinket swatted two of the creatures down with his paws as Vesper shot another one out of the air before it could add to the pileup on Wax.

She turned to him, triumph lighting her face, only to see the two dead ones crushed beneath his enormous paws. Comprehension quickly flashed through her gaze, followed by renewed determination. "Bet I can take out more than you," she dared, if a little wearily.

Bring it, came Trinket's answering growl as she shot another before it could land on his back.

"You're welcome!" she called hoarsely as she readied another bolt.

As he swatted another of the annoying bloodsuckers to its death, movement from the corner of his eye drew Trinket's gaze, and he realized Wax was now on the ground. That couldn't be good. The boy was chanting something to himself, too, over and over, almost like magic.

"Stop, drop, and roll."

The gnome rolled across the tunnel like he was on fire and desperately trying to put it out, crushing all the bloodbats until there were none left on him, and those left alive seemed wary of landing on such an erratic target.

Vesper shot two more bloodbats out of the air, neatly piercing them on the same bolt, but Trinket stopped swatting and waited until a whole flock of the creatures had alighted on his back before he, too, dropped to the ground like Wax and used his bulk to crush the unsuspecting bloodbats as he rolled around.

"What—?" Vesper panted, but her attention was quickly pulled away as she slammed a bloodbat against the wall with a particularly impressive shot.

Audra and Juni had caught on, too, and the four of them rolled around until Vesper had used up most of her bolts and the tunnel floor was a wet, furry mess.

She started toward Trinket, who had the majority of the casualties scattered around him. He showed off his teeth in what passed for a grin, and Vesper shook her head. "You totally cheated. I win by default," she declared firmly, despite her obvious exhaustion.

But a small smile quickly crossed her lips just after. They both knew no one had set any rules here, and she could clearly see the sentiment echoed in the way Trinket's eyes crinkled.

As she crouched by the grizzly and started to brush him off, pulling out a few more bows along the way, he reached up and swatted one remaining bloodbat off her back, an attachment she hadn't even noticed in the heat of battle.

Nearby, Audra slumped against a surprised Wax; he caught her around the waist, his cheeks ablaze in the faint glow of Juni's light. That must have been more magic than the Ashari was used to doing in a day.

This time, Vesper didn't even try to ask if everyone was okay; Juni's light flickered feebly as she pulled out a healing salve to dab on everyone's little bloodbat bites. Trinket guessed it was one of Pike's own mixtures.

Next, Juni laid a hand on the dark, leaking spot on Vesper's back. That one had struck deeper and needed true healing, something that took the girl several minutes to accomplish in total focused silence while Audra borrowed the salve to rub on Trinket's scrapes, too.

Yet the pleasant coolness of the salve didn't distract Trinket from the obvious in the slightest: it was past time to go home.

They had walked for what felt like miles, their feet ached, and they were all covered in a combination of their own blood and the creatures'. All of them would need to thoroughly wash up before their parents came home, Trinket included, to have any hope of hiding the evidence.

But when Vesper opened her mouth, it wasn't to suggest that they turn around. Instead, as her eyes met Trinket's, she pointed through the torn webbing and summoned a weary smile. "Before we go," she told them all, "I just want to check out that cave up there. If there are any souvenirs to bring back, even if it's just rocks, we've earned them."

Just a short march down the tunnel through the river of bloodbat bodies, Trinket and the others glimpsed what Vesper had been seeing as the path opened up into a large cavern. With long stalactites bearing down on them like daggers and stalagmites jutting up all over the floor at random like sharp teeth, Trinket couldn't help but imagine they were caught in the jaws of yet another hungry creature.

Several yards away on the other side of the cavern, an ancient, arcane light set into the stones cast a bluish glow over what looked like a small storeroom of sorts carved into the rock wall. As they drew closer, with Trinket in the lead, he realized it was more like a large hidey-hole someone had dug out with a couple of shovels and a shitload of determination.

The nook was full of crates of curious things that seemed to revive everyone's spirits better than healing salve. Even Wax seemed to be intrigued by a pouch he dug out from behind some tattered books; it smelled like cinnamon and anise and all sorts of good things to Trinket's sensitive nose.

"Ooh, strawberry jam," Audra exclaimed softly, beaming as she pulled some old, dusty glass jars tied with ribbon from one of the crates. "And it's *historical.* It must be good." She started trying to unscrew one of the lids, but Juni put a hand on her arm to stop her, and Trinket was relieved. He couldn't have the young Ashari getting poisoned on his watch.

"If you're going to taste that, at least let me purify it first. Mom showed me how last week," Juni rasped worriedly.

"Tomorrow, after you get some sleep," Vesper cut in, eyeing Juni with concern. The glow of the Everlight that she had kept floating along with them all this time was getting dimmer by the second as she dusted off a heavy rabbit made of gears and brass, some kind of windup toy that Trinket suspected would be useful for detecting traps.

As Wax shoved a little glass vial of what looked like bacon grease into his front shirt pocket, Vesper picked up a slender dagger and turned it this way and that, giving one of the wooden crates an experimental jab.

The dagger screamed as it was swung, making all five of them jump—even Trinket, who barely fit into the room to begin with. He flinched and bumped his head on the top of the doorway as the cubs all turned to look at him; their eyes widened, and what little color was left in their faces after the tunnel fiasco now drained completely away.

There was that singing again. The cool, ancient voice that wasn't Juni or Vesper.

Trinket didn't want to look behind him, but he backed fully out of the room and turned around all the same. There, crossing the cavern as if summoned by the dagger's cry, was the transparent form of a woman in a long gown with lavish embroidery at the cuffs and neck. Her hair swirled around her face in a nonexistent breeze as she wove between stone pillars, the floating locks held in place only by the gem-studded crown she wore. She had to be a ghost, a past ruler of Whitestone, most likely.

She stopped suddenly, turning to lock eyes with Trinket, and unleashed a bloodcurdling scream that chilled him all the way to the marrow.

Not a ghost, then.

"Banshee," Vesper whispered to the others just before Trinket answered the horrible woman with a bone-shaking roar of his own.

He didn't have time to glance at Vesper again, but he didn't need to. He knew she understood it was time to flee, and she ushered the others out of the storeroom and past Trinket. He acted as rear guard as the others broke into a flat-out run, shoving their treasures into their pockets as best they could along the way.

The spectral woman became a distant pinprick of blue-white light as they scampered back into the long, dark tunnel, all following the sound of Vesper's footsteps, her breathing, since she was the only one who could see now that Juni's light had fully died.

Trinket nudged the gnome along with his snout, trying to urge her on when she stumbled, too exhausted to even think about carrying on. Then Audra's steps started to falter, too, and he crouched low to allow both cubs onto his back while Vesper held tight to Wax's hand, sweeping him along behind her through total darkness.

Only, as they rounded another bend, the darkness didn't last.

There were lanterns burning brightly just past the narrow opening where they had killed the bloodbats and giant spiders, several smaller ones still scuttling here and there as the unfriendly flames drove them back.

Blocking the path home were three figures: a tall, unsmiling half-elven woman with scarlet hair, a smirking black-and-white-striped katari, and a stout and surly dwarf who leered at them and said, "Isn't it past your bedtime, little ones?" before he lifted a slender dart gun to his lips.

Trinket leapt just before the dart flew, dumping the girls quickly and unceremoniously to the ground so they wouldn't get hit.

The dart found its mark, sinking into Trinket's side, and he tried his best to angle himself in front of the cubs to block them completely from further harm before he started feeling the effects of whatever toxin he had just been shot with. But for now he could still feel his paws, so he charged toward the strangers, trusting Vesper to hold the others back while she readied a bolt.

Where had the katari gone? Trinket no longer saw the catlike figure anywhere in the tunnel's gloom. That was going to be a problem.

The dwarf fired another dart, this one missing and sinking into Juni's leg instead. As Trinket barreled toward them, he recognized the flash of regret in the stranger's eyes, the dwarf clearly realizing the mistake he had just made.

Behind Trinket, Juni collapsed into Wax's arms. As Audra sank ungracefully down beside them, Trinket heard her murmur frantically, her voice nearing a pitch of panic, "What do we do? What do I do? I can—Oh, I don't *know*! Juni, talk to me. I—I've never healed poison before. . . ."

The half-elf and the dwarf both effortlessly dodged Trinket's claws and teeth despite the grizzly taking up most of the tunnel. Realizing the effects of the poison were beginning to slow his movements, Trinket howled in frustration as the katari dropped from the ceiling onto his back. This was somehow worse than the bloodbats or spiders hitching a ride.

Vesper fired off a bolt at the menacing figure despite the challenging angle, yet the katari contorted himself out of the way without breaking a sweat.

"Narya, what's taking that poison so long to work?" Trinket's unwanted rider demanded as he pulled out a rope, and the grizzly tried to throw him off. "Shouldn't the bear be dead by now?"

Vesper cried out at that and unleashed another bolt; she had only one left.

"Look, girl," the katari crooned at Vesper, whose face was streaked with tears as she watched Trinket's legs wobble unsteadily. "We don't want to hurt you. We just want you to come with us for a little while, until your parents give us a nice pile of gold for returning you safely after rescuing you from this dungeon that unfortunately killed your big fuzzy guard dog."

Trinket snarled weakly at the stranger. He sure as hell didn't plan on dying like this in front of Vesper and the others.

Looking over each of their suddenly terrified but still battle-ready faces—even Juni's, tight with pain as the poison set in—he saw echoes of Vox Machina in the set of their jaws and the fight in their eyes. These cubs belonged to Vex and Percy. To Pike and Scanlan (and Grog, really). To Keyleth.

And they were also Trinket's. He had crawled through the Belly of Dragons, he had witnessed the fall of a god, and he had learned a thing or two about how to put unruly creatures in their place. He wasn't going to lose a single one of his cubs to these second-rate kidnappers, poisoned or not.

He had to shake this off.

"Gilly, can't you do *something* to keep this damn bear down?" the katari spat.

The half-elven woman had been staring at one of the giant spider corpses with a clear line of worry cutting between her brows, but now her eyes began to glow with some sort of spell.

Trinket thrashed harder, trying to unseat the katari and finally sending him flying. The grizzly dropped to the ground just after, no doubt thanks to the effects of the dart still in his side. He struggled back up, barely. If they could just draw the kidnappers deeper into the tunnel, back toward the eerie, transparent figure they had seen, maybe the cubs could escape before Trinket fully collapsed.

Before the woman's muttered enchantment could take effect, a sudden fog rolled over the tunnel, obscuring the lanterns' glow.

Audra, Trinket realized dimly. Despite being shaken and exhausted, she was trying to help them flee unnoticed.

Through the thick mist and the darkness, Vesper crawled her way forward to Trinket until her hand was buried in his fur, pulling the dart free. Then she put a hand on his shoulder and nudged gently. She wasn't trying to urge him forward, he understood, but back the way they had come.

Back toward the cavern and the ghastly, keening woman.

"This way!" Vesper called to the kidnappers as Trinket padded down the tunnel on unsteady paws. "Come on, catch me if you can!"

She was drawing the sinister trio away from the other cubs, giving Audra a chance to heal Juni. After a while, Trinket noticed Wax creeping along beside him, too, but there was no time to growl at him to go back to the others.

"There's all sorts of treasure down here, not just me!" Vesper called in a light, teasing voice despite her otherwise ragged breathing. They had finally reached the cavern, breaking free of the enchanted fog.

The spectral woman was nowhere to be seen.

Nor did Trinket hear any eerie singing. But they couldn't go looking for her now; the three kidnappers spilled out into the cavern, having easily kept pace despite the thick swirls of fog, with the still-smirking katari leading the way.

"You could stop all this nonsense anytime, you know," he said silkily to Vesper as he slowly strode closer, flanked by his companions on either side. He frowned, his whiskers wilting, perhaps trying to look sympathetic. "I know you're tired. You're hurt; so are your friends. We'll feed you while we wait on all the gold from your parents. My colleague Gilly here can even patch you up, I believe. Just come with us. Stop fighting."

Trinket caught movement out of the corner of his eye as Wax crouched behind one of the rock columns growing out of the floor, taking cover.

Vesper leaned against Trinket, trying to keep him upright as the scarlet-haired half-elf began to chant again—and it didn't sound like words of healing to Trinket. Vesper's skin was warm against Trinket's side, and despite the poison telling him he really ought to lie down and close his eyes, despite all his lingering aches and pains from battles past, despite too many comfortable days of eating pie by the hearth, with Vesper here he was as battle-ready as ever.

Together, they were young, eager, and invincible.

Trinket growled lowly at the kidnappers as Vesper put an arm around him, narrowed her eyes at the rotten trio, and asked coolly, "Hey. Have you ever done it with a bear?"

With that, she shot her last bolt up toward the cavern ceiling, waking several more slumbering bloodbats as the stalactite she hit broke off and came plummeting toward the ground. Trinket leapt at the kidnappers from the other side, forcing them to either embrace him or risk getting stabbed by the large shard of pointy rock.

Even sluggish and sick, he was still a better hunter than the scarlet-haired half-elf, who screamed as she received a tattoo in the shape of his bite, and the dwarf, who now found himself trapped beneath the massive paws of his quarry and promptly passed out.

"Vesper, Trinket, hurry up!" Wax shouted. He had snuck back toward the tunnel, and as Trinket shuffled toward him, he glimpsed a glass vial in the young gnome's hand. Clearly, Wax knew what he had taken from the storeroom and had a plan to use it.

Trinket growled for Vesper to join them, to abandon the fight (if not for the poison, he would have liked his odds here, even three on one. The dwarf was fully unconscious, and the half-elf looked too shaken to come back for a second round anyway). But Vesper shook her head, pulling something from her belt. The screaming dagger she had taken as her souvenir.

He knew she had never stabbed anything more than a straw dummy, but she brandished the knife fearlessly at the katari all the same. The kidnapper cowered against the rocks, looking truly afraid for the first time as the blade made its horrible shrieking again. Still, he snarled, "You brat, you're just wasting everyone's time. You're out of bolts, your friends are useless, and your bear is almost out of time. You can't win."

Trinket realized in a flash of appreciation what Vesper was trying to do as the katari kept talking. Giving the kidnappers something else to tangle with would certainly buy them more time to escape.

A cool, ancient voice filled the room as the spectral woman's glow faintly illuminated the cavern.

With a shudder of relief, Vesper tossed the blade at the katari's feet and backed slowly toward Wax once she saw Trinket put another paw, however unsteady, in the same direction.

Together, they edged into the tunnel as the wandering spirit held the bloodied half-elf and the slack-faced katari transfixed with her icy stare, the dwarf still passed out and oblivious on the cavern floor nearby.

Slowly, the katari reached down and plucked up the dagger, brandishing it at the approaching specter.

"S-Sparks," the half-elf stammered, unable to tear her gaze from the spirit that had them in her sights as she floated slowly closer. "You *idiot.* You should have listened to me. We should have just grabbed the de Rolo girl while we had a chance and called it a night."

As soon as they were in the tunnel, Wax hesitated, no longer following Vesper. Trinket turned, stumbling but determined to nudge him along, and watched for an awed moment instead as a flash of fear then determination crossed the young gnome's serious features. He tossed his vial back into the cavern, having firmed up his resolve to save his friends.

The vial exploded in a cloud of colorful flames and began to burn even against the wet stone, blocking the trio from using the tunnel for a potential escape as the fire spread.

"Look, we can easily cut you in on what we've got going here. Split the profits four ways, instead of three," the katari crooned back in the cavern—to the specter, no doubt. "No? Well, then . . ."

The katari gave a battle cry, and Trinket could just picture him lunging at the spirit with that dagger on the other side of the magical flames.

The spirit's answering shriek was loud enough that Trinket was sure it ruffled his fur as he lumbered down the tunnel, with Vesper and Wax supporting him on either side, urging him on to find Audra and Juni. The sound was still ringing in his ears by the time they found the exhausted Ashari resting in the circle of the lanterns' glow, a mouse on her shoulder curiously sniffing her face. Vesper hurried over to make sure she was okay.

Wax ran to his sister where she sat, still dizzy but no longer poisoned, and threw his arms around her. "Guess I'm doing all your chores for a month," he breathed. And she hugged him back tight.

One exhausting, lantern-lit walk later, with all four cubs pushing him up an uncountable number of stairs, Trinket saw six familiar faces framed in the light at the top and promptly collapsed just on the other side of the oak door.

Scanlan had the plate of Audra's leftover cookies in hand. "What?" he asked when Pike shot him a disapproving look, holding out her arms to the filthy and exhausted Juni and Wax as they ran to her. "You know I eat when I'm stressed." Still, he threw the plate aside to grab up his daughter and son (and kiss Pike's cheek).

"I made a new friend tonight," Audra told Keyleth through a yawn as the older druid knelt beside her, frantically checking her over. Keyleth paused, strands of shiny tinsel still wrapped around her antlers from their wild night, and glanced at the mouse on Audra's shoulder.

But Audra, gently beaming, was looking at Vesper, Juni, and Wax . . . and, longest of all, at Trinket.

Maybe it wouldn't be so bad after all, having a cub of his own one day. He was starting to suspect, as he gazed at each of his young charges, that he might really enjoy being a father.

Pike laid a hand on the grizzly's fur and started to heal him as Vesper hugged her bewildered parents, who smelled strongly of lavender wine and flowers and the fragrant smoke from a bonfire. "I found something really cool in the dungeons," she told Percy. "But I lost it again. This dagger, you should have seen it, Dad—or, rather, heard it. . . ."

Trinket, watching Percy's face, wasn't sure the man had heard anything but the word "Dad."

"Anyway," Vesper continued, her eyes meeting Trinket's again, "I wasn't ever really scared. Trinket had everything handled the whole time."

Weary as they both were, Trinket's eyes shone as they looked back into hers.

Vesper winked, a promise of more pie in her tired grin.

They were going to be partners in crime for a long time. Trinket could sense it already.

"Rough night, huh," Vex said knowingly as she knelt beside him, tugging gently on a half-undone braid. Her voice was low and scratchy, which meant she'd had a rough one, too; someone had convinced her to try singing solo at the tavern again.

Trinket grumbled, full of understanding and sympathy.

"Exactly," Vex agreed, carefully pulling the bows out of Trinket's fur. "Anyone can fight a dragon with the right tools, but parenting isn't for the weak."

Trinket nodded and flicked his ears.

Vex laughed hoarsely. "You're right, especially when it's four on one. Six, really—next time I'll leave the twins with you, too."

Those were terrible odds. But somehow, Trinket was already looking forward to it.

ACKNOWLEDGMENTS

JESS BARBER

I would like to thank everyone who helped "Take This Down" to exist: Becca, Dayna, and Sara, for all the encouragement, brainstorming, and inspiration. Cherae, for the same, with added love and gratitude for getting me the gig in the first place. Itoh, for tireless cheerleading and day-brightening. CWF and BSpec, for long-term writerly support. My agent, Maeve MacLysaght, and the whole crew at PRH, especially Lydia Estrada, for being such a delight to work with. AJ, for being the best partner in the world as well as an absolutely brilliant first reader. And of course, everyone at Critical Role, especially Sam Riegel, for inviting others into their sandbox to play with all their amazing toys.

MARTIN CAHILL

For Paul in college, the first to put a D20 in my hand, who promised me D&D had everything I loved and more; how right you were, my friend. To my fellow college heroes of Eberron, thank you for saving the world with me several times over. And to the Fogtown Five, the Fructuglies, (yes, they really chose that as their team name), and my Queens, to all I've rolled dice with, thank you for playing with me. Thank you so much to Sarah Peed and Lydia Estrada for their help bringing the Sun Tree to life. And a special thank you to Matthew Mercer, Dani Carr, and the entire Critical Role cast and team. Without Exandria and the stories of those who defend it, I would not be the storyteller I am today. Let's keep telling stories together, all of us.

REBECCA COFFINDAFFER

First and foremost, my many thanks to the teams at Critical Role and Random House Worlds, both for this opportunity and all your guidance in making this story the very best it can be. To Lydia and Sarah, your notes both encouraged me and pushed me in fantastic ways. To Lara, my agent, for her constant support and enthusiasm. To my family—both those who "got it" when I shared the news about getting to write for Critical Role and those who didn't but were very excited for me anyway. And always and forever, to Dave, my partner in life and occasionally crime, receiver of all my excited, all-caps texts.

AABRIA IYENGAR

Bidet! I would love to thank Matthew Mercer and the entire Critical Role cast for inviting me into a world so lovingly and masterfully rendered that I have, on many occasions, dreamed in it. The chance to tell this little tale of a shopkeeper's heart and hopes has been an absolute dream, and I'm delighted to be included among such brilliant storytellers here. I'd also love to thank my darling husband, Ryan, for first introducing me to D&D, and to truly every person I've ever shared a table with: your creativity has inspired me endlessly, and it's an honor to carry our stories in my heart!

SAM MAGGS

Thank you to my agent, Maria Vicente, my staunchest supporter and massive Critter. Thank you also to editor extraordinaire Lydia Estrada and the whole Random House Worlds team (including Tom Hoeler and Elizabeth Schaefer) for their brilliant direction and unwavering kindness. And finally, thank you to my dear friends and colleagues at Critical Role, especially Kimallura himself, Matthew Mercer, for trusting me with their babies and for the best job and community I've ever had. Finally, I'd like to thank lesbian yearning, the fire behind all my writing.

SARAH GLENN MARSH

To my own merry band of adventurers, without whom I'd be lost in the dungeons for quite some time, as we all know I can't read a map: Lydia Estrada, whose brilliant editorial insights and commentary kept spirits high as we saw this quest through to the end; Katelyn Detweiler, my wonderful agent, who joins me on oh so many adventures; the real Sparks, with apologies that I'm still working on finding you that dragon; Chris, my favorite wizard, who's always got the party's back. And last but not least, my sweet cub, Dawn, who holds Juni's light and rivals Vesper's daring spirit, and who has inherited many of my best druid qualities. You make this parenting thing really fun, even on days when I've got to dodge a few poisoned arrows.

RORY POWER

Thank you so much to Sarah and everyone at Random House Worlds for all your hard work. And, of course, thank you to Critical Role for ten amazing years! I'm so honored to have been part of this wonderful anthology.

NIBEDITA SEN

To Martin Cahill, my first DM, and the rest of the Fructugly V (yes, I stand by that name); to my wonderful nerdy spouse; to Sarah and Lydia at Random House Worlds; to Matthew Mercer and Dani Carr and the whole Critical cast and crew—to everyone who understands the power and delight of making up stories, thank you. Let's keep building weird and wonderful worlds that teach us how to make *this* world better.

IZZY WASSERSTEIN

Getting to tell Kaylie's story was a great honor. Many thanks to the Critical Role team for including me in this project, and to Lydia Estrada, whose insightful editing made the story stronger, and to my amazing agent, Dorian Maffei. I'm grateful for the insights and feedback provided by A. T. Greenblatt, Alexandra Manglis, Christian Opperman, Vina Jie-Min Prasad, Adam R. Shannon, and Emma Törzs. And thanks most of all to my spouse, Nora E. Derrington, who has always believed in my work. This story wouldn't exist without their wisdom and extensive musical knowledge.

KENDRA WELLS

Thank you first and foremost to Liam O'Brien, who showed so much kindness and placed so much trust in me right from the beginning, and who opened the door to the wonderful folks at Critical Role in the process. To Dani Carr (tireless champion of everyone she loves, and singular talent, to boot), thank you for welcoming me into your gigantic heart. And to everyone else at CR too numerous and darling to fit in a few short sentences: thank you for changing the direction of my life. XOXO

ABOUT THE AUTHORS

JESS BARBER can be found flitting sporadically between Boston and Los Angeles, though she originally hails from the mountains of northeast Tennessee. She is a graduate of the Massachusetts Institute of Technology, where she studied physics and electrical engineering, and the Clarion Writers' Workshop, which involved less math but just as much sleep deprivation. Her short fiction has appeared in publications such as *Clarkesworld*, *Lightspeed*, and *The Year's Best Science Fiction*, and has been long-listed for the Hugo Award.

jess-barber.com

MARTIN CAHILL is an Ignyte Award–nominated author living just north of New York City. His novella *Audition for the Fox* will be published Fall 2025. He is a graduate of the 2014 Clarion Writers' Workshop, and his fiction can be found in *Reactor*, *Clarkesworld*, *Lightspeed*, and many other publications. His short story "Godmeat" appeared in *The Best American Science Fiction and Fantasy 2019* anthology, and his nonfiction can be found in *Catapult, Ghostfire Gaming, Reactor,* and others.

martincahill.wordpress.com

Rebecca Coffindaffer grew up on Star Wars, Star Trek, fantastical movies, and even more fantastical books. They waited a long time for their secret elemental powers to develop, and, in the interim, started writing stories about magic and politics, spaceships, far-off worlds, and people walking away from explosions in slow motion. Coffindaffer is also the author of the YA space opera duology *Crownchasers* and *Thronebreakers.* These days, they live in Kansas with their family, surrounded by a lot of books and a lot of tabletop games and a very spoiled dog.

rebeccacoffindaffer.com

Aabria Iyengar is a gamemaster, performer, writer, and podcaster, and a trailblazing force in the world of tabletop role-playing games. In addition to her groundbreaking roles on prominent TTRPG platforms such as Critical Role and Dimension 20, she is the author of the comic book *THE FADE* with artist Mari Costa and the co-founder of the acclaimed podcast *Worlds Beyond Number*. Iyengar has also contributed her talents as a voice actor and performer to a diverse range of projects, from off-Broadway's *Dungeons & Dragons: The Twenty-Sided Tavern* to the hit game *Starfield.*

Instagram: @quiddie

Sam Maggs is a *New York Times* bestselling author of books, comics, and video games. Her novels include *Star Wars Jedi: Battle Scars* and *The Unstoppable Wasp: Built on Hope;* she's written for games like *Call of*

Duty: Vanguard, Tiny Tina's Wonderlands, and *Marvel's Spider-Man;* and her comics and graphic novels include *Marvel Action: Captain Marvel, Critical Role: The Mighty Nein Origins,* and *Tell No Tales: Pirates of the Southern Seas.* She is also an on-air host for networks like Nerdist. A Canadian in Los Angeles, Maggs misses Coffee Crisp and bagged milk.

sammaggs.com

Sarah Glenn Marsh is the author of several young adult novels including the Reign of the Fallen series. She has also written almost a dozen picture books including *A Campfire Tail, Ninita's Big World: The True Story of a Deaf Pygmy Marmoset* (an Amazon Best Book of 2019), and the Junior Library Guild selection *Dragon Bones: The Fantastic Fossil Discoveries of Mary Anning.* Marsh lives with her husband, daughter, and menagerie of pets in Richmond, Virginia.

sarahglennmarsh.com

Rory Power lives in Rhode Island. She has an MA in prose fiction from the University of East Anglia and is the *New York Times* bestselling author of *Wilder Girls, Burn Our Bodies Down,* and *In a Garden Burning Gold.*

itsrorypower.com

Nibedita Sen is a Hugo, Nebula, and Ignyte Award–nominated queer Bengali writer from Calcutta, and a graduate of 2015 Clarion West Writers' Workshop whose work has appeared in *Uncanny, Podcastle, Nightmare,* and *Strange Horizons.* She accumulated a number of English degrees in India before deciding she wanted another in creative writing—and that she was going to move halfway across the world for it. These days, Sen can be found in New York City, with her spouse and their sweet, toothless old cat, where she moonlights as an editor to fund her TTRPG and craft supply addiction. She has too many hobbies, enjoys the company of puns and potatoes, and is always hungry.

nibeditasen.com

Izzy Wasserstein is a queer and trans woman who was born and raised in Kansas and currently lives in California. She teaches writing and literature at a public university, writes poetry and fiction, and shares a house with a variety of animal companions and the writer Nora E. Derrington. A Lambda Literary Award finalist, Wasserstein is the author of two poetry collections, the short story collection *All the Hometowns You Can't Stay Away From,* and the novella *These Fragile Graces, This Fugitive Heart.*

izzywasserstein.com

Kendra Wells is a writer, illustrator, and cartoonist. Their published works include *Tell No Tales: Pirates of the Southern Seas* (written by Sam Maggs), *Real Hero Shit,* and contributions to the Ignatz Award–winning anthology *Be Gay, Do Comics.*

kendrawcandraw.com